LOVE'S LIE

"I hate you," Jody said, wishing with all of her heart she meant it. "And I won't be forced into something that I'll only live to regret."

The venom in her words ripped at Chase, but he hid his disappointment behind a sardonic smile. "Well, you do have a point. If and when we get back to the future, we certainly don't want any embarassing reminders of what happened here, now do we?"

"No," she readily agreed, her heart shattering. "We'd both regret it, I'm sure."

Her prim attitude only fueled his lusty frustrations. "Are you so sure?" he asked, backing her up against the door. "Are you so sure you'd regret this, Jody?"

Before she could answer, his mouth captured hers, taking her breath and her resolve away completely. The kiss was savage and punishing, exciting and demanding. All the things he was, all the things he made her want to be. Not understanding the mass of emotions taking over her soul, Jody moaned and fell back on the door, letting him press close to her, letting him show her just how aroused he really was. But she didn't care. She blocked out all her doubts, all her fears, and for a brief moment, let the feel of his mouth on hers overtake her sense of duty and decorum, while his hands on her body overtook everything between the lace at her neckline to the padded bustle of her backside.

Finally, winded and dazed, Chase lifted his mouth away, only to whisper raggedly in her ear. "You torture me, in this century and the next. You'll torture me until I have you, and I won't rest until I do."

Other *Love Spell* books by Lenora Nazworth:
CARLY'S SONG

Home Again

Lenora Nazworth

LOVE SPELL ◆ **NEW YORK CITY**

LOVE SPELL®

April 1997

Published by

Dorchester Publishing Co., Inc.
276 Fifth Avenue
New York, NY 10001

Printed in the United States of America.

To Pelham, my own little piece of Georgia, my home.
To Stephanie Nelson, for the original idea for this book.
To Janet, for finding a set of eyes staring out at her in a
gift shop in Stone Mountain, Georgia. Major Pelham was
calling to you and I have the photograph to prove it.
To Jeanette, a true friend, a good soul, and underneath all
that bluster, a sweetheart. We love you, Aunt Nette.
And to Major John Pelham...may he rest in eternal peace.

AUTHOR'S NOTE

While this book is strictly fiction, I did base Hampleton on my own hometown of Pelham, Georgia. The history of Hampleton is based loosely on the history of Pelham, which I saved from old newspapers. A house such as Spence House did exist in Pelham, but it was torn down when I was in high school. I hated to see the beautiful old house go, so this is my way of bringing that particular house back to life. Pelham was named after a Confederate war hero, Major John Pelham, who died on Saint Patrick's Day in a battle near the Rappahannock River in Kelly's Ford, Virginia. The town was named after him at the request of a railroad surveyor who had attended West Point with Pelham. The surveyor had a close relationship with John Pelham, much like Jackson's relationship with his brother John in my story.

Many thanks to those who remembered this colorful history. This book is my gift to all of you.

Lenora Nazworth

Prologue

Spring, 1863
South Georgia

"I'm not leaving!"

The young woman looked up at the giant, dark-skinned man towering over her, the stubborn glint in her crystal-blue eyes blurred by the mist of tears she wouldn't allow herself to shed. "He said he'd be back today, Ali, and I won't leave until he comes."

Ali-Rasheem sighed heavily and stalked to the black stallion his master had given to him, along with his freedom, for Christmas. Pulling a small sheepskin rug off the horse's broad back, Ali-Rasheem placed it on the ground and kneeled, his many robes bunching around his muscular body as he turned toward the east. Ali was of mixed blood—part African, part Arabic—a Muhammadan who conducted his prayers thrice daily, no matter what the circumstances.

The circumstances this misty morning did not bode well.

"Say one for me, Ali," the young woman whispered, closing her eyes to commune with her own God, hoping,

11

praying, that John would soon be there.

They were to be married that day. Looking down, she pulled back the lightweight blue wool cape protecting her high-necked muslin and lace dress from the dampness, her hand automatically reaching for the gold-and-pearl filigree brooch that John had given her so long ago. Again, her eyes closed, and she allowed herself to be washed in a sweet memory: the memory of John's lips on hers, right here underneath this magnolia tree; the memory of their bodies urgently joined together, because he had to go back to Virginia, back to his regiment, back to the horrible war.

"We'll meet here again, my love," he'd whispered in her ear. "We'll come back to this very spot and one day, I promise you. I'll build us a grand house right here and you'll have the loveliest garden in the whole state of Georgia."

"And children," she said, pressing her face to the crisp collar of his Confederate uniform. "We'll have lots of children, won't we, John?"

"As many as you want." He kissed her again, and then, having been summoned by his adjutant, turned to mount his impatient stallion. "I'll be back, my love, and we'll be married, this spring. I'll send you word."

"I love you, John."

"I love you, with all my heart."

That had been a week after the New Year. Two weeks ago, she'd received his letter telling her when to meet him. And now, she waited, guarded by John's own personal bodyguard and servant, the ever-faithful Ali. And like the mysterious Muhammadan, she'd pledged her heart to John Hample Spence.

Except this war was getting in the way of her heart's desire.

"Please," she pleaded to the wind. "Let him find his way back to me."

After everything they'd been through together, after everything they'd faced and overcome, surely, now they deserved what little happiness they could find. Surely, they would indeed be married as they'd planned.

She waited all day, with Ali by her side. Thrice, Ali-

12

Rasheem prayed to Allah, while her own prayers had been constant and repetitive. She'd given up everything, every tie she'd ever held dear, to be with this man. Her love for him was stronger than anything in this life.

"The sun is sinking low, Mistress," Ali said in his exotic voice. "We must go back. It is dangerous."

Her fingers clutching the brooch that covered her heart, the woman refused to give up. "No," came the whispered refusal. "No."

Then the sound of horses charging up the nearby road brought her head up and brought Ali into a swift protective stance just in front of her, his menacing sword raised in defense.

"It's him!" She pushed past the big man, running to the road.

Ali-Rasheem called after the woman he'd vowed to protect. "No, Mistress, wait! It isn't safe!" The giant rushed forward, throwing himself in front of her again.

But it was too late. Several shots rang out and Ali fell to the ground like a thundering giant. He'd taken the musket balls meant for her.

And now, in the dusk of a crisp spring day that had come to a cruel end, she was faced with a terror she'd only experienced in her worst nightmares. She was surrounded by Union soldiers. And she recognized their leader immediately, as he did her.

"My dear lady," he said, sweeping off his plumed hat to salute her. "Just the one I've been searching for. My men and I request a few minutes of your time. There are ... questions, you understand?"

She understood more than he would ever know.

She understood that her life was about to change, and that John wasn't ever coming back.

As she accepted the horse a soldier brought before her, she took one last look at the spot underneath the magnolia tree where she'd fallen in love with John Hample. Ali-Rasheem lay dead at its base, his blood running red over his muslin robes.

Somehow, she knew, she'd never be the same.

And somehow, she knew, she'd never make it home again.

Part One
Jody and Chase

Chapter One

"They're doing what?"

Jody Calhoun whirled around from the cash register at The Treasure Chest Antique Shop. The tourist to whom she'd just sold a stack of baseball cards stepped back, away from the flash of fire he saw in Jody's crystal-blue eyes. When the freckles along Jody's pert nose brightened with indignation, the wary customer took it as sure sign she wasn't pleased. But Jody wasn't upset with her customer. Instead, she turned her attention back to her grandfather.

Slamming the cash drawer shut, she eyed the old man sitting in a rocking chair in front of a noisy floor fan by the open screened doors. In a voice as sultry as the humidity hanging in the air like an unseen net, she said, "Grandpa, tell me all of that again,'cause I don't think I heard you right."

The stout white-haired man kept rocking, the twinkle in his eyes matching the heat of his granddaughter's look. Taking a long draw on the polished mahogany pipe that was a permanent fixture in his wizened mouth, he cleared his throat. "I said some company from Florida is going to take

17

the land the old Spence House is sitting on and build a new shopping center there—right smack in the middle of Hampleton. They're planning to tear that old house down.''

Jody gave her grandfather a sharp glare, her breath stopping in her chest. Outside, the early Monday morning sunshine worked its way toward afternoon, its heat waves creating a steamy mirage on the asphalt of US Highway 19 as it made a hot ribbon through the rural Georgia countryside.

"That's what I thought you said," she murmured. With a brisk nod, she thanked the confused customer, handing him his package and his change. Grabbing her bottle of Coke, Jody hopped up onto the wooden counter, her cut-off jeans revealing long, tanned legs. She took a greedy sip of the soft drink, her eyes scanning the huge, cluttered shop to make sure no other customers needed her immediate attention. "Look's like I missed a lot while I was away. Why'd they decide to go and do that?"

Mitchell "Mitt" Calhoun rose up in his rocking chair, stopping to take off his glasses and rub a speck of dirt out of one of the lenses of his sturdy bifocals. "I reckon because the town of Hampleton, Georgia is sinking faster than a lead weight on a fishing line, girly. Lord knows, we could use some new business around this place. All those fancy shopping malls along the interstate are sucking the life right out of us."

Jody held her Coke to her cheek, hoping to find a bit of cooling wetness on the bottle's glassy curve. "I couldn't agree more, but tear down Spence House?" She shook her head. "You know how I feel about that old house."

"Yes, I know how you feel about Spence House," Mitt echoed as he lifted his arms to let the fan's pitiful air circulate around his khaki work shirt. "But it'd take more money than you and me will ever see to redo that run-down place. Tearing it down is the best thing for everyone. It's just an eyesore."

Jody hopped down from the counter. "Grandpa, it is not an eyesore. It's an historic landmark. It just needs someone to take care of it, to paint it and fix it up." Letting out an exasperated breath, she pushed back the thick bangs tickling her forehead. Not even her grandfather knew of Jody's secret dream to buy Spence House and renovate it. No, only the president of the local bank knew of that dream, and he shot it down each time Jody went to him to ask for a loan. "I could do it, if I had the loot," she added, thinking out loud.

Mitt shot her a knowing look. "Now, Jodelyn, don't go getting any fancy notions in that pretty head of yours. It would take a lot more than money to fix up that old house. The Spences have abandoned the place; it's time it came down. Especially what with all those stories circulating about the place. Ghosts don't exactly attract visitors to the area, now do they?"

"Pooh," Jody snorted. "I don't see how a family could just leave their home to ruin. Whatever's haunting that old place is probably just lonely. Somebody ought to talk to them and make them see how important that house is— ghosts and all."

Mitt scratched his tuft of wiry white hair. "And I suppose you'd be the one to do the talking?"

Jody nodded, her eyes dancing a little jig. "Yes, for starters. But I'd also get the whole town involved. The Spence family started this town. They built the first trading company here. There's a lot of history surrounding that house. I don't understand why someone can't step in and save it, that's all."

Mitt shook his ruddy head. "Someone is going to step in all right. Ted Patterson told me yesterday, after church. The company from Florida—it's owned by none other than what's left of the Spence family—ol' Jackson Spence's great-great-grandson, Chase Spence. He's probably over at the Farmer's Bank right now, sealing the deal to build the shopping mall."

Jody shot a look across the street toward the Farmer's Bank, located past the train tracks on the corner of what had been appropriately named West Railroad Street. In 1881, the town of Hampleton was founded, mainly because it was one of several stops built at seven-mile intervals along the

Georgia-Florida railroad line. What started out as a railroad station had quickly grown into a small southern town, complete with a main street and a corner drugstore that still served the best chocolate malts in the world, according to Jody's way of thinking, anyway. And located at the head of West Railroad, behind an ornate once-white iron lace-work gate and a jungle of trees and shrubs that had once been a breathtaking garden, stood the Victorian mansion know as Spence House.

Years of being empty and neglected had taken its toll on the rambling old house. Now vagrants and vandals—mostly the local teens innocently searching for a good spot to have some fun—wandered through the house on a regular basis.

Jody had been inside the house, but not to vandalize it. Oh, no. She had often walked through the unlocked doors, alone, to sit for hours absorbing the loneliness and sadness the house evoked. Indeed, she knew all about loneliness. Maybe that was why she felt so protective of the old mansion. It was as if it cried out to be filled with laughter again, to hear the voices of children, to know love and happiness.

Jody dreamed of the house often, for reasons she couldn't even begin to understand. And after everything she'd been through in the last few weeks, she didn't need to hear her favorite hideaway was going to be demolished, or that the very bank executive who'd turned her down consistently was in cahoots with the person planning to do it.

"Chase Spence," she said, remembering the stories circulating around Hampleton regarding Jeanette Spence's favorite great-nephew. An up-and-coming land developer, a confirmed bachelor, a Florida playboy who wouldn't have any qualms about knocking down a piece of history to add more money to his already growing coffer of wealth. What a jerk! Jody hated him already. "Well, I guess it'll be easy for a high-and-mighty Spence to come in and take over. Heck, they used to run the whole town. Maybe this Chase fellow is planning on bringing back that tradition."

"He is the last of the line," Mitt replied, a frown slicing his aged face. "Don't know why he'd want to bother though. From what I hear he owns half of Florida already."

"Maybe he has a hankering for a little piece of Georgia, too," Jody said, wishing she had money and power and all the clout needed to restore Spence House herself.

But in a town this small, the haves and the have-nots were greatly separated, as they had been through the decades. Her own grandfather's grandfather, Tucker Calhoun, had worked for the Spence family, overseeing their vast farmland, until his death. Heck, even Grandpa's small farm just outside of town had once been Spence land.

Mad all over again at Ted Patterson for wanting her to put her grandfather's land up as collateral for her loan to purchase Spence House, and forgetting the old place wasn't actually for sale, she decided on the spot that she had a bone to pick with this Chase Spence. She was on the outside once again, looking at a situation she couldn't begin to control.

"I don't understand why he'd be interested in a sleepy little town like Hampleton," she said, her thoughts popping out with the same lack of tact as the sweat beads on her freckled nose.

"Probably because that particular corner of prime real estate will fetch him a solid return on his investment," Mitt said, rocking confidently in his creaky cane-back chair.

Straining her neck, Jody could see the round, ornate wooden cupola sitting atop one side of the three-storied mansion, reminding her of a turret on a castle. Once, in high school, she'd climbed all the way to the top of the cupola with a boyfriend, and she'd never forgotten the view or the melancholy feeling of isolation surrounding the tiny rounded structure. Being in that little room had left the strangest sensation in her mind, a feeling that still haunted her each time she slipped away to explore the old house.

Of course, her boyfriend had had other ideas, so the visit had been cut short by her hand slapping him across the face.

But her high school days were over, and from the looks of things, her great hope for Spence House would have to end soon, too. Unless . . . she tried to reason with its owner.

Jody called out to her grandfather, "I've got to go out for a while, Grandpa. Can you hold down the fort?"

" 'Course I can," came the indignant reply. "And bring

me back a cheeseburger from Siwell Drug, will you?''

Smiling, Jody called out, ''You know those cheeseburgers are bad for your cholesterol, old man.''

''Who're you calling old?'' came the answer. ''And where are you headed anyway?''

''No place special,'' she shouted. ''Just to talk to a man about a house,'' she mumbled under her breath.

Five minutes later, Jody entered the cool air-conditioned quietness of the town's only bank, her eyes taking in the updated decor and efficient elegance of the building's interior. An expert on things old, Jody didn't really like the modern furnishings, but she knew even an antique lover like herself had to move with the times. This building was one of the oldest in town, but in order to serve as a bank, it had to be in tune with its time. And that meant swivel chairs with rollers attached to their metal legs and computer screens blinking a greeting each time she made a business transaction.

Today, she didn't dwell on her distaste for business equipment, however. Instead, she strolled with purposeful intent to the desk of the bank president's secretary. ''Hi, Katie,'' she said, her smile pleasant as the other woman looked up from her filing.

''Well, hello, Jody. Heard you got back yesterday.'' Katie Winston's grin was one of the reasons people liked to do business there. ''How's your mother, anyway?''

''All settled in, at least,'' Jody replied. ''She's out at the farm. We got Erma Smith to sit with her, just in case.''

''Erma's a good nurse. Tell your mother I said hello,'' Katie said. ''Now, what can I do for you?'' Tossing her dark curls, she waited for Jody to reply, her brow furrowing in concern. ''What's the matter?''

Jody hated the way Katie read her like a book. But they'd been friends and co-conspirators since kindergarten, so she supposed there was no way around it. ''Nothing's the matter. I need to talk to Mr. Patterson,'' she said, her dimples crinkling into an attempt at an innocent smile. ''Is he in?''

Craning her neck, Jody peered around the heavy wooden

door to Mr. Patterson's huge office. When she heard voices from within, her heart started pounding a warning. What was she doing here, anyway? How could she possibly expect to talk Mr. Patterson into getting Chase Spence to sell her Spence House, when she'd failed every time before?

"Yes, he's in," Katie confirmed, her eyes questioning. "And I know that look. Jody, you look like a woman on a mission. Is everything okay?"

Plopping down into one of the navy vinyl chairs in front of Katie's desk, Jody gave up trying to be coy. "I heard they're going to tear down Spence House," she said, her eyes wide with dismay. "Is it true, Katie? Is Chase Spence in there with Mr. Patterson? I need to talk to both of them."

Katie relaxed back in her chair, a faint look of amusement on her porcelain-colored face. "Yes to the first question, and no to the second one. You just missed the hunk of the year. Mr. Spence was headed to his temporary offices in the Spence Building last time I saw him. And believe me, I stared long and hard, so I know of what I speak."

"You're married, remember," Jody reminded her friend. "Happily, last time I checked."

Giving her a disappointed look, Katie stuck out her tongue. "Oh, yeah. I am, aren't I." Then grinning again, she added slyly, "But you're not."

Ignoring Katie's dreamy expression and total lack of tact, Jody hopped out of the chair. "Never mind about Mr. Patterson. I'm going to talk to Mr. Chase Spence instead."

"Why?" Katie got up, her dark eyes widening as realization dawned on her. "Good Lord, you're not seriously thinking about trying to stop him, now are you, Jody?"

Jody fluffed her bangs. Then she shrugged. "Maybe."

"Maybe not," Katie snorted. "Sugar, he's already getting the paperwork together for the permits, so he can begin construction. He's hiring local crews and he's got big plans for that corner. Big plans." When Jody didn't seem convinced, Katie pointed a finger in her friend's face. "He was in here all morning, setting up payroll and expense accounts for his workers. He's going to build that shopping mall, Jody. It's too late to stop him."

"We'll just see," Jody said, her ponytail flapping behind her as she bolted toward the door. "Thanks, Katie."

"Jody?" Katie called after her. "I probably should warn you—he's a city slicker and he's all business. Remember, he wasn't raised here. He doesn't feel as strongly about that old house as you always have."

"I intend to change that," Jody said, her crystal eyes sparkling with challenge. Mr. Chase Spence had picked the wrong corner of the earth to stake a claim on. She ignored the little voice that warned her *she* didn't have any claims on Spence House. Her claim came from the soul, and in her eyes, it was every bit as legitimate as any legal deed of ownership.

Five minutes and five hundred heartbeats later, Jody stood in the hot sun staring up at the Spence Building. The inscription over the awnings still read "Spence Trading Company," but that title had been dropped long ago, even though the old timers still referred to it as that. Once billed the "world's largest rural department store," the Spence building now housed a clothing store on its bottom floor, a furniture store on its second floor, and business offices on the two remaining floors.

"I guess he'll come in and redo this building, too," Jody said to herself as she pushed at one of the heavy glass doors opening into the lobby. But she hoped he wouldn't cover the beautiful domed ceiling with its stained-glass panels or change the sturdy iron railings surrounding the three open floors above the central staircase. Surely the man had enough sense to realize beauty like this needed to be protected.

Glancing to her right, she spotted Spence House. Jackson Spence had built his mansion on the street that ran alongside his trading company. Spence Avenue was still one of the most exclusive streets in town. With its gnarled live oaks, fragrant magnolias and pure white dogwood trees mixed with hot pink crepe myrtles, it made for a lovely evening stroll. Mitt Calhoun had taken his granddaughter for many long strolls up Spence Avenue, always with ice cream cones from Siwell's in hand.

But Jody couldn't imagine taking that stroll without being able to see her beloved Spence House. From the very first time she'd seen the house, over twenty years ago, she'd felt a connection with the old place. That sense of déjà vu had been hard to explain as a child; no one wanted to hear her crazy stories regarding the house. A child's vivid imagination, they'd all said. She'd been dragged around too much; she was a wild child, they whispered. Pure fantasy, Grandma Rose used to say.

"It's just a house, Jody," Grandpa would remind her. "Just a big, old run-down house."

What a sad sight it was. It really was spooky looking, but she understood it needed a lot of attention. It could be a home again, and she was determined to prove that to Jackson's great-great-grandson. Right now, she needed a purpose, and saving Spence House would be a definite challenge, taking her mind off her never-ending problems with her wayward mother.

Squinting in the sun, she looked up at the turret room, imagining what it must have been like when it was new and shining. The July sun beamed down on her, reflecting off the roof of the huge house. Blinking, Jody reeled in her erratic musings, images of a bygone time flashing through her mind only to be replaced with the very real sight of a construction trailer crammed into one corner of the overgrown garden.

"Hell's bells, he certainly didn't waste any time!"

Look's like Katie was right. Glad that she'd come home in time to stop this fiasco, Jody clenched her teeth, her determination burning as hot as the sun on asphalt. Ever since this latest round with her mother's mental health, she'd been spoiling for a good fight. Might as well be with Chase Spence. Why not go all out and go for one of the big guns?

Entering the block-wide building in front of her, Jody looked up at the black marble staircase that always reminded her of the one at Tara in *Gone with the Wind*. It even had worn red carpeting covering its steps.

Traipsing across the tiled floors, she waved and nodded to people she'd known all her life. Taking the stairs two at a time, she headed to the third floor where she knew the Spence family used to keep an office. She was in too big a hurry to ride in the rickety old elevator with the intricate wrought-iron picket gate, something she'd loved to do as a child.

When she finally reached the office she was looking for, located on the right-hand corner of the building so its original occupant could have a bird's-eye view of the old mansion across the street, she was out of breath.

"Calm down," she told herself, straightening her faded tee shirt and fluffing her bangs across her forehead. "Just be reasonable and state your case, Jody. Surely you can make the man listen to reason."

But as soon as she heard the booming "Come in" following her hearty knock on the partially opened door, reason went right out the window. Jody opened the door and stared into a pair of eyes as gray and stormy as the mansion she'd come to fight for. That mansion stood as a backdrop for Chase Spence's penetrating eyes and irritated look, his own mood apparently equaling that of the house behind him.

In spite of the hot day, a chill went down Jody's spine and a cold sweat popped out along her backbone. Just nerves, she stubbornly told herself. Just the jitters. She'd never had a problem speaking her mind. Why should things be any different with Chase Spence? And why was Katie always right?

He stood leaning against a long, narrow credenza, a set of official looking documents clutched in his right hand, while with his other hand, he held a plastic Atlanta Braves cup up against his temple, apparently enjoying the cooling effect the condensation on the side of the cup provided against the summer heat beating at the closed windows. The irritated look clouding his tanned face vanished the minute he looked at Jody, to be replaced with a puzzled expression.

"I'm sorry," he said, tossing down the papers and taking a quick drink. "I thought you were my assistant. She went to the drugstore to get me some aspirin. I've got a booming headache.''

And what a good looking head it was, complete with thick curly dark brown hair.

Jody smiled. "This humidity can do that, especially on a day like today." Moving farther into the spacious room, she extended her hand. "I'm Jody Calhoun. I own The Treasure Chest."

Giving her another puzzled look, Chase ran a hand through his already tousled hair. "The Treasure Chest?"

"The antique shop across the tracks, on the other side of town," she offered, feeling more and more foolish by the minute. "Well, actually it's part antiques and part junk, but we do a fair amount of business."

He looked down, his gaze searching his desk calendar. "Do we have an appointment?"

"No, we don't," she said, wishing she'd learn not to act on her impulses so much. "But I'd like to talk to you."

At that precise moment, high noon, the sun's intense beam lit up one of the aged glass window panes nestled underneath the tarnished spires of Spence House's rounded cupola. The bright light hit Jody right in the eyes, blinding her with its brilliance. Squinting, she raised a hand to her eyes.

Chase looked at her as if she'd gone daft. "Are you all right?"

"Yeah." Jody tried to get out of the path of the reflection. "The sun—a glare."

Chase came around the desk, moving her away from the shaft of light, his hand gently pressing into her elbow. His eyes focusing on her with a brightness as intense as the sun, he asked, "Is that better?"

Looking around as if she'd just come out of a trance, Jody nodded. "Yes." Just to be sure she wasn't hallucinating, she peered out the window toward Spence House. The glare was gone now. But the hot sun still beamed down on the widow's walk adjacent to the cupola, making it seem hazy and surreal, like a too bright dream.

"That was strange." She shook her head to clear her vision and her mind.

Chase looked over toward the mansion, then back toward her. "Well, I've heard a lot of strange things regarding my ancestor's house since I've been here. Probably why no one wants to help me get rid of the thing." Shrugging it off, he turned to her. "Now, Ms. Calhoun . . . what exactly did you want to talk to me about?"

Jody looked up at him. He didn't seem to be having the same reaction to that piercing light as she'd had. The goosebumps were only now beginning to settle on her arms. Then again, maybe it wasn't the house she was reacting to, but its gray-eyed owner. Suddenly feeling disoriented and off balance, she said, "I . . . it's about the house." Thinking her intelligence had finally "flew the coop" as Grandpa would say, she added, "I came here to talk to you about Spence House, Mr.—"

"Chase, just Chase," he cut in. "And if you're hoping to find some antiques in the house, I'm afraid there aren't many left. Everything's either been packed up for relatives or stolen away."

And you don't give a hoot, Jody thought grimly. His whole demeanor spoke of his cavalier attitude toward what he was about to do.

"It's not that," she said. "That's not why I'm here."

Leaning back against his cluttered desk, Chase loosened his paisley silk tie, his actions revealing a nicely scattered array of golden-brown chest hair. Rubbing his temples absently, he said, "Then why don't you tell me why you're here."

Taking her eyes away from the contrast of his crisp white shirt against all that glorious tanned skin and swirling hair, Jody focused on the imposing house watching them from across the street. "I'm here because I heard you're going to tear down Spence House," she said, her crystal eyes blazing like blue flame. "I'm here to ask you to reconsider. Don't tear down that house, Chase. If you do, you'll regret it for the rest of your life."

Giving her an amused look, Chase folded his arms across his chest. "Gee, we haven't even had our first date. Don't you think you could wait a little while before asking me to hand you the world on a platter?"

Angered at his flippant response to what she considered a very serious matter, Jody moved closer, coming eye to eye with him. "You think this is funny?" she asked, feeling the flush rising up her neck and face.

Chase watched her, his eyes moving right along with her telltale climbing blush, settling on her lips before they caught her gaze. Giving her a direct look, he asked, "Am I laughing?"

"You're laughing at *me*," Jody replied, tossing the hot thickness of her long ponytail off her shoulder. "And I'm dead serious."

Coming up off the desk, Chase once again rubbed his temple. "Let me get this straight," he said as he strolled to the window to stare out at the house across the street. "You don't want me to tear down that old, practically condemned house standing over there? You realize, of course, what I'm proposing to do with that particular corner will bring new life into this town? I'm talking about new business, new jobs, new growth. I suppose none of that matters to you, so long as I don't tear down that ugly old house?" He pivoted, shooting her a frown that clearly stated his disbelief.

"I know it sounds crazy," Jody conceded, "but I'm not asking you to stop your plans completely. Heaven knows, I want new business in this town. I am a member of the Chamber of Commerce you know. But I believe in compromise, too. By all means, build your shopping center—somewhere else. Just don't tear down Spence House to do it."

Seemingly amazed at her gall, Chase shook his head, his hair reminding her of rich mahogany. "Excuse me," he said. "But I don't recall asking your opinion regarding this venture. And if you are a member of the Chamber of Commerce, than you'd know this deal was brought before the planning commission and the city council a few weeks ago.

Why didn't you voice your concern then?''

Embarrassed, Jody squirmed for a split second before giving him an answer. "I was out of town," she explained, not ready to reveal her whereabouts to a complete stranger. "I had to take care of some personal business in Louisiana. I got back late yesterday."

Chase watched her, his expression bordering between bemused and annoyed. "And nobody bothered to update you?"

"Not really," she replied, sighing. "I just heard about it this morning. I can't believe somebody didn't try to stop you."

"That's because I presented a good, solid plan," Chase replied. "I presented the proposal to the City Council and explained what I hoped to do. At the time, no one knew who I was—exactly."

"So you tricked our town into letting you do this?"

"No," he groaned. "I didn't trick anyone." Letting out a long breath, he added, "Look, it's a long story, but I'll try to make it simple for you. I didn't want anyone to jump on this just because of my name. I know it might be hard for you to understand, but I wanted to win this project based solely on my abilities as a developer, the way I do any place I decide to invest in property."

"I see," she said, a flicker of admiration melting some of the thaw around her heart. "But why here, and why now?"

"Why am I telling you all this, anyway?" he said, sticking his head out the door. "And where is Betty with my aspirin?"

"I've got some Ibuprofen," Jody offered. "It works just as well."

"I'll take it," he said, a look of gratitude replacing the pinched look on his face. "And some lunch, too."

"Lunch?" Jody held the bottle of pills she'd found in her huge purse out to him, her jaw dropping open. She wanted to talk and he wanted lunch. He was giving her the brushoff, big time. Typical snob versus poor farm girl. Same old story.

"Yeah, low blood sugar," he replied, gulping down a

30

couple of the tablets. "I need to eat something. Where's the best place to get some good food?"

Realizing she wasn't getting the results she hoped for, Jody headed for the door, turning just in time to see Chase's obvious admiration of her backside. "Well, we have a couple of fast food joints, but Siwell's serves the best burgers in town."

"Siwell's. But that's a drugstore," he exclaimed. "What do they do, lace all their food with instant antacid?"

Jody shook her head. "You have a lot to learn about small town life, don't you? They have a soda fountain and diner on the side."

"Wow," Chase said, looking like a little boy. "You mean like that diner in *Back to the Future*?"

"Something like that," she said dryly. "And speaking of back to the future, what are you going to do about saving Spence House?"

Lifting his brows, he reached out to take her hand. Thinking he was about to boot her out of his office, Jody braced herself.

But instead of throwing her out, he guided her out. "I'll tell you what I'm going to do about Spence House. I'm going to take you to lunch at Siwell's and I'm going to try and persuade you to see things my way."

Telling herself she was crazy, Jody stared him down. "Okay, I'll go to lunch with you, but only because I intend to persuade *you* to see things my way."

He grinned. "Should be an interesting lunch."

Anytime a stranger ate lunch at Siwell's, it proved to be interesting. That day was no exception, especially since the stranger was eating with none other than Jody Calhoun—a young woman some of the townspeople lovingly referred to as "the last unmarried woman in Mitchell County, Georgia." Old traditions died hard in the deep South, and Jody, being a local girl with very modern ideas about her independence, was a puzzle to the people who'd known her all her life. She'd come here on a dark cloud of scandal, and over twenty years later, she still didn't fit into any niche the townspeople tried to carve out for her. And now, here she sat in the heart of town, during the lunch rush, with a descendant of the town's legendary founder. This would be fodder for the garden club to dig through, and a juicy tidbit for the bridge club to toss around with their bids.

They'll have us married with children by sundown, Jody thought as she bit into her bacon cheeseburger, trying hard to ignore the stares and snickers of her fellow diners and the regulars who frequented the drugstore. *Or worse, they'll have us carrying on a torrid affair and I'll have to hang my head in shame.*

Not likely. She'd never once hung her head in shame. In spite of their wariness, the townspeople had given her their unspoken respect. It had been hard earned, but she intended to keep it. So she glanced around now, daring anyone to doubt her right to be seen associating with Chase Spence.

Even old "Doc" Siwell himself had one eye on mixing prescriptions and the other cocked toward the booth Jody and Chase sat in. Jody fervently hoped he wouldn't poison someone with an overdose simply because she was having lunch with the new kid in town.

While Doc Siwell mixed and watched, his faithful assistant of twenty years, Miss Edith, stood by his side, ready to call out to the next customer. Her eyes were glued to the couple in the booth.

Chase, too, seemed to notice the slow, simmering commotion surrounding them. The clatter of stoneware plates, the whine of the milkshake machine, the sizzle of hamburgers hitting the grill, and the banter of the lunch crowd all merged together; the same old routine to Jody, but completely foreign to him, judging from the look on his face.

"Do I have a piece of lettuce between my teeth?" he asked, his grin revealing a perfect set of white teeth.

Jody eyed him curiously, then laughed. "Relax, city boy. They don't get much excitement around here. You're already the talk of the town and you've only been here how long?"

"Two days this trip," he said, nibbling a crisp french fry. "I was really hoping I could get in and out without anybody making a fuss about my name.''

"Too late," she said, pushing her plate away. "Your name preceded you by about a hundred and thirty years. And why would you be embarrassed by it? The name Spence carries a whole lot of weight around here. You should be proud."

"I am proud," he replied. Taking a sip of his iced tea, he nodded. "But I want people to look past all that—and see me as just another businessman. A good businessman."

Jody made a wry face. "Touching, but unrealistic. Your ancestor started this town from nothing but a few thousand acres of pine trees. People don't forget a legend like that. And they're sure going to notice when his great-great-grandson comes in and starts rearranging things."

"I'm not him," Chase countered, "and I'm not rearranging things. Just trying to make them better."

"Who invited you?" Jody couldn't help the resentment in her voice and couldn't help but notice the restraint in Chase's.

"No one. I mean, my great-aunt . . . well, she wanted to do away with the land Spence House is sitting on. Only she wanted to sell it. She's never coming back to Hampleton, so she decided to make a quick profit and invest the money."

"And turn her back on her heritage!"

Chase lifted his head, as did several people sitting within earshot. The whole place quieted as if they were in church waiting for prayer.

Well, it didn't get any better than this, Jody reasoned. She could already feel the seeds of gossip sprouting around her like tender peanut shoots. Giving Chase a determined look, she whispered, "I can't believe your aunt would do that."

"You don't have to get testy," he said, irritation in his stormy eyes. "Aunt Jeanette has traveled the world, but now she just wants to settle down in her retirement home in Florida. She hasn't forgotten her heritage, but she can't take care of the property anymore."

"So instead of selling it, she handed it over to her favorite nephew?"

"You catch on pretty quick, don't you?"

He grinned again, and Jody felt the same pull she'd felt when he'd touched her elbow after that episode with the sunlight. He wasn't making this an easy battle. "Is that really the way it happened?"

Chase glanced around, as aware as Jody that every single ear in the small diner was straining to hear his next words. Leaning across the booth, he crooked his finger, motioning for her to come closer.

Knowing she was about to make a spectacle of herself, but unable to resist that "come hither" command he so arrogantly sent her way, Jody sat up over the table, her face mere inches from his. For a few seconds, she forgot why exactly she was here. She also forgot that everyone was staring at her. She forgot everything, but the powerful pull of those stormy eyes that drooped in a sexy laziness and that smug square jaw that spoke of a quiet strength and an inbred arrogance.

Chase had such an interesting face, she couldn't help but study him, her eyes taking in the brownish colored scar underneath his right eye and the lush length of his brown lashes as they curled over his deep-set eyes. But the moment ended when he grinned, causing little crows-feet to crinkle his face and causing Jody to fidget in embarrassment for openly making goo-goo eyes at a man she'd just met.

"What?" she whispered, her impatience apparent. When he only stared at her, as if he'd forgotten completely what he wanted to tell her, she kicked his shin underneath the table. "For pete's sake, Chase, everybody's staring holes right through us."

"Let 'em stare," he whispered back. "We're already the talk of the town anyway. Might as well make the best of it."

"What do you want to tell me?" she asked, irritated that he was making her sweat, in more ways than one.

"Only this," he said, cupping his words between his hands. "My aunt didn't give me the land. I suggested she keep it and let me develop it. Then she can make a profit and still have a solid investment."

Jody stared back at him, wondering exactly how many surprises Chase Spence could pull out of his hat. But before she could ponder the answer to that question, and before she could pull away, he wrapped his hand around hers and tugged her even closer.

"Oh, I need to tell you one more thing," he said, his words as smooth as a chocolate milkshake. "You have absolutely the most incredible eyes I've ever seen."

Jody jumped up with a groan of frustration that echoed through the still drugstore. All activity ceased and all eyes were on Jody and Chase. Giving Chase a look that would have killed a lesser man, she slapped a five dollar bill on the table. "If you think you can sweet talk me out of trying to save that house, Chase Spence, you're living in a fantasy world. I intend to fight you on this. And I intend to win." With that, she whirled and without stopping to look back, called to the scrawny teenaged boy working behind the counter, "Curtis, throw me Grandpa's cheeseburger."

Curtis didn't have to be told twice. He aimed the white bag at Jody's uplifted hand and was rewarded with a perfect one-handed catch. Jody didn't dare turn around, but she heard the waitress's reassuring words to Chase anyway.

"She gets a bit high-strung at times, suga'. Would you like another iced tea?"

"No," Chase replied rather loudly. "But I'll take two aspirin."

You'll need more than that before I'm finished, Jody thought as she pranced out the door.

Chapter Two

How could she possibly win? Jody wondered later that afternoon, as a hazy summer heat settled over the sleepy town. Business was slow at the antique shop, which wasn't unusual for a Monday, since most of her traffic was from tourists who traveled US Highway 19, headed to Florida on the weekends. But this particular Monday seemed to be dragging by like a lost log on the nearby Flint River, not in any great rush to get to its destination.

Jody, however, wanted this day to be over. Then she could forget the humiliation of that lunch with Chase Spence; she could forget the way his curly hair fell across his forehead; she could forget the way his eyes seemed to hold as many secrets as the house he'd come to destroy.

She finished dusting a rack of Roseville pottery, careful to place each piece back against the wall so the precious blue-tinged pitchers and vases wouldn't fall off and get broken. All afternoon, she'd pondered how to stop Chase from tearing down Spence House, but so far she hadn't come up with a solution to stop him. And what right did she have to stop him, anyway?

Her only defense was her love for the old house, a love she'd developed twenty years ago when, at the age of four, she'd come with her mother to live with her grandparents on their small farm just outside of town. Vivid impressions of that time crystalized in her mind, shimmering with an aged precision that held her like an old photograph. She'd been so afraid; the father she'd barely known was never coming home. And why wouldn't someone explain what war was? Why had her father gone to heaven, and what was wrong, so terribly wrong, with Mama?

Grandpa Mitt had taken her in his arms, hugging her close, his voice strangely husky. "Let's me and you go into town for some ice cream while Grandma takes care of your ma."

He'd taken her for a walk through the town, explaining that this was her home now, for as long as she wanted to live here. They'd walked up the main street, right up to the crossing where Spence House stood like a gingerbread castle waiting for a lost child to enter it.

"What's that place, Grandpa?"

"Just an old house, honey. Spence House. An old maid lives there and she doesn't like to be bothered."

"What's an old maid?"

"A woman who never married."

Visions of a wicked witch, or an evil stepmother came to Jody's mind. How sad, how sad, that someone was trapped in that house, waiting for her prince to come.

"It's beautiful."

Even when Mitt had tugged at her hand, trying to guide her past the sprawling mansion, Jody had held back to stare up at the cupola, all the fairy tales her mother had ever told her playing through her child's mind. Something had called out to her that day; something was watching her from those funny U-shaped windows in that rounded room high on top of the house. Yet she hadn't been afraid; the house had brought her a sense of . . . what? Belonging, peace, contentment? Even now, Jody couldn't explain it. She just knew.

At the sound of voices at the front of the long shop, Jody turned on the ladder she was perched against and almost lost her footing completely as she watched her grandfather shaking the hand of none other than Chase Spence himself.

"Yessir, Mitchell Calhoun, named after the county I was born in," her grandfather said, explaining his way through an introduction. "But just call me Mitt. Everybody does."

Then came Chase's clear response. "And everybody calls me Chase. Is Jody around?"

Now what's he doing here? Jody wondered, thinking she could duck out the back door before they spied her.

"There she is," Mitt said, pointing to Jody like a bird dog might point out a covey of quail. And that's what Jody felt like, cornered there on the latter, her left foot already posed and ready for flight. Giving her a meaningful look, Mitt called out, "Jody, somebody here to visit with you."

Oh great, she moaned silently. Grandpa had already been ribbing her all afternoon about that little fiasco at Siwell's, and he hadn't even been a witness to it. While he'd been talking politics with a man who lived across the street from the antique shop, Jody had been the source of the whole town's speculation. But by the time she'd gotten back to the shop, Grandpa had heard all the juicy details—thanks to his friend Miss Edith and the speed of a push-button telephone.

"Coming," she called, hoping nobody would notice Chase's car parked in front of the shop. One glance out the huge windows, however, showed her that would be impossible. The man was driving the brightest red Corvette she'd ever seen. Why not just rent a neon sign proclaiming his presence? And he claimed he wanted to keep a low profile?

By the time Jody reached the front of the shop, she was out of breath and thoroughly out of patience. What did he want now—to embarrass her even further? But she managed to bring out her best professional smile. After all, he could simply be here as a customer, though she doubted he'd know quality if it hit him between the eyes.

"Hi," Chase said, a sheepish look sweeping across his face. "I came to see if you're . . . uh . . . all right."

Before Jody could respond, Mitt cleared his throat rather loudly, causing her to glance at him in concern.

"I'll just go to the back and start locking up," the old

man explained. "You two take your time."

"Thanks," Chase said, giving Mitt an appreciative nod while Jody glared at her grandfather's back.

"I'm fine." She said through gritted teeth. "Why wouldn't I be all right? I mean, the whole town watched me make a complete fool of myself today, but other than that, things are just peachy around here."

"You're still ticked-off at me, right?"

Watching the way he lowered his head to give her a little boy smile, she knew she was a goner. How could she be mad at him for her own treacherous feelings? He was a mighty Spence, after all, and he had the good looks and breeding to back up his right of heritage to Spence House, but that had nothing to do with the instant and acute attraction she felt toward him. That was purely primal and almost predestined, as if she'd been waiting for him to show up. Which was silly. He was the enemy, she reminded herself with a heavy frown. She just needed to get her head straight, and focus on the task at hand, instead of the intriguing bronze-colored hand now resting casually on her counter.

"It's not your fault," she admitted. "I lost my cool, that's all. It won't happen again."

"Are you sure about that?"

"Positive."

"Good, then maybe you'll listen while I explain about the house."

"What's there to explain? You want to tear it down; I want to save it. And neither one of us is willing to give in." Sighing, she placed her hands in the pockets of her shorts, then quickly removed them when she saw the direction Chase's gaze was taking. The way the man looked at her— there went those goosebumps again!

"Look," she said, trying to find a place to put her hands and finally settling on leaning them against the counter separating her and Chase, "I know you have the upper hand. I mean, you do own the house and the land. I don't really have any business telling you what to do with your own property. I simply came to you, hoping we could discuss this like two adults. I thought maybe we could come up with something that would work—for both you and the town.''

She felt a little flicker of triumph at the look of admiration in his eyes.

''You seem to know a lot about the business world,'' he said, finally taking his eyes off her long enough to study the shop. ''Didn't you say you own this place?''

''Yes, I do.'' She couldn't help the proud grin on her face. ''Grandpa helped me get it started—co-signed the loan at the bank. We've been open almost four years now, and we're doing okay.''

''What made you decide to go into the antique business?'' he asked, picking up a miniature glass bottle that was dated 1910. He looked down at the red-colored glass then back up at her, his intense eyes making her feel shaky again.

''I've always loved old things,'' she explained, memories clouding her mind. ''Guess that comes from living with my grandparents, off and on, all my life. They taught me to appreciate the past.''

Chase set the bottle down, giving her his full attention. ''What do you mean off and on?''

Jody glanced away, then back at him. ''When I was four, my mother and I moved in with Grandpa Mitt and Grandma Rose—my father's parents.''

''Why?''

''Because my father died in Vietnam.''

Chase let out a breath, his eyes colliding with hers in the gathering dusk of late afternoon. ''I'm sorry.''

Jody didn't dare indulge in his sympathy. ''After that, my mother was never quite the same, according to what they tell me. I don't remember how she was before, except for the singing. She loved to sing. I'll always remember that part of her.

''When I was five, my mother left me with my grandparents. For almost two years, no one knew where she was. Then she showed up one day, married to a drummer in a rock band. She wanted to take me on the road with her. We made it as far as Tallahassee, and the drummer said either

I had to go or he would. She called my grandparents to come and pick me up.''

Chase stood perfectly still, his eyes telling her he understood the heartache she must have felt.

Not wanting his pity, she backed away. ''That was just the first of many such episodes,'' she said, her voice husky. ''And I really don't want to talk about it anymore—except to say that when I first laid eyes on Spence House, I fell in love with it. I guess it represented everything I dreamed about—a home to live in, a family to love me, something solid I could depend on.''

Chase spoke at last. ''But you've always had your grandparents, right? I never really knew mine.''

Jody didn't miss the touch of sadness in his admission. Maybe money and power didn't bring complete happiness, after all.

''That's too bad,'' she said. ''Grandparents are wonderful. Especially when you don't have reliable parents. But my grandmother died a few years ago—it's just me and Grandpa now. And my mother—she just moved back here.'' She wasn't ready to discuss the details of *that* relationship. ''So when you ask me why I opened up this shop, I can only say because it's something that belongs to me. I can make it or shape it; I can control it. And I can walk away from *it*. It's just wood and concrete. It can't ever desert me.''

Chase reached a hand across the counter, but she saw the restraint behind his tentative gesture. ''Like your mother did?''

Realizing she sounded like a charity case, Jody moved her own hand away before she did something really stupid like cry on his shoulder. ''I'm sorry,'' she said. ''I don't want you to think I sit around wallowing in self-pity. I know I'm lucky. I've had a basically good life and I've got a lot of people around who care about me. And I'm probably overreacting about the house, but still . . . I just wish we could find a way to save that old place.'' Giving him a wry smile, she added, ''That house is a source of strength; it's empty now, but once it was loved. It's seen neglect, it's been deserted—but it's still standing.''

His eyes held a warm liquid light that brought a rush of heat to her skin. ''Just like you.''

Jody couldn't help her response to that light. ''Just like me.'' Then, realizing she was acting like a silly teenager again, she quoted Chase's words to her earlier, ''And why am I telling you all this anyway?''

''Touché,'' he said, grinning. Then his eyes grew serious again. ''Look, Jody, I'm sorry about the house. But there's really no other way. It would take a lot of time and money to repair it and then it'd be sitting there empty anyway. I can't live there; I travel too much and I have a home in Florida. My aunt is the only Spence left, except for my parents. And believe me, they could care less about an old house in a small town. Why not build something in that spot that can benefit the whole town, as my great-great-grandfather's actions benefited Hampleton when it was just getting started?''

''I thought you weren't him?'' Jody countered, frustration blazing through her words.

''No, I'm not.'' He looked as aggravated as she felt. ''But I have a vision, a plan to make this town stronger and better. I promised my aunt that piece of property wouldn't go to waste and I intend to honor that promise.''

She lowered her head, closing her eyes for a calming minute. ''I can't argue with that kind of logic,'' she conceded. ''And it's awfully noble of you to try and make things better in a town you know nothing about. But then, I suppose that's what makes a man like you a success—always looking at the big picture. Your great-great-grandfather was a visionary. But what are you, exactly? Why are you really here?''

Thunderclouds moved through his gray eyes. ''I told you—although I don't normally explain my actions to anybody. I might not be a visionary in the traditional sense, but I know what I'm doing. I've done extensive research, market surveys, cost analysis and plenty of projections. This is a strong proposal. It'll bring new commerce to this area, give people jobs, or do you even care about all that?''

Jody faced him nose to nose. "Of course I care. And I also care about this town's heritage, your heritage. I've got some plans of my own, just no cash to back them." Then, ideas springing up in her head like spider lilies, she asked, "Why can't you build around the house?"

Chase shook his head in wonder. "You expect people to shop at a place with a dilapidated old house sitting right in the middle of it?"

"But if you fixed it up . . ." Knowing he was right, she backed down, for now. "Okay, okay. I had to try at least. When will you start taking it down?"

"In a few days, if everything goes according to plan." He gave her a quiet, steady look. "You're welcome to salvage anything that's left inside."

"Thank you." She gazed up at him, a hesitation in her next words. "Chase, you're going to think I'm crazy—I guess you already think that—but could I buy the cupola? Could you make sure it gets taken down in one piece? I'll fix it up—maybe make a gazebo out of it to go in the yard out at Grandpa's farm."

"You can have it," he said, his gaze warming her body temperature. "Consider it a gift from me to you—for caring." Then he said something that threw her completely off guard. "I'm leaving the big magnolia, the one in the far back garden. I used to climb that tree on the rare occasions my parents brought me to visit my aunt. I've given orders that it isn't to be touched."

So he didn't particularly love old houses, but he sure had a thing for magnolia trees. It was a start. At least he was willing to preserve something.

For just a minute, Jody admitted to herself that he really was a nice guy, and that he was only doing his job. But the pain of having to witness that great house falling down was too much to bear, nice guy or not.

Before she could voice her thoughts, Mitt ambled up the aisle from the back of the store, clearing his throat again.

"It's quittin' time," he said, his eyes as innocent as a new-blooming petunia. "Suppertime, too. Chase, want to come out to the farm for a mess of fresh bream? I caught

43

them right in the creek that runs by the house.''

"Grandpa," Jody protested, shooting him a meaningful look. "I'm sure Chase has a thousand things to do before getting started on his project."

Chase looked from the old man to Jody, his own eyes devoid of anything near innocence. "Actually, I am kind of hungry. And I haven't had fresh bream in a long time. That sounds great."

"Great," Mitt echoed, his smile a study in politeness as he herded them out the door.

"Great," Jody murmured, her smile as fixed as the dead bolt she turned on the set of double doors.

"I'll take the truck," Mitt offered. Turning on surprisingly spry feet for a man of his age, he told Jody, "Maybe you can ride with Chase, so he don't get lost."

"Sure," Jody said, wishing her grandfather wouldn't try to fix her up with every eligible man who happened to drop into town. But then, eligible men were rare around here. Not that she was looking, of course. Groaning inwardly, she motioned to Chase, noting the smug look on his handsome face. "Let's go, city boy. If we wait much longer, the mosquitoes will carry our fish off before we get the first bite."

An hour later, Jody stood at the kitchen sink, slicing fresh cucumbers for a salad, listening to the sizzling sound of fish being fried outside on the fish cooker she'd given her grandfather for Christmas. Smiling, she mentally gave her grandfather a hug, her love for the old man always a source of strength when she was feeling blue. Mitt Calhoun could make a mule laugh, she thought as she listened to him regale Chase with stories of his fishing excursions.

"It's the honest truth," Mitt was saying, his hands moving in story-telling banter. "I sneezed and out flew my false teeth. Happened back about five years ago. I'm telling you, somewhere on Lake Seminole, a big ol' bass is swimming around wearing my teeth. Had to buy a new set!"

Jody eyed Chase for signs of boredom, but his little-boy grin didn't look anywhere near bored. He was actually enjoying himself. And what a grin! It sizzled as hot as the bream turning over in the cooker.

Drying her hands on a towel, she walked out of the kitchen, passing through the long central hallway where the dining table was set up to collect cool breezes, making a quick check on the table setting before she slipped through the squeaky screen door to the back porch. Mitt and Chase were sitting under a billowy chinaberry tree, each in rusty metal lawn chairs, sipping their beers while the bream browned nicely in the bubbling-hot peanut oil.

Walking down the wooden porch steps, Jody couldn't help but notice the way Chase's eyes crinkled up when he laughed at her grandfather's colorful stories. He was really well-mannered and civilized. But what else would she expect from a Spence? The surprising part was that he was even here with her and her grandfather in the first place. Someone had obviously neglected to tell him old money didn't mix with dirt farming. The Spences and Calhouns of old had never traveled in the same circles, except when her great-grandfather Tucker Calhoun had worked for the Spences.

As she looked down at Chase, he glanced up, his eyes catching hers in the pinkish-blue dusk. Jody's heart did a somersault as that same surreal feeling she'd experienced in his office came over her again. There was something there, in the depths of his eyes, that made her shiver in the heat of the day. It wasn't that she was scared of him, it was more that she was scared of *herself* when she was around him. She felt she already knew what his lips would feel like on her mouth, as if she already knew what his big, tanned hands would feel like as they moved over her body. He was forbidden. This she knew even though he was right here and very real, very accessible. Lord, she had to stop inventing these Gothic fantasies!

Tugging at the wide straps of the faded print sundress she'd changed into, Jody skipped down the last porch step, determined to push these feelings about Chase Spence away. After all, the man had come here to tear down a house that she held dear. And he'd soon be gone just as quickly as that brilliant sun setting over the pastures to the west. No point in dreaming about what she couldn't have. The man was as unattainable as the house—out of her league.

"Well, well, don't you look pretty," Grandpa said, pulling up another old chair, motioning for her to sit.

"Thank you," she said, her eyes on Chase. His look seemed to indicate he felt the same way. Jody squirmed into the chair, well aware that she rarely went to this much trouble to get dressed up, and silently reprimanding herself because she'd done it tonight. Well, heck, a girl could get all whimsical every now and then, couldn't she? And they hardly ever had company for supper, so where was the harm?

The harm was in the way Chase continued to look at her. The harm was in the way his boyish grin slowly turned into a very adult male predatory stare. The harm was in the way she was responding to that stare, chill bumps popping up through the fine sheen of sweat trickling down her backbone.

Jumping up out of the chair, she tossed her ponytail back over her shoulder. "I just came out to tell you the salad and potatoes are ready. How much longer on the fish?"

" 'Bout five minutes," Mitt said, his eyes filled with an amused light. "Some things can't be rushed, girly."

"I'll get the ice and tea ready," she said, already headed back to the house, the smell of fried fish telling her nervous stomach her appetite was gone.

"Let me help," Chase called, hopping out of his chair to follow her.

"You're company," she protested, as he rushed to hold the screen door open for her. "You don't have to help."

"I want to," he said, following her into the house, squinting as his eyes adjusted to the muted kitchen light.

Jody watched as his gaze swept over their surroundings; did he think her grandfather's hundred-year-old farmhouse was too quaint and old-fashioned? But his next words had nothing to do with the farmhouse.

"Your dress is pretty," he said, his eyes settling back on her. "You look nice."

"Thanks." She smoothed her hands over the soft cotton skirt. "Actually, it's my mother's. One of the many things she left behind." At his raised brow, she laughed. "Yes, I like old clothes, too."

Chase took the pitcher of tea from her, pouring it into the tall glasses filled with ice. "Where's your mother now?"

Jody didn't look up. "She's upstairs, asleep. She's been ill. I just moved her back here from Louisiana."

"So that's why you were there?"

"Yep." She glanced out the window, hoping to change the subject. "Looks like Grandpa's just about ready."

Chase didn't push her for any more information regarding her mother. Instead, he looked around the kitchen, his eyes taking in the modern appliances mingling with old, traditional country furnishings. Jody let him look. This was a homey room, all blues and whites, all chipped enamel and cast iron. She certainly wasn't ashamed of it.

"No wonder you love old things," he said, surprising her with the warmth of his words. "This place is beautiful."

"Not what you're used to, I'll bet," she said, unable to voice her gratitude that he didn't look down on her way of life.

"No, I'm used to coming home to an efficient beach house, usually with a bag of take-out food in one hand and a briefcase full of paperwork in the other. I've got an ocean view, but I can't remember the last time I actually took the time to enjoy it." His expression filled with remorse. "You're lucky to live such a simple life, Jody."

Jody stopped stirring peas, her eyes locking with his. Why did she sense a loneliness about him that equaled her own? Curiosity caused her next question. "You . . . live alone?"

"Most of the time," he said, a teasing light cresting in his eyes as he set the tea glasses on the table. "My mother says I have one of the prettiest homes on the Gulf coast, but it badly needs a woman's touch."

"She didn't help you decorate it?" Jody wondered just how many woman had seen the inside of his beach pad.

"My mother refuses to meddle in my life," he replied, his eyes losing some of their luster. "My father's an executive for a large real estate company, so they travel a lot. She claims she doesn't have time to baby me anymore."

"Sounds like a wise woman," Jody said, laughing up at him. "But what about your father? I mean, he is a Spence. And if he's involved in real estate, why didn't he come back here to take care of Spence House?"

Chase stood silently staring out into the night, his light mood evaporating. "He prefers going after bigger fish," he said, that stormy darkness shadowing his eyes.

"Did someone mention fish?" Mitt entered then, breaking the bleak moment with his boisterous call. "Here they are, so just sit yourselves down for some of the best eating this side of the Florida line."

"He's very modest about his cooking," Jody said, motioning for Chase to have a seat.

"It sure smells good." Chase took the platter of fish, picking two of the biggest ones to put on his plate. Jody watched as he waited politely for her and Mitt to serve themselves before he dived in with both hands, pulling the crispy fishtail away so he could strip the backbone from the fish and get started eating the flaky, white meat. After taking a hefty bite, he leaned back in his chair, his smile that of a happy man. "Thank you," he said, glancing first at Mitt, then back at Jody, his eyes flowing over her like the warm summer wind pushing through the screen door. "I really appreciate you having me to supper."

Mitt beamed. "Well, son, you're welcome back anytime."

"I might just take you up on that," Chase answered, his eyes still on Jody.

Jody's stiff smile belied the inner turmoil whirling through her mind. She didn't want to like this man. She didn't want to feel the strange feelings she couldn't push away every time she was around him. And she didn't want to watch him destroy his heritage. Because she knew, once he tore down Spence House, he'd also tear down whatever feelings she might have had for him. And that made her wonder what might have been.

Which was something she never wondered. Unlike her mother, Jody wasn't a dreamer.

Or at least, she hadn't been—until now.

Home Again

* * *

It was well past midnight, but Chase Spence knew he wouldn't be getting much sleep that night. Standing at the open window of his office, he cursed the hot night and the mosquitoes buzzing hungrily around his neck. His eyes settled once again on Spence House looming across the wide expanse of street separating it from the empty, creaking office building he alone inhabited at this bewitching hour.

The large house seemed to be watching Chase just as intensely as he had been watching it for the past half-hour. But Chase didn't really see the moonlight reflected in the aged window panes of the imposing mansion. Instead, the crystal flow of moonbeams spilling through the still summer night reminded him of a pair of crystal-cut eyes that had caught his own and held him in a timeless grip of sheer need and longing.

Jody Calhoun's eyes. Haunting, luminous eyes that had given him a sense of knowing, almost a sense of recognition. Had he met her before somewhere, seen her in a crowd? Was he remembering those eyes from another place, another time?

Impossible, he thought now, smiling over at the silent house that watched him struggle with the night's secrets. He would have remembered *her*. You didn't forget a face like that, so seductive in its pure innocence. You didn't forget hair the color of yellowed straw, golden with promise and lush with sunlight. And a man could never, ever forget those country girl curves, built from nature's own exotic bounty, as fresh and earthy as the red clay she'd obviously been molded from by a sculpturer's hand. Mother Nature had endowed Jody Calhoun. She was the epitome of earth mother and flower child, all rolled into one luscious, ripe package.

And she wanted to stop him from tearing down the house he now stood confronting.

Why? The businessman in him asked what was in it for her. Why would she bother with a house nobody else wanted to fool with? Why was it so important to her to save the old, gaudy house that looked like an aged cancan girl, well past its prime. And why, oh, why, did Jody Calhoun's feelings suddenly seem so important to him?

It was the connection he'd felt toward her, maybe a purely physical attraction, maybe a connecting of souls, but when she'd walked—no, pranced—into his office with her lovely smile and her long, tanned legs, the jolt had hit him in his gut and had stayed to spread like warm honey all over his body.

And tonight, hours after he'd shared a meal with Jody and her grandfather, the jolt was still there, tugging at his consciousness, screaming like a siren through the logical planes and angles of his mind, humming like an electric buzz over the tired recesses of his brain, interrupting his thought processes so he was unable to focus on his work. This scared the hell out of him. Nothing ever came between Chase Spence and his work.

What was it Marcy, the model, had said in parting? "Good luck with your latest venture, Chase. Stay curled up with your charts and graphs, baby, cause they're about as emotional as you and you're about as flat and hard to read as them."

Very insightful words from such a shallow mind. Or maybe Marcy had gone deeper than he'd given her credit for. Actually, he'd never taken the time to delve any further. Same old story. He didn't love them, so they left him. So he turned back to his work, always shooting ahead to the future, always trying to stay ahead of the pack—just to show his father he could do it faster, better, and more successfully than any of the rest.

And always falling just short of victory.

Turning back to the bright desk light illuminating his plans for the prime corner across the street, Chase rubbed the back of his stiff neck, wishing he could be on the beach again, running, running into the wind, free from all his responsibilities and his commitments. But he had a job to do, and crystal eyes be damned, he intended to get on with it.

With an almost apologetic glance, he looked back at the house behind him. He wouldn't feel guilty about its demise. He wouldn't sweat his decision; he never looked back.

Yet, he reminded himself grimly, he just had. And he could have sworn he'd heard a sigh emitting from the old house. Or maybe it had just been a stray bit of wind pushing through the open window at his back.

Chapter Three

Two days later, Jody stood staring at a set of wicker furniture she'd purchased from an estate sale in Thomasville. She always had good luck finding antiques in Thomasville. The larger town located farther south of Hampleton was full of old, antebellum homes loaded with antiques and collectibles, sometimes junk, sometimes real treasures.

Hope you find a good home again, she silently told the sturdy brown rattan loveseat and chair. There was also a matching desk and smaller chair.

"Of course, you'd be perfect at Spence House," she said.

"Talking to yourself again?" Mitt said from his rocker. He was reading the latest edition of *The Hampleton Journal*.

"Just thinking out loud." She shot him a glance through the wicker. "Anything interesting in the paper?"

Mitt eyed her over the paper's edge. "Yep. A whole write-up about your young man's big plans for that corner up the road."

As soon as the words were out of his mouth, Jody was standing by his side, looking at the paper. "He's not my young man. What's it say?"

"He's planning an outlet store, a couple of doctors' offices, some craft and specialty stores. All neat and compact, and as it points out here, centrally located right in the heart of town."

"All located right where Spence House is standing," Jody replied, her tone huffy. "He's already had it re-zoned, so it's too late to declare it a historical landmark. I don't think I can bear this."

"Better bear it," Mitt said, his eyes gentle. "It's scheduled to come down Friday."

"Friday?" Jody couldn't believe it was actually going to happen. And Chase hadn't even been by to tell her, which showed how much he cared about this town and her feelings. Well, he might be the best at dealing with designs and futuristic layouts, but the next time she saw him, he'd learn a thing or two about dealing with her emotions. She ran her hand through her hair. "Doesn't anybody besides me care about that house?"

Mitt reached out a hand, patting her on the arm. "Now, girly—that house is long past its prime. That's why Jeanette Spence up and left it; you know she was an old maid. Mercy, the kids used to tease her about that. I heard she did a lot of traveling after she retired from teaching."

"So they say," Jody replied, "but it's strange to me that she's never come back to her home, especially now when it's being demolished. Maybe I ought to call her up and ask her why she's letting Chase do this."

Mitt shook his head, his mouth set in a solemn line. "Stay out of it, Jodelyn. You've got enough on your hands with this place and your ma."

"I know—I need to mind my own business," Jody said. "But, Grandpa, what if I had a plan . . . what if I could convince Chase that he could have his cake and eat it, too?"

Mitt took a long swig of soda, then leaned forward to stare at his granddaughter. "You're talking dangerous, girly."

"No, I'm talking business. If I can just make Chase listen to reason. I've been thinking about this a lot."

Pulling up out of his chair, Mitt said, "I know that look,

53

Jodelyn. It's the same look you used to get when you wanted candy at Siwell's and I'd already told you no.''

Smiling, Jody dipped her head. "But I always got the candy, didn't I?"

"Yep. And that's what scares me." Coming to stand in front of her, he said softly, "I know I've spoiled you, honey. But I only did it out of love. Maybe I was wrong to give in to you so much,'cause now you think you should get your way all the time. And it just don't happen that way. Sometimes, you have to give up and accept things . . . like now.''

Jody gave her grandfather a bear hug and a big kiss. "You didn't spoil me so bad that I'd go and do anything stupid, Grandpa. You raised me right. And you also raised me to fight for what I believe in. And I believe in that old house. Somehow, I have to make Chase believe in it, too."

Mitt lifted his eyes to heaven. "That boy don't stand a chance."

"Not if I can help it," Jody replied sweetly.

Two hours later, Jody stood at the door of Chase's office, her hair falling down past her shoulders, her new sundress pressed and starched, and her picnic basket full of fried chicken and potato salad. Hoping she wasn't about to make a complete idiot of herself, she took a deep, measured breath. She'd never before tried to use her feminine wiles on any man, so she wasn't quite sure if she was going about it the right way. But she had learned a thing or two from watching her wayward mother.

"Men like you to look pretty," she remembered Maria Calhoun saying as she'd sat combing her own long strawberry-blond hair. That had been before husband number two. The next time Jody had seen her mother, both the attitude and the hair color had changed.

"Don't ever trust a man, honey," had been her sage advice, the voice jaded and husky, the hair a bright auburn. "He'll tell you you're pretty, when you know he's lying. But the mirror never lies, and when the man leaves, the mirror is still there."

Home Again

You were always pretty to me, Mama. And what am I doing here?

She was about to make a fast getaway when the door to Chase's office opened and he stood looking down at her, his eyes filled with that delicious light she was beginning to like.

Chase gazed on the vision that had haunted his dreams and nagged at his waking hours. But the flesh and blood woman standing in front of him now was lovelier and more poignant than any dream. And her fresh-faced beauty put Marcy and all the other sophisticated women he'd ever known to shame. Feeling as awkward and tongue-tied as he had the day his mother'd made him attend his first soiree, he simply said, "Hi."

"Uh . . . hi." No chance of running now.

He leaned a little closer, his momentary lapse of sanity passing. "I thought I smelled fried chicken."

She held up the wicker picnic basket. "You do. I . . . I thought we could go on a picnic. To Spence House." At his surprised look, she added, "You did promise me I could salvage anything from it I wanted. I thought we'd take a look."

He lifted a brow. "Now? Together?" He wasn't so sure he could handle another meal with this luscious creature, since food was the last thing on his mind.

Nodding, she said, "Yes, unless you're busy. Here, why don't you just take the chicken." Shoving the basket toward him, she added, "This was probably a bad idea."

Pulling her into the office, he laughed. "No. No. In fact, this is the best idea I've heard all day. I've been meaning to come by the shop . . . to let you know about things." *Only I was trying to concentrate on my work, and not that little beauty mark on your left cheek.*

"But you couldn't find the time." It was her turn to lift a brow. "I understand."

He could tell by her tone she didn't understand. And neither did he. He'd come here on a mission, intent on getting the job done, intent on cashing in on another venture. Now, this bundle of curves and lips and hair had him afraid to venture out of the safety of his office. Not something he wanted to share with his vice-presidents and department heads at the next corporate meeting. Telling himself she was just a woman, a mere mortal just like him—although he had been accused of being an unfeeling robot once by a Palm Beach socialite—he gritted his teeth against his lust.

"I'm sorry." He inched closer. "That chicken sure smells good. But your perfume smells even better." *Now, how did that slip out?*

Now we're getting somewhere, Jody thought smugly. *I'll have to tell Miss Edith her choice of fragrance paid off.*

She gave him her best smile, the one she used to finagle antique dealers into to coming down on their lofty prices and junkyard vendors into practically giving her their dubious treasures. "So you'll go to lunch with me?"

"I'd love to." He stuck his head out the door, not stopping to analyze anything or evaluate why he was doing what he said he wouldn't do. "Betty, do I have anything scheduled for the next couple of hours?"

Betty, a petite black woman with a short fashionable hair cut and large intricately carved wooden earrings, eyed them curiously. "No, sir. You've got contractors coming in at three."

"Then I'll be back around three," Chase said, ushering Jody out into the hallway, past Betty's wide-eyed stare.

They took the elevator and Jody could feel the eyes upon them with each creak and groan of the ancient open-weaved iron-gated mechanism.

"We're being watched," Chase said into her ear, his warm breath tickling her neck.

"I know." She made a quick sweep of the building, wondering why no one seemed interested in getting any work done. "You know, there's an old rumor that says your ancestor had a secret tunnel built from the cellar of Spence House to this building. Maybe we should have gone that route instead."

Thinking of the possibilities involved in being lost in the dark with her, he chuckled. "They'd really get a kick out of that, but I think it is just a rumor, I haven't seen any evidence of a tunnel.'' Nodding toward a cherubic saleslady eyeing them from the houseware department, he said, ''Of course, we're starting a whole new set of rumors.''

''So, what else is new?'' Jody enjoyed the feeling of doing something forbidden and out of the ordinary. Maybe she was enjoying this a little too much, she thought, straightening her back and making herself presentable as the elevator reached the bottom floor. She didn't mind raising a few eyebrows, but she didn't want to get a bad reputation, either. The one she had—respectable and hard-earned—suited her just fine.

As if sensing her withdrawal, Chase nudged her out of the elevator. ''Hey, where's that drop-dead smile you were wearing a minute ago?''

''Guess I'm a little nervous,'' she admitted. ''I don't normally push myself on people.''

He stopped right in the middle of the store, his gaze moving over her face and hair. ''Who's complaining?''

''Well, no one that I can see,'' she said, giggling in spite of the eyes watching them. ''But everyone will be talking. I don't want you to think I'm . . . loose.''

He gave her an astonished look. ''Loose?''

''Yes, you know . . . a wild woman, a man-chaser.''

Good Lord, he didn't know this kind of innocence still existed in the world. It was refreshing, but disturbing, too. He wasn't exactly sure how he was supposed to deal with it. ''Is that just small-town mentality?'' he asked, real worry in his eyes, ''or are you really afraid to be alone with me?''

''I can handle myself,'' she replied huffily, marching for the door. ''And I expect you to behave.''

He rushed to catch up with her. ''Yes, ma'am. I wouldn't dream of doing anything to compromise your reputation.'' And he wouldn't tell her that in his dreams, he'd done exactly that.

''Now you're getting the idea,'' she said, swinging through the heavy glass door with one push of her hip. ''Life's just a little different here, Chase. It doesn't matter how modern the real world is, some things never change.''

''Which is why I prefer city life,'' he stated, squinting up at the clouds. "Here, let me carry the basket. Is that allowed?"

Jody eyed him curiously, thinking he was making fun of her. "Believe it or not, we do have indoor plumbing here, and cable TV, just like in the big city. And even though women are liberated here, just like in New York or Atlanta, we do want to be treated with respect."

"I see." He swung the basket, looking sheepish as they crossed the street toward Spence House, his eyes following the natural sway of her hips. "And I'll punch the guy who doesn't give you every bit of the respect you deserve."

Jody laughed, the indignation leaving her face. "You don't have to. I was a tomboy, growing up. I've punched out a few bullies in my time."

"I can believe that." He could also believe she'd probably wound up bringing those same bullies to their knees years later at high school dances and weekend hangouts.

They reached the iron gates of the house. Chase pushed at one of the heavy rusting bars, then looked up at the imposing mansion, trying desperately to put his mind to work on something sound and sure. "It is impressive," he said as he guided her through the over-grown driveway.

She stopped, catching her breath as she gazed up at the three-storied house. "Have you even been inside?"

Lifting his head to stare at the spires shooting up around the widow's walk, he said, "Only to consult with the demolition team. But I used to come here with my parents when I was younger. I can't remember much about it, except that my father always complained about having to drive up here to visit Aunt Jeanette. I'd make a quick, polite appearance at Sunday dinner, then spend the rest of the time out in the gardens. That's how I found the magnolia—I loved to climb up inside that tree. That particular spot was my fantasy land, where I could slay dragons or charge with the cavalry, typical little boy stuff." He shrugged. "It seems so silly now. I haven't been here since I turned twelve. That's when Aunt Nette moved to Florida."

She again felt a glimmer of hope. "Why haven't you been back?"

"Oh, I don't know. Time and circumstances, and a feeling of loneliness. This is such a gloomy place."

Jody took in his story, wondering why he seemed so intent on getting rid of this house. Again, she sensed a loneliness in him that matched her own. Except she had Grandpa to cushion her falls. Whom did Chase have? Shrugging off her curiosity, she set her mind back to the task at hand. "So you haven't really had a good tour of the entire house?"

He shook his head. "Not yet. I've been so busy getting zoning permits and building permits. Starting a new project is always hectic. My construction foreman, Wade Holland, has been dealing with the house. I just haven't had time to really explore it."

"Now's your chance." She tugged him along, knowing the way much better than he did. "We'll eat first; then we'll have a look around. There's a spot out back near an old broken fountain. It'll be cooler there."

Carefully, they made their way through the overgrown crape myrtles that continued to bloom a bright pink in the midst of all this decay, adding a melancholy beauty to the once perfectly landscaped gardens. Wisteria vines threatened the whole house, their fragrance cloyingly sweet in the hot sun. Thick, lush camellia bushes burst forth at each curve of the sandy driveway.

"You should see these camellias when they bloom in the fall," Jody said. "They're so beautiful—and I've been told they were your great-grandmother's favorite flower."

"It must have been some garden back then." Chase stopped, again looking around the large lot. "A lot of work went into this old place."

Jody thought she sensed a tad of regret in his tone. She leaped on it like a cat on cream. "Yep. And in a few days, it'll all be gone."

"Jody?" He lifted a brow, then leaned his head to one side. "You didn't bring me here hoping I'd change my mind, now did you?"

Shocked, Jody almost panicked. Whether it was because he was right, or because she was so obvious, she didn't know.

But she had to tread lightly, or he'd bolt like deer. "Chase, I know I can't do that." Tossing her long hair back, she shook her head. "Heavens, no. I just wanted you to see it— to understand why I'm going to miss it so much."

"All right." He relaxed a little. "There's a bench. Want to break into that chicken?"

"Sure." *Good,* she thought, *get his mind off the house for now. Maybe after we eat, I can tell him about my ideas.*

Heading for the stone bench Chase indicated, she ducked underneath what remained of a grape arbor. A few puny muscadines clung to a skinny vine, their neglect evident in the limp way they shifted in the sultry breeze. Nearby, the fountain she'd mentioned sat crusty and dry like an un-washed dinner plate, its pool overgrown with thirsty ivy, a broken Cupid figurine lying as if asleep on its upper tier with its arrow pointed toward the spot Chase had chosen.

Jody sensed the sadness shrouding the place, a little shiver going down her spine in spite of the sun's warmth on her skin. Tossing off the gloom, she became even more deter-mined to win Chase over to her side. "You know," she said, pulling a white table cloth out of the basket to spread across the bench, "your great-great-grandfather Jackson Spence used to make his own wine. The story goes that he had twenty-thousand gallons of wine locked in the basement of Spence House when a prohibition law went into effect. Because the county was "bone dry" the wine couldn't be used. So when he died, the wine was still sitting here."

Thinking he could use a good stiff drink, Chase asked, "It's not still in there, is it?"

"Of course not, silly," she continued as she spread their food out on the bench between them. "When he died, he left instructions for the wine to go to the University of Geor-gia. He thought the school could get some money out of it. But the university honored the prohibition law and finally decided to dump all the wine down the gutter. It was worth about forty thousand dollars."

Chase sat down, eyeing the dirty windows of what ap-peared to be the basement of the house. Taking the can of soda she offered him, he said, "You're kidding, right?"

60

"Now why would I make up something like that?" she asked, wondering if he'd ever read a history book. "Didn't your daddy tell you any of this?"

He picked up a chicken leg. "No. He doesn't talk about our family history very much. I don't think he enjoyed small-town life. According to what my mother's told me, he left Hampleton when he graduated from high school. He met her at Florida State University and they got married. He got a job selling real estate, went on to form his own company, and they've lived in Florida ever since." *And they'd never had time for their only son,* but he didn't bother telling her that story. Somehow, he didn't think he'd get any sympathy with his poor little rich boy melodrama.

Jody watched his face, saw the shadow of tension passing over his features. He sure didn't want to talk about his folks. But then, she didn't want to discuss her mother with him either. So she changed the subject somewhat. "Is that why your Aunt Jeanette lives in Florida now?"

"Yes. She's the last one—the baby daughter—out of Jackson's seven children. She was born in 1908, and she never married. She actually lived here until the early seventies."

"About the time I came to town," Jody reasoned. "That's about how long the house has been vacant."

Chase took a hefty bite of potato salad. "I think she tried to keep it up for a while, and my father was supposed to help her, but he stayed busy with his own career. Looks as if they let things slide."

"I'll say." Jody couldn't understand why these people would turn their back on their roots, but then her own mother had refused to live in Hampleton until recently, so who was she to judge? "Well, there are lots of stories about your ancestors," she said. "Did you know the town was named after Jackson's older brother, John Hample Spence?"

"I've heard that much," he said, chewing his chicken with a look of absolute pleasure. "This is good."

"Thank you." Jody took a swallow of her drink. "Yeah, John Hample loved this spot, but he never made it back from the Civil War." Leaning close, she whispered, "They

61

say his ghost haunts this house."

Chase looked skeptical. "If he died in the Civil War, how could he haunt a house that wasn't built until the 1880's?"

"You have been doing some research."

"Yes, I have," he had to admit. "Aunt Nette's told me some of the family history. And when I hired Betty, she filled me in on a lot of the legends, but she didn't mention a ghost." He cupped his mouth with his hands, then whispered, "Tell me why old John Hample haunts Spence House."

Jody sat back, her eyes dreamy. "Because he and Jackson used to go hunting right here on this very spot, before the war. Legend has it that John Hample loved it here so much, he vowed to come back and build a town—and a grand house—right here."

Chase could believe that much. "Aunt Nette said he died a hero's death, so Jackson built the town and this house in honor of his brother. I've always wanted a brother myself."

"See, you do know a few things. And why don't you have a brother or sister?"

Chase looked up at the house, his eyes moving over the various porches and windows. "My parents hardly had time for me, let alone another child. I spent most of my childhood in boarding schools and with nannies—most of whom I terrorized simply to get attention."

Jody's heart went out to him. She certainly knew all about that. "We're not so different after all, city boy."

"I'm beginning to see that," he said, his eyes softening. "Tell me some more about John Hample."

Feeling triumphant, she went on. "Well, he and Jackson were very close. They had big plans for this area. But only one of them lived to see it all happen." She looked around, the sadness of the place shrouding her. "The other one's still trying to get back here, apparently."

"He never got to build his house," Chase finished, understanding coloring his eyes. "So his brother did it for him." For reasons he couldn't begin to understand, this tale of two brothers and their dreams was really getting to him. Maybe it was because the woman telling it was getting to him. Not a good sign; he couldn't let Jody's romantic embellishments sway his decisions or his determination.

Jody enjoyed watching him get caught up in the stories. Maybe he'd see the value of the house if she kept pumping him with its history. "And named the town after him."

Chase grinned then. "Heck, where'd he get that name? Hample? It sounds like something the Spence family would saddle a kid with. You see, we're all so very proper and upstanding."

"Oh, you!" She tossed her paper napkin at him. "It was probably someone's maiden name. Do you want some more potato salad—in your face?"

"No, on my plate, if you don't mind."

They continued the light banter until all the chicken was eaten, then Jody pulled out her special weapon. "Would you like a slice of fresh peach pie?"

He had to wonder if any peach could taste as fresh as her lips looked. Groaning, he patted his stomach. "All this country cooking will kill me. Or is that the plan?"

Trying to maintain an air of innocence, Jody only smiled. "I can't take the credit. A woman who helps us out at the shop cooked all this. I'm lousy in the kitchen."

"I get it," he said, testing a sliver of peach. "Ummm, good. You ordered up all this, delivered it in person, so you could watch me die a happy man?"

"I'm not trying to kill you," she said, giggling again. "Haven't you ever heard of southern hospitality?"

"Yeah, and I've also heard of 'killing someone with kindness,' " he retorted, a teasing light in his eyes. Unable to look at him, Jody decided right then and there that she wasn't cut out to be a vamp. She hated conning him like this, but she had to make him listen to reason. She couldn't let him destroy this house.

"Are you ready to see the place?" Finishing her own slice of pie, she hopped up. At his mouthful-of-pie nod, she said, "I'll just toss our remains back in the basket, then we'll go. It's getting late and Grandpa will be needing his afternoon nap."

Chase jumped up. "All right." Lifting his head to stare

up at the cupola, he squinted. "Look at all that ornate trim. All those swirls and curly-cues make me think of a gingerbread house. The plans were designed by a German architect."

"How'd you know that?"

He shrugged. "I guess Aunt Nette told me."

Pleased that he had some knowledge of the house, Jody said, "It's very Victorian, though, isn't it?"

He nodded. "From what I remember studying about the Victorian age, I'd say this is a prime example. But I'm used to dealing in concrete and steel."

And that's the difference between us, Jody thought. *I'm too old-fashioned for my own good.* "Well, come on," she said, her tone lighter than her mood. "We can go through the back."

Leading him through the garden, she found what had once been a path to the back steps of the wrap-around porch. The wood had been painted white at one time, but the banisters and porch posts were now a rustic gray.

"Be careful," Chase warned her as she climbed the broken steps." Taking her by the elbow, he guided her up to the porch. "That's something I do know about. This place should have been condemned years ago."

She hid her disappoint. "Maybe, but it's still pretty sturdy. I know. I come here a lot by myself."

"That's not wise," he pointed out, his tone reprimanding. "But I don't suppose you'd listen to my advice regarding this place, huh?"

"Probably not," she replied, smiling up at him. "But thanks for your concern."

Slowly, she pushed open the heavy back door, leading him into a wide central hallway. A hot, musty aroma greeted them, its perfume aged and mellowed by the years. Mounds of trash and bits of broken glass told the tale of the house's demise.

"The kitchen's to the right," she said, waving a hand toward the long room. "See all the paned windows? Or what's left of all the paned windows."

"I remember the kitchen." Chase stood staring around

him, his eyes wide with wonder. "So many rooms."

"Twenty-five," she replied reverently. "There's eleven down here, counting the bathrooms, servants' quarters, and the butler's pantry. And six bedrooms, three baths and a sunroom on the second floor, a third floor bath and the large third-floor room, then a small attic off to the side of the widow's walk, and of course, the cupola. I've counted them all."

"And been in all of them, no doubt," he added, smiling.

Directly in front of them, running along one wall, was the back side of the wide staircase, its banister and railings every bit as ornate as the rest of the house's trim.

Opening a door behind the staircase, she pushed him into a long room with a large window serving as its only source of light. "This is the study." Pushing open a smaller door off to one side of the room, she added, "And a small bathroom. I guess they added the modern fixtures later."

"Not modern enough," Chase said, looking over the rusted porcelain furnishings and the water closet over the commode. "I can just imagine the plumbing problems involved in a house like this."

Tugging him along, Jody headed past the stairs toward the formal parlor, where an ornate fireplace opened like a cave on the back wall of the room. "Across the way is the formal dining room" she said. This reminds me of that movie, you know, *Cheaper by the Dozen*."

He laughed, nodding. "It is Victorian—and Gothic. I can see why a ghost would like hanging out here."

She put a finger to his lips, the contact bringing his gaze to hers, and quickening her pulse. "Shhh. We wouldn't want to get him riled."

His eyes still on her, he wrapped his hand around her finger. "You don't really believe all that, do you?"

"I'm not one to question the great beyond," she explained, the pressure of his warm hand on hers as unnerving as the other worldly presence she knew existed in the house. For a long time, Chase stood there, watching and waiting, his gaze on her, a soft smile resting nicely on his full lips. "Boo!" He laughed as she jumped. "Gotcha."

"That's not funny," she said, glancing around nervously.

Giving her an amazed look, he said, "You really think he's listening, don't you?"

"Yes, I do," she said fervently. "I believe he's searching for what he lost." She looked up the stairs. "I can almost see all of Jackson's children running up and down these stairs. John Hample should have had children, too." Jody envisioned children running, all right. But they'd always belonged to her. Living in this house had been the only dream she'd ever allowed herself. Which brought her back to her original purpose for bringing Chase here. "This house was meant to be filled with children."

Chase's gaze swept over her, his eyes sending her messages that had nothing to do with touring an old house. His next question surprised both of them. "Do you like children, Jody?"

Something sure was stirring in the humid air, Jody thought, that shiver of anticipation slipping down her spine right along with a trinkle of sweat. Again, she felt disoriented and off center. Swallowing hard, she croaked, "Yes, I do. I want a big family—one day."

He stared down at her, his eyes as haunting as any ghost. "Another thing we have in common," he finally said. "But in my case, one day will be a long time coming."

"Oh, me too," Jody agreed, her eyes lifting to his. "Who has time for babies, right?" Then quickly changing the subject, she asked, "Do you want to see the cupola room?"

"That turret thing? Is it safe up there?"

"If we're careful." With a flounce of her floral skirt, she was off up the stairs. But she wasn't sure what she was running from—Chase's tempting lips, or her own need to give in to his charms. Finally, winded and sweaty, she reached the third floor landing, hanging her head over to make sure Chase was still with her. "Hey, city boy, you okay?"

"Just fine," he panted, dragging himself up by the last newel post. "And I thought I was in shape."

You are, Jody thought, her eyes dipping over his button-down cotton shirt and blue jeans. *At least he'd dropped the*

*business suit persona. And as good as he looked in a suit,
he looked twice as good in jeans. Sweat and all.*

"If I owned this house," she said, ignoring that little
tickle running rampant down her backbone, "I'd turn this
room into my bedroom."

Pushing Chase ahead of her, she walked him through an
open door into a wide, high-ceilinged room with alcove windows at each corner. In the center of the spacious room, a
large multipaned bay window overlooking the back garden
rose from the floor, dainty oriel-shaped fan lights crowning
its circular design.

"Look." She pulled him to the right, pushing at cobwebs.
A wide arched entranceway spanned the ornate steps opening to the rounded sitting room of the cupola. "A sunroom," she stated, decorating it in her mind as she'd done
a hundred times before. "I always see green and yellow in
this room—you know, lots of wicker and ferns and bright
printed cushions around the window seats. Sunflowers. Yes,
definitely sunflowers."

Chase took the two steps up to the octagon-shaped room.
"It's bigger than I thought," he said, stepping carefully over
a rotted board in the floor. "Not bad."

"It's beautiful," Jody whispered.

As if called by her words, a breeze pushed through the
broken panes of the eight upside-down-U-shaped windows,
lifting her hair away from her face. Turning, she raised her
arms, letting the breeze sweep over her body, her eyes
closed in appreciation as she forgot her plan to seduce
Chase. Indeed, she forgot everything but how this house
made her feel. Enjoying the way the wind whipped at the
flowing skirt of her dress, she sighed with a peaceful contentment, unaware of the effect she was having on the man
standing beside her until he spoke.

"*You're* beautiful."

Jody's eyes snapped open at Chase's whispered words.
How had he gotten so close? He was there, that stormy look
in his eyes again. And all around them, the eerie wind
whipped and whined, its song mournful and filled with longing. Off in the distance, Jody heard thunder. Or maybe it

was her heart trying to break out of her chest.

"I want to kiss you," he said, moving closer to her.

"What's stopping you?" she asked, her famous directness coming through loud and clear, even though her practical nature told her to keep her mouth shut.

Slowly, as gracefully as the warm wind dancing around them, Chase leaned forward, lifting her chin with one hand. Then, his eyes still on hers, he lowered his head, his eyes closing as the soft padding of his lips touched her mouth.

Lightening flashed through the air.

Thunder rolled through the heavens.

His mouth on hers was like coming home again. In her heart, she knew she'd touched this man's mouth with her lips before. He tasted so right, so fresh, so hot, so good! He kissed her with an intimate knowing that left her both contented and wanting at the same time.

Shivers went up and down Jody's spine, but somewhere in the midst of this earth-shaking event, reality groped back into focus. Dragging her lips away from his, she stared up at him. "I think it's going to rain."

Chase's groan shocked her out of her stupor. "I kiss you, and all you can say is it's going to rain?"

Giving him a level look that completely contradicted the unbalanced shift rocking her to the tips of her toes, she said, "Well, it is. I heard thunder."

"That was some kiss," he replied, his surprised eyes tracing the flush rising up her cheeks. "You're blushing."

Fanning herself with her hand, Jody said, "It's hot in here. I think we should go back downstairs."

Groaning again, he took her hand, pulling her through the room. "You're driving me crazy. Ever since I laid eyes on you, I can't think. I can't work. I'm a mess."

Jody smiled secretively at his broad back. "I'm sorry," she huffed as he yanked her down the stairs. "I just wanted to show you the house; I hoped you'd maybe change your mind."

They reached the bottom of the stairs and Chase whirled around so fast, he nearly knocked her backwards. "What did you say?"

"Nothing." She tried to scoot past him. "Let's go."

"No, you said you were hoping I'd change my mind. About the house, right?"

No longer able to play coy, Jody sighed long and hard. "Well, how can you still want to destroy it after seeing it?"

His piercing eyes went one shade grayer. "How can you stand there and even look me in the eye, after what just happened?"

"Nothing happened," she tried to reason. "We got caught up in the moment, that's all."

"Well, you're probably right," he said, running a hand through his clinging curls. "I . . . I got caught up in your magic, in some sort of spell. I knew I shouldn't have listened to you; hell, I shouldn't have even eaten lunch with you. You're nothing but trouble, and I knew it from the very beginning."

Feeling the sting of his words, she lowered her head. He was right. She'd always been trouble, for her mother, for her grandparents, for this town. Why should it be any different with him? Yet, she wanted it to be different with him, Lord help her. She tried to reach out to him. "Chase, I—"

"You brought me here deliberately, didn't you, Jody? You thought you could charm me into saving this house, right?"

Unable to look at him, she nodded. "Right. That's right, Chase. I don't want you to tear this house down—and I've got some ideas—maybe a way to save it and still have your shopping area."

Throwing both hands up in the air, he laughed bitterly. "Oh, that's just dandy. Two days before I'm scheduled to tear it down, you come up with a plan. Well, guess what? It won't work. This place is coming down—and you can just stand back and stay out of the way."

Watching his departing back, she rushed after him. "But Chase, if you'd only listen—"

He pivoted at the open back door they'd come through earlier. "No, Jody. I'm sorry you wasted your time and a good meal on me. But I'm here to do one thing—build that shopping center. Right here!" He pointed down at the floor.

She wanted to scream and stomp her foot, but knew that wouldn't get her any sympathy. "Look, Chase," she said through a breathless rush, "what I tried to do is no worse than you sweet-talking me in the drugstore the other day."

He walked back a few steps then, his hands on his hips. "Oh, yes it is, Jody. For one thing, I meant what I said. You do have incredible eyes. And you came to me, with those shattered-crystal eyes . . . and peach pie . . . and all that hair." He stopped, his gaze sweeping over her. "Jeez, your hair alone could make a man go stark-raving mad, and you use all that to try and get me to . . . to stop a project I've spent months working out."

"I'm sorry," she said, genuinely ashamed of what she'd tried to do. "Chase, I don't usually act like this. It's just that—"

A groaning, creaking sound stopped her next words. Looking over at Chase, Jody watched his expression change from mad to confused to disbelieving as the very floor beneath his feet seemed to sway and bend.

Before she could move, Chase's sharp intake of breath hissed through the air at about the same time his right foot pushed through a breaking board in the hallway floor. Watching in horrified fascination as the wide plank splintered then crashed through the floor, Jody screamed while long-settled dust flew up around them and startled pigeons roosting in the eaves fluttered away in confusion.

"Chase! Are you all right?" She rushed over to where he lay with one knee buried underneath the floor and the other twisted at a funny angle behind him. She kneeled down beside him, her heart racing with fear.

Chase groaned, pain etching his suddenly pale face. "Well, this is just great, really great!"

"What? What?" Jody didn't know if he was being cute or sarcastic, but he looked angry, very angry.

"My leg," he said, his teeth gritted. "Jody, I think I broke my leg."

Jody looked down at him, shock registering on her face. The wind pushed at her back; dust and cobwebs coated her skin, and she knew she'd just ruined any chance she might have had with Chase Spence—both in saving Spence House and in ever being able to kiss his incredibly sweet lips again.

Then she heard it. A man's hearty laughter echoed through the house, rumbling as loudly and clearly as the thunder booming off to the west.

John Hample Spence had just greeted his visitors in his own special way.

Chapter Four

"Tell me everything," Katie Winston said, her brown eyes wide with anticipation as she plopped down in a red vinyl booth at Siwell's.

Jody sat across from her, nursing a tall glass of lemonade while she toyed with the petal of a silk daisy that leaned out from a cluster nestled in a Mason jar in the booth's center.

"Well, what have you heard?" she asked, her whisper about as useless as a fly swatter in a hornet's nest. Everybody in the place wanted to know all the juicy details of Jody's latest escapade with Chase Spence.

Katie squinted, then sat back to go into deep conversation. "First, he burst into The Treasure Chest, demanding—no, begging—you to forgive him. Then you invited him to supper—bream, I believe. Then you marched into his office and whisked him away for a romantic picnic at Spence House and then he accidentally fell through the floor and you had to leave him there while you ran through a rainstorm to get help, and now you're fighting to save the house—that was a real slam-banger of a letter to the editor of the Journal, by

72

the way—and Chase has a broken leg and a slight concussion?''

Jody put her head in her hands and moaned softly. "It's worse than I thought." Lifting her shoulders, she sat up straight. "That's not exactly the way things happened, but you're pretty close. He doesn't have a concussion, just a migraine. His leg isn't broken, but he twisted his ankle, really bad." With a grimace, she added, "But you were right about supper."

Katie's face lit up like a marquee. "You did invite him?"

"No, Grandpa invited him. But we did have bream."

"So . . ." Katie ran a hand through her clipped curls, "what's going on here, Jody-girl?"

Jody's smile was bittersweet. "He's very angry with me. He's had to delay everything, and the letter to the paper didn't help matters. But," she grinned. "He says I have eyes like shattered crystal and he seems to really like my hair."

Katie slurped the dregs of her soft drink; then she clapped softly. "Things are progressing right along."

"Except he won't even talk to me."

"And you care." When Jody didn't deny it, Katie's big brown eyes sparkled with realization. "You've got a thing for him!"

Jody tried to look shocked. "No, I don't. I don't give a hoot either way. The man's as stubborn as a yard dog."

"And you aren't?"

Slumping back against the squeaky vinyl booth, Jody sighed. "Maybe I did go a tad too far, but I want to save that house."

"Have you tried talking to him?"

"I'm heading out to the Dogwood Lodge tonight after work."

Telling herself she at least owed Chase an apology for causing him to hurt his ankle, Jody closed up the shop a few hours later, and headed out to the lakeside lodge where Chase was staying, just on the outskirts of town. Her hands gripped the steering wheel with white-knuckled tension. Lord, she dreaded facing him again.

That was because of the darn kiss. The kiss haunted her about as much as John Hample seemed to be haunting Spence House. She had dreamed about that kiss, and in her dream she and Chase were the same, but different. They were once again standing in the cupola, but the house was new and brilliant with sunshine, and they were dressed in different clothes, clothes from another era.

Only the kiss had been the same. It had been everything she'd remembered, and Chase's lips on hers had somehow changed her, rearranged her, leaving her longing and needy for something she knew she'd never have.

So on the wings of a kiss and a dream, and sweating profusely, she headed off to humble herself and try once again to reason with Chase.

Dogwood Lodge sat back deep in a forest of tall pines, which sloped like sentinels over the more delicate dogwoods sprinkled throughout the lush woods. The lodge itself was a rustic two-storied structure complete with a social hall, a lounge, and a gameroom. Smaller cabins made of the same dark, rugged logs were set in a semicircle around the lake. The secluded spot was a perfect hideaway for a man who didn't want to be found.

Except that Chase's bright red sportscar looked completely out of place sitting among the battered pick-ups and bass boats. Not his usual accommodations, Jody bet, as she pictured him in some high-rise, five-star hotel conducting business with a laptop computer and a cellular phone. Of course, he wouldn't find any of that here. He was probably sitting there flipping channels on the two local television stations, going mad with boredom. And he'd probably be glad to have some company.

She was wrong. On both accounts.

The minute she approached the door, she heard his deep voice, talking no doubt into a phone, before he turned to bark orders at someone else in the cabin. Hesitating a split second before knocking, Jody was surprised to find Betty peeking out the door at her.

"It's not a good time," Betty said by way of a warning. Chase's voice boomed out into the soft dusk. "Betty, what'd we do with that printout of the projected budget?''

Betty turned around, calling calmly, ''On the table by your left hand, Chase.'' Then she turned back to Jody. ''Get out of here while you can, girl. And send help back to rescue me.''

Jody whispered, ''I really need to talk to him.''

The petite woman came out the door, carefully shutting it behind her. ''No, ma'am, you don't need to talk to him.'' Her nose barely reached Jody's chin and her hoop earrings shimmied with each bob of her head. ''You know something, Jody Calhoun, I liked this job. Even though I knew it was only temporary, I really liked it—for the first two days, that is. Until you came along, that is.'' Jabbing her red lacquered nails at Jody's chest, she didn't miss a beat. ''Ever since that man in there laid his gorgeous gray eyes on you, child, he's changed. He went from being a nice boss to a big ol' grizzly bear.''

Advancing so close Jody was forced to step back, Betty didn't let up. ''This growling and snarling mess has got to stop. And I figure the only way that's going to happen is if you just step out of the picture. You're irritating that man, honey. And if I didn't need this job so bad, I could be enjoying it. But I have to work with him, you understand? So there's no way I'm letting you in there with Mr. Chase Spence!''

From the cabin door, loud applause escaped through the night, echoing around the swaying pines over Jody's head. Chase had listened to his feisty secretary's tirade, silently agreeing with each and every word. He had turned into a monster. True, he'd always been a tough taskmaster, but he never pushed anyone any harder than he pushed himself. Only this time, poor Betty was the lone sufferer of his wrath, since his Florida staff was holding down the fort at the corporate headquarters in Pensacola. Longing for the good old days before he'd become obsessed with Jody Calhoun's luscious curves and peach-flavored lips, he watched her now, wondering what feminine tricks she had up her sexy sleeve this time. Whatever she had planned in her cute pleated shorts and crisp white-cotton summer blouse, he wasn't falling for it. He was back to business, in spite of the pain throbbing throughout his tired body.

"Bravo, Betty," he said, balancing on one foot as he leaned heavily into the doorway. "I couldn't have said it better myself. Remind me to give you a raise."

Jody advanced a couple of steps, the sight of him tearing her heart into little pieces. He looked haggard and tired, a day's worth of beard growth covering his face. "Is that really how you feel?"

He almost lost his balance as he tried to rake a hand through his hair. "Honestly, right now, I don't know how I feel, except maybe a little woozy from the pain medicine Doc Siwell gave me."

"Let me help you," she said, hoping he'd forgive her.

He ignored the pain in her luminous eyes. "No, thanks. You've done more than enough already."

Grandpa always said she didn't know when to back down. Maybe now would be the best time. "All right. I'll leave you alone. I just wanted to say I'm sorry."

"Does that mean you'll stop interfering with my work here?"

Giving him a level look, she said, "No, that just means I'm sorry you got hurt. From now on, I intend to focus all my energy on saving Spence House."

"Then I guess we'll just see who wins this fight."

"Yes, we will." With that she went back to her car, slamming the door hard.

Betty turned to give her boss a sympathetic look. "You sure you're up to this, Chase?"

Chase stared after the car pulling through the sandy driveway, torment raging throughout his entire system. "I don't let anything get in the way of my work, Betty."

Betty cautiously skirted around him to go back inside. "Yeah, right."

Chase lifted his head skyward, reminding himself this job was supposed to be routine and simple. Only, nothing about Jody Calhoun was routine or simple. She was going to make his life a living hell—this he knew from the bottom of his soul, almost as if he'd dealt with her somewhere, somehow, at another time.

Which was ridiculous. He only dealt in logic.

Of course, up until now, he'd mainly worked from his head, not his heart.

The next day after spending hours researching Spence House in the cool confines of the library, Jody decided to pay the house one last visit. Her findings at the library hadn't been much help, except to confirm what she already knew. Jeanette had left the house in a swift run and hadn't looked back.

Mrs. Brinson, the librarian, and an authority on local history, had recounted the legend of John Hample but with a new twist. "He was such a handsome man, and a hero—Jeanette showed me a picture of him once. They say he had a secret lover. Did you know about that? And I swear, Chase reminds me of him. I still remember those eyes from the picture."

Something about knowing that had disturbed Jody. A secret lover? Gray eyes? A ghost? Somehow, she had to find something in all of this that would convince Chase to keep Spence House.

Her heart thudding, she headed up the street to the waiting mansion. The church bells struck six o'clock as she entered the rusty gates, her eyes centered on the cupola.

"Hope you're in the mood for a visitor," she told the house.

Her mind on war and death, Jody felt a strong empathy for the legendary ghost. War and death had separated her from her own father, and in a sense, from her fragile mother, too. She longed for the same peace John Hample's ghost obviously needed to find.

Moving through the weed-infested carriage entrance to the back porch of the rambling mansion, Jody began talking to John Hample. "Could you be specific about what you want from me? Do you want me to save this house?"

Her only answer was a sultry summer breeze that didn't even bother to ruffle the hair on the back of her neck. Hesitating a fraction of a second before stepping up onto the creaking porch, she breathed in the scent of the delicate purple wisteria blossoms swinging from a nearby vine. She would always think of Chase when she smelled wisteria, and she'd always remember Spence House standing solitary and sad, waiting for someone to come along and love it. The pity was that she'd have to remember both the man and the house with bittersweet fondness. Because one had come to destroy the other.

That only reminded her of being here with Chase, and only refueled her determination to put him out of her mind and get on with the task at hand.

She entered the wide back door, which at one time had been encased with stained glass panes. Gaping holes were its only encasement now. With a burst of nervous energy, she headed for the stairs, slipping around the spot where Chase had fallen through the rotted floor.

Her throat dry with dread and doubt, she pushed her way through dustballs and cobwebs, glad for the feeble shaft of late day sunlight trying to penetrate the house's gloom.

Finally, winded and sweating, she came to rest on the top landing. Inching her way through the door, Jody glanced around, envisioning a large Victorian-style bedroom, all sunny white and dainty. She'd put a big brass bed right smack in front of the huge bay window overlooking the back gardens. A vision of Chase and her curled together in that bed came to mind. The vision was so powerful and so real, she had to catch her breath. "Stop dreaming," she muttered.

Still the image stayed with her. Out of nowhere, the thought came—*I wonder how golden brown hair and gray eyes would mix with strawberry-blond hair and "shattered crystal" eyes?*

"So far, not very well," she reminded herself. But the dream stuck and held; she could hear children's laughter echoing through the house; could see little golden-haired boys and girls racing up the polished mahogany staircase. Dashing the unbidden tears brimming at her eyes, she whirled around toward the cupola room. That's when she heard something on the stairs.

Heavy footsteps came slowly and steadily up the stairs.

"Good grief." Her pulse pounded in her ears and her mouth went completely dry. Maybe John Hample was ready to show himself at last.

A shadow cut through the arch of golden sunlight pushing into the room. The shadow stepped forward. In the growing dusk, Jody could only see the silhouette of a man until he moved completely into the room.

The man standing before her had sad gray eyes.

"Chase Spence! You scared me to death!"

"Mitt told me you'd walked down here." He moved across the room to where she stood, his rugged workboots skidding on the worn wooden floor. For a long time, he just stood staring at her, as if remembering the last time they'd stood here together. "I didn't mean to scare you."

Taking a calming breath, Jody turned away. "I just wanted to come here one more time—"

"I don't mind you being here, Jody." Pulling her around, he handed her a trailing vine of wisteria blossoms. "I came to apologize. I'm sorry I wouldn't talk to you the other day at the lake."

Taking the flowery sprigs of lavender into her arms, Jody sniffed the sweet fragrance, wanting to cry all over again. "Me, too. I've always blurted things right out, getting myself into trouble. I shouldn't have pushed you so hard."

He smiled then, a soft shimmering smile that took the gloom away. Taking her into his arms, he pulled her close. "Jody, I'm so sorry things can't be right between us. I wish we could have known each other under different circumstances. I wish this house didn't have to drive us apart."

She saw the sincerity in the depths of his eyes, and her heart blossomed like the dainty flowers crushed against her chest. *When did I start loving him?* she wondered, awe filling her soul. *Was it when he kissed me right here in this room? Or was it the first time I saw him standing there with Spence House behind him?* It really didn't matter, she mused, unable to voice all the feelings cresting inside her like a newborn sunrise. Standing here, it seemed as if she'd loved him for all time; as if she'd been waiting an eternity for him to walk up those steps and find her here.

Swallowing back fresh tears, she tried to smile. "Maybe if we'd known each other a long time ago, before there was ever a Spence House . . . maybe things could have been different for us, Chase."

Chase took in the sight of her hair flowing in the hot wind, the way she clutched the wisteria to her chest, the sadness in her bright eyes. God, she was so very beautiful, so ethereal, so genuine and real. He felt as if he'd been destined to walk up those stairs and find her here, waiting for him.

Groaning, he pulled her close. "I can't settle for that, Jody. Don't let this come between us. Dammit, we can make things work, if you'll just forget why I'm here and let me do my job."

"No." Pushing him away, she looked down at the crushed wisteria resting in her arms. Afraid that he'd see the love brimming over in her eyes, she stepped up into the cupola. Looking out at the quiet town, she wondered how things down there could look so serene and rosy, when her heart was shattering. "I can't do that, Chase."

He followed her, trying to comfort her, but she pulled away. "I can't let go of this place," she tried to explain. "I don't know . . . I was only around four or so when I first saw it, but I still remember how it fascinated me even back then. And when I got older, I felt some sort of connection with these lonely rooms." Unable to stop the pain catching in her throat, she whirled to stare up at him. "You see, this house was abandoned at about the same time I was. And I guess I just need to know why. Why did your aunt leave her home? Why did my mother leave me? What's so wrong with this house?" Clutching the wisteria, she whispered, "And what's so wrong with me?"

"Oh, Jody." He took her into his arms, gently rocking her, the scent of wisteria floating around them to mingle with the scent of decay and neglect. "Jody, sweetheart, I can't speak for this house, but I do know that there's nothing wrong with you. And if you'll give me a chance, I'll prove that to you.''

She wanted to believe him, wanted to tell him that she loved him enough to watch him demolish her only dream. But she'd been waiting all her life for some sort of proof, proof that she was worthy of love. No wonder she doubted his promises. She'd seen too many broken ones. And she'd rather take a chance on saving this house than risk everything by loving him.

Lifting her head, she braced her heart against the intense pain slicing through it and said, ''I can't let you tear this house down, Chase. I know it means losing you; I know how much restoring this old place would cost, but some things are worth the extra expense and trouble.'' Sadly, she realized that was really her only dream. She wanted to be worth someone's extra trouble.

Releasing her, Chase rubbed his forehead. ''Then, we're right back where we started. The house is coming down first thing tomorrow morning.''

A great ripping pain cut off Jody's breath. Was this it, then? Was this her answer? To do nothing. To give up and simply watch him tear down all her hopes and dreams? Moving away from the intensity of his eyes, she sat down on one of the wooden window boxes. It was useless, as useless as her love for him. She was about to admit defeat, something that didn't come easily for her, when her eye caught an object over Chase's head. There almost hidden in the inch-wide casing of one of the tiny window frames, was a leather strap holding a large gold key.

Seeing the direction of her gaze, Chase twisted around. ''What's that?''

Jody wiped her tears, then hopped up to grab the key. ''Let's find out.'' Silently, she thanked John Hample Spence.

Chase's dubious gaze clashed with her hopeful one. ''We don't have time; the light's almost gone.''

A new energy coursed through Jody. ''Then we'd better hurry.''

*   *   *

A voice from downstairs stopped Jody cold.

"Hey, Chase, you up there? I need to go over these demolition plans with you. Hey, boss?"

Eyeing Jody apologetically, Chase called down the stairwell. "Yeah, Wade. I'm here. Be down in a minute." Taking Jody by the arm, he said, "Come on. I need to finish up some last minute details with the construction foreman. It's getting dark, anyway."

"No," she stated firmly. "I want to find out what this key fits."

"Jody, it doesn't matter." He took her hand to pull her along, an uneasy feeling leveling off in the pit of his stomach. He'd been with her enough to recognize the stubborn glint in her eyes. When she refused to move, he added, "Jody, listen very carefully and try to comprehend what I'm about to tell you. This house is coming down tomorrow, with or without your permission."

Undaunted, she gave him an incredulous look. "But Chase, how can you say that now? You said we'd go through the house together. What if this key belongs to a jewelry box or a safe?"

Shaking his head, Chase sighed long and hard. "I've checked the house several times already. Everything worth keeping is out. I just used that as an excuse to talk to you." Taking her hand, he held it up so they could both see the ornate brass key dangling from the worn leather strap she gripped between her fingers. "It's just an old key, Jody. An old key someone lost long ago. You can have it."

Aggravated by his high-handed tone, she yanked the key back. "Oh, I intend to have it. I intend to search this house to see where this key fits. And you can take the place down around my ears, if you're so determined to demolish it!"

"Don't tempt me," he said, pinching the bridge of his nose with a scowl. "You've been nothing but trouble. And I've tried to be patient with you, really I have. I've tried to understand your obsession with this place, but I can't." Holding his hands out like a lawyer stating his case, he took two steps toward Jody. "It's time to get on with things. I have to get this project back on track, and I can't do that until this place is knocked down.''

"And that's what you want, isn't it?" She faced him squarely, her chin held high. "To wipe any trace of your past off the face of the earth. Why are you so afraid of this house, Chase?"

"I'm not afraid of this place," he said, clearly stunned by her accusation. "But I don't have the time or talent to rebuild it."

"You are scared," she said, latching on to the doubt clouding his eyes. "You'd love nothing better than to tackle this old place, but you don't think you can do it. Are you so afraid of failure, that you can't take a risk—a real risk, one that isn't calculated in your charts and projections?"

"I don't know what you're talking about!" He started for the door. "I'm leaving. I should have known it was a mistake to try and make you listen to reason." Pivoting at the entrance of the cupola, he motioned to her. "Now come on, it'll be dark soon. I won't leave you here by yourself."

Jody dug her heels in to stay. "I don't need your protection. I've been in this house alone lots of times. I'm perfectly safe."

"Well, what if you fall through the floor like I did?"

"That won't happen. I know my way around better than you."

Wanting to scare her, he retorted, "And what if John Hample decides to make mischief again?"

She gave him a doubtful look. "He won't bother me. He wants me to find whatever this key opens. Can't you see, he's trying to tell us something."

"You're crazy," Chase said through gritted teeth, his patience clearly gone. "And you're making me crazy! I'm leaving—now!"

"Good. Close the door on your way out!"

Giving her a sharp scowl, he said, "If I have to come over there and carry you out of here, I'll do it."

Shaking her head, she laughed. "You can't manhandle me, Chase. I can take care of myself." On a calmer plea, she added, "You'll never understand, so please . . . leave me alone."

Throwing his hands up in the air, he said, "Well, you're certainly right about that. I don't understand. I don't understand how I feel about you, or how you feel about me, and I don't understand how you can let a house comsume you like this."

"This house means a lot to me," she said on a low, still voice. "And if you can't see that, there's no future for us."

"Oh, I think I'm beginning to see," he replied, his voice devoid of any emotion. "You care more about this place than you'll ever care about me. And you've made that very clear."

With that he was gone, the echo of his footsteps grating across Jody's bruised nerve endings.

"You're wrong, Chase," she whispered, holding the key to her heart. "I care about you a lot. And that's why I have to do this."

Waiting until she was sure he'd left, she looked around. Twenty-five rooms and a million cubbyholes and crannies waited for her careful inspection, while the sun seemed to be zooming to faraway destinations over the western horizon.

"Where is it?" she said out loud, hoping to hear some comforting noise. Maybe Chase was right. Maybe her obsession was getting out of hand. But she had to try, didn't she? She had an instinctive feeling that this key was important to her future—and to Chase.

When she didn't find any place the key might fit in the cupola or the third floor room, she moved to the second floor, quickly opening and shutting bedroom and bathroom doors and inspecting closets and ornamental nooks. But nothing caught her attention. Checking every step of the staircase, she slowly made her way downstairs, squinting at the leaping shadows rising up out of the growing darkness.

Reaching the bottom of the stairs, Jody stood between the massive dining room and the formal parlor, the wide central hallway stretching away from her on either side. Still clutching the key, she tried pulling the paneled sliding doors of the parlor together, to see if perhaps the key fit one of them.

But they only had latches for protection. No need for a key such as this one.

Careful to watch where she stepped, she peered at the arched bookshelves surrounding the cavernous fireplace, but nothing looked out of the ordinary. Conducting the same search in the dining room, she checked the window alcoves, trying to pry open window boxes as she went. But none of the hiding places needed this key. After glancing over the empty pantry between the dining room and kitchen, Jody headed back to the central hallway.

"Maybe the kitchen, or the basement."

Eyeing the small basement door built into the back of the staircase, Jody decided she wasn't brave enough to go down there alone. She opted for the kitchen.

Pushing at debris, she frantically searched the unhinged kitchen cabinets, banging doors and unsettling long-dormant dust as she went. Darkness wrapped around the house, and off in some distant corner, she heard scurrying noises as the night creatures began gathering in the gloom.

"Okay." She was winded, her words were high-pitched and nervous. "I give up. Chase was right; I am obsessing." On a whispered plea, she said, "Please, John Hample, if you want me to help you, you'd better show me where this key belongs."

Only the silence of a tired day coming to an end answered her.

Backing out of the kitchen, Jody tripped over the spot where Chase had fallen, crying out in pain as her foot slipped into the jagged hole left in the floor. Standing with one foot inside the shallow hole and one out safely on solid wood, she suddenly realized her lowered foot was resting against something, something hard and cold.

Yelping, Jody quickly jerked her foot away, rubbing the deep scratch rising on her ankle. Falling on wobbly knees, she tried to see into the black hole, but it was too dark and shadowy for her to make out what she'd touched upon.

"Only one way to find out."

Closing her eyes, she shuddered as she lowered her hand down into the small space between the hall floor and the large beam supporting the basement ceiling.

Cobwebs caught between her fingers, making her draw her hand back as chill bumps popped up on her arms. Trying one more time, she braced herself, feeling around until she could find a means of grasping the object.

"There," she said triumphantly as she pulled the heavy rectangular box out onto the floor, her eyes straining to see it in the darkness.

"A tin box." The whispered words barely hissed through the tightness in Jody's chest. Excited now, she flipped the dusty foot-long box around. It looked to be about six inches deep, with a lid designed out of intricate beaten metal—a lid that was locked tight.

Her fingers shaking, Jody took the key and carefully placed it through the keyhole on the lid, holding her breath as she slowly turned the key against the hard metal. A gentle, unprotesting click sounded throughout the house.

The box was open. The house sat perfectly still, holding its breath, silent and waiting. And outside, a rising moon cast an eerie light on Jody's shining silvery discovery.

Realizing she couldn't see what the box contained in the dark, she grabbed it up, locking it back before putting the key's strap around her neck. Then she ran out of the house, not stopping to look back until she was safely out on the wide sidewalk in front of the looming mansion. She didn't see Chase or Wade Holland anywhere in sight.

"Thanks," Jody whispered to the wind.

Then it hit her. Spence House would be demolished the next day.

"Oh, Chase," she whispered. "Please don't do it."

Taking one last look at the house, Jody hurried down the deserted street, a humid wind misting her with perspiration. But as she turned away, a shadow on the long front porch caught her eye. And she knew—Chase had come back to the house, to make sure she'd gotten out safely. He'd watched over her, in spite of his fierce denial that he cared.

You do care, Chase, she thought. *But had he started caring a little too late?*

She looked from the shadow on the porch, up to the cupola. A lone shadow loomed there, too. Startled, she glanced back at the porch. Was Chase upstairs then? Was that Wade on the porch? No, she would have seen Chase if he'd gone back upstairs. She would have heard him. She'd heard or seen nothing, no one. Yet the figure stood, the exact silhouette of the one on the porch below, the exact shadow Chase had cast when he'd found her in the house earlier. Jody looked from the cupola to the porch. Someone was still there, leaning against a weathered post. But when she looked back to the cupola, it was empty. The moon could be playing tricks on her mind.

But she knew better. She glanced back up to the windowed room. "Thank you, John Hample."

Chapter Five

Jody sat cross-legged on the old tester bed in her room at the farmhouse, a pot of lemon-mint tea steeping on the nightstand, a fresh cup—her third—clutched in her hands as she once again looked over the contents of the tin box she'd found at Spence House. She wanted to read all of the letters.

Letters. The old, battered box had been stuffed with letters, love letters to John Hample Spence from a woman who only signed each one of them with a beautifully looped set of initials: A. J.

Carefully setting her tea cup down, Jody lifted the first set of aged papers from the stack she'd gently unfolded and laid out across the peach-colored chenille bedspread, a hint of cedar from the small chest's lining wafting out around her. Outside, a midnight wind lifted over the chinaberry trees, whining for her attention, but she hardly heard it. All her thoughts were focused on the hidden cache she'd discovered from another time and another set of lovers.

She'd rushed through the first few letters, eager to hear every detail of the life the woman who'd written them had led over a hundred and thirty years before. This time, she wanted to read each elegantly scrolled word slowly, so she could savor her newfound treasures right along with her tea. From an antique standpoint, she knew the letters were extremely valuable. From a personal viewpoint, Jody considered them priceless. They were the key to Spence House; they told the secret of what might have been, what *should* have been. These letters would convince Chase that he couldn't tear the house down. Spence House had been part of this woman's dream.

April 3, 1861

Dear John,

I am healing just fine. Thank you for sending the food and the writing papers. You are truly so kind and you really did not need to go to all that trouble. Papa would punish me severely if he knew I were sitting here writing you instead of doing my studies. He sets such high store in learning, and since I am his only child, and a girl at that, he is determined to teach me everything he knows so I can carry on with the school once he is too old to teach.

Frankly, I believe he is too old right now. Yet, he refuses to let me take over. He says I need to find a suitable husband and settle down. But with all this war talk . . . well, that might be hard to do right now. Of course, he keeps reminding me of Cousin Will's proposal. At one time, I thought Cousin Will was indeed the husband for me, but now, I am not so sure. I am not sure of anything anymore, the world is so crazy right now.

I have truly enjoyed talking to you about these things, John. You have taught me so much about what this war could mean to all of us. Papa and I, being teachers from the North and not farmers, have never owned slaves. I cannot imagine what it must feel like, to be owned by another. Your assurances that you treat your slaves at Camille as part of the family has eased my mind a great deal.

When will you be coming through again? Let me know, please, and I will be sure and bake you a fresh peach pie to thank you for your kindness since my accident. Our newfound friendship means a great deal to me—more than you will ever know.

Good wishes,
A. J.

P. S. I know it was an accident. You do not have to feel so indebted to me. I am truly glad we met, even if your stallion did overreact to my running into his path.

Jody put the yellowed page down. Apparently, John Hample's horse had run the woman down, and John Hample had felt responsible. Digging through the notes she'd taken at the library, she reread the history of John Hample's family. They'd owned a large plantation several miles southeast of Hampleton.

Camille Plantation. The house had been demolished in the nineteen-twenties and the land sold off to build a subdivision.

With visions of a white-columned rambling mansion in her mind, Jody continued reading her notes. John Hample and his younger brother, Jackson, had discovered what was to become Hampleton when they'd come hunting on the land located near the planned Georgia-Florida railroad station. Jody wondered if that's how he'd met the mysterious A. J. Apparently, after the war, Jackson had carried on the dream the brothers had concocted during that first hunting trip.

And somewhere in Virginia, John Hample Spence has lost all of his dreams during a bloody Civil War battle that had ended his life.

No wonder his ghost couldn't rest.

Jody read another letter, hoping to piece together the rest of John Hample's story.

April 18, 1861
Dear John,
    I don't know where you'll be when you receive this letter. We heard that Confederate troops have gained

control of Fort Sumter, and that most of the Georgia regiments will be sent to Virginia. We've also heard that President Lincoln says this war should be over in ninety days. I pray he is right. I pray also, for your safety, John. I so miss our conversations. Of course, we do not agree on the politics of this dispute, but we both agree that we do not want to see a long and drawn out war.

Papa, however, is a different matter. He is taking his role as an abolitionist very seriously. I am fearful he will become involved in something very dangerous to both of us. I wish I could make him go back to New England. As for myself, I find I am happy here in Georgia. Oh, John, is it wrong, this feeling I have found since knowing you? Is it wrong to care for someone who stands for everything I've been taught to detest? I should not speak of these things; we did agree not to mention our true feelings, but I think of you every waking moment. I am now married to another. I should not even be writing to you. Please, keep my letters safe and let no one see them. For the sake of my marriage to Will, for your own sake. I only write you to give you hope and to let you know I pray for your safety daily.

You were brave to carry on at Camille while your father served in the home guard, but I understand you felt honor bound to enlist and fight for your beloved Georgia. I wish you Godspeed, wherever you are. My prayers and concerns will continue to be with you.

I cherish our last moments together underneath the magnolia tree, as I cherish the lovely brooch you gave me as a token of your love. It really is exquisite with its pearls and gold filigree. What an extravagant gift! I am wearing it right now, and I shall wear it forever.

Papa doesn't know you gave it to me. He is so involved in war talk, he thinks it is an old one I found in Mama's things. (Since her death, he refuses to go through anything of hers.) Says I can have it all, to do with as I see fit. Poor Papa, so sad, so disillusioned.

He is frustrated that he cannot run off and join up with
the North. His talk scares me; I keep reminding him
he is no longer in New England. He should be cau-
tious of how he speaks about freeing the slaves; someone might misinterpret his opinions. Old age makes
him irrational. In addition, he can barely walk across
the cabin.

I am wearing the brooch you gave me close to my
heart, until we meet again. Do not try to write me
back; it is too dangerous. I hear little from Will. He
is not a man of words. I know so little of my new
husband, but I had to honor my father's request. Forgive me, John. Please, forgive me.
Good wishes,
A. J.

A brooch. Jody sat back, wondering why the description of
the brooch had brought such a sense of familiarity. Had she
seen such a brooch somewhere? She bought a lot of old
jewelry for the shop, true. Maybe she'd actually seen a
brooch similar to the one described in this letter.

No. That wasn't it. This piece of jewelry seemed as familiar to her as the rings on her fingers. Pearls and filigree.
Pearls and filigree. She had so much old jewelry, maybe she
had a brooch like this.

Jumping up, she ran to the replica Queen Anne vanity
table to rummage through the old jewelry box her grandmother had given her years ago.

"Some of it is valuable; some of it is junk," her grandmother had stated in her matter-of-fact way. "A lot of it
came from Mitt's mother. She loved jewelry, especially
brooches and pins. Her mother gave her a lot of it. I gave
your mother a few pieces last time she was here, but I saved
the prettiest pieces for you."

Digging through the carved wooden box, Jody felt around
in one of the compartments. Now where had she put that
brooch? Tossing out a pair of peace symbol earrings and a
charm bracelet some suitor had given her for high school

graduation, she leaned close to see what was left in the deep, velvet-covered box.

"Aha!" Smiling triumphantly, she pulled out the large heavy brooch her grandmother had unknowingly given her. Jody remembered admiring the brooch all those years ago, and she'd worn it occasionally, but lately she'd had neither the time or the inclination to go anywhere that required dressy jewelry. Now, she took the brooch out to bring it to the lamp's bright light, her hands shaking slightly with the significance of her discovery.

Pearls and filigree. A cluster of pearls set in an oval frame of intricately twisted gold wire. Delicate and very feminine—something a man might give to a woman he was falling in love with. Jody held the brooch in her hand, rubbing the shiny yellowed pearls with her thumb.

No. This was impossible. This couldn't be the same brooch. Yet it seemed so familiar; it looked like the one described in the letter. Maybe someone in her family had picked it up at an estate sale or in a flea market. Maybe there were hundreds around, just like this one and she'd just gotten lucky. Maybe. Maybe not. What if this were the only one of its kind?

What if this particular brooch had belonged to the woman who'd written to John Hample Spence? A woman who'd been married to another man; a woman who had secrets. What if?

Jody held the brooch up to the lamp's soft light, her gaze transfixed by the aged, winking pearls.

"What happened back then, John Hample?" she wondered out loud. She had no answers. But she had a feeling she'd soon find out.

At dawn, Jody was still trying to decipher the letters. Some of them seemed to be missing. There were obvious gaps between the writings, causing most of what she'd read to make little sense. One thing was clear, however. John Hample and this woman had fallen in love. And that love had remained strong, even after the woman had married another man—a Union soldier who'd died in the war soon after the marriage. And with that love, the dream of building a great house had been nurtured, nurtured, but never fulfilled.

She had to find Chase and tell him. Looking out across the pecan grove behind the farmhouse, she saw the first rays of day gliding through the sleepy mists.

But Jody wasn't sleepy. Instead, she was determined. Quickly, she checked on her sleeping mother across the hallway, then stopping only long enough to wash her face and brush her hair, she threw on her mother's old sundress, grabbed the tinbox and the brooch, and ran for her car, ignoring her grandfather's open-mouthed surprise as she rushed past him on the back porch. She had to get to Chase, before it was too late.

Speeding all the way out to Dogwood Lodge, Jody skidded her car into the winding gravel lane leading to Chase's cabin, her eyes searching for his Corvette. When she didn't see it in front of his cabin, she hopped out, running for the door, her fists raised to beat it down if necessary. But all her banging only brought a fisherman bunking in a nearby cabin out to his porch.

Fully dressed and sipping a cup of coffee, the man eyed her sharply. "He left about a half hour ago, suga'."

"Thanks," Jody said, her words breathless. In seconds, she slammed her car in reverse and sped toward town, praying she wouldn't be too late.

As she turned down West Railroad, she saw Spence House looming ahead and her heart lurched in her chest.

The wide iron gates stood broken and open, while workmen wearing hardhats swarmed over the grounds like angry hornets gathering around a nest. Heavy equipment was gathered ominously around the house, the big rubber tires of bulldozers and wrecking balls crushing delicate magnolia blossoms and century-old camellia bushes. Some of the surrounding gardens had already been destroyed, leaving a red clay emptiness where great trees had stood for so long.

Up on the roof, several men made ready to unhinge the cupola, their massive hammers and unrelenting crowbars al-

94

ready prying apart the aged wood. Nearby, a huge crane was hoisted into place to lift the octagonal-shaped room off the top of the house.

"No!" Jody whispered, her throat so dry the one word wouldn't even form into a sound. "Chase, please don't."

Finding an empty parking space, Jody whirled her car into the nearby depot parking lot, her eyes scanning the area for any sign of Chase. Spotting his car parked in front of the Spence Building, she tried to find her next breath. She had to talk to him, to tell him what she'd found in the box.

Clutching the heavy box against her chest, Jody headed for the house.

"Have you seen Chase?" she asked a workman, a man she recognized as a local contractor. When he shook his head, she moved on, noticing that the whole town had turned out for the big event.

Shoving her way through the growing crowd, Jody heard the whispered words hissing through the air.

"There's Jody!"

"What's she got in that box?"

"She's here to stop him!"

Right, she thought grimly. Frantic now as she heard one of the hardhats telling another one to "crank 'em up," she ran up to the house, hitting the porch at a skid. Turning to look out over the crowd, she still didn't see Chase.

"Where are you?" she said, her eyes adjusting to the growing light. Hurrying to the side porch, she looked toward the back gardens, still holding the metal box tightly to her chest.

Chase stood in the far back garden underneath the big magnolia, his eyes shifting from the house to something on the ground. At the precise minute he looked up to find Jody watching him, the mighty engines surrounding the house roared to life, drowning out Jody's shouts.

"Chase!" she called, unable to move. He seemed to see her; there was something there in his eyes—a discovery, an awakening—that held Jody, making her wonder if he, too, felt the charge of energy rushing through the proud house.

His eyes still on her, Chase tried to say something, but

the noise of straining tires and monster engines made it impossible for her to hear. Desperate now, Jody knew there was only one way to stop this.

Whirling, she ran back to the front of the house where the crowd of onlookers watched in fascination as the big machines inched toward the front steps. As soon as the cupola was torn away, the porches would be stripped, and then the rest of Spence House would come tumbling down.

Unless she stopped them.

It didn't take long for the observers to see Jody standing there, her long hair flying out in the wind, her chin held high in defiance.

"Hey, lady!" one of the workman hollered, waving his hands in the air. "Get out of there!"

Jody stood her ground, her eyes roaming the crowd. Mitt Calhoun came running through the open gates, his old eyes wide with disbelief, his lovable wrinkled face a mixture of pride and fear. And . . . oh, Lord . . . Mama? Her mother was with him.

Please, Mother, don't let this upset you. Jody watched her slender, fragile mother as Maria clutched Mitt's meaty arm. Surprisingly, Maria was smiling, not the half-mad smile of depression Jody had learned to hate, but a serene, encouraging smile aimed at her daughter. Lifting her hand, Maria waved and nodded, giving Jody the extra burst of courage she needed. Without a backward glance, she pivoted and ran inside the house.

"I'm not leaving," she vowed, taking the steps two at a time. "I won't let it happen again, John Hample." Tears blurred her vision as she made her way to the cupola. Finally, winded and frightened, she looked out over the grounds, watching defiantly as fingers began pointing up to where she stood.

One of the workers on the roof came face to face with her, jumping back at her expression.

"Hey, get outta here," he said through the broken glass of the window. "This is coming off."

"I'm not leaving," Jody replied stubbornly, recognizing the man as an old schoolmate.

96

"Jody?" he questioned, rubbing red-clay dust off the mangled glass. "Oh, boy. Guess you meant what you said in that letter to the editor."

"Every word," she replied with all the calmness of a belle at a tea party.

Backing away, her friend signaled to his pals, halting the destruction on the cupola. Then, shaking his head, he started climbing down the roof, his expression telling Jody he knew when to call it quits.

A ripple went through the crowd, and in a matter of seconds, all eyes were on the woman with the flowing strawberry-blond hair, standing in the cupola of Spence House. If she hadn't been so flustered, Jody might have enjoyed the shock waves descending on the crowd below her.

She saw Katie Winston standing next to Grandpa and Miss Edith, Katie's brown eyes wide with fear. Next to them, old Doc Siwell and the bank president, Ted Patterson watched, talking erratically to each other, probably plotting to have her committed, no doubt. Every store owner, every town regular, every hired worker, now watched as Jody stood looking down over them, a defiant light in her crystal eyes.

Yep, this will take care of my reputation for a long time to come, she thought, not caring.

Except for Chase. Where was he?

The tractors and bulldozers still hummed, their fumes wafting out over the morning air. The men inside them sat, their gloved hands resting on gear sticks, their booted feet holding groaning brakes, unsure what to do next.

And then, Jody saw Chase. Chase, in work jeans and a black tee shirt, his workboots crusted with clay and grass, his own hardhat thrown to the wind as he rushed around the side of the house, hobbling on his bruised ankle, his eyes looking up, up to find her.

In one bright sunlit instant, all the noise and stares died away. And there was only him and only her, their eyes locking in a battle of wills, in a battle of longing and regret, in a battle of love. Chase stood, staring up at her, a look of wonder and grudging admiration rising in his eyes. Jody held his look, sending him a silent plea, hoping the love surging through her heart would win out over progress and money and concrete and steel. Hoping that what she'd known all along was finally dawning in his eyes even as the new day dawned behind him.

Behind him, too, the whole crowd waited and watched, their eyes wide, their breaths held.

Jody didn't move.

Chase didn't move.

And then Chase waved a hand to the crew foreman.

In a matter of seconds, the noise of revving engines died down, and in its place, a silence louder than any engine filled the morning air, followed by the cheers and applause of the watchers.

Amazed, Jody watched as the townspeople laughed and slapped each other on the back. So they'd been behind her all along! Wanting to hug all of them, she wondered why in heck nobody else had stepped forward, voicing what she'd felt the whole time. Her eyes settled on her grandfather and he gave her the thumbs-up salute. Beside him, Maria held her hands to her face and grinned. That was all Jody needed to see. Shifting the tin box to one arm, she gently stroked the pearl brooch she'd brought along to show Chase.

The sound of heavy footsteps threading up the stairs caused her to spin around.

Chase stood looking up at her, his hard hat in one hand and a sprig of wisteria in the other. Emitting a long, hard sigh, he cocked his head to one side. "Uh . . . Jody, I think it's time we discussed those plans of yours."

Gulping back tears, she said in a husky whisper, "I thought you'd never ask."

He gave her a resigned look, his gaze taking in the box and the brooch. "Let me just tell Wade. . . ." He turned to the window, his back to her.

Jody swayed; the room started shifting. "Chase?" she said, her voice echoing inside her head. "Chase?"

He didn't turn around. She tried to move, to get to him, but her legs crumbled into mush and she felt herself falling, falling, as if she'd been sucked into a puddle of quicksand.

"Chase!" she said, her voice weak and distorted, panic pushing through her. She saw him turn, waited for him to catch her; but when the figure before her came into full focus, she shrank back, confused. The man coming toward her looked like Chase, but he was wearing a Confederate uniform.

"Chase?" she said, so frightened now, she could feel the prick of the brooch's fastening pin as she clutched it tightly in her palm.

The man moved forward, bowing at the waist. "Major John Hample Spence, CSA, ma'am. Please don't be afraid. You must go now, take the letters and go back. You're the only one who can right the wrong we did. You're the only one who can save my Agnes and put my soul at ease."

Dizzy and afraid, Jody tried to focus on the swaying figure. "Where's Chase?"

"He's here, right here," the soldier said, holding his hand to his heart. "And he'll be with you soon."

The figure vanished, then she saw Chase at the window again.

"Thank goodness," she said, although the words seemed forced and measured. She tried to move toward him. It would be okay now. She was just so tired; she'd been up all night, after all. But Chase was here now.

She took a step, and the heavy brooch slipped out of her grasp. It hit the floor with a noisy clatter, landing in a far corner. The sound caused Chase to spin around.

The last thing Jody saw was the surprise on Chase's face. Then everything went black.

Part Two
Agnes and John

Chapter Six

"Do not be afraid."

The words echoed through Jody's throbbing head, the dark void around her brain vanishing to be replaced by white-hot streaks of annoying light. Sunlight.

She opened her eyes and sat up, holding a hand to her head. "Where am I?"

"Right where you belong, my dear."

The voice held a familiar ring, and if she could just get over this headache and focus, she'd remember who was talking. Shifting to try and stand, she hit a hard object lying on the ground next to her—the tin box.

Shocked awake, Jody opened her eyes wide. A pair of dusty black leather boots greeted her. Jody looked up the gray clad legs, her gaze stepping over each of the shiny brass buttons on the Confederate uniform.

No. This couldn't be happening! If this were Chase's idea of a joke, it wasn't funny at all. Closing her eyes again, she blocked out the man standing before her. "Go away," she muttered. "Stop this, right now."

"I cannot go away, at least not yet," the figure said, the

soft southern drawl comforting and frightening at the same time. "I have to explain why I brought you here."

Jody had had enough. She tried to get up, and not even stopping to think, took the hand offered down to her. Standing, she got her first good look at Major John Hample Spence. It sapped the breath right out of her. "You look exactly like Chase," she said, almost to herself. Then, "Or are you Chase? What's going on?"

He seated her on the stump of a fallen oak, underneath the welcoming shade of a young magnolia tree. Then he stood before her, his intense gaze moving slowly over her, absorbing her, it seemed.

"I need your help," he said, his voice hushed and muted. "Did you bring the brooch?"

"What?" Jody looked around, grabbed the tin box, then looked back up at the man . . . ghost . . . waiting for her reply. "The brooch—where is it?" She searched the ground, but didn't see the piece of jewelry in the patchy grass and dirt. "I had it in my hand, I know I did. I wanted to show it to Chase." Opening her hand, she saw the blood at the same time she felt the pain. The brooch had left a deep scratch in the center of her palm. Scared now, she rose off the stump. "Where are we? Where's Chase?"

"Oh, dear," John Hample said. "We really should have that brooch, but not to worry, my dear. I will get it back to you, somehow."

"You'd better tell me what's happening," Jody warned, her tone threatening, in spite of her confusion.

"I will, but you must listen." He pushed her back down on the stump, a chuckle rising from his chest. "You are so like her, you know. I've been watching you for some time now, and you are her—you have her soul."

Not liking the implications of that, Jody stared up at him. "Who? Whose soul?"

He strolled around the clearing, his gaze settling on the magnolia tree moving daintily in the slight breeze. "This was our spot. When we first met here, I picked her a blossom from this very tree. And over there," he pointed into the forest, "is the wisteria vine—the one she loved so much.

She was partial to wisteria.'' He walked to the lush purple petaled vine and broke off a sprig, bringing it back to Jody. Then in a faraway voice, he said, ''My dear Agnes Jodelyn, how I miss you.''

Jody listened to him, fascinated, her fingers curling around the wisteria sprig. Agnes Jodelyn? A. J.? No. It couldn't be possible. ''Did she write you letters?''

''All the time; everyday,'' he replied, his memories clear in his stark gray eyes. ''My wonderful, sweet A J.''

Good grief! Her very own three-times great-grandmother had been John Hample's secret lover!

''I was named after her,'' Jody said, too shocked to realize the redundancy of her declaration.

''I know.'' He smiled down at her. ''And you are the very essence of her. That is why I had to bring you back, you see?''

No, she didn't see. ''What do you mean—bring me back?''

''To this time, to this place.'' He held his plumed hat to his brass-buttoned chest, causing his shiny buttons to shimmer in the sun. Bowing down on one knee, he grasped Jody's hands. ''There is not much time, so I will try to explain. You only have a few days.'' He looked down, then lifted his gaze to hers. ''I might as well tell you right off, you are the reincarnate soul of my Agnes. You are sitting in the spot where she died. I tried to find her, tried to save her.'' He looked away toward the woods then. ''But I was too late.''

Jody saw the pain in his watery eyes, but she didn't buy that bit about reincarnation. ''I . . . I wish there were something I could do, but—''

He looked back up at her then. ''Ah, but my dear, that's precisely why you're here. There is something you must do . . . have to do. You will become Agnes, for just a short period, and your Chase will become me, so we can fix things, so my tortured soul can be reunited with hers. I have to be with her again, but I cannot, unless you help me.''

Pulling away from his grasp, Jody shook her head. ''Wait a minute. Are you telling me . . . I have to act like my great-grandmother?'' At his nod, she laughed. "Please, people already think I'm as loony as a goose—they'll really send me away if I start dressing in hoop skirts and corsets. No, thanks.'' She tried to get up. "Now, I'm going to find my way back to Spence House and Chase. I really need to talk to him.''

"He will be along soon," the ghost said. "But I have to make you understand—he will take possession of my soul.''

Jody's laugh bordered on hysteria. "No, he'll take possession of me. He's going to murder me.''

"Well, he can't," John Hample replied in all seriousness. "You see, he's my reincarnate. And he can't come yet—I have to release my soul to him.''

Jody stared down at the ghostly presence at her feet, her eyes wide with disbelief. "You're sure about all of this?''

"Oh, yes. I've waited a very long time, for just the right moment to make this exchange. I assure you, it's now or never. Even now, Agnes's soul has merged with yours. You'll have her memories. And Chase will have mine. Soon, it will all begin to make sense. You see, she died right here and I found her. I tried to make it home to get help, but I only made it to the front yard. I died in my brother's arms.''

He looked so wistful, Jody felt sorry for him. "How awful.''

"I gave him a set of final instructions, though," he explained. "He knew what had to be done. He kept our secret hidden . . . that is until you found the letters. Now it is time to proceed with what has to be done.''

The ghost stood to help Jody to her feet. "If you follow the Stagecoach Road, you will find Camille. You must go there. You must play your role before it is too late.''

"Camille?" Jody gave him an open-mouthed look. "Camille is gone.''

"No, it is still standing, so far," he replied. "The war has not affected this area very much, thank goodness. Of course, you might meet a few troops on the road, so stay hidden. It would not do for you to tangle with them, dressed like that.''

Looking down at her sundress, Jody tried to block the

sick feeling in the pit of her stomach. "What war? What troops?"

He stood, backing away. "The War Between the States, my dear. Watch out for any troops, Union or Confederate. Now, I must go, so that he may come to you. You will be all right; let the letters and your memories be your guide. You must go to Camille and serve as governess to my brothers and sisters."

Jody rushed after him. "No, wait a minute. You can't just leave me here in the middle of nowhere! I want to go home, to Hampleton, to Chase!"

"You will find your way back. He shall have to bring the brooch with him when he comes for you," he said, giving her an eloquent salute. "And do not worry, you shall have your Chase, I promise. I let my dear Agnes down, but I will not let you down." He started walking through the woods, then turned back to her. "You will never know how much this means to me."

Still in a state of disbelief, Jody called after him. "Don't leave me here. Please, tell me some more about Agnes Jodelyn." He kept walking. Running a hand through her tangled hair, Jody shouted, "Well, at least tell me what year it is!"

"1863," he replied. And then he was gone.

She had vanished.

Chase stood in the cupola once again, his head throbbing from two hours of tension and anxiety. He'd searched for Jody all over Spence House. Even now, he could hear people downstairs looking in every corner, calling her name.

The woman was driving him completely insane.

Why would she do it? Why would she go and hide away? It wasn't like Jody to play the coward. Especially when he'd called off the demolition and sent everyone home. It was the strangest thing. One minute she'd been there, the next, gone. Just like that. He'd heard her call his name; he'd turned from the window, but she hadn't been there when he'd turned around. His frustration had changed to concern in the hours since. Worried that she'd fallen and now lay somewhere in the depths of the mansion, unconscious and needing his help, he'd called back a few people to help him search. They'd found nothing.

Now, he was back where he'd started, holding the wilted sprig of wisteria he'd given her this morning. Giving her one last chance, he called, "Jody, damn it, stop this. I'm not mad, really. Can't we just talk about it? I won't take the house down, Jody." He wanted to tell her about the grave he'd found. He wanted to tell her he understood. "Jody, are you all right?"

At a sound behind him, he whirled in time to see a blur of gray on the cupola steps. "Jody?"

No answer. Angry beyond words, he kicked his foot against the window seat; then he watched, amazed, as a small rounded object clattered across the floor, stopping at his feet. Bending down, he picked it up.

A brooch. A rather exquisite piece of antique jewelry that suddenly seemed so familiar, so right in his hand. He'd seen this brooch before—Jody had been holding it right before she disappeared.

His hand shook, his empty stomach hurt. His headache was getting worse with each pulse beat. Chase held the brooch tighter, trying to steady his shaky hand, then looked down, his gaze following the path the brooch had taken. His heart went still at the sight of the bright red circle of blood staining the boarded floor. Turning the intricate brooch over, he saw the blood spots encrusting its foundation.

"Jody?" He whispered her name, unconsciously curling his fingers around the brooch. "Where are you?"

She was walking along Stagecoach Road, which she realized would soon become the same path of the railroad. She and John Hample had been standing right smack in the spot that would one day be the back garden of Spence House, underneath the magnolia tree that Chase now loved so much. She'd guessed this by judging the distance she'd had to walk to find the road. An abandoned way station had indicated she was on the right track, just a couple of city blocks away from the stump and the magnolia.

"But you're not in the city now, Jody girl," she reminded

108

herself. "Oh, no. You're in worse trouble than you've ever been in your life, only this time, you're not even in your life."

At first, after John Hample had left, she'd just sat there, thinking she'd wake up and roll over, laughing at the incredible dream she'd had. But all too soon, she'd realized she wasn't dreaming. The woods were too alive, too vibrant, for a dream. And the bugs biting her neck and arms were very real. She'd tried calling the ghost back, but only the echo of her own voice had answered her. So, alone, hot and thirsty, she'd done the only thing left to do. She'd started walking.

Lord, she wanted to be back in Spence House, standing there when Chase had come up those stairs with that sprig of wisteria. What was it about the Spence men and wisteria, anyway, she thought, glancing down at the drooping sprig John Hample had given her.

Oh, Chase, what have I done? she wondered, her eyes scanning the deserted road. He'd stopped them from destroying the house, because of her. That one thought had given her the strength to go into action. That one thought had given her the courage to find out what wrong John Hample expected her to "right." Chase cared. She knew he did.

Only she was about a hundred and thirty years too early to celebrate, and right now, she felt like the last person on earth. The woods were so dense, so deserted, and so very beautiful.

Lush honeysuckle bushes fought with cloying ivy and tangled oak saplings along the narrow clay lane. Wild Cherokee roses, their white blossoms cascading like a waterfall along the path, vied for attention underneath pines and oaks wrapped with purple wisteria vines. Sparrows flew from the sweet-scented woods, and somewhere in the dense forest, a blue jay fussed over her nest. Occasionally, a cricket's shrill chirp would rise up from the forest floor, followed by the drone of a hungry bumble bee. And underneath all these sounds, she heard the soft cooing of a dove, perhaps calling its mate. Some things never changed, Jody supposed.

Seven miles. She knew she had to walk at least that far

to find another inn or way station, since they were set up at seven mile intervals in anticipation of the emerging railroad. And she also knew Camille Plantation had been—was—near one of those way stations. Right now, she was literally taking this one step at at time, her mind still numb with the realization that she had somehow stumbled through a time warp. And she'd thought living in a small southern town was time-warped enough!

Well, at least she had the letters. John Hample was right. They would help her piece things together, for a little while. The letters had stopped in mid-1863. You only have a few weeks, John Hample had said. What happened after that? Jody wondered. And more important, would she ever get home again?

Hot and tired, she walked on, squinting at the shifting sun. How long had she been walking? Forever, it seemed, and not a house or living being in sight—just bugs and birds—the wild creatures, to guide her. But no soldiers yet, thank goodness.

A sound on the road behind her caused her to pivot around. Not taking any chances, Jody headed for the woods, her sandals flapping in the dry clay. Ducking behind a cluster of honeysuckle that grew underneath a misshapen dogwood tree, she hoped her floral dress would blend in with the white and yellow blossoms. She tried not to think about how snakes liked to curl up in honeysuckle vines, or that the sprig of green curling against her ankle looked suspiciously like poison ivy. She held her breath and leaned her head against the support of the dogwood's gnarled trunk.

Wagon wheels squeaked across the rutted road, followed by voices echoing through the forest. Laughter, young and fresh, filled the air. Why, it wasn't soldiers at all, it was children, two young boys. One was driving the wagon while the other one sat on the back, dangling his little legs after a large red dog that barked, played and ran after the wagon.

At the sound of Jody's footfalls rustling the bushes, the dog's ears shot up and he started barking ferociously. The younger boy hollered, "Hush up, Sport," but the big dog kept on barking, all the while dancing around in circles.

After spotting Jody, however, the animal bounded off into the woods.

Delighted and relieved, Jody sprang out of the trees to wave them down. Why walk when you could ride? "Hey there, can I have a lift to Camille Plantation?"

The oldest boy, the driver of the wagon, stood up to bring the two ancient mules to a dust-lifting halt. "Holy—"

"Jackson, I'm telling Mama if you cuss," the younger boy said, his wide-eyed gaze on the startled driver. "You dang near threw me outta this wagon. Whatcha see anyway, a bunch of blue bellies?"

When the older one refused to answer, the smaller boy hopped off the wagon to come running around, then stopped in his barefooted tracks at the sight of Jody standing there. "Holy—"

"Shhh," the one called Jackson said, hissing the word. Then, "Ben, don't she look like Miss Agnes?"

Ben grabbed the side of the wagon, his eyes studying Jody with a hard, all-encompassing squint. "Yeah, only Miss Agnes wouldn't be caught dead half-naked like that." Putting a hand to his mouth, he cupped the words in a whisper. "Jackson, her arms and legs are showing."

Shushing his talkative brother again, Jackson pinned Jody with a questioning stare. "Who are you?"

Trying to stifle the smile creeping across her lips, Jody accepted that this was really happening. She was staring into the face of the founder of Hampleton, Jackson Spence. She supposed now would be a good time to start playing her part, as John Hample had advised.

Giving the boys a confused look that wasn't hard to play at all, she said, "Don't be scared. It's me—Agnes—Miss Agnes. I need your help. I need to get to Camille."

Setting the brake on the wagon, Jackson shot off the seat. "Is it really you?"

"Yes," Jody lied, "It's me." Coming up with the first plausible excuse she could think of, she added, "I . . . I'm afraid I've been lost and my memory's a little cloudy. Maybe you boys can help me get my bearings."

They both started talking at once.

"You went to see your kinfolk."

"You ran away."

"You left a note."

"You been gone a powerful long time."

"We were worried something awful."

"Yeah, them renegade Yankees are everywhere and John'll tan our hides when he finds out we let you go."

" 'Specially since you snuck off without Ali. He tried to find you, though. He followed you."

Ali. Agnes had mentioned that name several times in some of her letters. He was apparently a servant on the plantation, a bodyguard of sorts. Right now, though, she was more concerned about John Hample, since she knew he'd died in 1863.

Finding an opening in the boys' chatter, she asked, "Is John . . . is he safe?" It was important to her, very important; she could certainly feel Agnes's worry for her true love. That would require no acting.

Ben spoke up first. "Sarah thinks he ran off looking for you."

Jackson added his own opinion. "That ain't so, though. He did leave shortly after you did, but we all know he was heading back to Virginia—some place called Chancellorsville." He made a rebel fist. "He's riding with Jeb Stuart—the best of the Cavalrymen. John got promoted just before he got hurt—to Major. 'Course, Mama's worried something awful. He got hit with a piece of shell, dang near shattered his ankle. But I guess he tried to get back to the front. He was still limping, is all."

Jody soaked up all this animated information, her mind clicking. John had possibly gone after Agnes? John was hurt. Chase was also hurt, in almost the same spot. She got goose bumps in spite of the warm day. Concerned, she said, "I've got to find him, somehow."

Jackson shot a look toward the boy Jody guessed was his younger brother. "Ben, go call Sport. That dang dog's chasing squirrels and we need to get going."

Ben scurried into the woods, calling loudly for the big dog. "Here, Sport!"

Jackson stepped closer to Jody. "John tried to find you, but he had to go back. We're just worried that we ain't heard from him." Giving her a pleading look, he said, "Why'd you try to go back up North, anyway. Don't you still love Camille? Don't you still love John?"

Jody swallowed the lump in her throat, her heart brimming with love for Chase. "Completely," she stated. Wanting to know more, she asked, "How did you know?"

The teenager gave her a surprised look. "I'm the only one who does know, besides Ali. Remember, you swore me to secrecy after I caught you and John . . . kissing. And I ain't told a soul, I swear." When Jody could only stand there, stunned, he asked, "Are you all right, Miss Agnes? Did you lose all of your memory—I mean, meaning no disrespect, but the way you're dressed and all . . ."

Jody's heart went out to the boy. She didn't want to be here, playing this strange game. But she was, and until she could figure out how to get home, she might as well do a passable job of it. "You're right, Jackson," she said, holding a hand to her head. "I don't feel quite well. I . . . I fell and I must have hit my head or something. I've got this terrible headache and I can only remember bits and pieces of things."

It was only a half-lie. She did fall—through time—and that was enough to give anybody a headache, she reasoned. And strangely enough, she was getting flashes of memory—strange, foreign scenes—playing through her head with a vague familiarity.

Jackson relaxed, then called after Ben. "Come on. We'd better be getting on—you never know when a Yankee'll show up and Mama don't even know we're gone. We need to get you home, Miss Agnes. You'll feel better after you've rested." His gaze darted over her revealing sundress. "Hey, I've got some old clothes in the wagon. Mama told me to give them to the Sanitary Committee to make bandages for the soldiers, but you can borrow one of the dresses if you want."

"What a wonderful idea," Jody said, impressed with the boy's fast thinking and tactfulness. No wonder he would go on to build a town. Taking the worn blue-sprigged calico dress he handed her, Jody waited as the red-faced boy turned away, then hastily tugged it over her head. "It's just right," she told Jackson. "A little snug in places," she added, glad the the rounded neck of the button-front dress wasn't cut too low, "but much more becoming than this thing I was forced to wear."

Jackson turned around, clearly relieved that she was decent once again. "Must be some new-fangled deal from Paris, huh?"

"Something like that," Jody said. "I'll explain later."

When Ben came back, dragging the reluctant Sport with him, the big dog lunged away from the boy to run up to Jody. Two paw steps away from her, however, the animal halted then circled her warily, sniffing the air with a snarling growl.

"Hey, Sport," Jackson said, rubbing the dog's coarse straight coat, "you remember Miss Agnes, don't you?"

Sport's almond-colored eyes settled on Jody, and whimpering, the dog backed away, then turned and hopped up on the wagon by Ben.

Breathing a sigh of relief, Jody decided she'd better be nice to Sport. That old cow dog was smarter than he looked. If the dog had figured out something wasn't right simply by sniffing the wind, then it wouldn't take long for everyone else to think the same thing.

An hour later, Jody caught her first glimpse of Camille Plantation and was immediately caught up in the beauty and opulence of the antebellum era of the South. She thought of all the times she'd dreamed of the past, sometimes wishing she could step back into it, just to escape her troubles. Well, now was her chance, only she still had troubles. But right now as she sat looking up at this beautiful mansion, they seemed far away.

"Stop for a minute," she said, placing a hand on Jackson's brawny arm. "I want to look at it."

Giving her a puzzled glance, the boy did as she asked. "Heck, you've seen it before."

"I know," she agreed, longing to tell him the truth. "I just want to remember it, just like this."

Shaking his head, Jackson relaxed the reins and looked up at his home while the woman beside him did the same.

Camille Plantation hadn't yet been touched by the war. From where the wagon had stopped at the welcoming arch of a white-columned entrance gate decorated with wild pink running roses, Jody had a perfect view of the panoramic gardens and the majestic white mansion centered behind the circular drive.

Dozens of fat Doric columns lined the house, rising up from the raised bottom wraparound porch to the second floor balcony that also encompassed the entire house. Tall, green-shuttered windows opened wide across the expanse of the front and sides of the mansion, while a massive double door with cascading fanlights made up the welcoming front entrance.

"Things aren't quite the same," Jackson stated, giving the reins a click. "I might as well tell you now, Miss Agnes. Pa is dead."

Jody heard the crack in his voice. Not knowing what to say, she patted his arm. "Oh, Jackson. What happened?"

Jackson lowered his voice so Ben couldn't hear. "He got real mad right after you left—not because of that, even though he was worried about you. It's just this war—heck, we've had to start selling off stuff just to get provisions— prices are sky-high, you know, and the Yankees are keeping the blockades tight, so we can't get supplies. Plus, a lot of our people have run off. This time, it was Ali. He followed you, and we ain't seen him since. I guess Ali's leaving was the last straw for Pa. He never figured Ali would desert us. Anyway, he had some kind of attack . . ."

The boy stopped speaking, his eyes misting over. Regaining his composure, he added, "I sure miss him. John's off at war, Pa's gone, and Mama, well . . . she's been in her bed for days. Me and Ben snuck off to find the doc, but he's done joined up and headed to Virginia. I swear, Miss Agnes, I can't take much more."

Jody automatically wrapped an arm across the boy's

hunched shoulders. "I'm back now," she said. "I'll do whatever I can to help." And she meant that. Good Lord, this boy needed someone to help him shoulder the tremendous responsibility that had been pushed off into his lap. "We'll be okay, Jackson."

"And you won't leave us again?"

She had to look away. The hopefulness in his eyes was more than she could bear. How could she promise him something like that? "I'll be here as long as I'm needed," she said, hoping John Hample had taken his brother's feelings into consideration when he'd hatched up this grand scheme to change history. "Now, take me to your mother. I'll see what I can do for her."

Jackson slapped the reins again and the wagon rattled up the worn clay driveway. Jody sniffed the scent of magnolias and honeysuckle, mixed with mimosa and roses. The garden was in full bloom and on either side of the drive, large arched live oaks shot across the way, their branches reaching out like great green umbrellas to offer a cool passage from the sun's glistening heat. Toward the back of the house, she saw several rows of blossoming fruit trees: peaches, plums, a grape arbor, a couple of fig trees and a row of sapling pecan trees.

Well, if she had to be dropped back a century, spring was the perfect time to land. The whole place was like a picture in a fairy tale. But like a fairy tale, it had a dark side. It was a facade, covering a tragic scenario of war and death and destruction.

A commotion from the house brought Jody out of her depressing musings. The front doors burst open and several children of various sizes, some boys, some girls, spilled out onto the wide porch.

Trying to remember the children Agnes had mentioned in her letters, Jody tried to figure out which name went with which child. Mentally sizing up each child, she recalled the names—Sarah, oh, probably the tall, shy blonde who stood back with a haughty air, her cornflower blue eyes summing Jody up. Lizbeth? The giggling one with the caramel-colored hair, of course. Lizbeth was the mischief maker.

And Rachel, little five-year-old Rachel, what a doll! Okay, that left Ben. Oh, he was the twin to Lizbeth! But what about the other one, the baby Agnes had mentioned time and again—Tucker? Had her own ancestor been named after a Spence?

She didn't have time to figure that one out. Probably asleep in the nursery, anyway.

Lizbeth rushed down the steps, running up to the wagon. "It's Miss Agnes! It's Miss Agnes! She's come home!"

Jackson hopped down, helping Jody. "Get back—you'll scare the mules to death, screaming like that."

Unheeding, Lizbeth threw herself around Jody's legs, holding on with the firm, trusting grip of a child. "I missed you, Miss Agnes."

Touched, Jody said, "I missed you, too . . . Lizbeth?"

"You're starting to remember," Jackson said low, his smile reassuring.

"Yes, yes, I am," Jody agreed, relieved that things were advancing so smoothly. One by one, the children came and hugged her close, excluding the haughty Sarah. She just stood looking down on the whole group, her blank gaze never wavering.

Wondering what was eating her, Jody looked up at the pretty blonde. "Sarah, is everything all right?"

"Why, of course," the girl replied in a stilted, formal tone. "I was just wondering if you'd show any concern for little Tucker, that's all."

Confused, Jody looked to Jackson for support. "Is Tucker ill?"

"No, ma'am," Jackson said, lowering his eyes. "It's just that . . . well, you left in such a hurry, and with Mama being sick and all. Sarah's pouting because she's been having to take care of him, is all."

Jody gave Sarah an understanding look. "Well, I'm back now and I'm sorry I worried everyone. Sarah, I'll take over my duties again as soon as I've rested a bit, okay?"

Sarah folded her arms across her lacy white bodice. "Fine. You take all the time in the world. Tucker's young, maybe he won't remember that his own mother abandoned him."

"Sarah, be quiet," Jackson admonished, then looked at Jody, his own gaze questioning.

Shocked, Jody could only stand there, her mouth dropping open. "What are you talking about?"

Jackson gave his younger sister a harsh look. "Sarah, she's been sick. She got hurt and she's lost some of her memory."

Sarah lifted her exquisite brows. "How convenient. So I suppose she has no memory of giving birth to Tucker?"

"Oh, oh." Jody grabbed the wagon, clutching the splintered wood to keep from toppling over. No wonder Agnes had gone on and on about little Tucker. Of course, she'd never come out and said he was hers. Why would she? John Hample obviously knew the boy belonged to Agnes. But did he belong to John Hample, too? Was this part of Agnes's secret life?

Jackson glared up at his sister. "Now see what you've done? You've upset her. I told you she's not feeling good."

Sarah turned and walked away into the house. The other children rallied around their older brother and Agnes.

"I'll be all right," Jody said, her heart thumping in her chest. "I want . . . I want to see Tucker."

"Get back," Jackson said to his siblings. "Let me get her in the house."

The children obeyed, parting to rush open the front door.

Jackson offered Jody his hand. "C'mon, Miss Agnes. Don't pay no mind to Sarah. She just thinks she's above taking care of children, including her own brothers and sisters. She's still pining away for Pa. She was his favorite, you remember."

"Of course," Jody said, her knees still weak as she made her way up the wide stone steps.

So much to comprehend, and so many unanswered questions. Such as: who was Tucker's father, and why in the world had Agnes left her baby with the Spence family?

Then there was the one overriding question.

How was Jody supposed to fix all of this, anyway?

Chapter Seven

He just wasn't sure how to fix this one.

Chase once again stood in the cupola of Spence House, watching the sun set in the west behind a crimson sky. They'd searched for Jody all day; she simply wasn't anywhere to be found. He'd even had workers tearing away at some of the basement walls to see if she'd found the tunnel everyone thought Jackson had built between the house and the trading company.

Nothing. No tunnel. No Jody.

Nothing left of her existence, except the brooch he'd found this morning. Mitt, noticeably shaken himself, had told Chase the brooch once belonged to his wife. She'd given it to Jody years ago, an heirloom passed on from Mitt's own grandmother.

Worried, his head pounding a painful beat, Chase now stood in the small round room, retracing the days events for the hundredth time. There wasn't any explanation for Jody's disappearance. And the worst part was, even though the whole town knew about it, everyone was trying to keep it from Jody's volatile mother. Mitt had told him that something like this could push Maria right over the edge. So.for now, Maria was under the assumption that Jody had been called away on an emergency estate sale.

Shaking his head, Chase wondered what had possessed him to abandon his other, more pressing projects, to come here and try to take on this house anyway. Now he was knee-deep in a peck of trouble: a ghost, a missing woman, a depressed mother, an angry grandfather, and a house that seemed to be drawing him farther and farther into its melancholy gloom.

But he knew deep down inside that Jody had been right about him. He'd always been drawn to this house, even as a child, but now he was afraid of taking it on. Looking out over the back garden, he saw the huge magnolia tree that dominated the far corner of the yard. He'd found John Hample's grave marker there, hidden by overgrown camellia bushes and thick wisteria vines. All those times he'd climbed that tree, he'd never noticed the grave. But he knew it was there now.

And he also knew something, some force, was working against him. Holding Jody's brooch in his hand, he casually rubbed the time-polished pearls, his callused thumb tracing the smooth, intricate cluster. "Whatever it takes, Jody. I'll do whatever it takes to find you and make you mine. I'll even try to rebuild this old house, somehow."

Darkness settled over the creaking mansion. The evening star rose through the trees. The wind picked up, blowing a mournful song through the long hallways and broken, jagged windows.

Chase turned to leave, the brooch still in his hand. Then a terrible pain shot through his head, and clutching his temple with one hand, he fell back onto the window seat, a cold sweat popping out on his forehead.

Too much stress, he thought as he tried to regain his balance. *Damn these headaches!*

The pain increased. He groaned, closing his eyes to block out the sensations inside his brain. Then his whole world turned as black as the night outside, and he found a peaceful oblivion.

Home Again

*　　*　　*

Jody stood on the upper balcony of Camille, gazing out on the summer night and listening to the many sounds of plantation life. Lord, so much to do each day; so many mouths to feed, so much responsibility to cope with.

Pulling the thin gauze wrapper around her white cotton gown, she wished Agnes's clothes didn't fit her so tightly. Marveling that she was even here, she reasoned Agnes had probably been more petite than her, since people weren't as large back then anyway. But that wasn't the most marvelous thing about being thrown into this past world. That would be Tucker. He was beyond marvelous. The toddler was asleep inside the nursery which adjoined Agnes's cozy bedroom. Tucker was beautiful, a bundle of pure joy and innocence. Upon seeing him, her need to nurture had taken over, making her long for children of her own. Jody had fallen in love with the boy immediately, temporarily forgetting that in reality, Tucker was her great-grandfather.

Oh, it was all too confusing to comprehend anyway. But at least she'd put on a convincing act. She'd even managed to fool the shrewd Sarah. That girl was as spoiled as week-old bananas, but Jody couldn't really blame the child. She herself couldn't understand why Agnes had left her baby for a whole month. Deciding she'd pull out the final letters and read them more carefully, she thought over the day's events again.

She wondered where Chase was right now.

Was he looking at the same evening star she saw in the open sky between the twisted live oaks? Was he wondering what had happened to her? Jody was also worried about her grandfather and her mother. She tried to understand what she was doing here.

She'd met Miss Martha, albeit briefly, since the woman was quite weak and not really in the mood for visitors.

"Agnes, you've come home," the feeble voice had called. A thin, white hand, lined with bulging blue veins had reached out to Jody. "Why did you leave us, dear? I promised John we'd take care of you until he comes back."

That seemed to be the question of the day—why had

Agnes run off in the first place? Everyone here was chalking it up to the war; it made people crazy after all. Confusion reigned everywhere as people became refugees or runaways. And it would only get worse, Jody well knew, but she still couldn't figure her part in all of this. She only knew that while she was trapped here, she would do the best job possible. She'd love little Tucker, and teach the rest of the children. She'd nurse Miss Martha back to health, and first thing tomorrow, she'd get everyone lined up to help her. This place needed organizing, and heck, she had lots of time on her hands.

Leaning over the wooden gallery railing, she sighed into the night. Such a beautiful night. The few remaining servants were settled in their cabins behind the great house. All of the children were tucked into crisp white cotton sheets in ornate mahogany and rosewood tester beds that would be worth a fortune back at The Treasure Chest. And poor Miss Martha had had her dose of whiskey—the only thing in the house Jody could find with any medicinal purposes—and was now snoring softly into her mounds of lacy pillows.

An exotic perfume, scented with many different aromas, wafted through the trees. In the woods beyond the gardens, an owl hooted softly. Jody lifted her face to the gentle breeze rustling through the live oaks, closing her eyes to reality for just a moment.

Such a tranquil, lovely night.

Then something went thud, as if someone had fallen across a tree root. This noisy action was followed by the single word, "Damn!"

A prickle of warning rose along Jody's backbone. The voice uttering that bit of profanity sounded so familiar. Squinting into the darkness below, she looked across the drive, her gaze searching for any signs of movement. There, three trees away, a figure rolled in the dirt. Whoever it was seemed to be writhing in pain.

Jody's first instinct was to go to the hurt person, but logic told her to be careful. Running into her room, she grabbed an ornate silver hairbrush, intent on using it for a weapon if need be. Then after hearing several more moans, followed

122

by a whole row of intense profanity, she hurried down the winding stairway, her bare feet treading across the richly woven carpet that padded the stairs. Gold-framed portraits of generations of Spences watching her progress lined the walls. Making her way across the cool marble floors, she paused at the Hepplewhite chest by the front doors, the rich fragrance from a bowl full of fresh-cut magnolia blossoms filling her senses. Taking a breath, she lifted the bolt to open one of the heavy doors, then slipped out onto the broad porch, her eyes searching the shadowy front lawn.

Following the sounds of the intruder, she ran down the drive, her feet freezing in the dewy grass. Listening, she watched for any signs of movement. Heck, if he was trying to sneak up on them, he wasn't doing a very good job of it!

Spying her mark near a clump of bushes underneath one of the trees, she tiptoed up behind the man, her gaze sweeping him from head to foot for clues as to which uniform he might be wearing. Before she could decide if he was friend or foe, the dark shape groaned again and tried to rise. Startled, Jody reacted with a swift whack of the heavy hairbrush, hitting the stranger dead-center on the skull.

"Ooouch!" He fell back down, rubbing the top of his head with one hand while he braced himself on the damp grass with the other.

Jody waited, her breath coming in little puffs, to see if he would try any tricks. Probably a deserter, looking for loot. Only the man lying in the dirt at her feet wasn't wearing a uniform. He wore a black tee shirt and a well-worn pair of blue jeans.

Jody's heart started pounding so hard, she was sure the man could hear it from where he lay with his face down in the dirt. It couldn't be! She struggled to control the sheer joy rising inside her stomach, giving him the once-over again.

It was him. She'd know that fine set of buns anywhere, even one-hundred and thirty years into the past.

"Chase!" she said, dropping the hairbrush, then throwing herself down on top of him to plant feathery kisses along the back of his neck. "Oh, Chase, I'm so glad to see you!"

Fully awake now, Chase rolled over, taking her with him until he had her pinned underneath the length of his body. Then, pulling away, his face mere inches from hers, he said, "Jody? Jody, is it really you?"

"In the flesh, city boy," she replied, jubilant. "Did you just drop in to say hello, or are you planning on staying awhile?"

Looking around, Chase seemed to realize all was not as it should be. Then he shot Jody a scalding glare. "That depends," he answered in a tone that didn't bode well, his warm breath tickling Jody's collarbone. Lifting her hands above her head, he held her pinned to the ground. "Why don't you tell me what in hell's going on here, Jody."

Glaring up at him, Jody decided maybe she wasn't so glad to see him after all. Geez, he had the disposition of an old bear. You'd think he'd be at least halfway happy to find her safe and sound and in one piece. "There you go," she huffed, trying to pull out of the knuckle grip he had her in, "blaming me already, without even hearing what happened."

Chase closed his eyes, squinting hard to work the throbbing pain out of his head. "I didn't say I blamed you," he managed between gritted teeth, even though all of this was her fault, of course. "I just would like to know where we are and how we got here. I think I deserve that much at least, considering I've halted a major project, again, so I could please you."

Thinking the only thing he deserved was a another good konk on the head, Jody lifted her chin to a haughty position. "I never asked you to do me any favors."

He did let go of her then, pushing himself away while he debated whether to shake her or kiss her. "Oh, no? Well, early this morning, you sure looked as if you wanted me to do you a big favor. So, like the sap I'm turning out to be, I stopped the demolition, just so I could talk to you, just so we could maybe reach some sort of compromise." Before she could put in a word, he went on, "And what do you do, but disappear! And now, somehow, you've managed to drug me and drag me here in the dark.'' Glancing over at her discarded hairbrush, he added, ''And to top it off, you tried to kill me with that thing.''

''I was only trying to protect myself,'' she said defensively.

''As if you needed protecting.'' Leaning close, he positioned himself over her once again, his breath a whisper across her nerve endings. ''What'd you have in mind, another seduction scheme?''

Anger flared inside Jody, replacing the joy she'd felt at having him here with her. Oh, he'd never, ever understand this little predicament, and even if he did, he'd swear she'd somehow cooked up the whole thing. But she had to tell him the truth, since he'd find out soon enough. Sitting up, she pushed back her hair, only to reveal the lace-edged, scooped-neck gown she was wearing.

Chase's eyes moved from her face down to her throat, settling on the soft hollow of her cleavage. ''Why are you dressed like that?'' he asked in a voice gone husky and soft. ''And . . . where are we, anyway?''

Taking his questions in the order in which he'd asked them, Jody worded her answers carefully. ''I'm wearing a nightgown, because I was just about to go to bed, and . . . we're on Camille Plantation.'' *There, that had gone okay*.

Chase gave a slight nod. ''Oh.'' Then, ''What did you say?''

Shifting away from him, she started repeating her answers. ''I said, I'm wearing a nightgown—''

''I can see that,'' he interrupted, his gaze following the line of the crisp white gown while he rubbed the rising bump on his head. ''I didn't quite get the second part.''

She scooted a few inches further away. ''We're on Camille Plantation.'' Hurrying on, she added, ''Oh, Chase, wait until you see it in the daylight. It's so beautiful. You'll really like it.''

Chase shook his head and laughed. ''Jody, you're too much. Whatever plan you've got, drop it. I told you, I'm not going to tear down Spence House. You didn't have to kidnap me, you know, and you certainly shouldn't have brought me to some secluded spot . . . unless of course, you want to have your way with me.'' He winked at her, his stormy eyes flashing like lightning in the night.

"I don't have a hidden plan," she tried to explain through the haze of desire his suggestion provoked. "And I didn't bring either one of us here." In a muffled voice, she added, "John Hample did."

To her amazement, Chase threw back his head and hooted with laughter. "Good one, Jody." Rolling away from her, he chuckled again, putting a hand to his nose so he could pinch his nostrils. "Listen, I'm tired, I've got a roaring headache and, silly me, I forgot to pack my pain pills. So could we stop playing games and get home. We'll talk about all of this tomorrow. Right now, I want to crash and try to regroup. This has been one long day."

Jody stood up, brushing grass sprigs off the back of her billowing gown. *Longer than you realize, buster!* "We have to talk now, Chase. We can't go back home, not for a while. John Hample won't let us. And I've got to figure out what he wants us to do while we're here."

Chase shot her an incredulous look. "You've really lost your mind, haven't you? I pushed you too far, about the house, didn't I?"

Angry, Jody stomped around him. "I'm perfectly sane. And you'd better start believing me,'cause I need your help. Take a good look around, Chase, and you'll see I'm telling the truth. We're at Camille Plantation and . . . we're not exactly in a position to go home. Somehow, we've gone back in time!"

"Whoa!" He jumped up, wincing at the dueling pains in his ankle and his hammering head. "This is too farfetched even for you, Jody."

Grabbing him by the arm, she twisted him toward the house looming nearby. "Look, you stubborn mule. See that mansion? That's your ancestor's home. And inside it right now, sleeping, is Jackson Spence himself, and his mother, Miss Martha, and his four brothers and sisters.'' Shoving him forward, she added, "If you don't believe me, take a good look."

He did. Staring up at the splendid whitewashed mansion, Chase had the strangest feeling he'd been here before. Without thinking, he knew the entire floor plan of the house; knew where each room was and how many rooms there were in all.

"No, this is crazy," he said out loud. He was probably remembering all the antebellum architecture he'd studied in college. Turning back to Jody, he said, "What's going on?"

"I honestly don't know," she admitted, twisting her hands together. "I was standing in the cupola, waiting for you to turn around, then the next thing I knew, I was here."

Trying to make sense of this, Chase nodded. "Last I remember, I was in the cupola, looking for you."

"And you wound up here, right?"

"Right." Giving her a hard stare, he realized she might actually be telling the truth. He could see the doubt and fear in her luminous eyes. Belatedly, he asked, "Are you all right?"

Jody closed her eyes, pushing back the tears of relief. "I'm better now that you're here. Just glad to see someone I left behind, I guess."

Still confused, he rubbed his head again. "Left behind? Don't make it sound so morbid. We'll just go home."

"We can't." Frustrated, she wrapped her arms across her chest. "We're stuck here for a while. Chase, we've traveled through time. It's 1863."

That really stopped him. "All right, Jody, this isn't funny anymore. I don't care what it takes—witchcraft, black magic, or a fax machine, but do whatever you did to get us here and get me back to Hampleton—now!"

Throwing up her hands, she stared him down. "I told you, I can't do that. John Hample said . . . he said I have to have the brooch—did you bring it?"

Dropping his jaw in disbelief, Chase looked down at her. "I found a brooch on the floor of the cupola, yeah. It had blood on it." Turning sarcastic, he said, "What happen, prick yourself trying to travel through time?"

"Stop teasing me," she admonished, glaring back at him.

"I scratched myself with the brooch when . . . when I saw John Hample standing there."

He snorted. "Well, that explains everything. Of course, you'd scratch yourself, what with having to deal with a ghost and all." Walking a few feet away, he pivoted to point a finger at her. "I've had just about enough of this—"

The front door of the house opened, stopping his next words.

A voice called out into the night. "Who's there?"

Grabbing Chase by the arm, Jody pulled him behind the trunk of a massive live oak. "Shhh. I don't want the family to see you."

The voice called again. "You'd better answer me. I've got a rifle and I'm a pretty good shot."

"That's Jackson," Jody explained, urging Chase to be quiet. "Stay put while I get rid of him."

Too amazed to do anything else, Chase leaned into the cover of the tree, watching as Jody popped out onto the drive.

"It's just me, Jackson." She waved and let our a deep sigh. "I couldn't sleep, so I decided to take a walk in the garden. I'll be in soon."

Jackson answered her with his own sigh of relief. "Goodness, Miss Agnes, I thought you were a Yankee. You be careful out there, all right?"

She laughed softly, belying the fluttering beat of her heart. "I will, sugar. Go on back to bed, now."

With that, the sound of the front door shutting echoed into the night. Jody hurried back to Chase, then stopped to calm her frayed nerves. "That was close."

Chase pulled her into his arms, leaning her into his body as he braced himself on the tree's sturdy trunk. Sounding doubtful, he whispered, "That was Jackson, I suppose. My, my, Jody, you'll go to any lengths to convince me, won't you?"

She glared at him. "You still don't believe me, do you?"

"Stop playing games, Jody, and level with me."

Moaning, she pulled away from him. "I am leveling with you. That was Jackson Spence, and we're in the year 1863."

"You've really lost it, haven't you?"

Putting her hands on her hips, she sighed. "I'm telling the truth."

Chase thought back over the brief conversation Jody had had with the boy. Trying to trick her into admitting that this was all a scam, he said, "He called you Agnes. Why?"

Oh, boy. He'd never believe any of this. "He . . . they all think I'm Agnes Jodelyn Calhoun—my three times great-grandmother. Remember the key I found in Spence House," she glared at him. "After you left me there, I found a tin box and the key opened it. There was a packet of letters inside, to John Hample from someone named A. J. I didn't know until I arrived here that A. J. was my ancestor. John Hample told me. And he told me Agnes was governess of Camille, so now I have to pretend to be her."

"I see," he said, not seeing at all. *Good Lord, I've somehow landed in the Twilight Zone.* Playing along, he asked, "What else did John Hample tell you?"

"That I had to right a wrong, fix something he didn't get to fix before he was killed. And he told me I'd see you again soon. Did you bring the brooch with you?" Maybe they could just get out of here right now.

Chase shook his head. "I don't know; I might have dropped it. It's not in any of my pockets." He ran his fingers through his disheveled hair. "I can't believe I'm actually falling for this." Grabbing her arm, he tried to drag her toward the house. "You're going to go in there and tell that boy you hired that the one-act play is over."

Stepping away from him, she said, "I'm not acting, Chase. And I'm serious about that brooch. Look again. We've got to find it. It's our only chance of getting back."

"Wonderful," he said, his hands digging through the pockets of his jeans. "Okay, I'll play along, and then I'm going to get the truth out of you somehow. I don't have your precious brooch."

Jody punched his arm. "How could you lose it?" She conveniently forgot she'd lost it herself.

Angry and tired, Chase gave her a hard look. "Well, excuse me. I forgot to call my psychic friend to see just exactly where I'd wind up before this hellish day was over, so I didn't know I'd need to pack an ancient piece of jewelry as my frequent flier award.''

Hurt by his sarcasm, she stepped away from him. ''You don't have to be so mean about all of this. Lord knows, I didn't expect things to turn out this way. I only wanted you to read the letters, to see that we need to save Spence House.'' Lowering her head, she mumbled, ''I've really made a mess of everything.'' She couldn't admit how glad she was to see him again; she couldn't voice her need to fall into his arms and never let go.

Heaving a long sigh, he moved toward her, tugging her back to him. Somehow, in spite of all the trouble she'd caused him, he had a spot in his heart that softened each time she was near. And right now, it was pure mush. ''Come here,'' he ordered, noting her resistance, but pulling her close anyway. Maybe if he calmed down a little, she'd break down and tell him she'd rigged this whole scenario just to prove something to him. What, he wasn't sure, but he'd get it out of her soon.

He wrapped his arms around her, urging her head down on his shoulder. ''It'll be all right, Jody. We'll figure this out together. After all, we're stuck with each other, huh?''

''Yeah,'' she said into the worn cotton of his shirt, her senses filling with the scent of him. He didn't want to be stuck with her, but he was, maybe forever, the way things were going. This would be pure torture, but at least she wouldn't have to deal with everything alone. And it did feel wonderful to have a shoulder to lean on. For no apparent reason, she started to cry softly, trying desperately to keep her tears silent. But the dampness penetrating his shirt gave her away.

''Oh, now, don't do that,'' he begged, knowing her tears would do him in for eternity—if they were real. ''Jody, Jody, what am I going to do with you?''

''Hold me,'' she said, ashamed that she'd asked him for any type of comfort.

He did, long and tight and hard, crushing her to him, his eyes closing in tired relief that he'd found her safe and all in one piece, in spite of the fact that she claimed they were in another time and another place and things were just getting stranger and stranger. *Another time, another place.* The words echoed inside his head, as if he'd said them to her before.

"Somehow, my love, we'll be together again, if not soon, then in another time, and another place."

The vow sounding in his head, he lifted her chin with a callused thumb, then slowly, as the soft midnight wind blew over their heated skin, he lowered his head to kiss away her tears, his mouth touching her satin skin inch by agonizing inch, until he could stand it no longer, and hungry now, he found her lips and covered them with his own.

Jody melted against him, forgetting that she should be mad at him, forgetting that he was mean and stubborn and hateful, and that he didn't believe a thing she'd told him. She forgot everything but being in his arms, everything but his mouth covering hers, everything but her love for him that seemed to be getting stronger and stronger with each passing minute, no matter the time or the place.

Too soon, he lifted his mouth away from hers, his gaze searching her face. To hide his own amazement at how the kiss had affected him, he asked, "Better?"

She nodded and sniffed. "I see you brought your kissing skills with you."

He laughed then, loving the way she could bring a smile to any situation. "I see your sense of humor is still intact."

"Well, heck, this is laughable, or it would be if it were happening to someone else." Then turning serious, she asked, "Chase . . . is Grandpa, is he all right? And my mother?"

"Mitt's worried," he admitted. "And we didn't tell your mother anything." Wanting her to open up to him, he added, "Let's just get this mission accomplished and try to get back to our real lives, okay? Tell me what's happening here, Jody."

"I told you," she insisted, angry that his kiss had momentarily sidetracked her. "We've gone back to the year

1863. I didn't want to believe it at first, either, but it's real. It's happening."

Deciding to call her bluff, he said, "Okay, prove it to me, then."

"Okay," she agreed, wondering if in spite of his heated kisses, he couldn't wait to be rid of her once and for all. "I'll take you to the house and let you read some of the newspapers and books I found—and the letters. I'll show you the entire house, if I have to." When he shook his head, his eyes sparkling with disbelief, she turned the tables. "What about Spence House?"

"I gave strict orders to halt everything until I found you," he explained. Then trying a different approach, he added, "You know, the sooner we get back, the sooner we can discuss your big plans for Spence House."

She pulled away, wiping the last of her tears. "Right, but we have to have the brooch. I guess the only thing we can do now is go to bed. And until I can decide how to introduce you to the family, I think it'd be best if I hide you."

"Oh, c'mon," he said, rolling his eyes. "Enough is enough, Jody. Is all of this really necessary?"

She lowered her head, not wanting to break the sweet truce their few moments of intimacy had provided. "I think it is, until I can figure out what to do with you. I think you're supposed to be . . . John Hample."

He looked toward the heavens. "Here we go again."

"Are you going to help me," she asked, "or make fun of everything I tell you?"

What choice did he have? "I'll help," he said, taking her hand in his. "But only because I want to speed this up and get you home to a good psychiatrist."

"I don't need a shrink," she replied, hurt that he wouldn't at least try to believe her. "I'm not crazy, Chase. Just wait, you'll see soon enough."

"Okay." He raised both hands, then dropped them in defeat. "Whatever you say. But we're wasting precious time here."

"Then let's get some rest. She yawned. "I'm so tired. I didn't think I'd be able to sleep, but now I'm exhausted."

"Me, too." He smiled wickedly, thinking she'd soon be telling him this was all a hoax, because he knew exactly what to say to make her confess. "I just have one more question, Jody. Where am I going to sleep?"

Chapter Eight

Jody stopped with one foot on the porch and one on a step, her brows arching in a question mark. Seeing the dare in his eyes, she informed him, "Well, certainly not with me, if that's what you're thinking."

Oh, he was thinking it all right. But right now, he just wanted a straight answer. "I wouldn't dream of compromising you like that, Miss Agnes."

They both stared silently at each other after his off-handed remark. Somehow, Chase knew he'd said this to her before, right here on these same steps. Not liking the eerie sense of déjà vu creeping over him, he turned cranky. "Just find me a spot, will you? Traveling through time has zapped all my energy."

Ignoring both the memories rising like smoke in her mind, and his sarcastic attitude, Jody shook her head. "We'll put you in the attic."

"The attic? It's hot up there."

"How do you know?"

Not willing to admit that he knew more than he could

explain, he shrugged. "It's at the top of the house. Heat rises."

You can say that again, Jody thought. Having him near was certainly making her heat rise. Oh, she didn't need this distraction right now. She needed to go home! Getting more irritable by the minute, she said, "Stop whining and come on. I'm tired and I've got to think about what to do with you. As far as I know, Agnes left a few weeks ago and nobody's heard from her since. John Hample is somewhere in Virginia fighting Yankees—he's a cavalryman with Jeb Stuart, and good at artillery, too. If you're supposed to be him, then why are you home and not off fighting the war? Oh, I'm so confused."

"I'm home on furlough," Chase said, then looked over at her in surprise. "I mean, we could use that excuse. I am hurt," he reminded her, pointing toward his throbbing ankle. "And these headaches are real enough to convince anyone I need a good long rest."

She bobbed her head. "Yes, Jackson told me John had been hurt." Her eyes went to his leg. "His left ankle."

Laughing to himself, he was pleased with how calmly he was playing along with all of this. "There you have it."

Worried, Jody touched his temple. "Are they worse—the headaches?"

"I had a really strong one right before . . . right before I was beamed back."

Shaking her head, she dropped her hand. "Well, all we've got for pain is some mighty expensive bourbon—the last of Papa Spence's private stock—or so Jackson told me when I gave some to Miss Martha. Daniel died a few weeks ago, and she's not taking things too well. Jackson's trying to run this place by himself and, well, we can help there at least."

In spite of the ludicrous situation they were in, Chase couldn't help but smile. "I see you haven't wasted any time forming a plan of action." He rubbed his forehead. "Whiskey sounds wonderful. I could use a good stiff drink." *And apparently, you've already had several yourself.*

"I'll take you up to the attic, then I'll bring you one. Are you hungry?"

Wishing he had a double decker hamburger from Si-well's, he nodded. "Maybe a little."

Jody clicked open the massive door, cautiously stepping into the dark hallway to make sure no one was about. Motioning to Chase, she brought him into the house.

Chase stood in the middle of the entrance hall, amazed that he *knew* this house. He knew the pink and white marble on this floor had come from Italy, as had the marble on most of the mantels over the dozens of fireplaces throughout the large home. He knew every pilastered and corniced doorway, each rosette patterned circle centered over the elaborate sparkling crystal chandeliers in the drawing room and the long dining room. In his mind, he saw the mural of the hunting scene covering one wall of the library. When the giant grandfather clock down the hall chimed the hour of one, Chase remembered the clock had come from England.

The timber used to build the house had been soaked in a millpond so it wouldn't shrink and the bricks around the bottom foundation of the house and in the kitchen fireplace were made from red Georgia clay. He knew these things, knew them in his heart, and wondered how he knew them. Turning back to Jody, he saw the questioning look on her face.

"Are you all right?" she asked, her hand on his arm.

"Yeah," he managed, his gaze sweeping the stairs. "It's just so—"

"Beautiful?" she finished, her own gaze following his. "Isn't it amazing?"

"Yes," he said, more amazed by his vivid memories than the house itself. Not wanting to share anything yet, he decided he was just tired; he probably was doing some associating again. After all, the antebellum period had been one of his favorite subjects in school. "Quite an impressive home."

Jody found her way up the stairs, letting the moonlight streaming in through the circular fanlight over the doors serve as her only guide. She'd already made her way around most of the rooms on the first and second floors of the house, and Jackson had reminded her that the attic was just off the third floor landing. Maybe Chase would be safe there until she could decide how to handle this situation.

Following her, holding one of her hands, Chase enjoyed the way the moonlight streamed through her thin wrapper and billowing white gown. A vague silhouette of her long legs and rounded bottom greeted him as they turned the curve in the stairway. When she stopped on the second floor landing, holding a finger to her lips to entice him to be quiet, he nodded, his gaze taking in the sweet shadow of her luscious bosom. A ceiling to floor window centered over the back door of the long, wide hallway, giving him plenty of light by which to enjoy viewing her body through the thin material of her gown.

Heck, he was becoming uncomfortable in more places than just his head and his ankle! This was maddening. Trapped in time—hah—with the one woman on earth he needed to get as far away from as possible, and her running around in a gown that rivaled anything out of Victoria's Secret. Of course, he reminded himself, his eyes still caressing her curves as she moved on up the stairs, it was all her fault he was here in the first place, wherever they were. If she hadn't meddled in his affairs, if she'd just let him do his job, none of this would have happened.

His mood blackening, he whispered, "Are we ever going to get there?"

"Shhh," she admonished. "Don't wake the whole house."

Motioning to him, she stepped off the stairs and onto a little hidden alcove at the very top of the house. "This way, I think."

"You think?"

"Well, excuse me, I haven't had time for a formal tour of this whole place!"

"I can't believe I'm doing this," he whispered, his tone bitter. "Why couldn't you just leave well enough alone?"

Whirling, Jody smacked right into his hard body, gasping as he steadied her to keep both of them from falling down the stairs at his back. The closeness brought an instantaneous reaction, making Jody squirm away from him. "Let me go!"

But Chase, tired, frustrated, mad, worried, and downright disgusted with himself for wanting to touch her so badly, didn't want to let her go just yet. No, not yet. She'd played games with him, caused him major problems, and now, she wanted to hide him away in the attic.

Pushing her back against the small door, he looked down at the woman trapped against him. "What if I don't?"

Seeing the determined glint in his stormy eyes, Jody wondered if she'd finally pushed him too far. "Well, I can't scream," she reasoned on a breathless whisper, "as you well know. And I won't beg." She shot him her own determined look here. "So, we can stand here all night, or you can be a gentleman about this and . . . let me open this door."

He looked down at her, his eyes sweeping over her enticing peachy lips. The scent of her honey-hued hair filled his nostrils, making a heat flare deep inside the pit of his empty belly. She'd do it, just for spite. She'd stand here all night, torturing him, taunting him, making him want her when he knew he shouldn't want anything to do with her. The dare in her eyes, coupled with the expectation that parted her full lips, made him as weak as a pup. But he wouldn't let her see that weakness.

Laughing low, he ran a finger down the hollow of her throat, then backed away. "Just playing. Take me to my bed."

Sighing in relief, Jody turned away before he could see the need clearly written on her face. Lord, how would she ever survive this? The man was absolutely the sexiest thing she'd seen in this century or the next.

Venting her frustrations on the squeaky door, she pushed it open, not caring if she woke the whole countryside. The attic, as expected, was dark and shadowy, filled with the clutter of the mansion's castaway furnishings and multiple odds and ends.

Trying not to think about what might be living up here with all this junk, Jody waited for her eyes to adjust to the scant light coming through an alcove window at the front of the long room. "I think I see a bed over there," she whispered, taking Chase by the hand. "Go lie down and I'll be right back with your food."

Giving her an amazed look, Chase whispered, "Just like that, you expect me to go over there and go to sleep like a good little boy."

"That would be nice."

"I can barely see that thing, let alone lie on it."

"It looks perfectly safe," she said, making her way toward the old iron bed. "Probably an extra bed for when they have company. You know, back then, I mean, now, in this time period, people stayed a spell when they came to visit."

Stomping through the stacked baskets and old trunks, Chase glared down at the small bed. "Well, I don't intend to stay a spell. You'd better think of a way to get us out of here."

"Well, if you hadn't lost the brooch—"

Grabbing her by both shoulders, Chase thought about shaking her, but let it go when she gave a breathy sigh that only made him want to kiss her. Using what little restraint he had left, he moved away. "Look, we're both tired, this is strange, and we can't settle this by fighting in the dark. Just bring me something to eat and drink, and I'll try to figure this out. First thing in the morning, we're going home."

"All right." She knew all this snipping wouldn't get them anywhere, and if he touched her one more time, she'd crumble. "Sit down. I'll be right back."

"I think I'll just shake this mattress around a bit before I get comfortable," he answered, watching as she made her way to the door.

Once out of the room, Jody leaned against the wall to regain control. At first, she'd been thrilled to have Chase back in time with her, but the more she was around him, and the more she thought about John Hample's scheme, the more frightened she became. If Chase were here for the same reason as she, that could only mean one thing.

She and Chase were destined to become lovers, just as John Hample and Agnes had been.

"Well, at least I know part of my mission now," she whispered to herself, resolving that she'd have to work hard to keep that particular destiny from coming to pass, no matter about John Hample's fierce need to fix things.

"Miss Agnes?"

"Oh!" Whirling, Jody came face to face with Sarah. The smug look on the girl's freckled face only added to Jody's worries. "Yes, what is it, Sarah?"

"I heard voices—what are you doing in the attic?"

Not liking the accusing tone in the child's voice, Jody reminded herself she was in charge of disciplining the Spence children. "What are *you* doing up?"

Sarah lifted her chin. "I told you, I thought I heard voices."

Shooing away the girl's doubts with a wave of her hand, Jody replied, "I thought I heard something, too. In the attic. Must have been a big, old rat." She said this last a bit too loudly, hoping Chase would hear it.

"Rats don't talk," Sarah replied coolly.

"Well, I talk to myself, as you well know," Jody said, hoping Agnes did talk to herself. "Now, go back to bed. Would you like me to walk you to your room?"

"I'm not a baby," the girl said, snatching away from Jody's hand on her arm. "And I know what you're doing. You might have Mama and Jackson fooled, but I know the truth."

Startled, and momentarily caught off guard, Jody stopped in her tracks to stare at the girl's hazy features in the moonlight. Had Sarah figured out she wasn't really Agnes? Would she tell everyone? Maybe she even knew about Chase.

Deciding to take a firm hand, Jody looked down on the girl with what she hoped was a stern face. "Don't be silly, Sarah. I'm not up to anything but checking the attic. You're tired, you must be imagining things."

"I am not imagining anything," the girl said, glaring up at Jody. "I know where you went on your little journey. And I know the real reason you left Tucker with us."

Relief mingled with fear in Jody's mind. So, Sarah was talking about something entirely different from what she'd thought. But what? "Sarah, *dear*," she said, trying to stay completely calm, "whatever are you talking about?" She really needed to know, and maybe Sarah did know something about Agnes that would help Jody. "I was trying to visit relatives, and I suffered an accident." *Didn't I?* "I left Tucker here because it wasn't safe." It was the only reason she could come up with.

"Well, at least you've admitted that," Sarah said, her tone still wary. "And you and I know why it was not safe, do we not, Miss Agnes?"

Fed up and worried that Chase would come looking for his food, Jody took the girl by the arm, exerting just enough force to propel the slender teenager along ahead of her. "Now listen to me, young lady, I don't know what you're prattling on about, but it's late and I've had a very trying day. I won't stand for this, Sarah, do you hear me?"

Giving the surprised Sarah a gentle shove as they reached the landing of the second floor, Jody whispered harshly, "Now get yourself to bed and not another peep, or . . . or I'll make you help Faith wash all the bedclothing tomorrow." She didn't know if tomorrow was wash day, but she had heard the kitchen maid named Faith complaining to one of the other servants about having to carry the extra load of washing, now that half the servants had run off.

The threat seemed to impress Sarah. Bursting into tears, she rushed into her room, slamming the door behind her.

"There," Jody said, making her way down the stairs to the library to retrieve Chase's bourbon. Feeling a slight bit of remorse for being so firm with the girl, Jody again wondered what Agnes had done to make Sarah so suspicious. Maybe she should seek the girl out and try to bond with her, so she could glean some sort of explanation. The sooner she figured all of this out, the sooner she'd be back where she belonged. She hoped.

Sinking down in a leather chair by an exquisite Chippendale gaming table, Jody opened the crystal whiskey decanter and poured a good dollop into a matching crystal glass. Instead of taking it up to Chase, however, she drank it down herself, then instantly regretted her impulsive action.

Coughing, tears streaming down her face, she sank farther into the soft chair, one hand held to her head. "Lord, I needed that more than Chase, even if it did just about choke me to death."

She also really needed to find out what John Hample expected her to do next. She had a feeling she wouldn't like it, whatever it was. Resigned, but determined, she took Chase his food and drink, shoving it in his hand with a hasty good night before he could question her any further. He still didn't believe her, she knew. But he would soon enough. As her grandmother used to say, "Everything always looks different in the morning."

"I'm telling you, she's different," Sarah whispered to Jackson at the breakfast table the next morning. "Haven't you noticed anything?"

Giving his sister a hard stare, Jackson shook his head. "All I noticed is that she's a little confused. The woman hit her head, Sarah. Give her some time to get well."

Slamming down her linen napkin, Sarah waved away Jackson's explanation. "Hit her head! Hah! It's more than that. I think she remembers more than she's letting on, and I think she's up to something. She was downright rude to me last night. Miss Agnes was never rude or overbearing before. She was firm, of course, but not in the same way she seems now. She even sounds different."

"Well, maybe she's changed," her brother responded. "This war's making it hard on everybody, and you'd be smart to pitch in and help out, instead of expecting everyone to bow down to you."

Glaring at him, Sarah pointed a finger in the air. "I will not let that woman boss me around. Why, she was already overstepping her place anyway, just because John likes her so much. Now, she acts as if she owns the place."

Tearing a fluffy biscuit in half, Jackson rolled his eyes and leaned close to his annoying sister. "Well, she just might come close one day, if John comes back and they get married.''

Jumping up, Sarah rushed to the hallway, then turned to face her brother, her eyes misting with angry tears. ''That won't happen. Mama won't let that happen. You know how she feels about Miss Agnes.''

''Yeah, I know,'' Jackson admitted. ''She likes her well enough as long as Agnes stays in her place.''

''That's right,'' Sarah said, her eyes wide. ''And John will change his mind, too, when he comes home. He must find a suitable girl and they will marry and they will take care of all of us. He will never marry the daughter of a known abolitionist. Why, she was married to a Yankee, for heaven's sake!''

''He loves Miss Agnes,'' Jackson gently reminded his hardheaded sister. Why was he the only one who could see that, and why was he the only one who approved wholeheartedly?

''I don't care,'' Sarah insisted, tossing her blond curls. ''All I know is . . . something isn't right. Miss Agnes looks different. I swear, she's taller, and . . . more rounded.''

Turning red, Jackson shoved another biscuit in his mouth, chewing wildly to hide his embarrassment. He'd certainly seen too much of Miss Agnes's curves already. He didn't dare tell Sarah about the strange-looking dress their governess had been wearing when he'd found her yesterday. ''Hush, Sarah. You don't know what you're saying.''

''I know more than you do, big brother,'' the girl said coyly. ''You're just so sweet on her yourself, you're blinded by it. That woman is not the saint you think she is, and I'm going to prove it to you, somehow.''

Jackson didn't doubt that. Sarah had never liked their new governess, but she did like bossing people around, especially the servants. Maybe Miss Agnes had just gotten a bellyful. Shaking his head, he watched his sister prance out of the room, then he grabbed another biscuit to take to the field with him.

''Good morning, Jackson,'' Jody said from the door leading into the kitchen, her tone friendly in spite of the look of concern on her face. "I'm afraid I overheard some of your conversation with your sister. She doesn't like me very much, does she?" She didn't tell him that she'd heard more than enough to clue her in on a few things.

Wanting Miss Agnes to give his sister every chance, he said, "She doesn't seem to like anyone very much. And she's gotten worse since Pa died. I think she's just scared."

"I can certainly understand that," Jody said, moving into the room with all the grace she could muster in the heavy skirts of the lemon-colored ruffly gown she'd found in Agnes's closet. How women ever wore such things was beyond her, but she was enjoying playing dress-up. "Why does she distrust me so much, anyway?"

Jackson shot her a surprised look, then said, "I guess you don't remember, huh?"

"Remember what?" Afraid she'd let something slip, Jody casually sipped her coffee, grimacing at the weakened state of the brew. Touching her head, she added, "I declare, everything's still so fuzzy. I'm sorry, Jackson." She was sorry, sorry she was here, telling tales, sorry she was having to play a role she wasn't sure of, sorry she'd ever tried to stop Chase from tearing down Spence House, but she couldn't change any of that now. Best to get on with things and get back to her own time. "Please tell me how I can make Sarah my friend."

"Miss Agnes, you don't remember about your father?"

Jody lifted her head, wishing Agnes's letters had been more thorough. "He's dead, yes, I remember."

"But do you remember how he died?"

Looking down, Jody tried to think about what Agnes had written. Her references to her father had been vague, because John Hample and his entire family had not approved of Adam Calhoun's northern ties and his apparent loyalty to the Union.

Mistaking her hesitation for grief, Jackson patted her on the shoulder. "I didn't mean to pain you. Those men, they didn't give him a chance, gunned him down without even listening to his side of things. Sarah doesn't trust you be-

cause of him, and what she believes he stood for. I don't
believe a word of it myself.''

"Thank you for that," Jody managed to whisper. Oh,
what was the big mystery, anyway? What kind of web had
John Hample thrown her into? So Adam Calhoun had been
shot, but why? She was just about to ask Jackson to fill her
in when Ben came running into the room.

"Jackson, hurry. It's Mama. She's a'moaning and crying.
She thinks she saw John!"

Jumping up to follow Jackson, Jody raced up the stairs
to the large, dark suite of rooms Miss Martha occupied. By
the time she managed to gather up the yards of fabric ham-
pering her climb, Jackson was already at his mother's bed-
side.

Out of breath, Jody stood at the door, watching as Jackson
tried to soothe his distraught mother.

"It's all right, Mama. You know John's away in Virginia.
He'll get another leave soon, maybe. Rest now. You just
had a bad dream, is all.''

"No, no," the frail woman lying on the big bed said,
rising up off her mounds of pillows to point a finger at the
door where Jody stood. "I saw John standing right there. I
know I saw him. He . . . he was shrouded in black.''

"Ohhh." Jody fell back against the door jam. Chase!
She'd been so wrapped up in eavesdropping on Sarah and
Jackson's conversation, she'd completely forgotten about
checking on Chase. He'd obviously decided to take matters
into his own hands.

Concerned for both his mother and her, Jackson dropped
his mother's hand to comfort Jody. "She's just dreaming,
Miss Agnes. We all miss John; don't get upset.''

"I'm all right," Jody said, swallowing, her gaze darting
around the room to make sure Chase wasn't lurking in some
shadowy corner. "I'll go get your mother something to
eat." *And find Chase, too!*

"I am not hungry," Miss Martha insisted. "I do not need
your help, my dear.''

Confused by the woman's haughty tone, Jody stepped

into the room. "I want to help you, Miss Martha. We all want you to get well."

"It's all this worry," the woman said, her eyes glassy. "Worrying about my son, worrying about those soldiers. They shall come back, you know. They will come looking."

"What's she talking about?" Jody asked Jackson.

Motioning Jody away from the bed, the boy took her by the arm. "Some Union soldiers. They rode through while you were away. Said they were looking for a spy, a traitor."

"Why here?" Jody wondered out loud, a sick feeling forming in the pit of her stomach. "Who were they looking for?"

From the hallway, Sarah's voice echoed in a loud hiss. "The spy they were looking for happens to be a woman."

Whirling, Jody saw the condemnation in the girl's eyes. Then a new thought occurred to her. What if the soldiers had been looking for Agnes! Watching Sarah's face, she was almost sure of it.

Had her great-great-grandmother been a spy for the Confederacy?

Chapter Nine

After helping Jackson to calm Miss Martha, Jody went out to the kitchen to grab a couple of biscuits for Chase, along with a wet cloth so he could freshen up. A whole hour passed, but still no sign of Chase. Worried that he was roaming around the big house, Jody slipped up the stairs, checking to make sure suspicious Sarah wasn't tailing her. If Agnes had been a spy, then Sarah must somehow know about it. Anxious to fill Chase in on this newest revelation, Jody rushed to the alcove door, then turned to peer down the stairs.

The small door behind her swung open, and with the force from one strong hand holding her arm in an iron grip, she was yanked inside the attic.

"Well, you certainly took long enough," Chase said, his hand stilled looped around her wrist. "I'm starving and it's getting hot up here. I'm tired of this nonsense, Jody. I was willing to indulge you last night, but now this little game is over."

"Good morning to you, too," Jody said, throwing the

napkin covered biscuits at him. "Are you always this cranky in the morning?"

"Only when I've supposedly been swept back in time over one hundred and thirty years," he growled. "You were right about that whiskey. I've got one helluva hangover."

He didn't tell her that somewhere in the dead of night, he'd started to believe she might be telling the truth. He had to admit, not even Jody could have gone to so much trouble just to delay his work on Spence House. But this was all still too surreal to comprehend. Giving her a hard look, he said, "Just tell me what's really going on here."

"I'm sorry," Jody said, noting the beard stubble covering his jawline. "I had a hard time getting up here. I can tell you still don't believe all of this, but Chase, this is real, very real. We'd get through it a lot better if you'd just take the time to listen to what I've been trying to tell you."

Looking her over, he could only nod. In spite of their unbelievable circumstances, she looked right at home and as lovely as a spring morning with her yellow dress and upswept golden curls. Was this real, or was she putting on some elaborate act?

His attraction to her only made him yell at her. "Well, I tried to find you earlier and I think I scared some poor woman nearly to death."

"That woman is Miss Martha, John's mother," she told him, her tone full of reproach. "Why didn't you stay put?"

"I got tired of being cooped up in here. What's the plan, anyway? I'd like to go home before I have to spend another night in this stifling place."

Closing her eyes to the fatigue settling over her, Jody shook her head. "I don't have a plan. In fact, I found out something this morning that makes this even more complicated."

"What? How could this get any worse?"

"I think Agnes was spying for the Confederates."

His bitten biscuit forgotten, Chase stared at her. "You're kidding, right? I mean, this is the part where you tell me its all a joke, a scheme to keep me away from Spence House?"

Irritated, and impatient with his refusal to believe her,

Jody tugged him over to one of the dormer windows. "Look out there, Chase, and tell me what you see?"

Still dazed and hungover, he did her bidding, leaning forward to hold back the yellowed lacy curtain. The scene laid out down below brought him out of his daze rather quickly.

A cotton field stretched like a plush green comforter, out away from the formal gardens behind the house. And in that field, hoeing and pruning the cotton plants, a handful of slaves worked steadily. A young man moving along with them, supervised the work from the back of a shiny roan. Chase watched as the young man issued an order, his tone gentle and his demeanor one of concern.

"That's Jackson Spence. And those people are the only slaves who've stayed with the plantation. This is Camille, Chase, and I swear, this is real." Touching him gently on the shoulder, she turned him around. "I want to go home as much as you. But we can't, not yet."

He watched her closely, searching for some shred of deceit in her shimmering eyes. But, Lord help him, he couldn't find anything to prove that she was lying. All he saw was an abiding sincerity, and a touch of fear.

"What makes you think Agnes was a spy?" he asked.

"Do you believe me?" she asked.

"Do I have a choice?"

"Right now, no." She sighed long and hard. "Something happened here, something that John Hample couldn't stop. Why he chose to roam Spence House is beyond me, but he can't let go until we fix things for him."

"Do you know what happened?"

"No, I'm not sure. Jackson's haughty little sister, Sarah, has already hinted at something shady going on, and Miss Martha mentioned some Union soldiers coming by here looking for someone."

Plopping down on the lumpy mattress he'd wrestled with all night, Chase looked down at the floor. "We're in a big mess here, Jody. War, spies—this isn't safe. Whatever your ghost told you, forget it. We're getting out of here today, somehow."

"Not without the brooch," she reminded him. "John

149

Hample told me we had to have it. I've got to go look for it.''

He jumped up. "I'll go with you." If this was some sort of trick, he'd find a way to break her.

"And risk being seen? No. You need to stay hidden until I can figure something else out. It might not be safe for you either.''

"You mean, if someone mistakes me for John Hample? Come on, Jody, get real.''

"Exactly. Chase, this is real, as real as being dragged through time can be. We're supposed to play some sort of roles here. I just don't know how or what we're supposed to accomplish.'' Wanting him to understand, she handed him the bundle of letters she'd brought through time with her. "Read these. It'll give you something to do. And, here, wash your face.''

"Yes, Mother.'' He grimaced, his eyes on the letters. "Is this what you found in the tin box?''

"Yes, but the letters are sporadic. Some of them are missing, and I need to fill in the blanks. Just read them and maybe it'll help you see why I wanted to save Spence House.''

Snatching the cool rag from her, he said, "Well, that's something I'd certainly like to understand. Do you realize how much trouble you've caused me?''

"How can I forget with you reminding me every time we're together? I can't help it that a ghost decided to use us to change history!'' she said.

Running the cloth over his tousled curls, he retorted, "If you hadn't insisted on meddling, he wouldn't have gotten all stirred up.''

"Right, and your taking down his house wouldn't have bothered him either, I suppose?''

"That would have gotten rid of him!''

"You're wrong. That would have only made him madder, or sadder, in this case.''

Still unable to comprehend that he was indeed in the year 1863, Chase tossed the rag on a nearby rickety table. "Just get us back, Jody. I've got people wondering what's going on. I've got a business to run. I've got responsibilities!''

Hurt by his righteous tone, she looked away. ''And you think I don't have responsibilities? I'm so worried about my mother. This . . . my not being there . . . could really push her over the edge.''

He didn't miss the worry in her voice, or the throaty little catch that tore through her words. He lifted her chin and saw the fear and fatigue in her eyes. ''Did you eat breakfast?''

''I nibbled a biscuit. They're really quite good, but I don't recommend the coffee. It's in short supply and it's weak,'' she said.

Dropping his hand away from her silky throat, he backed off. ''I'd settle for a cool drink of water.''

''I'll bring you some,'' she said, letting out a breath, ''if I get a chance to come back up today.''

''Well, please try.'' He sat down, then gave her a soft look. ''And try not to worry about your mother, or anything back home. Let's concentrate on getting back and we'll deal with the rest then.''

''Sure.'' She swallowed away the lump in her throat. He didn't really give a hoot about her or her family. He just wanted to get this over with, so he could take up where he'd left off. Well, so did she. ''I've got to at least pretend to be Agnes, so that means spending time with the children. Don't come looking for me again.''

Frustration clouding his eyes, he picked up the letters he'd tossed on the bed. ''I'll read these while I wait.'' *And if you actually believe I'm going to stay cooped up in here all day, you really are living in a dream world!*

Looking around, Jody suggested, ''You could look through some of this stuff, too. Maybe you can find some interesting tidbits on your family tree.''

Shooting her a wry smile, he nodded. ''Yeah, I probably won't get another opportunity like this.''

''That's what this is all about,'' she said. ''Another chance. John Hample wants another chance, Chase.''

Still holding the letters, he gazed up at her. ''I don't deal in chances, Jody. I deal in logistics. I need charts and graphs

151

and five-year plans to convince me of something's worth. I like to see the bottom line.''

She threw up her hands. ''Well, city boy, the bottom line here is that we're stuck until we figure out what's expected of us.''

''Then let's hurry up and solve this problem.''

''Yes, Mr. Corporate America,'' she said, regaining some of the composure his fingers on her chin had shaken. ''I'll be back with a full report by the end of the day.''

''The end of the day? I'll go stark raving mad. And I need to find a bathroom, soon.''

Grabbing a rusty old bucket, she shoved it at him. ''Try this, and please, don't miss the pot.''

Back downstairs, Jody rounded up all the children. She'd learned enough from Agnes's letters to know that each morning was spent teaching the children. She'd have to work this in with her search for the brooch, or someone might get suspicious.

Deciding to combine her classes with her quest, she took the children outside for a nature walk. Little Tucker, blond curls clinging to his cherubic face, toddled along with the rest of them.

''Why does he have to come?'' Sarah asked, her hostility toward the child obvious. ''He'll slow us down. And why do we have to go on a silly old walk, anyway? It's hot out here.''

Looking toward the heavens for guidance, Jody smiled over at the girl. ''Tucker is coming along because he's my son and I want to spend time with him, and we're going on a walk because exercise is good for all of us and Miss Martha needs her rest, in a quiet house.''

''I don't mind walking, Miss Agnes,'' Lizbeth said, her short legs hurrying to keep up. ''I like being outside.'' Laughing, she chased her twin brother, Ben, as they followed the course of a vivid black-and-blue colored butterfly. Little Rachel trailed behind to pick wildflowers from the nearby yard.

''It's a shame Jackson has to oversee the workers,'' Jody said, hoping to glean information from the taciturn Sarah.

Sarah rolled her eyes. "What do you care?"

"I care a great deal," Jody admitted, her hand holding tightly to Tucker's. "Why would you doubt me?"

"You ran off and left us," Sarah replied, holding her head down to avoid looking at Jody. "And Ali's gone, too. You took him with you and now he's run off for good."

Her mind clicking to piece things together, Jody asked, "What do you mean? Ali's not here on the plantation?"

Sarah glared over at her, kicking dust with the toe of her kid leather walking boot. "Oh, did you forget Ali, too? Did you forget that he guarded you and that whiny child," her eyes flew to Tucker, "when he should have been watching over John instead?"

"No, I didn't forget." At least that much was true. "I've just been so busy since I got back. When was the last time you saw Ali?"

"The day he rode away after you," the girl said. "Nobody else knew you'd left, but I was watching. I saw you leave, then I watched Ali sneak after you. We haven't seen him since."

Okay. Think, Jody, think. Ali Rasheem had been John Hample's personal servant, a valet and bodyguard of sorts. A strange man of mixed blood, from what Agnes's letters had indicated. John had insisted Ali stay on the plantation, instead of going to war with him, which had been the custom between some of the gentleman planters and their personal servants. So Sarah was saying John had instructed his servant to watch over Agnes in his absence?

Stopping in the spot where she'd found Chase the night before, Jody fixed her eyes on the dirt. While casually searching the area, she asked Sarah, "Do you think he went north?"

The girl snorted, then carefully sat down on the grass, gathering her skirts up around her. "Ali would never desert us, or you, especially. Not when John left him specific orders. Something happened to him. And I think you know what it is."

Pulling Tucker close, Jody sat down with Sarah while the younger children frolicked in the grass. "Sarah, you must

153

believe me. I don't know where Ali is or what could have happened to him. Everything is so mixed up.'' Trying to enlist the girl's help, she added, ''You know, you could help me fill in the missing parts.''

''Oh, really?'' Sarah shook her head, her blond curls bouncing. ''You shouldn't try so hard, Miss Agnes. You're not very convincing.''

''I'm not acting,'' Jody replied, wishing she could just throttle the stubborn child. ''I need your help. I need to understand a few things.''

''What things?'' Sarah's angry words drifted through the trees. ''Things such as your father's loyalty to the Union? Oh, you pretend to be devoted to John and us, and the Southern cause, but you can't fool me. I know you were secretly helping your father. I know you still help runaways. And I also know that if you're not careful, you'll be shot just like Adam Calhoun was by Confederate troops!'' Seeing the genuine shock on Jody's face, Sarah smiled, then hopped up. ''Is it all starting to come back to you now? I bet you can even remember your little brat there had a Yankee father. You're such an impostor!''

Jody sat openmouthed, watching the girl stomp back toward the house. Sarah had inadvertently confirmed what she already knew about Agnes, and now, the fact that Tucker belonged to Will Calhoun instead of John. Something about that revelation made Jody melancholy, but she quickly dismissed it as another of her foolish romantic notions.

Going back over her conversation with the girl, she had to admit Sarah had accused her rightly, of course, but were the girl's accusations about Agnes also correct? Had Agnes been involved in the Underground Railroad? But how could that be? How could she be a spy for the Confederates if she'd been helping slaves escape?

Tucker's wail nearby brought Jody out of her confused musings. ''It's okay, baby,'' she cooed, soothing the child's chubby little knees where he'd fallen in the sand. ''You're all right. Such a sweet boy.''

Looking around, Jody didn't see any sign of the missing brooch. Taking Tucker in her arms, she rounded up the other

children, and under the pretense of searching for rocks, had
them look here and there in the grass and flower beds. The
children found several lovely rocks, but no pearl brooch.
So, for now, at least, she and Chase would have to stay here
and try to find their way through this everchanging intrigue.
That realization left a sick feeling deep in Jody's stomach.

He had a bad feeling deep in his gut. Chase dropped the
last of the letters Agnes had written to John Hample, at last
understanding the magnitude of everything that had brought
him here to find Jody. Out of boredom, he'd picked up only
one to skim over, determined to find a gaping hole in Jody's
carefully fabricated story, so he would have something logical and concrete to take downstairs to confront her with.
Now, hours later, he knew these letters weren't a fabrication.
In fact, he felt such a strong tie to the yellowed pages, he
could have sworn he'd read these very letters before.

He was no longer dealing in reality and logics. He was
dealing with something stronger than any computer printout
or new land development. Unbidden memories floated
through his head—memories of the way Jody made him
feel, memories of knowing how it would be between them.

This all boiled down to human emotions and unrequited
love, two things he didn't have much experience with.
Thanks to Jody, he was learning he had emotions, emotions
he hadn't even known existed! But unrequited love? Whatever had or hadn't happened between John Hample and Agnes Jodelyn, had somehow driven John Hample's ghost to
roam around Spence House, waiting for the right two people
to come along.

Apparently, his ancestor thought he and Jody the perfect
pair. But why them, and why now?

He'd spent the better part of the day doing his own roaming in the attic, trying to figure that out. He'd found lots of
interesting things in his wanderings. Clothes from another
time, portraits of people who'd come before him, old papers
attesting to the reality that he was indeed back in time. And
something else, something that had kept him here, in spite
of his vow to escape.

Buried here in this long, dusty, cluttered room, was his heritage, his past, a part of him that his glamorous, over-achieving parents had neglected to teach him about, a part of himself that he'd pushed away, that he'd deliberately ig-nored in his quest to be a futuristic man.

His great-aunt Jeanette had tried to tell him; she'd often sat and talked about the past, about things that had seemed only tolerably interesting to him at the time. Now he wished he'd listened, really listened, to the ramblings of the old woman. Maybe if he had, he'd be better able to grasp all of this now. And, maybe he wouldn't have been so hard on Jody.

Remembering earlier when he'd walked to the deep-set dormer window facing the front of the colorful yard, he thought of seeing her out there on the lawn with the chil-dren. Carefully, he'd lifted the old, torn lacy curtain away from the window. He'd only wanted to see the place in the light of day.

Instead, he'd seen Jody in a shaft of sunlight, her hair shimmering as rich as gold, her laughter echoing through the trees as she supervised the children's impromptu hunt. It didn't take him long to figure out what she was up to. They were looking for the brooch. He watched, fascinated, as she reached out to the toddler clinging to her skirts.

Ah, that must be Tucker. When Jody swooped the chubby baby up in her arms, rocking him close to soothe his tears, something caught and knocked in Chase's chest. That some-thing had pressed and squeezed at him, making it hard for him to breathe, making it hard for him not to open that door and run down those stairs and into her arms.

Looking back on the scene now, after having read Ag-nes's letters and having seen some of the family through pictures and other clippings and papers, he knew he'd wit-nessed a similar scene before. Again he got the distinct feel-ing that he'd been here, in this place, before.

Silly! All of this was preposterous, of course. Hell, being cooped up in here was enough to make any sane man start imagining things. If Jody didn't show up soon with food and something to convince him they were on their way home, he'd just have to take matters into his own hands. He wasn't used to being at the mercy of a woman's whims.

He took the whiskey bottle and fell back on the bed, intent on drinking himself into a more peaceful state.

Which is why when Jody came to him hours later, with darkness cloaking her in its nocturnal wrappings, he was just tipsy enough and just fed up enough, to act on some of his fantasies, combined with his baser instincts.

It would prove to be quite a combination.

With the light of a single small candle guiding her, Jody made her way to the attic, all the while looking over her shoulder to make sure no one was following her. The whole house had settled down for the night, the occasional creakings of floorboards and solid beams the only sounds within the mansion. Outside, however, the wind picked up and off in the distance, thunder echoed. It looked as if it might be a stormy night.

She reached the attic door, careful to shift the candle in one hand while she set the bundle of food and jug of water she'd brought down on the floor so she could open the door. Sure no one was watching, she managed to slide the stubborn door open without too much fuss. Then taking her rations up in her arm again, she entered the attic, waiting a moment while her eyes adjusted to the pitch black darkness.

"Well, come in, Miss Calhoun," a deep, slurred voice said from a far corner. "I've been anxiously awaiting your arrival."

Surprised, Jody held the candle up, her searching gaze falling on the man who sat in an old wing chair by a dormer window at the far corner of the long narrow room. Startled now, Jody blinked. The man looked like Chase, but something was different. For a moment, she thought John Hample himself was waiting to greet her.

Her heart pounding like the approaching thunder, she stared at the silhouette of the man sitting before her. He wore a white shirt with billowing sleeves and an open neck that revealed his bronzed chest. His pants were black and tight-fitting, and an old worn pair of black leather riding boots completed his ensemble. This, coupled with the two day's worth of beard stubble on his handsome face, made him look like a pirate. In one hand, he held what was left of a bottle of booze. In the other, he held the bundle of letters Jody had left in the attic earlier.

"Chase?" she said, stepping forward, her glance sweeping the room. Obviously, in his efforts to stay busy, Chase had organized the entire attic. The bed now had an old pink brocade spread thrown over its lumpy feather ticking. The various chairs and tables were arranged in a cozy seating order, with books and pictures setting at appropriate angles here and there to complement the grouping. Amazed, Jody called out to him again, "Chase?"

"The one and only," he replied, toasting her with his bottle of brandy. "Just little ol' me, waiting for little ol' you."

"Are you drunk?" she asked, stepping closer to give him a scrutinizing stare. "Did you change clothes?"

"Almost, and yes," he answered. "I decided if you could play dress-up, I might as well join you. I found this spiffy outfit in that old trunk over there." He raised his bottle toward an open trunk he'd moved to one of the windows. "I think I've got a complete wardrobe, so I'll be able to look my best at all times."

"You need to eat something," Jody said, worried at seeing him like this. "I brought you some water, too."

He rose out of the chair, dropping the letters to stumble toward her. "Who needs water? I have nectar from the gods."

"You've had too much nectar," she said, trying to reach out for the whiskey decanter he held away from her. "Give me the bottle, Chase."

He caught her arm with his free hand. "Oh, no. I haven't had nearly enough nectar. And you know, the more I think about this . . . situation, the more I think I might be able to enjoy this if I just go with the flow, so to speak. I've read Agnes's sweet letters to her lover." At Jody's shocked gasp, he smiled. "Oh, yes, I figured out that much, at least. Those two were hot for each other."

"They were in love," Jody corrected, trying to twist out of his grip. "There's a distinct difference."

He bowed his head. "Okay, call it love if it makes you feel better. Whatever. But I've come to a decision of sorts, based on all those endearments Agnes wrote to John."

Fear gripping her insides, Jody tried to stay calm. Maybe giving him the letters had been a mistake. "Oh, and what decision is that?"

"You and I . . . we have to fulfill our part of the bargain, right?"

"But we don't know what we need to do yet," she reminded him, closing her eyes as he set the crystal bottle down on a nearby table, then strolled closer to her.

He pulled her into his arms. "Yes, we do."

She almost dropped the candle, causing the flickering light to leap across the room like a set of phantom dancers.

Chase took the candle holder from her shaking hand, his eyes never leaving her face. "We both know exactly what's expected of us, don't we, Jody?"

Jody shuddered as he pulled her close, then lowered his head so his lips could trail down the column of her throat.

"Let me go, Chase," she pleaded, closing her eyes again to block out the sweet rush of desire coursing through her. "You've had too much whiskey. You need to eat."

"I'd rather nibble on you," he whispered. Then in a calculated demonstration, he did just that, starting with her earlobe and working his way down her neck to her shoulder. "Isn't this part of the plan?"

A soft moan slipped through Jody's parted lips, but she caught herself before the next one escaped. Yanking herself away, she glared up at him. "You can't be serious."

She watched as anger flared brightly in his eyes. "I'm deadly serious, sweetheart. If you think I intend to stay hidden away up here, like a prisoner, without some form of . . . diversion, you're sadly mistaken. I want to get out of here, and if fulfilling this destiny will bring that about, then I say let's get to it."

She didn't miss the cruelty or the crudeness in his suggestion. Stung by his callous summary of a situation she was following with her heart, she backed up against the door, covering her mouth with one hand. "I hate you," she said, wishing with all of her heart she meant it. "And I won't be forced into something that I'll only live to regret."

The venom in her words shook Chase out of his drunken stupor, but he hid his disappointment behind a sardonic smile. "Well, you do have a point. If and when we get back to the future, we certainly don't want any embarrassing reminders of what happened here, now do we?"

"No," she readily agreed, her heart shattering. "We'd both regret it, I'm sure."

Her prim attitude only fueled his lusty frustrations. "Are you so sure?" he asked, backing her up against the door. "Are you so sure you'd regret this, Jody?"

Before she could answer, his mouth captured hers, taking her breath and her resolve away completely. The kiss was savage, and punishing, exciting and demanding. All the things he was, all the things he made her want to be. Not understanding the mass of emotions taking over her soul, Jody moaned and fell back on the door, letting him press close to her, letting him show her just how drunk he really was, just how aroused he really was. But she didn't care. She blocked out all her doubts, all of her fears, and for a brief instance, let the feel of his mouth on hers overtake her sense of duty and decorum, while his hands on her body overtook everything between the lace at her neckline to the padded bustle of her backside.

Finally, winded and dazed, Chase lifted his mouth away, only to whisper raggedly in her ear. "You torture me, in this century and the next. You'll torture me until I have you, and I won't rest until I do."

With that, he moved away, turning his back to her, his head down, his breath still ragged. "Go, Agnes Jodelyn. Now!"

She did. She opened the door with a fling, not caring if the creaking wood woke the devil himself. She ran down the stairs and didn't look back, didn't let out a breath until she was safely in her own room. Then she doubled over, gripping her stomach. The physical pain of loving him was

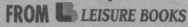

Get Four Books Totally FREE – A $21.96 Value!

▼ Tear Here and Mail Your FREE Book Card Today! ▼

PLEASE RUSH
MY FOUR FREE
BOOKS TO ME
RIGHT AWAY!

Leisure Romance Book Club
P.O. Box 6613
Edison, NJ 08818-6613

AFFIX
STAMP
HERE

so strong, she thought she'd die from it. She didn't want to love him. She didn't want to need him. She'd seen what this kind of need could do to a woman.

Yet, she couldn't very well avoid him. She needed his help. She needed him, for more reasons than she cared to admit.

Out in the shadowy hallway, a lone figure stood listening to the hard rain that now fell outside. As a flash of lightning colored the house, Sarah turned, her eyes lifting to the attic door. "What are you hiding up there, Miss Agnes?" she whispered to the night. "Whatever it is, I intend to find out. Soon."

Then maybe they'd all be rid of Agnes Jodelyn Calhoun once and for all.

Chapter Ten

Chase woke with a start. Something, someone, a noise, had startled him out of his alcoholic stupor. Raising up on one arm, he had to stop and remember where he was.

In the attic of Camille Plantation, in the year 1863.

Vaguely, he also remembered his inexcusable behavior toward Jody earlier in the evening. Had he dreamed of trying to seduce her, had he dreamed of her sweet lips clinging to his own, of her intoxicatingly lush body pressing against his. What a sweet dream—maybe all of this was a dream.

A soft sound stopped his dream memories. Someone was in here with him.

"Jody?" he called into the shadows. "Is that you?"

No one answered him, but the room went still. He listened and immediately heard the distinct sound of rapid breathing.

Rolling off the lumpy bed, he called out again. "Who's there?"

When no response came, he carefully made his way around the cluttered room, his eyes adjusting in the moonlight to give him a darkened image of his surroundings.

Stepping toward the doorway, he saw that the small attic door was partially open.

"You'd better tell me what you're doing, right now!" he called, hoping to scare away whomever was lurking in his private domain. Stepping closer to the door, he listened for the breathing again.

A small figure swooped out from behind an old armoire. Acting quickly, Chase lunged forward, capturing a tiny wrist in one of his hands. "Gotcha!"

A piercing scream greeted him, followed by an angry demand. "Let me go!"

Pulling his quarry out into the hallway so he could see by the light of the moon, Chase stood the small person up by the wall, all the while holding himself away from a pair of flailing arms and kicking feet. "Calm down, little one. I'm not going to hurt you."

Another scream. "Jackson, help me. Jackson!"

Doors everywhere immediately opened, and footsteps echoed up and down the hallways of the big house. Chase knew he should hide, but this person was trying to beat him within an inch of his life, and she—he'd identified her as such—had a set of lungs that would do the Florida State University cheerleading squad proud. Good Lord, what a little hellcat!

Before he could react, a lantern was shoved in his face and several sets of inquisitive eyes were fastened on him. Feeling like a pinned rabbit, he could only stand there, holding onto the scared child who was trying to punch him out.

The young boy holding the lantern looked hard at Chase, then let out a gasp. "John?"

Oh, boy. This must be Jackson and his entourage of brothers and sisters. But where was Jody, and why didn't she hurry and get him out of this mess?

The girl who'd been trying to defend herself against him suddenly stopped kicking and swinging, her blue eyes going wide as recognition colored her illuminated face. "John? Did you say John? Is it? Jackson, is it really him?"

Jackson circled Chase with the lamp held high, his smaller brothers and sisters following him like foot soldiers.

"I think so," he said, giving Chase the once-over. "You've cut your hair. And where's your beard?"

Not knowing what to say, and cursing Jody and her whimsical dabblings, Chase could only nod.

"Well, what are you doing hiding out in the attic?" the blond-haired girl who'd found him asked. "You nearly scared me to death, jumping out at me like that." Then, taking Chase by surprise, she threw herself into his arms to crush him in an affectionate hug. "Oh, John, I'm so glad you're home!"

He remembered it as being her jumping out at him, but he didn't argue the point. And what excuse should he give them, or should he simply tell them the truth. *I'm not John, I'm actually his great-great-great nephew, from the year 1995, and I'd really like to get the hell out of here.*

Looking around at the expectant faces watching him, he knew he couldn't tell them the truth. They'd probably take him out and hang him, with blondie personally kicking the bucket out from him. He was about to make up some elaborate lie, when another door opened and he heard a set of hurried footsteps coming up the stairs.

Jody rounded the landing, her white robe billowing out behind her like the petals of a magnolia blossom, her eyes wide with apprehension. Scanning the crowd, she found Chase in the center. "I heard screams," she managed to say, her skin going as white as her robe.

Chase saw the workings of her brain in her shimmering eyes. In spite of the dire circumstances, he couldn't help but smile. Let her do some fast talking now. Maybe they'd at least be able to get out of here and get back to Spence House.

"What's going on?" she asked, a firm tone in her voice.

Sarah stepped forward, a finger in the air. "I knew you were hiding something up in the attic, so I decided to see for myself what it was. Why didn't you tell us John was home?"

Relief washed over Jody. So they believed Chase was John. So far, so good. Had Chase let anything slip? Looking over at him, she could see the twinkling light in his eyes.

Why, he was enjoying watching her squirm. Glaring at him, then putting on a sweet face for the sake of the children who'd all started talking at once, she managed to get her facts straight, based on what she already knew.

"Uh, well . . . John managed to get a few days leave." Looking at Chase, she added, "He got injured, remember. His foot is still bothering him, and he had a fever . . . he was disoriented for days . . . he barely managed to make it home. On the way, he had to hide from that same group of Union soldiers who came by here the other day."

"You mean the soldiers looking for a woman?" Sarah asked, proud to be the one to inform her older brother that his paramour was possibly in trouble.

"Yes," Jody said hastily, making things up as she went. "Anyway, when he showed up last night in the middle of the night, I was afraid for him, so I hid him in the attic until it was safe."

Taking advantage of the situation, Chase interjected, "I didn't think hiding up here was really necessary, but you all know how determined our Agnes Jodelyn can be at times."

"Probably the best place," Jackson said with a shrug. "So, that was you Mama saw this morning, huh?"

Chase's gaze flew to Jody's. "Uh, yes. I wanted to let everyone know I was here, but Miss Agnes insisted I rest and remain hidden for a couple of days."

Sarah snorted. "That doesn't make a bit of sense. This is your home, John. Why, you have a whole suite of rooms on the second floor. We could hide you in no time flat if any Yankees show up. And she knows that."

The girl had a point, darn her. "That's true, but Miss Agnes just wanted to be sure. I went along with her . . . she insisted my rooms needed to be aired and cleaned." Shrugging, he added, "Look, I'm sorry I scared everyone. Now that you all know I'm home, how about a hug for your big brother."

Jody watched, amazed, as Chase hugged each child, his eyes telling her he had no earthly idea who they were. Still, she was touched by his generous gesture and the way he'd played along with her story. Maybe he was actually beginning to believe her, after all.

Hoping to get him alone to discuss things thus far, she pulled all the children to her side. "Now that all the excitement's over, I think you all need to return to bed. John will be home for a while yet. Plenty of time to catch up on things."

Ben stepped around. "Does he have to go back to the attic?"

Rachel chimed in. "Please, Miss Agnes, we'll take real good care of him. We'll watch for the Yankees."

Jody looked from one child to the next, her heart turning to mush. "Well, I suppose it would be pointless to keep him hidden away up there. As long as we're very careful, I think we can let him run loose."

All the children laughed, except Sarah. She only stood there, staring at Jody with condemning eyes. "You just wanted him all to yourself."

"Sarah," Jackson said, giving his sister a warning look, "you know that's not so. I think Miss Agnes did the right thing, considering how dangerous it is around here right now."

"You would think that," the girl answered, her arms wrapped against her chest. "If I hadn't found him, she might have kept him away from us forever."

"I didn't intend to do that," Jody said, thinking she'd like to set Sarah straight on a few things. But now wasn't the time. She and Chase were too deep into this charade to back down now. And until they found that brooch, they'd just have to keep pretending.

Sarah perked up, pulling Chase along. "I'll take you down to your room, John. Dancy just cleaned it the other day. It's fresh still." Tossing a look at Jody, she pushed Chase by. "You can go back to bed now, Miss Agnes." Then underneath her breath, she added, "Or should I call you Jody?"

Shocked, Jody stood staring after the girl. How did Sarah know her real name?

As dawn colored the gardens and surrounding fields,

Chase stood at the ceiling-to-floor window in the spacious set of rooms that had belonged to his ancestor, still in wonder at the strange turn of events that had somehow propelled Jody and him back in time. Yes, he had to accept that they were indeed in some sort of different plane of existence, yet he still couldn't comprehend exactly why.

He did know that since he'd entered this room, memories, clear and precise, had moved like a computer printout through his confused mind. He'd been here before. This he knew from the depths of his being. In fact, since he'd arrived on these grounds, his mind had reeled with some sort of stored-up memories that refused to be squelched.

Turning to the massive, teakwood, four-poster bed, he knew he'd slept in that bed before. Everything was familiar to him, from the Turkish carpets covering the polished hardwood floors, to the heavy velvet and damask burgundy draperies and matching bed cover. The elaborate teakwood wardrobe and the matching dresser and bed had been a gift from his parents when he'd moved into the large suite of rooms.

Wait a minute! Not his parents, John Hample's parents. Holding his head between his hands, Chase groaned softly. Wishing he'd brought some Tylenol through time with him, he wondered why he had to suffer headaches along with his still sore foot on top of everything else he had to deal with.

Falling down on the bed, he decided he'd try once more to get some sleep. He was very tired. First thing tomorrow, he would mount his own search for that brooch. And once he found it, he was leaving here, with or without Jody!

Burying his face in the rich burgundy satin pillow case, he took a deep, cleansing breath and was instantly intoxicated by a familiar scent.

Apple blossoms and wisteria.

Again, just to be sure he wasn't imagining things, he sniffed the pillow. Yeah, no doubt about it. This pillow smelled like someone he knew, someone who continued to torment him and taunt him.

His pillow smelled like Jody.

His pillow held the scent of desire.
And his headache increased tenfold.

As the day wore on, so did Chase's many pains. Never in his life had he deceived so many innocent people. He'd always prided himself on being honest and hardworking, the complete opposite of his ruthless father. Oh, he could be ruthless when he had to, but Chase knew where to draw the line. He always managed to keep his integrity while increasing his bank account. A good, honest job well-done, with a fair amount of money changing hands, was the balance that had always brought him plenty of business.

This was a different situation. For one thing, Jackson seemed to worship the ground he walked upon. The boy had bounded into his room bright and early, pulling clothes out of the wardrobe, insisting John get dressed so they could ride through the fields together.

"I'll be real careful, John, I promise. I'll post guards at the entranceways and the roads. I'll take you on the back lanes, away from the main road. We'll watch out for each other, just like we always have."

How could anyone refuse an endearing request like that? Now, sitting at the long mahogany dining table, eating his biscuits and salty cured ham off of an exquisite china plate, Chase could only glare at the woman seated two chairs away, his thoughts as full of brine as the ham. He badly wanted to blame Jody for all his troubles, since she looked as sweet as fresh cream, sitting there in a ruffled blue hooped dress, with a matching blue ribbon tied in her hair.

"Have you seen Mama yet?" Jackson asked, his youthful eyes wide with concern.

Peeling his own eyes away from Jody, Chase shook his head. "Miss Agnes informed me she was still sleeping. I'll go up after breakfast."

"Maybe seeing you will perk her up," Jackson said, his tone bright with hope. "How long can you stay, anyhow?"

"That all depends," Chase began, wondering the same thing himself.

Interjecting, Jody said, "John needs to heal. He's been

suffering terrible headaches and he still has a slight limp. We'll just have to see how things go.''

Accepting that, Jackson pushed his chair away from the table. ''I'll go saddle up the horses. Phantom will be so glad to see you! You were right not to ride him into battle; he's too dang skittish.''

Phantom? Chase gave Jody a questioning look.

Laughing nervously, she said, ''Yes, that stallion will enjoy a good run. He's been chomping at the bit, but no one else has the nerve to ride him.''

''Ali wasn't afraid of him,'' Jackson reminded them. Then turning to Chase, he asked, ''Have you heard anything from Ali?''

Remembering the reference to Ali in Agnes's letters, Chase tried to ad lib his way through the awkward conversation. ''No, I'm afraid I haven't seen him.'' Well, at least that much was true! Trying to steer Jackson away from that subject, he added, ''I'll look forward to our ride, as long as this old leg holds out. I'll meet you at the stables.''

Jackson looked from Chase to Jody, then shot them a sheepish smile. ''I reckon you two want to talk privately.''

Chase nodded, his eyes cutting across the long table toward Jody. ''Yes, I reckon we do.''

Jackson left the room, his riding boots clicking on the polished floors. The other children had had breakfast earlier and were now upstairs doing their lessons, with Sarah in charge of making sure they all did what Jody had assigned for them. Putting the girl in charge had been a good idea, since she loved to boss everyone around anyway.

Chase leaned forward, elbows on the table, hands laced together so his fingertips touched, two matching silver rococo candlesticks set in the middle of the table framing his stern profile. Jody waited, watching the play of emotions across his handsome face, wishing the earth would just swallow her up and end all of this. Yet, she wouldn't give him the satisfaction of seeing her squirm.

''More coffee?'' she asked, clearing her throat so her tone would come off sounding halfway confident.

''No, thank you.'' He tapped his fingers together in a

169

steady rhythm, then let out a long sigh. "Well, Miss Agnes Jodelyn, this is certainly one fine mess you've managed to get us into. I haven't ridden a horse since junior-high summer camp!"

Sitting up, Jody leaned forward, too, to glare at him. "*I* didn't do this. You seem to have conveniently forgotten— John Hample put us here. When will you stop blaming me?"

Raising up to stalk toward her, he said, "When I get my life back!"

Jody rose out of her chair, meeting his heated gaze with one of her own. "I don't like this any better than you. I hate the lies, the mysteries; I wish I could tell these children the truth, but I can't. We're in too deep now, Chase. All we can do is play along until we find that brooch, or complete our purpose here."

"Which is?"

She lowered her eyes. "I don't know."

He stalked closer. "Oh, but you do know. We both do, don't we?"

She lifted her chin, her eyes defiant. "If you're referring to what happened last night—

"I was drunk last night." His eyes traveled down the column of her throat. "I suppose I owe you an apology."

His eyes were trained on the decolletage of her dress. She managed to say, "So you didn't mean any of the suggestive things you said last night?"

"Frankly, I don't remember what I said last night," he replied, his lie as white and smooth as the curve of her bustline pressing against all that lace. Lifting his gaze to her eyes at last, he added, "But we both know what good ol' John and prim little Agnes were up to, don't we?"

She pushed away from the table. "That doesn't mean we have to repeat history."

"But isn't that why we're here?"

He'd somehow managed to inch closer, close enough for her to see the flecks of midnight in his eyes. He'd bathed this morning, and Lord help her, he smelled deliciously fresh. But he'd left the beard stubble, making him look even

more like his predecessor. He was again dressed in a brilliant white cotton shirt and dark trousers. John Hample must
have been a bit smaller through the hips and stomach. The
pants fit Chase like molded clay, leaving very little to Jody's
overwrought imagination.

"Jody?"

Bringing herself out of her desire-drenched stupor, she
said, "Don't call me that!"

Anger sparkled in his eyes. "Well, excuse me, Miss Agnes." Groaning, he backed away to run a hand through his
hair. "Oh, hell, let's just get on with this, so we can find
that brooch."

"Fine with me." She brushed past him, but not before
he snaked out an arm to hold her back.

"We're not just dealing with Agnes and John here. You
know that, don't you, Jody?"

Looking down with disdain at his strong hand on her
wrist, she refused to let him see the need in her eyes. "Let
me go."

He stepped closer instead, the gleam in his eyes chal-
lenging all the resolve she'd managed to conjure up. "It's
not over; it won't be over, even when we get home."

Sarah pranced into the room, her eyes flying wide when
she saw them. Giving Jody a disgusted look, she trained her
gaze on Chase. "Mama's awake, John. She's anxious to see
you." Smirking at Jody, she added, "Alone."

Unable to do anything else, Chase nodded, then let go of
Jody's arm. "I'll be right up."

After seeing the man she thought to be her eldest son
home again, Miss Martha perked up considerably. Jody had
already informed Chase that Papa Spence was dead, so when
Miss Martha clung to him, pouring her heart out and la-
menting the loss of her husband, Chase played his part well,
struggling to contain his own frustrated emotions while he
comforted the frail woman. With the entire family gathered
around, he was reunited with John's mother. Jody stood
back, away from the tender scene, very much aware of
Sarah's disapproval of her even being in the room.

Later, Jody stood at an upstairs window, watching Chase ride away down a back lane with Jackson. The boy talked and laughed, innocently animated with the man he believed to be his brother, while Chase, still suffering from his hurt foot, somehow managed to calm Phantom down into a fairly sedate trot. Even so, the devilish stallion didn't seem to like its mysterious rider. Just like Sport, the horse seemed to sense something wasn't quite right. Well, she'd won the old dog over with a ham bone. She wondered how Chase would fair with the stallion.

Turning from the window, Jody found Sarah staring at her, a look of pure malice gleaming in the girl's cold, blue eyes.

Checking to make sure the younger children were doing their various assignments, Jody motioned for Sarah to join her at the window. Reluctantly, the girl pranced across the room.

"Why do you hate me so much?" Jody asked, pleased when the direct question brought Sarah's head up a notch.

Just as direct, the girl shot back. "Do you even have to ask?"

"Yes, I do." Jody nodded slowly, her eyes searching the teenager's taut face. "I'd really like us to be friends, Sarah."

"That can never happen," the girl insisted, looking away to watch her brothers disappear around a curve in the lane. "The minute John set eyes on you, our lives changed. You've brought nothing but pain to this house, and I can't forgive you for that."

"What have I done that's so awful?" Jody asked, really wanting to get to the bottom of Sarah's hostility. She felt all the answers she and Chase needed probably could be found in the girl's story.

"I do not have to explain anything to you!" Sarah whirled to walk away, but Jody's firm grip on her arm held her still.

"Not even if it can help your brother?"

"Are you threatening me?" the girl asked, a tinge of fear evident in her voice. "Don't you care about John? Or do you just want what little money this family has left to advance your precious cause?"

"What cause? What are you implying with all these accusations, Sarah?"

Sarah laughed, jerking her arm away from Jody. "You think you've got everyone fooled. But I'm not so stupid. You were married to a Union officer; your father was an abolitionist, and yet you expect us to believe you've changed, that you are now loyal to the South." Her eyes going glassy, she whispered, "The only reason you hid John in the attic was to protect yourself. If your Yankee friend comes back and finds you with John, you know what will happen."

Frustrated, and sick with fear, Jody pleaded with the girl. "Sarah, I honestly don't know what you're talking about."

Tears coloring her eyes, the girl leaned forward. "You just can't decide, can you, Miss Agnes? You're a woman caught in the middle, and now it's too late for you to get out. Oh, why didn't you just stay gone? Now, you're back—with John here, too. You'll wind up getting him killed. And I swear, I'll never forgive you for it, if you do."

Appalled, Jody could only watch as Sarah rushed out of the room. Determined to find out more, she went into her own bedroom to pull out the letters Chase had given back to her. She'd read them all again, and maybe she'd find a clue to support whatever Sarah refused to tell her. She didn't like the tone of the girl's accusations, and she honestly couldn't blame the child for being afraid. What if something happened to Chase?

"You're right, Sarah," she whispered, her eyes scanning the yellowed pages before her. "I'd never forgive myself either, if that happened."

An hour later, Jody put the last of the letters down, still as confused as she'd been after reading some of them before. The only sure truth in the packet of letters was Agnes's certain love for the man to whom she'd written them. The letters spoke of how Agnes and John had met—his horse had accidentally run her down—near the magnolia tree where Jody had met John Hample herself.

John had then taken Agnes back to her father's cabin, but her injuries weren't severe, just a few bruises and scratches. Her father had immediately disapproved of everything John Hample Spence stood for, forbidding his daughter to see the man again. The attraction between the two was undeniable, though, according to the intimate tone of the letters. The brooch sealed that love, while the war sealed their fate.

Shortly before the war broke out, Will Calhoun, a distant cousin, came to visit Agnes's father in hopes of starting his own school down south. Deciding Will was the man for his only daughter, Adam Calhoun forced Agnes to marry Will. Agnes gave up any hope of ever being with John Hample. While both John and her own husband were away at war, one fighting for the South, the other for the North, she must have given birth to little Tucker, and watched as soldiers shot her father down for his part in the Underground Railroad. Since some of the letters were missing, Jody could only confirm this based on what she'd learned since being here.

But one letter clearly stated Agnes's thanks to John Hample.

"I do not know how I'll ever repay you and your family for your kindness, dear John. Letting me move into Camille, and live there under your protection, is truly noble. I will not let you down. I will abide by your word. I cannot say here how I really feel, but soon, my love, soon."

Alone and afraid, Agnes had been near destitute, until John rescued her and brought her back to live at Camille.

Then, another letter, months later that indicated the strong attraction growing between the two.

"Seeing you again, being near you for even such a short time, has reinforced these forbidden yearnings. But we cannot give in. We both have obligations, loyalties. Yet, I count the hours until I can be with you, freely, and forever."

John had protected the woman he loved.

It was a kind gesture on his part, but one his family objected to vehemently, obviously, because of her northern ties. So, some of the pieces were beginning to fit in this continuing puzzle. Perhaps Sarah was partly right; perhaps Agnes had been loyal to the North because of her father and her husband, and perhaps, just perhaps, when she'd lost both of them, she'd lost any loyalty she might have had to the North. She'd then turned her attentions to loving John, protecting John. Her loyalties would naturally lean toward the South.

"You're a woman caught in the middle," she remembered Sarah saying. A nagging thought reared its ugly presence in Jody's frazzled mind.

What if Agnes had been playing both ends against the middle? What if dear Miss Agnes had been a double agent?

Chapter Eleven

Jody didn't get a chance to delve further into Agnes's questionable loyalties. A commotion downstairs brought her rushing to the window. Out in the yard, she saw Chase and Jackson, both dismounted, with another man lying across Chase's big stallion. The man was huge, and wore dirty flowing robes of various fabrics and colors. As Jody watched, he leaned over Phantom's back, resting his turbaned head across the thick black and grey speckled mane flowing around the snorting animal's neck.

"Let's get him inside," Chase called to Jackson. They both rushed forward to catch the big man before he toppled off the horse. Jody watched as they gathered him between them, half-carrying, half-dragging him up the broad steps.

Realizing this must be Ali, Jody hurried downstairs to see what was going on. As she reached the rounding curve in the stairs, a servant ran to open the front door. Sarah followed close behind.

"Mama would not want him in here," Sarah stated, waving a hand as Chase and Jackson struggled to drag the big man inside the house. "Take him to his own quarters."

"No," Chase stated in a firm tone. "He's hurt. Now stop prattling and move aside so we can take him to the sofa in the front parlor."

"Not Mama's best brocade sofa!" she said.

"Will you please stop worrying about the furniture," Chase said over his shoulder.

Proud of his firm tone, Jody came down the stairs and followed them into the room. "Dancy, get fresh water and some cleans rags, and bring me some of that herbal tea Miss Martha likes. Oh, and bring the whiskey, too."

"We will need two knives, Dancy," Jackson said.

Dancy nodded; then she scurried to do their bidding.

Sarah huffed, looking at Jody. "Well, who, pray tell, put you in charge?"

"Never mind that now," Jody shot back. "This man is hurt and obviously in need of our care. Now don't be a pain, Sarah. Get back upstairs and tend to your brothers and sisters."

Ignoring Sarah's hateful glare, Jody turned to Chase. "Where did you find him?"

"In the back pasture," Jackson answered. "He was trying to get back home. He must have collapsed near the pond. He said he wanted a drink of water."

"He's been shot," Chase told her, his eyes conveying a silent message. Did this have anything to do with them?

Jody returned his worried look with one of her own. "How badly?"

"There's a bullet in his shoulder," Jackson explained, pulling aside the cotton robes to reveal a big, gaping hole in the man's left arm. "We'll have to cut it out."

Feeling faint, Jody backed away. "Oh . . . I'll go get more fabric for bandages."

"We'll need your help," Jackson said, his eyes on the wound.

"Why not just get a doctor?" Chase said, his own face going pale. "We can't handle this by ourselves."

"Doc Fletcher joined up," Jackson replied. "There's no one else."

"Excuse us a minute, Jackson," Chase said, his jaw set

177

in a grim line. "Miss Agnes, could I have a word with you?"

Out in the hall, he whirled to face her. "What are we going to do?"

"Save his life, I hope," she replied calmly. "Come on, Chase, surely the sight of a little caked blood and guts doesn't make you squeamish?"

"You know it does, and you don't look so hot yourself, so don't give me that daring look. I won't do this. We need to find a doctor for that man!"

"We don't have time. Besides, the sooner we get him well, the better for us. He might know what's going on."

Chase paced a foot or two, then spun around. "Oh, great. Let him in on this little escapade, too! He doesn't look like the type we should get riled, and from everything Agnes mentioned in those letters, he could kill both of us simply by banging our heads together."

"Which is why we have to be extremely careful, and play our parts to the hilt. If that means performing surgery, then we're going to do it. I won't faint—how about you?"

"I don't like this, Jody. I really don't like this."

"John?" Jackson called from the other room. "He's calling for you."

Pushing Chase ahead of her, Jody followed him back into the room. "We're coming."

Dancy showed up then with the requested first aid materials, her eyes wide with fear. "My Mama says stay away from the Mohammadan. She says he has many lives; if he dies once, he returns again and again. I'm scared of that man."

"Nonsense," Jody said, shooing away the girl's fears with a wave of her hand. "Ali is a good man; he's just of a different background and religion. Now, scoot. We've got work to do." On a softer note, she whispered, "Ali is just a man, Dancy. Once we get him cleaned up, he won't look so scary."

The girl shot Ali a curious look. "Yes, ma'am."

Gritting her teeth, Jody inched over to where Jackson and Chase were tending Ali. For all her bravado with Chase

178

earlier in the hallway, she wasn't looking forward to being Ali's surgical nurse. She had to agree with Dancy; the man scared her, too. With his flowing robes and exotic jewelry, he reminded her of Merlin from King Arthur. How had such a strange man wound up here in antebellum Georgia?

"He's trying to say something," Chase whispered.

The big man lying sprawled against Miss Martha's green brocade sofa cushions moaned softly, then reached out a hand to Jody. "Who are you?" he grunted out in slow, measured tones.

She tried to smile. His iron grip on her arm frightened her. "I'm Agnes, Ali. Don't you remember me?"

"No. It cannot be," he insisted. "I saw them. I saw the blue men—they took you away."

"What's he talking about?" Jackson said, unable to comprehend the man's ramblings.

With a sinking feeling in her stomach, Jody continued to grip the man's big hand. "He's just concerned about me, I think. He's probably surprised to see me here when he thought I was gone."

Chase stepped forward. "We need to take care of that wound."

"Do you want to take out the bullet, John?" Jackson asked, as if offering his brother this job was some sort of honor.

Chase looked down at the boy's trusting eyes. He'd learned a great deal about Jackson Spence on their short ride over the plantation. The boy had talked on and on about the spot of land they'd discovered a few years earlier, the very spot where Hampleton, Georgia stood—or would stand—in the future.

"Yeah, all those pines; we'll make a fortune once the war's over. Timber prices will go sky high, won't they, John? Isn't that what you always said?"

Chase could only nod, listen, and gather information about the vision John Hample and his little brother had shared. "It's a nice piece of property, Jackson."

"Yeah. And what about the house, the one you want to build. Are you going to marry Miss Agnes, John? You told me when you came home on leave, you'd marry her. She'd sure love a big house like that—her own home. It'll be a grand thing, won't it, John? Are you still going to build it?''

''That all depends,'' Chase said, wondering if he'd ever get out of this mess. He'd looked for the brooch, searching in the gardens on his way to the stable, going over the spot where he'd tripped in the yard. But the piece of jewelry wasn't to be found.

''John?'' Jackson's expectant gaze brought him back to the unpleasant task at hand.

The boy had sterilized one of the knives by the flame of a candle, and now held it out to Chase. This meant he was expected to take that knife and . . . just thinking about it made him ill. He looked up at Jackson's youthful, trusting face, then shot Jody another this-is-all-your-fault glare. She raised questioning brows, then inclined her head toward Ali.

''Let's do it,'' he said, kneeling down to rip away the already tattered shreds of Ali's many garments. ''Jo—Agnes, hand me that wet cloth.''

Jody did as he asked, steeling herself against the queasy feeling in her insides. Watching as Chase gently washed the wound, she swallowed hard at the sight of the open, swollen flesh.

''Bet you've seen this type of thing a lot in the war, huh?'' Jackson said to Chase, his eyes full of admiration. ''I sure wish I could join up, but I know we agreed I had to stay and take care of things here.''

Sweat popped out on Chase's forehead and upper lip. Earlier, he'd stalled Jackson's many questions about the war, stating he really didn't want to talk about it. Now, he felt the added pressure of trying to measure up to the boy's hero worship. If he let Ali die, Jackson would never forget it.

''Hand me the whiskey,'' he said to Jody, the stress of the situation evident in his strained words. He doused a clean rag in the amber liquid and pressed it firmly over the wound. The effort raised Ali, bringing his onyx eyes wide open.

''Master,'' he said on a weak whisper. ''You are indeed safe?''

Chase nodded. "Ali, I'm going to try to get that bullet out of your shoulder."

Ali looked at the man kneeling beside him. "You are the same, Master, but you are different." With that, he passed out again, his hand falling away from Chase's arm.

Jackson chuckled. "He always did talk in riddles."

Taking a deep breath, Jody wished she could ask Ali about this particular riddle. Would she ever find out what was really going on here?

Not right now. Right now, she had to watch as Chase dug through Ali's skin with the knife, cleaning away torn flesh and bits and pieces of blood soaked material. After what seemed an eternity, Chase placed a finger inside the wound, looking away as he rummaged around.

"I found it," he said on a shaky voice, his skin pale underneath his tanned features. Lifting a blood soaked hand away from Ali's body, he held up the bullet. Sinking back on his knees, he handed the knife to Jackson and dropped the bloody ball in a nearby pan of water, then quickly washed his hands. "Give me the bourbon."

Jody did as he asked, her stomach churning from the smell of blood and flesh. Chase took a hefty swig of the liquor, then poured some on the wound.

"Here's the other knife," Jackson said, handing it over to Chase. "To seal the wound and stop the bleeding," he said to Jody's questioning look.

Telling herself she wouldn't be sick, Jody watched as Chase took a deep breath and held the white-hot knife to the wound. The sound of hissing flesh warred with the smell of charred skin. But the bleeding stopped almost immediately.

Now it was over. They'd done it. Chase silently thanked the gods for all the western movies he'd watched as a boy. Somewhere he'd seen this done before. How else could he have known exactly what to do?

Jody could see the fine white lines of fatigue circling his eyes. "You're exhausted," she said, urging him to his feet. "Go up and rest. I'll have someone move Ali to one of the bedrooms down here."

181

"I'd like to talk to him when he wakes up," Chase said. He agreed with Jody that maybe the Mohammedan could shed some light on their situation.

"I promise I'll come and get you." Giving him an imploring look, she added, "I'll bring you a bite to eat."

Jackson didn't miss the hidden meaning behind her gesture. "She's right, John. We need to get him cleaned up and in a comfortable bed. You're still recovering, too. Go on up and rest."

"I really don't want to rest," Chase insisted, his knees wobbly and his hands shaky, in spite of his brave words.

"Just for a while," Jody urged.

In the end, she wore him down, though he couldn't understand how she'd done it. He wanted to look for the brooch again, but once he reached the cool quietness of his rooms, he had to admit he was tired. Maybe he'd spend just a few minutes with his eyes closed; he felt another headache coming on.

The dreams came fast and furious, like an angry ocean surf. Horses running, soldiers everywhere, in a sea of blue and gray. Gunshots, cannon shots, dust and dirt and swords clashing. The sounds of anguish as men fell all around him. Then a pain so intense, it coursed through his system like a hissing snake, slick and hot. And throughout it all, throughout the hell of fire and dust and death, he kept seeing a face rising up before him. The face of an angel with golden hair and shimmering eyes. Agnes? He silently called out her name. *Jody? Where are you, Agnes Jodelyn. Please, don't leave me.*

"Jody!"

"I'm here. Chase, wake up, I'm right here."

He pulled her into his arms, wrapping his sweat-drenched body in the sweet essence of her open, welcoming arms. "Jody, are you all right?" The anguish in his voice showed in his eyes.

"Yes, of course I am. You were having a bad dream."

"You can say that again." He let her go long enough to get his bearings. "I . . . it was as if—"

"As if you were really John Hample?" She gave him an

understanding look, then handed him a glass of water.

He drank the well water down, savoring the rusty flavor. "How did you know?"

"I've had similar dreams. It's like I am Agnes. I guess we're really getting caught up in all of this."

Still slightly disoriented, Chase asked, "Do you ever feel as if you've been here before?"

She nodded, glad to be able to share this with him at last. "When I first saw this place, I felt as if I'd seen it somewhere, maybe in a book or a magazine spread."

"Or maybe in another life."

Her brows lifting, she teased him. "Don't tell me your logical, analytical brain is beginning to open up to the possibility of all of this."

"I'm not saying I believe any of it," he said, raising up to brush the hair off his forehead, "but we are here. And even though we're supposed to be playing roles, it's as if I already know my lines. I know what's expected of me. I have these strong memories, and now, the dreams." Shaking his head, he stared up at her. "This is getting downright creepy."

"Tell me about it." She fluffed his pillows, all the while aware of his close proximity and his magnificent hair-dusted chest. Was he wearing anything underneath that satin sheet? To clear her mind of the subject, she said, "Ali is certainly a strange one. He insisted in a groggy voice that we put him in his own quarters." Shaking her head, she shivered. "His decorating scheme is not for the squeamish. Very strange, indeed. He has some exquisite African artifacts, and various amulets and charms hanging around his bed. No wonder Dancy is scared of the man. He's very intimidating. It's as if he can see right through you."

Chase took a bite of the bread and cheese she'd brought him. Between chews, he said, "Ali strikes me as very wise and tough. Maybe he can help us."

"Or expose us for the impostors we are," she added. "I'm going back to the garden, to look for the brooch. Feel like walking with me?"

He hopped off the bed, revealing that he still wore his

trousers. ''Yes. I can't stand being cooped up in here. Let me get a shirt.''

She watched as he pulled on the same white shirt he'd worn earlier, her gaze slipping down his broad chest. When Chase glanced up, his gaze teasing, she quickly averted her eyes.

''See something you like, sweetheart?'' he asked, grinning.

''Don't be silly.'' She went to the door. ''You coming or not?''

''I'm right behind you.'' He took his time admiring her swaying posterior. ''Playing the southern belle becomes you. Maybe you were born in the wrong time.''

''Well, the way things are looking, I might be stuck in this one.''

He caught up with her on the stairs. ''Not if we find that brooch. What are we supposed to do with it, anyway, rub it like a magic lamp or something.''

''Lower your voice.'' She glanced around. ''There are big ears around this place.''

''Our little Sarah?''

''The very one. That girl doesn't trust me at all.''

''Can you blame her?'' To Jody's hurt look, he whispered, ''Don't take it personally. She's just extremely jealous. Until Agnes came along, her big brother focused all his attention on his siblings. Then she lost her father to boot. She doesn't like you being the center of attention.''

Jody scoffed. ''Since when did you become the sensitive big brother?''

Chase wondered that himself. ''I'm not sure. It's as if I know what's going to happen, but I don't have any control over any of it.''

Jody nodded her agreement. ''Whatever happened, or whatever is supposed to happen, it better start soon. I'm going crazy with worry.'' Stopping to rest a hand on his arm, she said, ''Chase, if anything happens to you—''

He smiled, lifting her hand to his lips. ''Ah, Miss Agnes, are you trying to tell me there's a spot in your heart for me, after all.''

Snatching her hand away, she sighed. "Of course there is. And besides, I want you in one piece, so you can rebuild Spence House."

Anger flared in his eyes. "Ah, yes, it always goes back to that, doesn't it?"

"Chase, I—"

He took her by the arm, dragging her the rest of the way down the stairs. "Let's find that damned brooch."

Once outside, he remained hostile and distant, his eyes scanning the grounds. "I remember waking up right here," he said, indicating the spot where she'd already searched several times for the brooch.

"But why here?" Jody asked. "I came back underneath the magnolia. Do you think you did too, and you just don't remember it? We could go look there."

"Maybe." He still refused to look at her. She didn't care about anything but having Spence House saved, and for some strange reason, he wanted her to care about more; he wanted her to fight for him the way she'd fought for that house. But he wouldn't, couldn't let her see that. "Can you get us back there?"

She nodded, aware that he was still angry with her. But why? He knew how she felt, he'd already agreed to save the house . . . unless he'd had a change of heart. After all, she had caused him a world of trouble, what with bringing him back about a hundred-and-thirty years, and plunging him into all this danger and intrigue. That was a bit much to forgive, even in her own eyes. He wanted to find the brooch as much as she did, so he could be rid of her. That realization saddened her, and fortified her at the same time.

Giving him a determined look, she said, "We'll need to take a horse. That would probably be safer than taking a carriage. We have to be very careful."

"We'll take Phantom." With that limped off to the stables, his broad shoulders held ramrod straight.

"Too bad we don't have the car," she whispered.

Much later, and with a huge protest from Miss Martha that it was too dangerous to go for a ride, they arrived at the spot underneath the magnolia tree. Chase brought along a fine set of revolvers as protection.

But on this particular day in late spring, the woods were quiet and peaceful, the only sounds those of the birds singing and the hungry bees searching for food amid the many blossoming forest shrubs. It was good to be away from the bustle of the plantation house where they'd both taken on the responsibilities of helping to run the place. The day was warm, but a cooling breeze made the ride pleasant, in spite of the tension whipping around them.

"So here we are," Jody said at last, as they strolled over the open patch of woods. Mounds of pine straw and fallen leaves had cushioned the little glade, giving it a carpet of lush browns, golds, and greens. "This is a beautiful spot."

Chase looked around. His sense of déjà vu experienced earlier came on again in a powerful way. "Jackson went on and on about this place," he said. Looking up, he stared at the young magnolia tree towering before them. "This is my tree, isn't it?"

Jody smiled. "Yes, it is. I should have brought you here right away."

He looked over at her. His eyes were gentle. "We've been kind of busy."

"You handled Ali's surgery like a pro," she said, hoping to regain some of the camaraderie they'd shared earlier.

"I was a wreck," he admitted, his tone bordering on gruff. Then he rubbed his backside. "And I'm sore from riding the stallion. I don't think that horse likes me."

"Animal instinct, I suppose," she retorted, reaching out to rub the animal's slick flank.

Not quite sure whether that had been meant as a compliment or an insult, Chase let it pass while he passed by her. Her fragrant scent didn't go unnoticed, however. His nostrils flared right along with Phantom's.

Jody moved through the mounds of pine straw. "If the brooch is here, it'll be hard to find." She kicked a path, the toe of her laced-up boot growing dusty from the effort.

Chase did the same, scanning the ground at his feet. Kicking the dirt didn't help relieve his tension. This day had gone from bad to worse. Like his horse, he felt like kicking and snorting.

So he kicked, each thrust filled with resentment and aggravation.

In her corner, Jody kicked even harder, wishing the brooch would appear, wishing Chase would stop being so ornery, wishing many things.

Which is why neither of them saw the other one coming, until with a gentle thud, Jody found herself off balance and in his arms.

"I'm sorry," she mumbled, trying to move away.

"Excuse me," he replied, about to push her out of his path.

Before he let her go, however, he let his guard down, just for a brief second, and their eyes locked. Chase took one look at her parted, expectant lips and caught his breath. Why did she feel so right in his arms, yet so wrong in his life?

Not taking the time to answer that question, he kissed her, putting all the frustration and anger he'd held in check into the frenzy of his mouth touching hers. He couldn't be brutal to her; her softness demanded he be kind. And her sweet response, her yielding surrender to his touch, only brought him more heartache, along with a hungry need.

Lifting his mouth away from hers, he searched her face, and saw that same need in her luminous eyes. "What's happening to us?" he asked in a hoarse whisper.

Jody looked away, fighting back tears of frustration. "I don't know. I only know that . . ." She stopped, unable to tell him that she was in love with him. She couldn't confess that deep, dark secret. Not now, not ever.

"What?" he asked, urging her chin up with his thumb. "Jody, tell me what's really going on here."

She didn't answer, so he took her silence as another opportunity to kiss her. Hard. In the time it took to wrap his arms around her, he had her pushed back against the firm trunk of the satin-leafed magnolia tree. His mouth braced against hers while his thighs pressed at her voluminous skirts. His hands went from her hair, down the delicious curve of her back where they met with what he guessed to be about twenty layers of crinolines and lace.

Lifting his mouth, he said on a voice drugged with desire, "You're wearing way too many clothes."

"A necessary evil," she said. "Better to keep the likes of you away."

Giving her a look that left her breathless, he whispered somewhere in the vicinity of her throat, "I assure you, your clothing will not stand in my way." As if to prove his point, he kissed her again, then let one hand trail down the column of her throat.

She managed to grab his hand before it inched even farther. Holding her hand over his, she pulled back. "We've got to find the brooch." *Before it's too late.*

He released her then, a blank look replacing the desire in his eyes. "Yes, of course."

Neither of them could admit that the brooch, or getting home, seemed of little importance right now. What did matter, what did cast them apart, even while it pulled them together, was that they were falling in love, just as John Hample and Agnes Jodelyn had.

And Jody had to wonder, were they caught up in John and Agnes's need to find a lost love again, or were they caught up in their own need, to find each other.

As they stood there, sizing each other up, a deep, resonating voice spoke from the trees. "Who sent you here?"

Jody and Chase turned to find Ali standing by a tree. He'd changed his robes and turban, and he looked well for a man who'd been shot and on the run.

"Ali?" Jody stepped toward him. "How did you—"

"I have my own remedies for illnesses," he stated, "but Madame Martha's herbal tea did prove sustaining. I should know. I gave her the recipe."

"You should be resting," Chase said, clearly as shocked as Jody to find the mysterious man watching them. "Can I take you back to the house?"

The Mohammadan made a slight bow. "In due time, Master. Right now, I think we need some time to talk. Things are not as they seem."

Jody's nervous glance moved from Chase to Ali. "What do you mean?"

"I mean," the Mohammadan said, stepping out into the sunlight, "I saw the Union officers take you away."

"Yes, but—"

He held up a bejeweled hand. "Wait, madame, I beg of you. There is more."

Jody did as he asked, her heart jumping in an erratic pattern. "What is it, Ali?"

Ali looked at Chase, his chocolate-colored eyes bearing down. Then he lifted a long finger, pointing to Chase. "You are not my master. I want to know who you really are?"

Chase looked shocked. "I . . . I'm John."

"Do not deceive the one who knows the truth," the Muhammadan insisted, his finger still pointing. "You see, I saw my master die. He was trying to get home to help her, he wanted to save her." His dark eyes bright with condemnation, he repeated, "Things are not as they seem, and I think I know why."

Chapter Twelve

Chase glanced over at Jody, then back to Ali. "What do you mean?"

The big man stepped forward, using a long cane with a wolf's head carving at its staff, to steady his gait. "I was standing at the entrance of the otherworld. I was going forward to the land of the dead, to another life. My soul was lifting from my body."

Aggravated with the man's overly dramatic descriptions, Chase waved a hand. "You almost died?"

Ali nodded, his dark eyes moving from one face to the other. "I think I did die. My master came to me in the form of a *jinn*." He pointed to Chase. "He came and told me to come back—to find my way home—to two who would be the same, but different."

Jody tried to reason with the man. "You were probably delirious."

The Mohammadan shook his head. "No. No delusions, madame. I know of what I speak. You see, I was shot right here underneath this very tree over a fortnight ago."

Jody gasped, then turned to Chase. He sent her a "here we go again" look.

Ali nodded, his long braids sweeping over his shoulders. "I tell you, I was with Mistress Calhoun right here, waiting for the master to come and take her away, so they could be married. But he didn't come."

Barely able to breath, Jody asked, "What happened, Ali?"

"The Union soldiers came," the big man explained. "They shot me, and they took her. They wanted to use her as bait to capture my master."

"And were they successful?" Chase asked.

Ali gave them a grim look. "Yes, I'm afraid they were. You see, this particular Union captain didn't obey orders. He left his post to come and search out Master Spence. It was an ongoing vendetta, partly because Master Spence was such a prize for the young captain to capture—a Confederate war hero—but mostly because Captain Markham had known Mistress Agnes for a long time, and he had designs on her after her husband Will's death. When she refused his advances, he became furious. She turned to Master John for protection, and they fell back in love. This only added to the captain's anger. In the end, it turned rather ugly, I'm afraid."

Remembering John Hample's declaration that he'd been too late, Jody pushed back the taste of fear in her throat. "Did they kill him?"

Ali continued his story. "I managed to track them to the old Calhoun cabin." He pointed off into the woods. "I was weak, but able to keep moving. I reached the cabin to find them taking Mistress Agnes away. Inside, I found my master." His eyes turned dark as midnight. "They had hanged him from the rafters."

Jody brought a hand to her throat. "Oh, my God."

"I tried to cut him down, but I was weak from losing so much blood. I finally managed to free him; then I thought I heard someone coming. I hid behind a cupboard. I must have passed out. Later, I awoke to find my master's body gone. I doctored myself with what little provisions I could find within the cabin, then I went in search of Mistress Agnes. But it was fruitless; after several days, I became weak and disoriented. I managed to make it back to the pond. That's when I had my vision." He stared directly at Chase. "And a little while later, you and young Master Jackson found me there."

Chase's mind clicked with all this new information. "But what about the story about Virginia? Everyone thinks he died there, on the battlefield. Do you think he survived, maybe, and somehow made his way back to the field?"

Ali looked puzzled. "I do not know. He was not there when I woke up, but I assumed one of the Yankees had come back to hide his body, perhaps. I tried to find him, but I failed. Perhaps his family does not know the true story. I wanted to talk to both of you, before I told Miss Martha anything. Information can become distorted easily in these times of war." He shot Jody a stern, menacing look. "I do know that Master John was concerned for Mistress Agnes's welfare, and if he did survive, he would have gone after her."

Jody didn't say a word. She wouldn't tell Ali about John Hample's ghost, not yet anyway. Instead, she waited to hear the rest of the giant man's story.

"After he was wounded at Chancellorsville, he took a brief convalescent leave, to come home and see about his family and his lover. He knew the crazy Union captain had been snooping around his lady. Master John wanted to marry her, but Papa Spence was dead set against such a union. So they were to be wed in secret."

Jody said, "So he came home only to be ambushed by this captain?"

Ali confirmed her fears. "Yes. He was a fine, brave soldier, but he wasn't quite well when they captured him. He had a fever and he was weak; they had him at a disadvantage." His accusing gaze stayed on Jody. "They knew his one weakness was this woman, and so they killed him because he wouldn't tell Captain Markham what he wanted to hear."

With a catch in her voice, Jody asked, "What did this captain want John to tell?"

Ali went silent and still, his whole countenance full of distrust. Finally, he held his head up, his eyes fixed on Jody. "That you were a spy; that you betrayed the Union by taking the side of your rebel lover. My Master gave his life for you!"

Chase stepped forward to shield Jody from the man's menacing wrath. "You don't know what you're talking about!"

With a sudden movement, Ali grabbed Chase, clutching his shirt with one hand. "I know you are not my real master, and that this woman is not the real Mistress Calhoun. Now tell me who you really are, or I'll crack you like a twig!"

Chase knew the man could do it, even with a hole in his shoulder. But he wouldn't back down either. He hadn't done anything wrong, and he was fed up with this whole wacky deal. Giving the giant a hostile, daring look, he said, "Are you willing to listen to my side of the story before you break me in half?"

Ali glared at him, measuring him inch by inch. "You look almost exactly the same. He told me another would come. He told me I had to help you. I could not accept this though, until I saw you today, riding toward me on the stallion. You do not handle the wild horse in the same manner my master did." Dropping his hand away from Chase, he said, "Please, explain yourself."

"Don't," Jody pleaded, trying to warn Chase. "He'll probably just kill us anyway."

Ali's menacing grin was all white-toothed and deliberate. "A very wise woman, this one. But you saved me—for now—so I am honor bound to serve you, not kill you. It was my master's command."

Chase had had enough of charades and reincarnation and games. "No, Jody, we need to level with Ali. He seems to know more about what's happening than either of us, anyway."

Ali studied Jody again. "What name is this?"

"Look, it's her real name," Chase said, glaring up at the

huge man. "And we're just as confused as you are. John Hample . . . your master, propelled us both back in time, claiming we're the reincarnate souls of him and his precious Agnes. He told Jody we had to fix some big mix-up. And now I think we all know what that mix-up was. He obviously did survive, and he must have gone looking for Agnes. Apparently, he never found her."

Ali stepped back, quite shaken by Chase's explanation. Looking at Jody, he asked, "Is this the truth, what this man speaks?"

"It's true," Jody said, bobbing her head. "John told me as much . . . when he brought me back. He said he tried to find her. He came back here a few days later, but he was too late. She was dead. He made it to Camille, and Jackson found him in the yard. He told Jackson everything just before he died." Swallowing the palpable fear choking her, she pleaded, "Please Ali, listen to us. We're from . . . from the future, over a hundred and thirty years away." Because it sounded ludicrous to her own ears, she hurried to explain. "I found some letters in an old house Chase was about to tear down, and I found a brooch—"

"Describe the brooch."

"Oval-shaped with pearls and filigree," she said, using her hands to show the size. "About the size of a hen's egg." When he didn't respond, she rushed on. "I found out it belonged to my three times great-grandmother, Agnes Jodelyn Calhoun."

"We both read the letters," Chase explained. "John Hample Spence was my great-uncle, two or three times over—I've lost count—but that's not important. What is important, and what is the absolute truth, is that John Hample's ghost is haunting the house I wanted to tear down. He brought Jody and me back to right some great wrong, and," he gave a dubious look here, "we believe we are the reincarnated souls of John and Agnes."

Ali stood so still, Jody thought he could easily be a statue, or a really bad figment of her imagination. Then in one elegant gesture, he sank to the ground and folded his long legs about him, in spite of the grimace of pain clouding his dark features.

"Please, sit with me," he said in a weak voice, his eyes closed as he concentrated on denying his pain.

They both did as he said, then waited for him to speak.

"I had a vivid dream," he began. "Master told me this would come to pass. He told me to come back to Camille, so I could bring the past to the present."

"Did he tell you what in hell we're supposed to do?" Chase asked, his impatience clear.

Ali nodded slowly, frowning at Chase's attitude. "Yes. He told me about the letters and the brooch—you described it exactly. He told me to trust you both and to help you, to protect you no matter what. He also told me that we'd have little time—only a few days—to end this once and for all. You both must bring the desired destiny into the future." Then smiling peacefully, he added, "And he told me what you need to do during this short time."

Jody's breath stuck somewhere in her diaphragm. "Which is?"

The Mohammadan opened his eyes wide, startling Jody. "You are to be married, as soon as possible!"

"Come again?" Chase said.

Ali gave Chase a direct, disconcerting gaze. "You are to be married; this was my master's greatest wish, to marry the woman he loved. You must understand, the soul is only borrowed by certain matter forms here on earth. My master's soul, and that of his beloved, were never connected. So they've both been drifting in the other world. In my many travels, I've learned things about humans." He leaned forward, his big hands clasped as if in prayer. "And I tell you this, the soul is always pure. But if the user fails to take proper care of the soul, he must suffer the consequences. So many wasted souls; so many lonely hearts. But the interior knowledge of the soul can never be denied. The soul is immortal."

"You're not making sense," Chase said, disgusted. "This is crazy. I mean, if we're here playacting that we're really

John and Agnes, where are they?''

"They're both dead," Jody reminded him with a worried frown. "John Hample told me that our souls would merge with theirs, that we would have some of their memories. Think about it. We've both had such vivid feelings about this place, and . . . what about our dreams? You can't deny the effect those have been having on each of us." She put a fist to her chest. "They may be dead, but their souls are right here. We must have come back at the exact moment each of them died. We've merged."

Chase wanted to laugh, but no sound would come. "Merged? Well, that explains everything, doesn't it?" He rolled his eyes. "So they sent their swami to tell us what to do, while they mess with our minds!"

Jody groaned in frustration. "He's telling us that in order for John Hample and Agnes to find peace, we must purify their souls. They weren't able to be together—because one or both of them, didn't leave this earth with a clean slate. So it's up to us to unite their mortal souls."

Ali beamed. "I told you she is wise."

"No," Chase argued, "She's a hopeless romantic who's done everything in her power to make my life a living hell. Talk about purified souls, she's messed up everything I've tried to do."

Ali smiled again. "Then being married to her should prove very interesting, yes?"

That brought both Jody and Chase to attention.

"I'm not going to marry him!" Jody stated, tossing back a wayward strand of golden hair. Since Chase had just very bluntly blamed her for all the ills of his existence, she'd walk through fire before she'd say "I do" to him!

"No way," Chase agreed. "Lord, we'd wind up killing each other."

The Muhammadan shook his head. "Please, I'm not your lord, just a mystic. And you are wrong. You can't kill each other. This time, remember, the intent is to survive, so you can find each other again."

Chase hopped up to point a finger at the imposing man. "We have found each other, and we don't agree on anything, except that we want to go home soon, and without any lost souls hanging on to us.''

"In due time," Ali said, his calm gaze sweeping both of them. "I did not return here to waste my time or my soul. You will fulfill your destiny. And I will see to it personally, by orders of my master."

"Well, go back and tell your master the deal's off," Chase said. "Jody, I'm going back to Camille. Are you coming?"

Jody scooted up to run after him. "But what about the brooch? We've got to find it."

Ali rose, too, leaning heavily on his sturdy cane. "You will, madame, when the time is right."

Chase whirled around to face both of them. "Do you know where that damned brooch is, Ali?"

Ali inclined his head slightly. "I know only that you will find it when the time is right."

Narrowing his gaze, Chase studied the strange man dictating orders to them like a king on a throne. "How in the world did you wind up here, Ali?"

The Mohammadan laughed. "Young John Hample saved my life once, in a faraway place. I was honor bound to serve him for the rest of my days."

"You could have kept running," Chase reasoned. "You don't have to be a slave, you know."

Ali looked affronted. "I am no man's slave, sir. Master John never owned me by law. No man can own one who controls his own way. We had an agreement. This past Christmas, he made it official though, so no law could challenge my freedom. I am free to go when the notion suits me. So far, it hasn't."

"Even though John's dead," Jody said on an awe-struck whisper. "You must really care a great deal about him."

"I will do this bidding," Ali said, bowing slightly.

Chase snorted. "Isn't this just great! First, I cancel every logical plan I have for building my shopping center, then I get tossed back in time and have to 'merge' with someone else, and now, I have my own personal genie telling me what my next move has to be." Laughing almost hysterically, he said, "I'm just not having a good week."

"Nonsense," Ali said, walking over to where Chase stood pouting. Slapping Chase on the back in a gesture of comradery, he said, "You are about to be married. Is that not reason to celebrate?"

The last eligible bachelor in Florida looked from Ali's knowing grin to Jody's fearful eyes. Married. In another time, in a place completely foreign, with strangers all around and a bitter war raging to a certain end. Suddenly, it dawned on Chase that he might be able to deal with this in a logical fashion if he just thought it through. After all, this was a means to a certain end, too.

Giving Ali a level look, he said, "If that's all ol' John wants from us, then so be it." It was simple, really, so simple, he'd almost overlooked it. He could go through the act, he could pretend. It didn't have to be permanent, after all. And if it would get him home any quicker, he'd do it. "I say, let the party begin."

Jody didn't like the smug tone in his declaration. "You can't be serious? Are you honestly thinking about going through with this?"

He smiled over at her. "Yes. If John wants us to get married, to ease his conscience and purify his flawed soul, then we should do it. I mean, how bad can it be?"

"Then you agree?" Ali asked, his whole face lighting up in spite of his pained state.

"Yes." Chase laughed, then grinned at Jody. "Will you marry me, please, so we can fulfill our destiny, so we can get on with our lives, so we can end this stupid charade once and for all?"

Jody stared at him, hurt and dazed by his flippant attitude. He didn't want her, let alone want to marry her. He just wanted to end all of this and he'd do whatever it took to get the job done. Why, the nerve of the man, to use her like so much garbage. If he thought she'd agree to this just to please him, he had another think coming!

Strolling over to him with a sickly sweet smile plastered on her face, she watched as the triumphant gleam in his eyes turned to a wary waning glow of doubt. Placing one hand on his chest as if to endear herself to him, she pushed at him instead. "You're a selfish, uncaring, unseeing jackass, Chase Spence, and I wouldn't marry you if you were the last man left in the South and the whole Yankee army was chasing after me."

Turning to Ali, she said, "No deal. I'm out of here." With that, she flounced her skirts and headed to the waiting horse, her march as precise and sure as the echo of her refusal.

Chase stood looking after her with his mouth open. "What in hell is wrong with her?" he said.

Ali shook his head, jingling an earring or two in the process, then expelled a long, winded sigh. "Oh, master, this is not going to be as easy as we thought," he said to the wind.

Chase heard him, and looked over at him, a grin of reassurance moving across his face. "She'll come around. I'll see to it."

"How?" Ali asked, his tone dubious.

"Good question," Chase said, worry evident in his words.

How could he convince Jody to marry him? And why, oh why, did it suddenly seem so important that she want to marry him?

The ride back to Camille was strained to say the least. Jody sat up front; she refused to look back at Chase. Instead she cast her eyes out over the sun-soaked woods and tried desperately to ignore the way Chase's thighs brushed hers with each beat of Phantom's hooves. Being caught in the saddle with Chase was like being caught between a rock and a hard place. And right now, she thought she knew exactly where the hard place was located.

Ali rode his own Arabian steed some paces behind, as noble as an African prince. "Madam, would you like to see where Mistress Agnes lived?"

Jody turned then, her eyes wide open. "Yes, yes, I would." She liked Ali in spite of his intimidating ways. And she especially liked the fact that he'd accepted their being here with a level head and a philosophical attitude—not the hotheaded, closed-minded view of some other person sitting too close to her at that moment. "Take us there, Ali," she commanded, liking her role as "madame."

He did, showing Chase an almost hidden path that led away from the woods to a small, desolate looking cabin and a burned out hull of what used to be a schoolhouse.

"Mr. Calhoun, he liked to teach. Come down from New England to teach the planters' children. When the war came, the Southerners no longer wanted a Yankee teaching their sons and daughters—too much Northern propaganda." Unfurling his long legs from his horse, Ali looked at Jody. "Mr. Calhoun had a strong sympathy for the North. It was his undoing, I'm afraid."

"He was shot by soldiers," Jody said, the statement ringing hollow in the silent woods. "Did he have anything to do with the Underground Railroad, Ali?"

Ali shot her a knowing look. "It was his highest cause, madame. He helped many slaves gain free passage to the North." His eyes brimming with his own memories, Ali sighed heavily. "I'll miss Adam Calhoun. In spite of his fanatical ways, he was a very learned man. I received many insights from my heated discussions with him."

Chase finally spoke. "Where did you become so educated, Ali?"

"In the Far East, master," the Muhammadan explained. "Master John always accepted that I craved knowledge; he allowed Mr. Calhoun and me to study together."

"Can we go inside?" Jody asked, her tone hesitant. She had an eerie feeling about being at the place where John was tortured and left to hang, yet she was drawn to the dank little cabin.

Chase sensed her fear, along with his own strong vibes. "Come on. Maybe we'll find something to help us."

"I shall stand guard," Ali said, finding a stump to prop against. "You both could very well be in danger, being here."

Finding no comfort in that warning, Chase took Jody by the hand, guiding her into the dark interior of the cabin. A smell of neglect greeted them, along with the overpowering sense of having been here before.

Jody glanced around the long rectangular room. "This feels very strange. I don't think any memories I have of this place will be good ones."

"Me, either," Chase said. A vague image was there in the back of his mind, but it wouldn't surface. "I think we're blocking, big time."

A coil of rope lying looped on the floor by a broken table told them both that Ali's story was real.

"John survived the hanging," Chase stated, his eyes fixed on the rope. "He must have wandered for days before he made it back to Camille."

"And collapsed underneath the oak tree where I found you," Jody finished, her hand automatically reaching for his. "And Agnes . . . she survived, too." Jody knew this immediately, standing there in the dusty, drab cabin. "Markham let her go after a few days, but she only made it to the magnolia tree." A great, ripping pain crested in Jody's insides, then disappeared as quickly as it had come. "She suffered before she died."

"This is too weird," Chase said quietly. "Let's hurry and get out of here."

Jody moved through the room, pushing at the dark images in her mind. Concentrating on her surroundings, she wanted desperately to find something good in all of this. "Chase, look!"

Chase stepped out of the shadows to see what she'd found. "Wow."

Books: volumes and volumes of books, along with various pamphlets and magazines, lined a rickety shelf leaning against the wall. Rushing forward, Jody grabbed at one of them. "They're first editions . . . and look, literary magazines, stories by Poe, Irving, Charles Dickens. These are worth a fortune. I wish we could save them."

"To take back to the Treasure Chest?" he teased, some of the tension between them disappearing. "You'd be able to retire on the money you'd get for these." He pulled out a leather-bound volume. "Thoreau. Quite impressive. It would appear Adam was a free-thinker, a transcendentalist.''

"Here's John Greenleaf Whittier—look, papers written by the man himself. Apparently, Adam was a member of the Society of Friends at one time. They were very much against slavery.''

Chase shrugged. "While they allowed child labor to go on in their Northern factories.''

"Taking sides, Mr. Spence?''

He smiled. "It sounds that way, doesn't it?''

His smile broke through the gloom of the cabin. He was really quite nice when he smiled; deliciously handsome, too. At this thought her breath caught in her chest.

Chase didn't miss the breathless quality of her silence. He took it as an opportunity to woo her. "I'm sorry if I upset you earlier, Jody. All of this has been so . . .''

"Unsettling?'' she finished, her hands moving lovingly over the worn books and magazines stacked haphazardly against the crude wooden shelf. "Do you think we'll ever get out of this?''

In a gesture that took both of them by surprise, he tugged her into his arms. "We'll find a way.''

Jody leaned against him, taking in the warmth of his broad chest, the scent of his body, the security of his arms. What would it be like to be married to him, to wake up next to him every morning, to go to bed with him every night?

As if reading her thoughts, Chase lifted her chin with one finger so he could study her face. Then he lowered his head until his lips brushed hers. The touch was butterfly soft, but the connection was like a bolt of white-hot lightning. Tremors of need coursed through Jody's body, bringing her both pain and pleasure.

Chase felt her shudder, felt the same shuddering deep inside his own soul. Again, that sense of knowing came over him. Had John Hample stood right here kissing his Agnes? Lord, Chase could understand how the man's spirit must be suffering. He knew the same torture, each time he touched the woman in his arms. Suddenly, he wanted to be married to her, to have her, to hold her, to keep her near. But first, he had to convince her to marry him.

Lifting his lips off her arched neck, he whispered, "Would it be so awful, being married to me?"

"No," she moaned, then coming to her senses, quickly added, "I mean, if that's what it takes to get us home." Putting some distance between herself and his wicked lips, she backed up against the leaning book shelf. "I suppose I could endure it, pretend that I like it, for the sake of John Hample's soul, of course."

"Of course." He spun around so she wouldn't see the physical effect being near her always produced. Damn John Hample's too-tight britches, anyway! Running a shaking hand through his hair, he laughed. "It would only be temporary, anyway. Just a couple of weeks."

"Sure." She gathered a few choice books and papers to take back to Camille. "It's the logical thing to do, the only thing we can do. Ali did say we have to be the ones."

He didn't dare look at her. "Then it's settled?"

"I suppose so." She walked past him to the partially opened door, her skirts flouncing out a saucy tune as they rustled by.

Chase watched her departing curves and smiled a triumphant little smile. She'd agreed. Easy as pie. The woman melted in his arms at the merest touch.

Then it occurred to him that he immediately turned to mush each time he looked into her crystal eyes. And touching her was another story altogether. How would he survive being married to her? He got a sick feeling in the pit of his stomach. Hurrying out the door, he gulped great breaths of fresh summer air.

Ali jumped to attention, pushing up off his stump. "Master, are you all right? You look quite ill."

Trying to sound confident, Chase chuckled. "I'm fine, Ali, just fine. She has agreed to the marriage. I won."

Ali stared long and hard at the basketcase of a man standing in front of him. "Master, are you sure you have won? Perhaps you have lost."

"Don't go making riddles for me," Chase replied. "I'm in no mood. What do I have to lose, anyway?"

"Only your heart," Ali replied, his shrug a study of indifference.

"But, Jackson, you don't understand," Sarah wailed, tears streaming down her blotchy face. "They can't get married. What will Mama say?"

Jackson sat back in his chair, then gave his sister a long-suffering sigh. "Mama will be just fine. I've been talking to her about this very thing."

"No, you've been taking advantage of her delicate state," Sarah huffed, her pacing around the parlor causing her to almost knock over a Waterford crystal vase sitting on a Queen Anne occasional table. "You know she can't tell night from day lately. She's still mourning Papa!"

Jackson looked out the window at the row of live oaks leading down the drive. "Mama is getting old, Sarah. She wants to see her first-born married and happy. She doesn't really hate Miss Agnes; she mostly just had to go along with Papa's wishes."

"And now you defy him," Sarah snapped. "How can you do that to this family, to Papa's memory?"

Angry now, Jackson stood up. "I'm trying to save this family! John loves Miss Agnes, and she loves him. Why is that so hard for you to accept?"

"She's a Yankee," Sarah reminded him with venom. "We can not trust her. You and I both know her father was involved with the Underground Railroad, and I believe she's been sneaking around helping our own people to escape."

"Well, heck, Sarah, it don't much matter now, anyway. President Lincoln's done freed most of 'em."

Sarah stomped her foot. "He's not our president, Jackson. And he never will be." Goading her brother further, she added, "Why, you're so understanding about this, I'm surprised you don't run off and join the Union army."

Jackson was going for her throat when Chase found them.

"Hey, what's going on here?"

Sarah shot him a tearful look. "Jackson's being mean to me, that's what. I swear, if you hadn't come in, I do believe he would have struck me."

204

"You need a good whacking!" Jackson said, looking down at the floor to avoid his brother's concerned gaze. "I'm sorry, John. She got me all rattled, is all."

Chase didn't need a full explanation to understand. Little Sarah seemed determined to ruin everyone's life. "It's all right, Jackson." Shifting his gaze to Sarah, he asked, "What's all the fuss about?"

Sarah hurled herself into his arms, almost knocking him off balance. "Oh, John, I don't want you to marry that woman."

"Ali told me," Jackson admitted sheepishly. "I've been trying to make Sarah mind her own business."

Patting Sarah's yellow curls, Chase lifted her out of his arms. "Sarah, honey, I want to marry Agnes. I need to do this." *More than you'll ever know.*

Sarah gazed up at him, a mortal fear in her eyes. "But she's a Yankee, John. She's not like us."

"Nonsense," Chase said, laughing. If she only knew. Jody was about as Southern-bred as they got. "She's lived here most of her life, Sarah. And she's a good woman."

"You don't know everything about her though," Sarah argued. "Please, John, if you marry her, I'm afraid something awful will happen to you."

If I don't marry her, something awful will happen, Chase wanted to tell her. "Don't be silly," he said. "I'm only going to be here a few days longer. You'll hardly realize we're married." What else could he say? It was the truth, since he hoped to be out of here very soon.

But Sarah couldn't be convinced. "I just know it's wrong."

"Not if we love each other," Chase responded.

He realized that much was true, and again, it seemed as if he'd said those very words to Sarah before. While he now had a certain knowledge that John and Agnes had indeed been in love, he'd never actually connected the term to what he'd been feeling toward Jody. Was he in love with her?

Sarah stared up at him. "You do love her, don't you?"

Chase shook himself to attention. God, did it show so clearly or was John Hample's soul doing a little bit too much merging with his? Unable to answer the girl, he could only nod. Luckily, Dancy called them to dinner then, and he didn't have any further chances of dwelling on his new-found feelings. But much later as he sat at the head of the elaborate dinner table, with the entire family gathered around, and Jody sitting at the other end by Miss Martha, he had to wonder. Was he in love with Jody? Or was he simply caught up in this thing between John and Agnes?

Miss Martha tapped on her glass, bringing Chase's head up. Giving Jody what he hoped was a blank look, he spoke at last. "Mother, did you want to say something?"

Miss Martha sat up stiffly in her Chippendale chair, her back never touching the damask covering. She looked pale and drawn, but her eyes held a glint of determination. "Yes, I do have an announcement to make."

"Go ahead then," Jackson encouraged, his eyes bright with hope.

"I love each of my children," the woman said, the candle light glinting off the premature gray in her dark hair. "I loved your father, too, God rest his soul. Jackson and John and I have been talking, and while I do not necessarily con-done it, I have agreed to give my blessings to John and Agnes, so they can be married."

At Sarah's gasp of horror, she raised a withered hand. "Hear me out, children, please. This war has changed all of us. There was a time when I would have been horrified at the thought of a match between my son and . . . someone so free-thinking and forward as our Miss Agnes." Her tired eyes settled on Jody. "I often dreamed of my oldest son's wedding. I always assumed he would marry one of the local girls, the daughter of a neighbor, someone to connect our land to an adjoining plantation, someone to carry on our Southern heritage. Now, most of our boys are gone . . . killed by this terrible but noble undertaking, and the girls . . . well, they've been sent away to safer places, or they're too busy trying to scratch out a living, or saddest of all, they, too, are serving the cause, as nurses to the gruesome carnage our boys are suffering."

Lifting a goblet of water, she nodded her head to prepare

for a toast. Waiting like a queen for the others to follow suit, she continued. "Our Miss Agnes has served us with kindness and dignity. She's taken care of all of you while I was . . . incapacitated. She and Jackson have seen to everything from the planting to the running of the house, to tending the sick. And for all of that, I am grateful. So, John, yes, you may marry the woman you have chosen and . . ." her voice cracked here, "be happy for the brief time you have together."

A hush fell over the candlelit room, then Sarah burst into tears and bolted for the door. All the others stared after her for a moment, then began talking excitedly.

"A wedding," Jackson said, beaming his approval. "After the war's over, we can start our town, huh, John?"

"May we attend, Mother?" Ben asked, with Lizbeth echoing his request.

"Me, too. Me, too," little Rachel shouted, giggling.

Miss Martha smiled, then tapped her glass again. "Settle down, children. You all can attend the ceremony. And I do believe we shall throw a party—just the family, of course, since we're still in mourning for your papa." She gave Chase a valiant smile. "We'll celebrate our blessings."

"Thank you," Chase said, admiring the strength behind Miss Martha's fragile demeanor. Finally, he looked at Jody. She'd been mysteriously quiet all evening. Now, by the light of the shimmering candles standing between them, he saw the glistening tears trailing down her face. Concerned, he raised up out of his chair. "Are you all right?"

Jody rose, too, to meet him as he automatically reached out an arm to her. For the benefit of Miss Martha and the children, she said, "Yes, of course. I'm just so . . . happy."

"Me, too," he said. As he pulled her into his arms, he whispered, "It'll be over soon. Hang in there."

"I know," she whispered back. "That's why I'm crying."

Hours later, alone in her room, Jody dried her tears and tried to put a reasonable, brave face on this turn of events. She was marrying the man she loved, and it was breaking her heart. Because he didn't love her. Because he was only doing this to fulfill a request. Because he couldn't wait to be rid of her.

Well, could she blame him? Her mother had always dumped her when the going got tough. Her grandparents had tolerated her, giving her as much love as they could, when they should have been enjoying their golden years. Now, Chase was barely tolerating her, until he could get away from her.

What ever happened to unconditional love?

Glancing into the next room, where a lamp burned a low-keeled glow, she saw little Tucker sleeping in the spindled crib, his world whitewashed in mosquito netting and creamy dimity, his little breaths causing his crocheted blanket to rise and fall with a steady consistency.

A surge of warmth filled Jody's chest. Wishing she could take the baby back into the future with her, she rolled over on her bed to stare at the empty pillow beside her. She wanted Chase there, more than her next breath. But she wouldn't give in to that want, not if he couldn't return the deep love she felt in her heart. She wouldn't settle for lust. She had to have more.

The wind lifted, blowing with grace through the open French doors. And around the corner, in another set of rooms, that same wind fanned its caress over Chase's body, as he lay in the moonlight, staring at the empty pillow next to his head.

Chapter Thirteen

"What do you mean, we can't find a preacher?"

Chase paced the length of the polished oak floors of Camille Plantation's formal parlor, John Hample's too-tight black jackboots clicking on the shiny wood with each step he took. "And why can't we?"

Jody and Jackson sat on the green brocade parlor sofa, looking up at him—one with admiration and determination, the other with dread and anxiety. Jackson wanted so much to please his brother, while Jody just wanted to curl up somewhere and lick her wounds like a cat.

"He joined up," Jackson explained again. "And there ain't no one else."

"There *isn't* anyone else," Jody corrected, then looked up at Chase again. "Except Ali."

That brought Chase's shoulders up. He stared at her as if she were a two-headed alien. "Ali?"

As if on cue, the big man popped around the open double doors. "Greetings, master. Did I hear you call my name?"

Jody motioned him in. "We were telling . . . John . . . about your offer to perform our marriage cermony."

"Ah, yes," Ali said, bowing deeply. "Remember, master," here he gave Chase a meaningful look, "I'm trained in the ways of Muhammad, and I am considered a mystic—"

"And he says that's as good as being a preacher," Jackson interjected. "Of course, Mama and Sarah are dead set against it. They think he's a heathen and that if he marries y'all, you'll both be cast into a life of eternal sin."

Ali took the innocent insult with his usual wry calm. "They do not understand the ways of the world."

Chase continued to stare at them, feeling as if he were lost in some *Arabian Night-Gone With the Wind* nightmare. "That's ridiculous—him marrying us. Would it even be considered legal?"

"Who knows?" Jody said, her nerves on the edge. "With this war . . . and the circumstances . . . who's to say what's legal anymore."

"Ali says he'll perform a proper ceremony," Jackson chimed in. "He promised me he'd read straight from the Bible."

"A very interesting and historical book," Ali said, his big hands clasped as if in prayer. "Master, I would indeed be honored to perform this much-needed deed for you."

Chase rolled his eyes and nodded slowly. "Well, just as with everything else, I don't have much choice. Heck, let's do it."

"When?" Jody asked, the word ringing out like a death toll.

"Mama wants to have it Sunday afternoon," Jackson said, raising up to shake Chase's hand. "Guess you're finally getting married, big brother." At Chase's absent nod, he added, "Want to go over those plans for your house?"

Chase glanced down at Jody. "Yes, I'd like to see Spence House. And yes, Sunday is fine."

Surprised, Jackson smiled. "Is that what you're going to call it, Spence House?"

"Uh, yes." Chase looked uncomfortable for a minute, then regained his composure. "Do you approve of that name?"

Jackson bobbed his head. "Sure. Spence House. It has a nice ring, don't you think?"

Jody got up, wiping her sweaty palms on her dress. "I'm sure it will be very beautiful. I can't wait to be there."

"After the war," Jackson reminded her. "Until then, Mama thinks it best you stay here since John will be leaving again in a few days."

"And I will stay behind to protect you," Ali said, the statement meant as an obvious further instruction.

Not wanting to think about what that entailed, Jody turned to go. "I've got so much to take care of."

Jackson stared after her, waiting until he was sure she was gone. "I think I upset her, reminding her that you have to get back to the war."

Chase knew she was upset, but it had nothing to do with the war. Jody had been unusually quiet and cool toward him since they'd decided to get married. Did she find it so distasteful to be wed to him? At the expectant look on Jackson's face, he said, "I'll talk to her. You know how women are."

"Right," Jackson agreed. "C'mon, let's go look at those plans."

Hours later, Chase sat at the massive oak desk in the downstairs library, once again looking over the blueprints of Spence House Jackson had shown him earlier. It was uncanny, but he felt as if he'd actually drawn up these plans. All his life, he'd been familiar with Spence House to the point where he'd taken it for granted. Its very essence had become ingrained in his consciousness, because he'd visited there so many times. It had never occurred to him that that essence was all the stronger because of events that had happened so long ago, or that he might one day become a part of those events.

He'd set out to destroy the house, and now it seemed he couldn't wait to get back and save it. And had it not been for Jody . . .

Jody. He was in love with her. There, he'd finally admitted it, if only in his mind. He wouldn't tell her yet, of

211

course. No, first he had to think this through and make sure what he was feeling was real. If they ever made it back home, then he'd decide how to handle his feelings—if they were indeed his feelings.

And he'd rebuild Spence House. He'd promised her that much at least. Right now, as he stared down at the intricate etchings that would one day become a home, he thought back over the few days he'd been here on Camille Plantation, so far removed from the life he'd known.

He'd learned a lot in his short time here. Jackson was a good young man. They'd grown close over the last few days, and Jackson didn't seem to notice that his "big brother" acted strange and dazed at times. No, Jackson possessed the same single-mindedness that Chase did. And right now, that involved getting his brother married, and getting through the war so he could help John build the community they'd so often talked about.

Chase could see Jackson going on to build Hampleton. The lad amazed him. He felt a certain affection for all the children, even little Tucker who played at his feet and tugged at his knee as well as his heartstrings. He'd shared long, quiet talks with Miss Martha, reassuring her that everything would turn out the way it was supposed to. That was the only comfort he could give her.

He'd learned that there were no guarantees in life. He'd always stayed the course, following the rules, sticking to his damnable plans, so rigid in his work and his self-righteous, one-minded purposes, that he'd almost missed out on the important things in life—the things this struggling family had clung to, and fought for, and stood for: home, family, love, loyalty, heritage. Why had he never taken the time to learn all these things? Perhaps his own soul needed to be purified as much as the tormented John Hample's.

A tentative knock at the door brought his head up. "Come in."

It was Jody, looking fetching in a muslin gown of the palest pink. She'd been avoiding him, so he was surprised to see her, and feeling guilty that he'd been thinking of her.

"Everything's set," she said, her eyes falling across the

plans laid out on his desk. "Miss Martha has reluctantly agreed to let Ali perform the ceremony. Sarah, on the other hand, is pouting in her room, and says she won't come out."

"Good," he said, lifting a brow. "Maybe this wedding will come off without a hitch if she stays away."

"She certainly hates me, or the woman she thinks I am."

"That I don't understand," he admitted. Then in a teasing tone, he added, "To know you is to love you."

"Oh really?" she said dubiously, all the while savoring his off-handed remark.

Looking a bit sheepish, he brushed a hand over the house plans. "Look, it's Spence House. Thanks to this, when we get back, I'll be able to restore it to the exact specifications. I've practically memorized them."

Jody studied the elaborate plans, then faced him. "Then you do intend to save it?"

He pushed up out of his chair. "Yes, I intend to save it. And I have you to thank for that."

"I hope it will all be worth it," she said as she turned to leave, not wanting him to see the love mixed with regret in her eyes.

"It will be, Jody," he called after her. "I promise."

It would prove to be one of the hardest promises he'd ever made.

Sunday dawned bright and sunny, a day so perfect Jody thought time had indeed stopped to allow them this brief moment of rare beauty. Everyone in the household walked around with a sense of joy, a sense of anticipation, a sense of contentment that hadn't been seen inside these great walls in many months.

Except for Sarah. She sulked, and sighed, and pouted to the extent that even Miss Martha threatened to give her a good thrashing. This only added to Sarah's already hostile attitude. Each time Jody crossed the girl's path, the teenager glared at her with pure malice.

One such time, shortly before the wedding, Jody stopped. "Sarah, I'd really like you to be a part of the ceremony. Won't you be my maid of honor?"

The girl bristled. "I refuse to be a part of something I cannot bear to watch. I shall stay in my room until this despicable event is over."

Jody sensed more than just malice in the girl. She saw fear in the girl's eyes. "Sarah, what are you afraid of?"

Clearly shaken, the girl stepped away. "I'm not afraid of you, if that's what you think."

Jody refused to give up. "Is something troubling you?"

"No," Sarah said through gritted teeth. "The only thing bothering me is you and what you've done to this family." Giving Jody a look that bordered on a plea and a threat, she lifted her chin. "It's not too late. You could still get away from here. You don't have to go through with this marriage."

Confused, Jody could only shake her head. "But I want to go through with this marriage, Sarah. I love him."

"You'll regret this," the girl insisted, then turned to slam her bedroom door in Jody's face.

"I know that," Jody whispered, "but I have to do it anyway."

Three hours later, Jody stood before a high-gilted mirror, looking at the woman who stood with wide, frightened eyes staring back at her. Blinking, she had to look hard to see herself in that woman. She was dressed for her wedding day, but she was making a mockery out of everything she'd ever held sacred.

She'd always dreamed of this day, when she allowed herself such silly notions. Never had she dreamed it would come about this way, however. Never had she dreamed that she'd find the one man that turned her upside-down, fall in love with him, and wind up marrying him on some quirky time trip into another era.

"Oh, Mama," she whispered as she gazed at the upswept golden curls Dancy had fussed over and the high-necked Victorian collar of the white muslin and lace gown Miss Martha had insisted she wear. "I wish you were here, Mama. I'm so scared."

Mentally chiding herself, she remembered there was

really nothing to be scared about regarding the actual marriage. This was a mock marriage, after all, a marriage in name only, a means to an end. And lordy, how she wanted this to end.

On the one hand, she loved living on this beautiful plantation, but logic told her this life wasn't as romantic in reality as it had been in her dreams. No, she had to get back to where she belonged, back to Hampleton and back to Spence House. This was her mission. And if marrying Chase would bring that about, then she could do it.

"Ready, ma'am?" Dancy asked from the doorway. "Everyone's waiting."

"As ready as I'll ever be," Jody said, heaving a deep sigh to steady her nerves. Saying a quick prayer, she gathered her lacy skirts and started for the door.

"You should wear your brooch," Dancy said. "It'd be perfect with that dress."

Jody stopped, giving the girl a sharp look. "Which brooch, Dancy?"

"Why, the one Mr. John gave you. Heck, everybody know's was him that gave it to you, and now I guess it don't much matter if you wear it out in the open, since you're marrying him."

Hope surging through her entire body, Jody nodded. "Yes, of course. I can wear it, can't I? Now, where did I put it?"

Maybe Dancy would actually help her find Agnes's missing brooch. That would mean they might be able to get back to Hampleton without the benefit of matrimony after all.

"What? You lost it?" Dancy seemed shocked. "You always kept it right there in the tin, under that false bottom." She headed to a large wardrobe to dig through hat boxes until she pulled out, to Jody's amazement, the very tin box Jody had brought with her through time. Jody had hidden it there for safekeeping.

Wondering how Dancy knew exactly where to find the box, she watched as the girl opened it and took out the few letters Jody had found in it. Then Dancy pressed hard on each side of the box and was rewarded with a faint clicking sound. The bottom of the box popped up, and there clustered in sky blue satin, lay the brooch Jody and Chase had been searching for.

Too stunned to question Dancy, Jody took the brooch from the girl's hands, but she was too shaken to pin it to her bodice.

"Let me," Dancy said, obviously noting the effect the piece of jewelry was having on Jody. "Are you all right, Mistress Agnes?"

Tears clouded Jody's vision, but she managed to smile. "I thought I'd lost this. Oh, Dancy, this will make all the difference. How did you know where to find it?"

Dancy finished pinning the brooch to Jody's high wide collar, then turned her around to face the mirror. "Why, you told me yourself where you kept it hidden, along with your letters to Mr. John. Remember, you had me sneak them to the way station for the mail carrier?" At Jody's blank look, she added consolingly, "You've had a hard time since your accident, haven't you?"

"Yes." Jody swallowed hard. Seeing the brooch on her dress gave her such a strong sense of dread mixed with hope that she had to turn away. "But today is a happy day."

"It sure is," Dancy agreed, although she had no way of knowing that Jody was happy for a different reason than she.

Outside in the hallway, Sarah held her breath and leaned back against the wall. She'd learned how to sneak about the house without being detected. Heck, it was as easy as pie around here, what with Mama so deep in mourning and the little ones constantly bickering with each other. Or at least, it had been easy until Miss Agnes had shown up again with a new attitude.

Sarah had always managed to get around Agnes before, telling the nosy nanny anything to make her stick to her own business. But prim little Agnes had changed; she was still putting on an act, but this one was different. Now, even John seemed different. He no longer had any patience; he didn't indulge Sarah the way he used to before the war, before *her*.

And now, somehow, all her plans were falling apart. Somehow, the brooch she'd found and hidden had disappeared from her jewelry chest. That Dancy! It'd be just like her to go snooping through Sarah's things. That brooch was hers by right; it had belonged to *her* grandmother, after all. Agnes had no business wearing a family heirloom anyway. Sarah was the oldest daughter, and until that uppity nanny had come along, she'd been the favorite of her older brother's.

Oh, I'll throttle you good for this, Dancy, she swore silently, her fist clenching. And Ali, too. That heathen had been watching her like a hawk. Lord, he made her nervous. But he couldn't outsmart her. *I still have my new suitor*, Sarah reminded herself, smiling at her smug reflection in a bulls-eye mirror as she tried to hear the rest of Agnes's and Dancy's conversation. The room fell silent, so she glanced around and moved quietly down the hall. Nothing more to gain there.

Checking the grandfather clock ticking away on the landing, she knew it would be only a few hours before the entire family went down to the garden for that stupid wedding. Mama was furious that she refused to attend, but Sarah didn't care. A little nip of that bourbon Miss Agnes had so graciously suggested to soothe Mama's nerves would take care of that.

And while everyone was down there fawning over precious Miss Agnes, Sarah would have some fun of her own with her new beau. Imagine, an Army captain, interested in her.

Prancing into her room, she squeezed her arms around her chest, then frowned deeply. Of course, he was a Yankee captain, but he'd been so kind to her that last time he'd come by with his patrol troops, looking for mean old Miss Agnes. And he'd really seemed so appreciative when Sarah answered all of his questions. Shortly after that, Miss Agnes had disappeared—probably doing that filthy Underground Railroad stuff again.

Of course, Miss Agnes wanted them to think she'd

stopped all of that. Now, she was pretending to have a change of heart, because of John. Sarah had told the captain as much the last time she saw him. He had not liked that bit of information, not one bit. Nor the fact that his friend Agnes Calhoun was in love with a Confederate soldier. Sarah hadn't told him that the soldier was her brother. That would put John in danger. No, she just wanted Agnes out of the way, and darn it, she'd thought her gone once and for all. Poor Captain Markham. Agnes had obviously used him, gaining his trust only to cast him away, now that she'd found a better catch.

Well, he'd be especially interested to know Agnes was actually marrying that same Confederate soldier. But, he mustn't find out it was John. She had to protect John. Nodding her head, she decided she'd only tell the captain enough to get Agnes in trouble. He didn't have to know everything, just that Agnes had turned against the Union and now was a spy for the Confederates. That should get her carted off right away.

Sarah smiled dreamily at her reflection. Captain Markham was her only hope. Papa was gone. John was honor bound to go back to the fight, and soon, Jackson would probably run off and join up. By then, maybe she and Captain Markham would be engaged, and she'd be safe. She'd be protected and pampered, and she wouldn't have to worry about her home being destroyed. She'd be a proper lady once again. And she'd be rid of Miss Agnes Jodelyn Calhoun, once and for all.

Regaining some of her pep, Jody decided not to tell Chase about the brooch. Let him see it on her dress; let him be as surprised as she'd been. How the thing had gotten back into the tin box was a mystery, but then this whole affair had a mystic quality. Soon, it would be over. Soon, she would be home. Then she'd deal with Mr. Chase Spence.

But as she made her way down the winding stairs, she saw Chase standing at the bottom with Jackson by his side, and almost lost her footing. He was wearing a Confederate uniform! And he looked so very handsome, so very Southern, that she lost her breath and her determination. She couldn't take her eyes off him, drat his hide.

His hair had grown longer, and his new growth of beard made him look exactly like John Hample. And she loved him with every fiber of her being. For as long as she lived, whether in this life or the next, Jody would never forget this moment, or the way Chase made her feel. For a brief time, she thought she saw a surge of the same strong love she felt, there in the depths of his stormy eyes. But like everything else about this whole interlude, she could have simply imagined his look of love.

When she stepped off the staircase, he took her hand and somewhere, a flute begin to play a sweet, enticing song. Chase's eyes held hers, while Jackson and the rest of the entourage whispered their compliments.

"We're going out into the garden," Chase whispered close to her ear. "The wisteria is blooming."

She understood. How could they be married without wisteria to decorate their altar, and magnolia blossoms as their audience?

Touched that he'd thought of such intimate and romantic details, she managed a shaky smile. "Thank you." Then, "Nice uniform, but don't you think you're carrying this a bit too far?"

He smiled too. "Jackson and Miss Martha, between the two of them, managed to alter an old one." Underneath his breath, he added, "So for now, I am Major John Hample Spence, CSA. I feel so eerie."

He hadn't noticed the brooch yet, she thought.

The back garden was in full bloom, with Cherokee roses trailing at random over whitewashed trellises and azaleas lifting their cotton-candy blossoms to the sun. Bees hummed greedily, and a golden butterfly fluttered in their path, acting as flower girl on the gentle afternoon wind. Chase brought Jody before an arched trellis adorned with heavy clusters of wisteria.

Ali stood just before the trellis—he was flute player as well as preacher. As they arrived, he finished the haunting tune and bowed down to them. "I am indeed honored to serve you on this fine afternoon, master." Giving Jody an elegant bow, he added, "You are lovely, madame." His dark eyes fastened on the brooch nestled in the lace at her throat. "It is time."

Jody didn't miss the hidden message he seemed to be sending her. Should she rub the brooch and chant over it, right now? That had been her plan—to get them back before they went through with this preposterous ceremony. Her gaze on Ali, she lifted her fingers to her neck, but something stopped her.

What could it hurt, to go through with just the ceremony? This was what John Hample wanted, after all. Where was the harm? It was such a beautiful day for a wedding, and if she couldn't have Chase in real life, why not for a few precious minutes in this life?

Ali smiled at her knowingly, then held up both his hands to the sky. "We are here today, oh, Great and Knowing One, to witness the union of John Hample Spence and Agnes Jodelyn Calhoun, two souls that will merge as one, for all eternity."

The impact of his words didn't escape the couple standing before him. Chase glanced over at Jody, hoping to give her an encouraging smile. It came out as a lopsided grin. He should be scared, about the future, about the past, about whatever was to come to past in the near future. But right now, all he could think about was the woman at his side and how radiant she looked. Jody Calhoun was a stunning bride.

Jody saw his grin, and managed one of her own. If he weren't so obstinate and aggravating, she could almost enjoy herself. Almost. Well, she'd have the last laugh. She had the brooch.

Ali continued, majestic in his robes and bright turban. "In the grand scheme of life, man can only borrow time here on earth. It is the eternal time that the great Allah allows us to keep forever. We must use it wisely, never squandering it with pride and deception; we must use it honestly to make the earth a better place, to make each other stronger beings."

Chase gave him an impatient glare, which Ali chose to ignore. "By coming together in this union here today, John Hample and Agnes Jodelyn will no longer squander their time separately with false pride and denied feelings. They stand before the Great One and their family, to announce their love and their commitment to the world. And so it shall be, forevermore."

With that, he whipped out Miss Martha's treasured family Bible and had Jody and Chase repeat their Christian vows. The "I do's" were said in weak, breathless whispers and in a matter of minutes, Jody was the new Mrs. John Hample Spence. In her deepest imagination, she preferred the title Mrs. Chase Spence, but she kept that dream to herself.

"Master," Ali said, nudging Chase along, "you may kiss your bride."

He did, long and hard and sweet, much to the embarrassment of Miss Martha and Jackson. Ali beamed like a proud papa.

Jody accepted the kiss, drinking it like water, savoring its sweet brutality, savoring the man she loved so dearly. When Chase finally let her go, she stood back to get her breath, her eyes brimming with happiness. Alas, it would be over the minute Chase laid eyes on the brooch.

He did, his eyes shifting from her flushed face to the high collar keeping her neck from his view, while his expression shifted from desirous to murderous in two seconds flat. "Where did you find that, my love?" he asked in a fake sweet voice for her ears only. "And how long have you been holding out on me?"

"I'm not holding out on you," she whispered a few minutes later after hugs and kisses from the family. "I only found it immediately before I came downstairs."

He gave her a dubious look. "You wouldn't tease me about something so important, would you, Jody? Knowing you, you've had it all along."

Angry beyond words, she plastered a fake smile on her face for the benefit of the family. Everyone was eating and drinking the sparse wedding food—mostly fresh fruits and vegetables with a scrawny side of the last of the cured ham as the main dish, and a real pound cake—a pound each of flour, eggs, sugar, and butter, precious commodities—as the wedding cake.

Nudging his foot with her slipper, she told him, "That's typical! Jump to the wrong conclusion; see if I care. After the party, I intend to rub this thing till my fingers blister, just so I can get away from you!"

He laughed, then shoved a piece of cake in her mouth to shut her up. "You seem to be forgetting one thing, sweetheart. I'll be right by your side on the trip back home."

"Fine, but that's where we part ways."

"Fine, but I'll still be around—restoring *my* house. We're bound to run into each other."

"I'll stay away," she swore. "My only concern was Spence House and now that you'll be taking care of it, I can go about my own business quite nicely, thank you."

Angry that she could write him off so nonchalantly, he dropped the china plate he'd been holding onto a nearby picnic table. Motioning for Ali to play, he waited for the sound of the flute to fill the garden. Dusk was beginning to fall over the scene, coloring everyone and everything with a golden light. The haunting music only added to the surreal feeling sweeping through Chase.

Taking Jody by the arm, he took the loaded plate of food she'd been nibbling at and set it aside. "Before you go on about your business, Mrs. Spence, will you dance with me?"

Mrs. Spence. He'd called her Mrs. Spence. Unable to breathe, let alone respond, she could only move her head slightly.

He pulled her into his arms, moving her in a slow steady waltz that brought cheers and whispers from the crowd of family and servants. Little Tucker clapped his hands and danced his own jig, with Dancy laughing down at him, and Sport barking around them. Everyone laughed, happy in spite of the war and the strange wedding ceremony.

Everyone except the bride and groom. They danced with each other, around each other, against each other, both trying desperately to hide their true feelings.

Jody smelled the wisteria, saw the glistening sunset, heard the children laughing, absorbed the enticing melody of Ali's flute, and was only aware of the man holding her in his arms. She was married to him—albeit pretend—but, oh, what a dream, what a wonderful, beautiful charade. She'd never forget the way being in his arms felt.

Chase looked down at the woman in his arms and felt a surge of love so strong it nearly knocked him off balance. Somehow, he managed to keep to the exotic beat of the flute's lilting music; somehow, he managed to guide her around the garden without taking his eyes away from her heart-shaped face. He'd never seen her so beautiful, yet he knew in his heart he'd seen her before—in another life? In this life? It didn't matter. The only thing that mattered was that he was hopelessly smitten with her, and he didn't have the guts to tell her.

So they danced, their eyes, their arms, their touch, saying what they couldn't yet say. The sun set, the spectators grew quiet, the wind picked up, and Ali finished the song.

Chase stopped moving, but he didn't let her go.

Ali stepped forward. "Master, you look like a man deeply in love. Don't you think it's time to retire?"

Chase moved his head, but kept his eyes on Jody. "Retire? What are you talking about?"

"To . . . the wedding chamber," Ali said with as much tact as he could muster. "Take your new bride to the honeymoon suite and celebrate your good fortune."

Realization settled over Chase while the sun settled down for the night. He smiled. "Ah, yes. How could I have forgotten the best part?"

Glaring at him, Jody stepped back. "You can't be serious?" Looking at Ali, she said, "That wasn't part of the deal."

Ali gave an eloquent shrug. "Did you expect separate bedrooms?"

Seething, she nodded briskly. "Oh, I not only expect it, I demand it!"

"And what would everyone think?" Chase chimed in,

enjoying watching her squirm. "Remember your place, sweetheart."

Giving him a look that could have melted steel, she hissed, "I know my place and it isn't in your bed!"

Looking like a bad third wheel, Ali held up a hand. "My apologies, madame. Apparently, I didn't make my master's wishes completely clear. You must consummate the marriage—yes, that is a very important stipulation—to carry the legacy into the future."

Shocked, Jody lifted a shaking hand to the brooch at her throat. Ali noticed, and smiled. "I see you recovered your brooch. Very good."

"You bet it's good," Jody said, flouncing away, her fingers frantically rubbing the polished pearls. "I've had enough. I've done everything John Hample asked me to do, but I'm going home now." She closed her eyes much like Dorothy in *The Wizard of Oz*, and started chanting, "Take me home; please take me home," all the while rubbing the brooch.

Chase held his breath, waiting, wondering if everything was about to change. Seconds turned into minutes. The family had broken apart, going back to the house while the servants cleared away the remains of the party. Still, nothing happened. Ali cleared his throat and discreetly walked away to help Dancy with the cleaning up. Still nothing happened.

Finally, flustered and frustrated, Jody opened her eyes only to find she was still in the very spot where she'd started out. And Chase was still standing beside her, a questioning look on his face.

"Ah, Jody, I don't think it's working."

"It has to work." She tried again, closing her eyes to concentrate. "Come on, John Hample, help me."

Finally, Chase, a little bit disappointed, a little bit relieved, took her by the arm to lead her inside. "Well, Jodelyn, looks as if you're stuck with me—for the night at least." Giving her a devilish look, he whispered close, "I'll warn you though, I like to snuggle."

Jody didn't answer. Instead she allowed him to guide her into the house while she held tightly to the heavy brooch at her throat. Then she said into the wind, "If you weren't already dead, John Hample Spence, I swear, I'd kill you!"

Chapter Fourteen

"Give up, Jody. That thing's not going to take us back to Hampleton. We might as well be asking Scotty from *Star Trek* to beam us up."

Jody stood at the open French doors, her fingers working frantically against the brooch still at her throat. She was already nervous enough, being here in his bedroom, without him teasing her in the process. And it didn't help that Miss Martha and the entire staff had fixed the suite up with a definite honeymoon flair. Normally, the freshly cut magnolias and trailing wisteria blossoms would have cheered her up. Tonight, she was too keyed up to enjoy the sweet fragrance wafting out across the summer wind.

She faced Chase at last, hating the smug look on his handsome face. "I'm not stopping until I wake up in my own bed, in my own house, in my town."

"It might not happen."

"It has to." She stalked around the room like a cat. "I can't believe this."

Chase's belly laugh brought her pacing to a halt. "Oh," he said, "that's rich, and what an understatement! You talk to ghosts, you read centuries-old letters; then you get yourself transported back in time, but you take it all in stride because you have to save Spence House. And now that we're down to the wire, you can't seem to believe it's happening.''

Raising up off the bed, he reached out a hand to grab her arm. "This is real, Jody. Probably the only really real part of this whole scam."

"And what's that supposed to mean?" she asked. Her whole body was quivering with the answer she tried to deny, her gaze avoiding the sight of him lounging there on those tempting satin sheets.

"Our . . . attraction for each other," he said his hand trailing down the column of her neck. That damnable high collar was in the way, so he stopped at her jawline. "We're here together; it's a beautiful night. Why not make the best of the situation?"

Lifting her arm away, she glared up at him. "Oh, that's just like you. You always manage to mess with my head when you get me alone. Well, it won't happen this time, Chase. Not the way it did in Spence House, or your cabin, or especially not the way it happened up in the attic. This is a marriage in name only, a way to get what we both want."

Angry that she despised being here with him so much, Chase forced her closer, his eyes flaring darkly as he pinned her inside his arms. "You know what we both really want, though, don't you, Jody? And it's this."

The kiss was punishment and pleasure all at once. His hands moved through her upswept hair, pulling and tugging at the curls until several dainty hair pins dropped on the Aubusson carpet and the soft tresses fell around her shoulders. Then, his mouth still searching hers, he moved his hands down her back to unbutton the long row of tiny pearl buttons holding her lace dress together. Frustrated at the slow pace, he seriously thought about yanking the darn thing off, but something in the soft moan he heard coming from deep inside her stopped him.

Pulling back, he cupped her face between his hands so

he could study her up close. The moonlight became her, lighting her face with an ethereal quality that took his breath away. "You are so beautiful," he said, the words husky and strained. "Why are you so frightened, Jody? Don't you know I would never deliberately hurt you?"

Not wanting him to see the vulnerability in her eyes, she looked away. "I'm not frightened, silly. Just worried. We've done everything John Hample wanted. I want to go home."

The small catch in her words was his undoing. Pulling her close, he tugged her into the cushion of his chest. "Me, too, baby. Me, too. But we have to consider the possibility that we might not make it back."

Startled, she looked up at him. "We have to. If we don't it means you might die. I . . . I'd never forgive myself if that happened, even though you do get on my nerves."

He kissed the top of her head. "Well, maybe you'll get lucky and be rid of me for good."

She slapped his arm. "Don't tease me, Chase. Not about that."

Smiling, he asked, "Does that mean you have a small amount of affection for me in your heart?"

She didn't dare admit anything. "No, that simply means that I want you in one piece in the next century, to take care of Spence House."

He backed away as if she'd really slapped him. "Of course. We can't forget our entire purpose for being here, now can we?"

Seeing the tenderness drain from his face, to be replaced with a bland expression, she regretted bringing up Spence House. Right now, she'd gladly demolish it herself if he'd just take her back in his arms and hold her close all night.

But that didn't happen. Instead, he grabbed a decanter of whiskey and a crystal glass from a nearby dresser, and saluting her with it, said, "I'm going to sit out on the porch and watch the stars twinkle. Why don't you get ready for bed," he said. To the questioning look in her eyes, he added, "Take my bed. I don't think I'll be getting much sleep this night."

The room went dead with his leaving it. Oh, Lord, she

thought, why did she have to go and ruin everything with her big mouth and smart-aleck attitude? Why couldn't she just run after him and tell him she loved him madly and she wanted more than anything to take him to bed?

Because, she wouldn't make love to him without the commitment of love. She'd been taught to value love, from her mother's bad examples and her grandparent's good example. She knew in her heart, mock marriage or not, she would never settle for mere lust. And, she wouldn't settle for going through the motions just to appease Agnes's tortured soul. It had to be real. Since Chase didn't love her, had never even come close to saying he did, then she had to keep her true feelings to herself.

And that meant she had to keep herself away from his touch, his bed, him. Struggling with the delicate dress she'd been married in, she managed somehow to finish the task Chase had started. Damn these buttons, anyway! Finally, she pushed the dress and its under-crinolines to the floor, stepping away with only her white corset and lacy drawers covering her.

Carefully removing the heavy brooch from the neck of the discarded dress, she clutched the pin in the palm of her hand, staring down at it as if it could give her the answers she needed.

Outside, Chase watched her through the veil of lace curtains, struggling with his self-control. When she stood, half-naked and oh, so very innocent in her sexiness, her buxom curves enhanced by the old-fashioned underwear, he almost went to her. But then she bent to retrieve the brooch, and the look of anguish on her face stopped him. He continued to watch her, feeling the frantic hope she felt as she clutched the brooch near. That she longed to be away from him only added to his misery, and made him want her that much more.

He loved her. But he wouldn't tell her. Not when she loved a house more than she'd ever love him.

"It's not the house, Jody," he whispered into the night, "it's the home that matters. But we'll never have that, will we?" Too late, he'd learned that lesson.

Jody thought she heard him speak. Glancing up, she called, "Chase, did you say something?"

"No," he answered on a voice raw with need. He took a swallow of whiskey, but its fiery burn did nothing to appease the thirst he was feeling. "Go to bed."

Hours later, a storm raged through the night. The wind howled its delight as limbs splintered and fell against the damp grass of the gardens, crushing delicate blossoms while the raging rain rushed past in glee.

On the small sofa he'd managed to prop himself against, Chase shifted and groaned. He didn't know which hurt worse, his head or his still-bruised foot. He was sore all over. Glancing over at Jody, he saw that she wasn't sleeping peacefully either. Her dreams raged as fiercely as the storm outside, but the presence she cast out over the room was every bit as powerful.

Good. Let her suffer. She'd sure worked him over, with her prim wedding gown and that country-girl innocence. He'd have to remember that she could be conniving as anyone when she wanted something. He'd have to remember—

"No!"

Her scream brought him up off the lounge. With a groan caused by his aching ankle, he hurried to the big bed. "Jody, wake up! You're having a dream, sweetheart."

Moaning, she raked a hand over her eyes and sat up abruptly, almost colliding with his bare chest in the process. "Where am I?"

"In my room," he whispered, taking one of her hands in his. "At Camille Plantation, remember?"

"Oh, God," she moaned. "It's not a dream. We're really here."

From the muted light of a single lamp, he saw the fear paling her skin and the disappointment darkening her eyes.

"Still." He shifted up on the bed, automatically taking her onto the pillows with him so they could sit the storm out together. "And all hell's breaking loose."

"When did it start raining?" she asked groggily, holding on to him as if her life depended on it. After that horrible dream, she had a feeling it did.

"About an hour ago," he said as he brushed her hair away from her eyes. "It's almost dawn."

"I dreamed about us," she said at last, her words shaky and unsure. "Or at least, I think it was us. Oh, maybe it was them—John Hample and Agnes. We . . . we were underneath the magnolia." Her voice caught and she became silent for a minute. She couldn't tell him that in the dream he was kissing her and that he'd told her he loved her. That part would have to remain a dream. Continuing, she said, "Ali tried to warn us, but it was too late. The soldiers came—Union soldiers." Looking up at him, she whispered, "They took you away."

Concerned for her, he tucked her into the cradle of his arms. "You're getting too caught up in this mess. I hate this! I hate having to sit here, waiting, wondering, what's going to happen next."

What happened next took them both by surprise. Jody looked up at him, wanting, needing to feel his presence, needing the security being with him always brought her. The dream had left her shaken and vulnerable. And it had also left her wondering.

What if they didn't make it out of this alive?

What if she never had another chance to be with the man she loved? That thought tore through her, making her bold. Raising up, she kissed him. "I love you, Chase." It no longer mattered that he might not love her in return.

Chase took a heavy breath, his gaze searching her face for any signs of trickery. What he saw in the misty depths of her eyes convinced him that she was being completely honest. She'd never looked more beautiful.

"You . . . love me?" he asked, awe coloring each word.

Feeling like an idiot, she wished she could take it back. He would probably just laugh in her face. But the dream haunted her. It had been so real, as if she'd lived it before.

Looking away, out into the storm, she nodded. "Yes. I think I fell in love with you that day you kissed me in the cupola room." Smiling shyly, she said, "You're one mighty fine kisser, Mr. Spence."

She'd *loved* him all that time! Boy, had he read the signs all wrong. Or maybe he'd been just as stubborn about this as she'd been. Maybe it was time to come clean himself.

Taking a finger to her chin, he lifted her face. "Well, guess what, sweetheart?"

Here it comes, Jody thought. *He's going to tell me to drop dead.* "What?" she had to ask.

"I love you back, probably twice as much."

"What?" she repeated, her eyes widening.

He kissed her lightly, his lips nuzzling hers in a new, more intimate fashion now that he knew she really liked it. "I'm so in love with you, it's driving me mad. I love your lips." He kissed her again just to prove his point. "I love your hair." He buried his nose in the soft tresses, inhaling the scent of her. "And I especially love the rest of you, even that off-the-wall logic you throw at me all the time."

Jody's heart sounded like a pounding drum in her head. Every fiber, every nerve in her body tingled to life. "In my dream, you told me you loved me."

He pulled her down, down onto the satiny soft sheets. "Well, you're awake now and I do love you. Wife."

Turning away, she struggled to control the warring emotions pushing through her. "But I'm not your wife, not really."

He forced her back to him. "We were married today. Granted, it was unconventional, but heck, we're living a facade anyway. But this," he kissed her neck, "this is real. And this, Jody, is between us—you and me—not John Hample and Agnes. What I'm feeling right now has nothing to do with anyone's destiny but my own."

His honest words, so poetic yet so logical, made her fall in love with him all over again. "What about . . . what about when we get back, if we do get back, to Hampleton?" She put a hand on his arm. "I've been so silly, pushing you to save Spence House. Now, I don't care about it all that much. I care more about you . . . about us. But how do you feel?"

He thought about that for a minute. That was all the time he needed to know how he wanted his future to turn out. Now that he knew she loved him, and not just his house, he could afford to be generous.

"Don't give up on your dream now, Jody. We've been through so much—that house is a part of us. We'll rebuild Spence House together, and we'll get married all over again, and we'll have lots of little girls with strawberry blonde hair and smart-alecky attitudes."

She grabbed him around the neck, pulling him down, her fingers moving over the corded surface of his back. "Husband," she said, the word trembling through her lips. "Are you sure, Chase? Do you really love me, or are you just caught up in this thing between John and Agnes?"

He stroked her cheekbone with one finger, his eyes warming her, heating her, making her believe. "I love you, Jody. I've loved you since I set eyes on you, and I think now I understand the torment John Hample must be suffering." His finger moved with a gentle flutter down the column of her throat. "I've never wanted anyone the way I want you— and I don't say that lightly, no matter what time zone we're in."

She watched his expression, saw the love and need in his eyes, felt that same love and need in the depths of her soul.

"Husband," she said again, her heart winning out over what little reasoning she had left, "love me."

"Yes, ma'am."

He moved over her, his hands testing her skin through the gauzy material of her white cotton nightgown. He buried his nose against a rising mound of creamy flesh. "So beautiful." Then he kissed her through the material, wetting the fabric so that it clung to the tight pink bud that sprung to life at his touch.

Jody moaned, then lifted her arms in a slow stretch, a sweet seductive smile crowning her lips. "I think I'm going to like being married."

His mouth enjoying the taste of her skin, Chase slowly pulled the gown up, up, over her head. Taking a minute to gaze at her body, he promised on a breathless whisper, "I'll make sure that you do."

He did. With his lips, with his hands, with his big body rising over hers. Jody felt as if her whole being were the tip of a flame, burning so hotly she thought surely she'd explode. While he caressed her and stroked her, she struggled with his pants.

"Hold on," he said on a winded breath. Moving off the bed, he gazed down at her. "You look like a dream."

She watched as he stripped. "You look better than a dream." When just a touch of reality hit her, she whispered, "Chase, I'm so scared."

He fell across her again, gathering her into his arms, their bodies molding together. "Don't be. I love you. And I won't let anything bad happen. I'll be here with you, Jody, no matter what. I promise."

She cried as they moved together. Nothing in her life had prepared her for the overwhelming feeling of love and need that stirred deep within her as Chase took her with a fierce tenderness. Outside, the storm reached its own climax, cresting and abating as the lovers joined together and became one in the soft, glistening rays of a fresh new dawn.

Jody had never known such power, or such peace. It was as if all the pain she'd ever known had at last found a release. And so she cried.

"Why are you crying?" he asked, still joined with her, still in awe of what had just happened. He'd been her first; now, come hell or high water, he intended to be her one and only, her last.

Jody hugged him close, pulling his head down on the curve of her bosom. "Because," she tried to explain, "I've waited for you all my life. No one's ever promised me anything, Chase. Until now."

"I'll make you one more promise," he said, his mouth close to her heart. "I won't let you down, Jody. No matter what. Go ahead and cry, love. You won't ever have to cry again."

She wanted to believe him with all of her heart. When the last of her tears had stopped, along with the rain outside, she snuggled close in his arms. "Well, we did it."

He chuckled. "Uh-huh, and how."

Lifting her fingers through his tousled hair, she lifted her mouth to his. "I guess John Hample's probably pretty darn satisfied with himself right about now.''

"Not as satisfied as I am with myself," Chase said, raising up on both elbows to look down at her. "Oh, wait, I need to rephrase that. I'm satisfied, but not nearly enough.''

She grinned. "Then husband, let's see what we can do about that.''

"With pleasure," he said. Then his mouth came down on hers once more.

Outside, birds fussed, looking for fresh breakfast in the aftermath of the storm. Sport barked and chased squirrels through the damp grass, and down in the quarters, a flute played a haunting melody. The lovers nestled in the big bed on the second floor didn't hear any of it.

Nor did they hear the sound of horses approaching swiftly over the muddy road leading to Camille Plantation.

Jody was lying contentedly in Chase's arms when a loud banging knock roused her out of his embrace. "My goodness. Just a minute!''

Grabbing her gown and a heavy cotton wrapper, she hastily donned both, her eyes meeting his over the persistent noise.

While Chase slid on his pants, she opened the door. Jackson rushed into the room, his eyes wide with fear. "They're back. The Union soldiers are coming up the lane. Quick, we've got to hide John.''

"Oh, my God," Jody said, fear slicing through her with the force of a blade. "What are we going to do?''

Chase stood perfectly still, his eyes on his younger brother. He was pretending to be a soldier, but he didn't feel so brave right now. "I'll talk to them, explain everything.''

"You can't," Jody said, whirling to face him, her skin pale. "They'll arrest you and take you as a prisoner of war. We can't let them find you.''

"Then what do you suggest we do?" he said, the whinnying of horses echoing across the yard even as he spoke. "It's too late to make a run for the stables.'' Not caring if Jackson heard, he asked, "Where's that damned brooch, anyway?''

"I've got it, but I doubt it will help us now." Jody hurried to the side door, where she could see down below. "They're stopping right at the house."

Misunderstanding, Jackson said, "They'll take the brooch, and all the rest of our valuables, and still come after you. How about the attic? We didn't find him up there; surely they won't either."

"They might search the whole house, though," Chase said, "and the way I organized that place, they'll suspect someone's been living up there."

Ali ducked through the door, his eyes on Chase. "Master, follow me."

Everyone did as the Muhammadan commanded.

"Where are we going?" Jody asked nervously as they moved down the servants' stairs toward the root cellar.

"In the cellar, a secret passage," Ali explained. "It was installed years ago in case of an Indian attack. Mr. Spence kept it a secret, thinking to use it in the event of a slave revolt." In his nonchalant way, he added, "Of course, I discovered it right away."

"Of course," Chase echoed, glad that Ali was so cunning. To Jody, he whispered, "So there really was a secret passage, just not at Spence House."

Frantic now, Jody looked around, then stopped, going still. "Where does this secret passage lead?"

Urging her on, Ali explained. "To the big fireplace in the kitchen. There's a small trap door underneath the floor directly in front of the fireplace."

"You're hiding me in a fireplace?" Chase asked, rolling his eyes. "Thank God it's summer."

"It might work." Taking him by the arm, Jody held tight as they hurried. "Dancy's been doing most of the cooking outside in the kitchen yard to avoid fires. With this heat, and so little food, it makes sense."

"Lucky for me," Chase said. "But is this fireplace big enough to hold me? I don't want to get stuck."

Jody nodded, all the while propelling Chase along down the back stairs leading to the cellar. "Trust me, it's huge. And Ali wouldn't put you in there if he hadn't checked it out ahead of time. Stop whining and hurry.''

In spite of the seriousness of their plight, Chase couldn't stop his smile. God, he loved this woman! He knew she was scared; he felt her hand trembling against his now. But he also knew she was strong, probably much stronger than he'd ever be. Her courage was that rare kind that real heroes— and heroines—possessed. It came straight from her heart. The poor Yankees didn't stand a chance.

Still, he worried. He loved her.

As they reached the darkened corner of the root cellar, Ali pushed on the handle of what looked like a pie safe. ''Through this door, master.''

''I'll go out and talk to them,'' Jody said. ''Maybe I can stall them.''

Chase took her in his arms. ''No. Would you two let me have a say in this, please?'' Giving her a look that expressed his newfound love for her, he said, ''I won't put you in danger like that.''

She lifted a hand to his face, loving him so very much it hurt to breathe. ''I'll be fine. We have to do it this way. We have to.''

''I don't like it.''

Jackson pulled at his arm. ''We've got to hurry. They're banging on the front door.''

''Please go,'' Jody begged him. ''I'll be okay.'' Giving him one last meaningful look, she whispered, ''It has to happen this way, Chase.''

Still watching her, Chase followed Ali into the black hole behind the false back of the pie safe. Slowly, they made their way on hands and knees through the long cobweb-covered passage. Directly over them, what had once been a porch connecting the kitchen to the house had been enclosed and made into a sleeping porch with wide encased windows on all sides. The passageway winded directly underneath this, Ali explained.

They'd barely reached the trap door in the kitchen when the sound of horses galloping around the yard greeted them. Stilling for a minute, they listened to the two soldiers talking in low tones just outside the kitchen.

"He has gone beyond his duties, I tell you," one of them said, his horse snorting and pawing in the mud. "This is insane. We're supposed to be halfway back to Pensacola by now. He'll wind up getting all of us court-martialed."

The sound of a horse prancing close echoed through the still kitchen. "All because of a woman," the other soldier said. "He is determined to have her now that he's eliminated Major Spence. That's the only thing that saved his hide with the commander. I say we ought to ride on back to our post; leave him while we've got a chance."

As the two men rode away, Chase and Ali heard the last of their conversation. "He's gone against orders one time too many. We can't trust him anymore."

Chase hissed at Ali. "Markham is a madman! I can't let her face him—he'll kill her." He raised up. "I'm going out there."

Ali stopped him with a hand on his arm. "I'll not let them harm her, master. You have my word on that." Giving Chase a determined look, he added, "What good can you do anyone if you wind up dead, too? The captain will not kill her; he only wants to toy with her. Use your head, Chase Spence."

Ali shoved Chase up, crawling behind him before they could be seen through the many windows. Chase didn't like it, but he didn't argue. Ali was right. If he rushed out without a plan, he'd wind up getting both of them killed. His heart pounding, he inched up into the blackened fireplace. With a quick look around, he scooted up inside the wide, dark chimney, bracing his hands on either side as he slowly propelled himself up the brick encasement.

"There are two bricks that stand out from the others," Ali explained as he hoisted Chase up into the sooty hole.

With a groan, Chase lifted himself higher, the pressure on his tender ankle causing him to grit his teeth. Finally, he found a slight slope in the bricks and, balancing himself in a spread-eagle fashion, managed to position one foot inside the small opening the loose bricks had allowed.

"There are such footholds all the way up to the roof," Ali said. "If you have to, you can climb even farther."

Chase wondered if his ancestor had considered how to get off the roof, but now wasn't the time to worry about that.

"I'm in," he told Ali on a winded whisper. "Now go and stay with her, Ali. And find Jackson. Tell him to stick with her, no matter what." His voice hoarse with emotion, he added, "Don't let anything happen to her."

Ali nodded. "I shall protect her."

Chase lowered himself into a squatting position, still bracing himself with his feet and arms. His whole body protested the awkward position, but he managed to balance himself into a fairly comfortable stance. Now all he could do was wait—something at which he'd never been very good.

Sarah stood at a window, looking out over the yard, her smile triumphant. He'd come! He'd said he would, last night at the cabin. Richard Markham was a man of his word, a true gentleman. He'd been so kind to her last night.

And he'd been very pleased with the information she'd given him regarding the return of dear Mistress Agnes. Now, maybe he'd arrest the meddling woman and take her away for good—and that brat Tucker along with her!

Hope you enjoyed your one night of wedded bliss, Sarah thought, watching as Agnes greeted the soldiers. *It's over now*.

Jody sent the leader of the soldiers a shaky smile. "Good morning, gentleman," she said, her nerves coiling so tightly she thought she might faint. "What can I do for you?"

Behind her, Jackson slowly made his way down the porch steps, his silent look reassuring her that Chase was safe. Nearby, Sport growled ominously. Knowing Ali had prearranged for just such an encounter, and that he and several armed hands were posted around the house, gave her the strength to appear nonchalant and at ease, even though the ruffle at her neck shook with the beat of her pulse.

The handsome dark-haired man who seemed to be in charge dismounted and came to stand before her, his brown eyes moving coldly over her entire body with deliberate

239

boldness. "So good to see you again, Mistress Calhoun. How have you been?"

Her heart pounding, Jody looked up at Captain Richard Markham, wondering how to answer him. Fear clutched at her, but she faced him, hoping she would have the nerve to do whatever she was supposed to do at this point.

"I'm afraid I haven't been well, Captain." Pulling her wrapper tighter against her body, she wished she'd dressed. She didn't like the way the man was looking at her. Repeating herself, she said, "It's early and I'm still not myself. What can I help you with today?"

Stepping forward, the captain gave her a scathing look. "Do not play coy with me, Agnes. You know what you've already done. I gave you every chance the last time we were together. Pity, I had to return to my duties."

Swallowing back her fear, Jody stepped back. "What are you talking about?"

He laughed, an ugly, deep-throated rumbling that made her skin crawl. "You bargained highly for your lover's life, didn't you, Agnes? Tell me, have you heard from him, or that big servant of his lately?"

Jody's heart did a somersault. If he found Chase here, he'd kill him for sure. Agnes's bargaining hadn't worked; he'd hanged John Hample anyway. She didn't dare tell him that she knew John had survived for a brief time.

Using all the wiles she possessed, she said, "You'll have to forgive me, Captain. I've been very ill these last few weeks. My memory is sketchy, but the last the family heard was that John Hample had returned to his regiment in Virginia. I swear to you, sir, I haven't seen him since the day I left with you. If I've wronged you in some way—"

He grabbed her wrist, twisting it so hard she cried out in pain. When Jackson made a move to help her, he held out a hand in warning. "Stay where you are, boy." Looking down at Jody, he said, "You wronged me, all right. And I was a fool to listen to your pitiful pleas. I should have kept you imprisoned, but even now, after all you've done, I still have a soft spot in my heart for you."

Taking that as an opportunity, she asked, "Is that why you let me live?"

He gave her a hard look. "You really don't remember our little bargain, my love?"

Jody's blank look seemed to convince him that she didn't remember. For a brief moment, his features softened with genuine concern. Then he turned hard again. "Let me remind you. Your agreed to come with me, in return for your lover's life. We had such wonderful moments together, didn't we? Then, alas, I had to return to my post and you, being the good, dedicated mother you are, begged to come home to Tucker."

His words sparked a flash of surreal images in Jody's brain. "Yes, I do remember," she said with such honesty, his entire expression changed. "We were at the cabin. You threatened to hang John, but I begged you to spare him. We rode away together, and you gave orders to one of your men, to let him go."

"Which I did, for your sake and the sake of your son," he lied. His dark eyes burned with a mad fire. "How is Will's son, my dear?"

"Much better, because of your kind gesture," Jody said, her mind trying to follow what he was telling her. "I thank you from the bottom of my heart for letting me return to my son . . . and for sparing John Hample's life."

He watched her intently, then relaxed. "I only did it to win your admiration, and because you promised me more information. I've come to collect on that promise."

Jody wanted to sigh in relief. Apparently, in spite of his demonic ways, the captain still had strong feelings for Agnes. Jody planned to use his weakness to its fullest.

"What else can I do?" she asked honestly. "I have no new information. I'm trying very hard to be a good mother to my son, to protect him. And I ask that you leave this family in peace."

He yanked her close, his burning eyes moving over her face and throat. "Are you hoping your lover will return, Agnes? Is that what you hope to gain from me—the freedom to sleep with your enemy again." His grip on her arm tightened. "You are a disgrace to your country and your husband's memory."

Jody knew enough to tell him the truth. Apparently, Agnes has been a Union spy, but her love for John had changed all of that. Feeling that same fierce loyalty now, she said, "I regret the things I have done, but I can no longer be a part of your intrigue, Captain. You must understand, this is my only home now. I'm responsible for this family. It's too risky to continue."

"Because of your lover?" He looked at two of his men, then laughed harshly. "I doubt you'll be bothered with him for a while. But, perhaps we should search the house in the event that he has come home to you."

The two soldiers laughed at the private joke, while Jody fumed. He knew he'd killed John Hample, or so he thought, yet he was so cruel, he continued to torture John's poor unknowing family.

"No," she said too quickly. "I told you he's not here. The only people here are a few servants and the children, and Miss Martha is not well. She recently lost her husband, and had to watch her son go back to the war. She doesn't know about our agreement, Captain. Please don't do anything to upset her."

"That will be entirely up to you," he said, his tone eager now. "Give me something to take back, something to show to my commander, and I'll spare the family and the house."

Jody couldn't believe the gall of the man, but then Ali had warned her this particular captain didn't play by the rules. The few men with him looked uncomfortable and frightened, probably because they'd witnessed his ruthless techniques, and probably because they thought John already dead.

"I don't know anything," she insisted. Then her knowledge of the Civil War clicking, she added, "Except that General Stonewall Jackson is dead; but before he died, he defeated General Hooker at Chancellorsville, with an army that was outnumbered, but apparently not outsmarted." There, let him chew on that bit of news for a minute or two!

She shouldn't have goaded him, she realized in the next instant.

"You little fool," he hissed. "There is no way you could have such knowledge so soon out here in the back woods, without the benefit of someone who has actually been there." A new, frightening light colored his eyes. "Perhaps your lover told you this?"

Jody sensed his fear and his doubt, and, her heart sinking, knew that he'd just realized John might still be alive and here. Seeing that he was scared of that possibility gave her new courage. This was a twisted, dangerous game, but she was in the thick of it now. She wouldn't let him win twice. "No, we heard from some neighbors."

"I don't believe you, my dear." With a loud, almost pained roar, Markham shouted, "Search the house! If you find him, drag him out to me—unharmed. And bring me what food and rations you find, as well as any silver and other valuables, of course."

Men rushed up the steps, whirling past Jody. "No, please," she said, then turned to face the smug captain. "Why are you doing this? I did as you asked before. Don't you have better things to do besides frighten a mother and her children?"

"Blame yourself," he said on a calculated whisper. "We had a deal, Agnes. If he is still alive, the deal is off."

Calling his bluff, Jody asked, "Did you let him go, Richard? Did you fulfill your end of the bargain?"

His laughter was as brittle as shattered glass. "What do you think, my love? Did you really expect me to spare that traitor's life?"

Trying to bargain yet again with him, Jody said, "If you killed him, why do you think he's here?"

The Captain's eyes went black. "Your fault again. I was too preoccupied with you, my dear, to make sure he was actually dead. I left that to one of my men." Holding her in a death grip, he said, "Now, we'll soon find out, won't we, dear, sweet Agnes. Soon, we'll know which one of us is the real betrayer."

As men scattered out around the house and yard, Jody

243

watched and waited, hoping desperately that Chase was hidden securely in the fireplace. And where was Ali? He was supposed to be protecting Chase, but they'd surely kill him if they found him still alive.

Sarah's smile turned to a frown. What was he doing? He'd told her he'd take Agnes Calhoun away. Why was he sending men around the house?

"John," she said, her hand going to her throat.

From behind her, a dark hand snaked out to cover her mouth. "Do not scream, Miss Sarah. I shall not harm you."

Ali pulled her kicking into the butler's pantry off the main dining room, buying some time. With his hand still over her mouth, he said, "I know what you've done. I know you found the brooch out in the garden. I have returned it, so no need to worry about that now. But we do need to worry about Captain Markham. What did you tell him?"

Sarah gave him a look of malice, then tried to no avail to wiggle free from his iron grip.

"Don't waste precious time, child!" Ali snapped. In a gentler tone, he added, "You have put your brother in grave danger. The captain has already tried to kill him once, and now he suspects John Hample is here. Can't you see, foolish girl, the captain is using you to get to Miss Agnes and your brother. He wants John dead. That is his only purpose."

Shock and fear surfaced in the blue waters of Sarah's big eyes. When she tried to squirm away, Ali leaned close. "Do you understand what I tell you?"

Her whole body shaking, Sarah could only stare at the frightening Muhammadan. When she didn't speak, Ali said, "I will remove my hand from your mouth, but you have to tell me the truth right now. Your brother's life depends on it."

The sound of heavy footsteps in the front of the house brought Sarah's head up. With a muffled sob, the girl collapsed against a shiny Duncan Phyfe oak cabinet.

Slowly, Ali lifted his hand from her mouth. "Tell me now, child, before it's too late."

Sniffing back a sob, Sarah wailed, "What have I done! Oh, Ali, what have I done!"

Chapter Fifteen

Outside, Jody watched, her whole body trembling, as soldiers trampled over Miss Martha's rosebushes and camellia trees, searching out every bush to make sure no one was hiding inside the many intricate flower beds. The sound of plates crashing, followed by the screams of frightened servants echoed from inside the house. Dancy and Miss Martha were with the children in the nursery, trying to keep them quiet. The guards Ali had posted could do nothing, for fear of causing a family member to get shot or worse.

Silently cursing her own stupidity, Jody felt responsible. If she'd only kept her impulsive mouth shut, he might have spared them of this.

"Please," she said to the captain who held her, "can't you stop them? I told you—we have no word of John's whereabouts. He is not here, I assure you. I've done everything you asked; spare the family of this, please."

"I could simply order them to burn the place to the ground."

The cruel tone in his voice left little doubt in Jody's mind that he'd do just that. Giving him a heated look, she shook her head. "There's no reason to do that, Captain Markham. None of this is necessary. I've done everything you asked and I've given you all the information I have."

"Really?" He pulled her close, then stared at her with hard, malicious eyes. "Before Will died, I promised him I'd take care of you. I even thought we'd marry and I'd send you back up north out of harm's way."

Swallowing back her disgust, Jody digested this bit of information. "I'm sorry things didn't work out that way."

"Yes, you're sorry." Her held her arm so firmly, she felt the imprint all the way to the bone. "And you'll be even more sorry for turning against me yet again, Agnes." Lifting her chin in a twisting grip, he said, "What happened to you? You were so against everything the South stood for, so determined to continue your father's work with the Underground Railroad. Until you met him."

"I don't know what you mean," she said, her eyes defying him even as he continued to inflict pain with deliberate pleasure.

"Yes, you do. You can't play coy with me, Agnes. I know you too well. You didn't love Will, did you?"

Angry now, Jody used her only defense. "He was my husband; I bore him a son. Isn't that proof of my love?"

The captain's brown eyes flared with hatred. "That proves nothing, except that you consummated your marriage in the short time you spent with Will. How convenient, to marry him, then watch him ride off to his death." Twisting her head around, he asked, "Is the brat even his?"

Agnes's love for her son gave Jody strength to defy him. "How dare you question Tucker's parentage! Let me go!"

"Never," he said in a deadly calm tone. "I promised Will, you see. I'll keep my promise, and I'll be your tormentor for all eternity, if need be. You must understand, my dear Agnes, you committed the ultimate sin. You turned against your country. You slept with the enemy. And now you must suffer the consequences."

In that one moment, everything became crystal clear to Jody. Now she knew exactly what Agnes had done; now she knew the torment John Hample had suffered, both in life and death. The woman he'd loved had given her loyalty and her soul to him, and she'd died because of it.

Agnes and John had been lovers, but without the benefit of marriage. They'd shared a brief encounter, maybe one time, together. Then just as they'd been about to be married, this monster had come along and tormented them, and they'd never found their way back to each other. They had come close, but it had been too late.

That same fate couldn't happen to Chase and her. Thinking about him now, thinking about how much she loved him and what they'd shared together last night, she knew she'd walk through hell to get back to him. Whatever it took, whatever the outcome of her fate, she'd be with Chase again.

Looking up at the man before her, she said, "If you will spare them, I'll come to you later. After I make provisions for Tucker's well-being. I'll go anywhere you ask, do anything you ask, if you'll grant me this one last request."

He stared down at her, then jerked her by the arm. "My God, your noble nature never ceases to amaze me. Even now you're thinking only of him. You're willing to sacrifice yourself yet again, for him. You don't care that I intend to kill both of you this time."

Somehow, she'd known that all along, but hearing him say it caused her to gasp. "Why would you torture me so?"

He pulled her so close, she could smell his rancid breath. "Because you tortured me, you teased me, bringing me contraband in the hems of your ruffled skirts, smuggling little tidbits of information through to me, nestled in your sweet-smelling petticoats, telling me you had to do this for Will, for your father's memory. For months, we communicated, Agnes. I thought we had an understanding. I thought I could trust you.

"Then he came back home, a Confederate war hero, the calvalry captain who manipulated his way to major—one of the best of Jeb Stuart's elite." At her look of surprise, he said, "Oh, yes, I know everything about him. Everything." He glared down at her, disgust clouding his rugged features. "And apparently, so do you. So much so, that you've forgotten your father's memory and your marriage vows. You took up with him again, even after your father's dying request that you stay away from him. Maybe you never really ended it. Maybe you were only bringing me information so you could extract better information to take back to him.''

His dark eyes seemed to turn black as night. "Maybe, my dear Agnes, you were a double agent all along.''

Fear pumped through Jody's body. This man was demented. There would be no reasoning with him. He'd kill her right here, right now, just to seek his revenge. And if he found Chase . . .

"I told you,'' she said, gritting her teeth to keep from breaking down, "I will do whatever you ask—if you spare this family and their home.''

Several Union soldiers rallied around their leader. "Captain Markham, we've searched the grounds and the house. There's no sign of Major Spence.''

"Really?'' The captain's smug expression told Jody he wasn't fooled. "Then I suggest you search harder. I know he's here. I can smell the fear on his lover's body. Did you check the master suite?''

The young man looked chagrined. "Yes, sir, Captain.''

His eyes centered on Jody, he asked, "And what did you find there?''

"The bed had been slept in, sir.''

"Did the room smell sweet, gentlemen? Did it smell like her?'' As he spoke, he thrust Jody forward into the circle of soldiers. "Maybe I'll let each of you have a taste of her, for the memories, after I play with her a while, that is.''

Jackson ran down the steps. "Stop it. She didn't do nothing wrong. She's been sleeping in that room because it's close to my mother's. She's been nursing my sick mother.''

The young soldier piped up. "There was an old woman across the hall with some children. She looked sick enough to me.''

"Shut up,'' the captain snarled, his anger causing the fearful soldier to shrink away.

"He's telling the truth,'' Jody said, her words breathless. "I've taken over the master suite only for convenience.''

"I suppose you would," the captain said, rage spitting through each word. "Do you dream of him when you're all curled up in his bed?"

Speaking from her heart, Jody said, "I dream of the day this war will end and we can all get back to normal. I dream of my future with my son, a peaceful future here on this plantation. And I beg you, leave them alone. They've done no harm to anyone."

He laughed, a low ugly sound. "I could almost believe you, you look so innocent." Looking around, he signaled to his men. "Mount up, boys. We've got plenty of time to flush out the good Major Spence. If he's here, we'll find him soon enough." Turning to Jody, he bowed low. "I expect you to be at the cabin at midnight. Or I will come back and burn this place to the ground. Dream about that, my dear Agnes." Still watching her, he slid onto his prancing stallion's back. "Oh, and please, my dear, keep me in your dreams, too, until I can claim you for my own."

Jody held her breath as she watched the party of men ride away, the horses leaving muddy paths in the lane. She let out a long sigh of relief and immediately started trembling.

Jackson ran into Jody's arms. "I can't believe he let us go. I was sure he'd burn the place."

"He's playing some sort of evil game," Jody said, rocking the frightened boy in her arms. "It's all right, Jackson. He won't be back today. But I have a feeling he'll keep pestering us until he tires of it, or he takes me away in chains."

"Why would he do that?" Jackson's innocent question tore through the still air.

Deciding the boy deserved as much of the truth as she could reveal, she explained, "Captain Markham was a friend of my husband's. After Will died, the captain promised to take care of me. I'm afraid he thought we might have a future together, but somehow, he's discovered that I'm in love with John instead. He thinks I've betrayed him and the Union, and he won't rest until he gets his revenge."

"Then we have to get John back to Virginia," the boy said, his eyes wide with concern. "Heck, he'd be safer on the battle lines than here with that lunatic running around."

"You're right about that," Jody agreed. "We'll keep John hidden today. But as soon as possible, we need to smuggle him away." *Chase and I both need to be away from here.*

"Just tell me he didn't hurt you?"

Chase looked down at Jody, his eyes full of concern and worry. "Are you sure you're all right?"

"I'm fine," she said, hugging him tight. "I was scared to death, but I've faced down lots of bullies—I was always the outsider in school, so I learned to defend myself. Captain Markham is one of the worst bullies I've ever seen. I'm just glad he didn't carry out his threats." She didn't dare tell him why the captain had backed down.

Chase pulled away to stomp to the curtained attic window. They'd decided he'd be safer up here for now, since the attic was closer to the small stairway leading to the servants quarters and on to the root cellar. Now, they were waiting for Ali to report back on the whereabouts of the Union patrol.

"I should have faced him. I've never walked away from a fight, but I've always done my fighting in the board room."

Jody wished he'd drop the male pride thing and concentrate on what they needed to do next. "Chase, please. It had to be this way. He wants revenge on Agnes, and that means he'll kill you. This has nothing to do with the war, and what's right. This man makes his own rules. His own men were scared of him."

He glared at her. "All the more reason for me to face him instead of you. He's dangerous, Jody, and we're playing a dangerous game, guessing as we go, piecing together the parts of Agnes's complex puzzle. I won't put you in that kind of jeopardy again."

From the doorway, Ali uncurled and stood in the darkened room. "You are both in jeopardy. And you have charming little Sarah to thank for it."

"What do you mean?" Jody pushed around a cypress

column supporting the long room. "Did you talk to Sarah?"

Ali nodded, his dark eyes widening. "Ah, yes, mistress, we talked. The poor girl is hiding away in her room, afraid to face her brother."

"What did she do?" Chase asked.

"She told Captain Markham that Mistress Agnes had returned to Camille, and that she had betrayed him by taking a Confederate lover."

Jody gasped. "She turned the Yankees loose on her own brother!"

Ali nodded his head, his eyes sad. "It would seem our young Sarah ran across the good captain the last time he was here, and they got . . . acquainted. She promised him information in exchange for his protection. That's probably why he didn't burn the house today."

Jody remained quiet. She'd worry about her own promise to Markham later.

Chase groaned. "What kind of information?"

"Regarding Mistress Agnes. The girl confessed she wants to be rid of you, mistress. You have threatened her status within the household, it seems. She's been charmed by the Union captain, and he's managed to glean all the information he needs from her to prove that you have become a traitor. Except who your lover really is, or so she thought. She believed she had cleverly diverted him there. She did not reveal that Master John was the one, or that he was home on furlough a few weeks ago. However, as we well know now, the captain figured all of that out. Young Sarah has no way of knowing that she inadvertently caused her brother's death."

"Poor Sarah," Jody whispered, her hand going to her heart.

"Poor Sarah, my foot," Chase said in a snort. "She almost caused you to be carried away and hung as a traitor, and Lord knows what Agnes suffered because of poor Sarah." His eyes flying to hers, he added, "They'll be back, Jody. We've got to get out of here before he comes for you again."

"I agree," Ali said. "Captain Markham defied orders to

to come here. I tracked his men due west. They were dispatched on a federal expedition from Pensacola and apparently they have been raiding at random as they go. These are dangerous, uncaring men, and they will be back. I suggest you both leave tonight, if possible.''

''And where do you suggest we go?'' Chase asked, thoroughly frustrated at being so helpless.

''To the tree,'' Jody replied before Ali could respond. ''We'll take the brooch and go to the magnolia. Surely we've completed our task; surely it's time to go home.'' In her heart, she knew she would have to somehow go to Markham first and do whatever had to be done to protect the family.

''Master said you would need the brooch,'' Ali said. ''I can not tell you what to do. My time is almost complete.''

''What does that mean?'' Jody couldn't bear the thought of something happening to the gentle giant.

''It means, mistress, that my reprieve has come to an end. I have served the purpose I was brought back to serve. I can go to my death in peace.''

''How can you be so calm about it?''

Ali bowed deeply, then took her hand. ''It is my destiny, madame. I accept that which I cannot change. Remember, the soul is eternal.''

Jody swallowed the lump in her throat. ''Are we all going to die, Ali?''

He smiled slightly. ''I cannot answer that, madame. You have the brooch; you have each other. The soul is eternal. And love . . . it transcends time.''

''It didn't save Agnes and John,'' she reminded him bitterly.

He lifted a hand in the air. ''Ah, but it did. You two are proof of that. The *mahabbah* between you two is strong; so strong you have the knowledge of the heart—you can read each other's thoughts—you instinctively knew Mistress Agnes's heart. You became her—indeed, you are her.''

''*Mahabbah?* What does it mean, Ali?''

''It means love, madame.''

Jody turned to Chase, her gaze locking with his, her heart

racing with the sure knowledge that in another life, in this time they were in now, they had known each other, had loved each other as Agnes and John, had suffered at the fate of a great, crippling war, had been torn apart as much as the country they both loved had been torn apart.

Their hearts had been torn apart, but their love had survived. Their love had transcended time.

"I will go now," Ali said discreetly. "I'll be back near midnight."

"All right," Chase said, his eyes still on Jody. "We'll be ready."

After Ali had gone, they stood watching each other in the muted light from a single candle, a thousand thoughts flickering through their minds, burning as hotly as the yellow flame that connected them to each other across the room.

Jody willed herself to stay calm. She could do this. Once they set out to the tree, she would simply sneak away, back to the cabin, to confront Markham. As long as Chase was safe, as long as he could get home and the rest of his family was safe, that was all that mattered to her now.

"Are you hungry?" she asked, her heart thumping like a wounded bird. "I could get you some bread—"

"I don't want food," he answered, his tone bitter and sharp. "I want you safely away from that lunatic."

Jody closed her eyes. "Lord, let this be over soon. I can't take much more."

When she opened them, Chase was there, pulling her into his arms. He kissed her with the same urgency she felt as she clung to him.

Lifting his mouth from hers, he whispered, "I won't lose you again."

They both realized he was referring to the past as well as the future.

Jody lifted her head up to see his face better. "I can't believe he'd bring us here to suffer the same fate he and Agnes did. Somehow, Chase, no matter what happens, we have to survive. We have to."

He held her close, his mouth moving across hers in a heated path. No words were needed. Lifting her into his arms, he carried her to the old bed in the corner.

Jody watched, fascinated, as he undressed and joined her there. Then, her breath held in anticipation, she lay still as he slowly undressed her, layer by layer. First her ruffled calico frock, then the layers of petticoats.

"Too many clothes," he said, smiling down on her when he'd finally stripped her to her cotton chemise and drawers. "At least you didn't wear a corset."

"No way," she breathed as his hands worked their way down her body. "Agnes was smaller in . . . certain places. The one I wore for the wedding just about cut my breath off."

"Mmmm," he moaned, his head falling between the curve of her full breasts. "Maybe she didn't eat as much cornbread and turnips greens as you."

"Probably not," she managed to say, her eyes closed in bliss as he kissed her in such intimate places, it made her weak. "Thanks to those soldiers, none of us will be eating much of anything from the garden now."

That brought back full force exactly where they were, and what might happen to them. Chase rolled over, pulling her on top of his naked length.

Cupping her face in his hands, he gazed up at her. "I'm so in love with you. When I was packed in that damned chimney, I kept thinking what if I never saw you again. How could I go on, what would I do?"

"Stop, stop," she said, feathering his jawline with little kisses to hide the fear and sorrow showing in her eyes. She refused to think beyond right now. "I'm here; I'll always be here. I love you, Chase. I love us. Nothing will change that. Nothing."

He lifted her up so that she fit against him. Then he unlaced her chemise, his fingers brushing her sensitive skin as he worked the satin ribbon apart and slid the garment over her body. Jody moaned softly, marveling at the way he made her feel—whole, complete, loved. She'd always been so scared of this, so afraid of falling in love. It was scary, but it was also beautiful.

"Beautiful," he said as he found the wide slit in her thin drawers. "So very beautiful."

Then he lifted her up and slowly, exquisitely, he centered himself to receive her body. The touch, the merging, the impact was electrifying and immediate.

"Jody," he whispered through the cloud of her golden hair. "Jodelyn."

"Forever," she said, meaning it with all her heart. "I'm yours, my love, forever."

He made love to her with all his heart, knowing they might not have forever. They had a few hours. He tried not to think past that. He only thought of the good, of the love they'd found, here in this strange time, faraway from everything they'd ever known.

Then he remembered he had known her before, and he loved her all the more because he had her in his arms again.

He'd crawl through hell before he'd let her go again.

Hours later, a muffled knock awoke the lovers with a start.

"It's Ali," Chase said, a finality in his voice that made Jody wish they could stop time, instead of travel through it.

"I'll get dressed," she said, raising up. She had to be very careful or he would suspect something. Praying for the strength to leave him so she could stop Markham, she closed her eyes to the pain ripping through her heart.

"Hold on." He tugged her back close. "Just another minute, that's all I want."

She kissed him and held him, savoring this precious memory. "Hopefully, it will be over soon and we'll have a lifetime together." *If not, at least you'll be safe again.*

"Hopefully," he echoed. Then with a determined resolve, he lifted her away. "Let's hurry. The sooner we get there, the sooner we can start our new life together."

A midnight moon cast shadows over the woods, giving a peaceful impression to the sultry summer darkness. But Jody felt anything but peaceful. She jumped every time a twig snapped or a wild creature scurried into the foliage. She'd tried, really tried, so hard to make a getaway. But between Ali's cunning and Chase's protective stance, she had not been successful. Short of telling him the truth, which could prove to be fatal, she had to find a way to leave Chase.

"All clear," Ali said, silently approaching from the road. "It would seem we made it here without the good captain following us. I covered our tracks, so we should be safe."

From where they stood underneath the magnolia tree, Chase looked down at Jody. "Well, I guess this is it. You have the brooch?"

"Of course." Her words were taut and hushed. She couldn't go with him, but she had to pretend she was doing just that. Turning to Ali, she said, "If . . . if this works, will you explain to the family. Tell them—"

"I'll tell them you wanted to be near your husband, madame."

She nodded, tears clouding her vision. "And Tucker? You'll make sure he's safe?" Her voice quivered. "I didn't get to say good-bye."

"Little Tucker will be just fine, Mrs. Spence. He'll grow up to rebuild the plantation, and his family will farm the Spence land for generations to come."

"How do you know?" she asked, amazed that he could predict so far ahead.

"Master John told me," he explained, bowing in his eloquent fashion. "I shall leave you now. I will watch the roads and sound a warning if all is not well."

Chase let go of Jody to walk over his friend. "Ali?"

"Yes, master?"

"My friends call me Chase," Chase said, taking the big man's hand to shake it firmly. "I'll never forget you."

Ali lowered his turbaned head, his hand grasping Chase's. "Perhaps we'll meet again, Chase Spence, somewhere in the great *sarmad*—everlastingness."

"I hope so," Jody said, rushing over to hug Ali. She was so terrified, she shook against him.

Chase smiled as the big, brave Muhammadan seemed to grope for words, his body stiff with formality.

"Madame, please."

"Ali, don't be silly," Jody admonished. "Where we come from, the color of the skin doesn't matter, and no man is a servant or slave to another. You're a friend, and that means you get a hug."

Relaxing, Ali smiled at last as he hugged her back. "What a wonderful world you must live in."

"It's not perfect," Jody admitted, "but I will be glad to get back to it." *If I can.*

Ali stepped away. "Then go, and seek the light of the sun. May you have a long and good life." With that, he bowed again and turned to hurry into the shadows.

Jody's nerves seemed to turn to mush. She leaned into Chase, her heart pounding so loudly, she was sure the Yankees would hear it echoing through the woods. She only had a little time left before Markham would come looking.

"Hey," Chase said, sensing her fears and doubts, "it's going to work, Jody. We've done what we set out to do."

"Have we?" she asked, her words muffled against his crisp cotton shirt. "Is it really about to be over?"

"One way to find out," he answered, taking her hands in his. "Where's the brooch?"

"Right here." She pulled it out of the pocket of her dress, then held it up in the moonlight, watching the luster of the aged pearls as they winked their secrets. Looking from the brooch to Chase, she whispered, "Hold me, just once more, just in case."

He couldn't say no to her. Groaning, he pulled her around, pressing her back against the trunk of the young magnolia tree, his hands on the small of her back. "How's that? Better?"

"Much better," she said, her mouth trailing kisses across the width of his chest. She couldn't leave him just yet.

"Jody," he managed to groan, "if we don't stop this now, I won't be able to stop at all."

"Then don't," she said, pulling his body close to hers.

Realizing what she wanted, he gazed down at her, his heart racing, his body taut with need. "Here? Now?"

"Yes." She placed the brooch back in the safety of her pocket, then lifted her skirts. Leaning back against the tree, she whispered, "Hurry. We don't have much time."

Amazed, Chase hastened to do her bidding. She certainly didn't have to ask twice. He needed this one last intimacy, too. Needed to remember the feel of her against him, around him one more time. *Just in case.*

"I want you, always," he said, his eyes searching hers.

With an urgent need, she came to him, lifting her body to fit his. He pressed her against the tree, his hands sliding up her thighs to hold her close. With her kisses, with her hands, with soft moans against his skin, she urged him on until he felt as if indeed he were traveling, hurling, through another time, another space, to a place where only love and pleasure existed. For one shining instant, there was no pain, no fear, no beginning and no end.

Jody felt it too—the spiraling feeling of being out of control. A fine flush of heat covered her body, warming her, making her feel safe and secure. Never in her life had she been so bold; never before had she so needed to be held, to be loved in such an erotic, intimate fashion. But something, some primal force that was far beyond her control, had overcome her, making her want many things. Now, as she came floating back to reality, she knew that no matter what happened, she'd cherish this time, this act of love, here underneath the magnolia tree that had stood as sentinel for Spence House—waiting, silently waiting.

"I'm sorry." She lifted her arms over his shoulders, locking his head in her hands, her body slumping against his in the aftermath of their lovemaking. "I don't know what came over me. I . . . I just had a bad feeling. I didn't want to let you go, ever."

"Please, don't apologize," he said, his heart pounding as he gave her a dazed kiss. "That was . . . incredible. You're incredible."

Hurriedly, she fixed her skirts, then watched as he adjusted his own clothes. "Will you hold me again? I won't seduce you this time." *I only want to say good-bye.*

"I'm here," he said, coaxing her close, wanting her all over again. "We'll hold the brooch together, okay?"

"Okay." She bobbed her head, then brought the piece of

jewelry out of her pocket. She'd fake it, willing him back home while she disappeared into the nearby woods. Silently hoping John Hample would go along with her plan, she looked up at the man she loved. "Take the brooch."

He did, their eyes locking in the shadowy night.

"Kiss me," she said hurriedly.

He did, his lips covering hers in a protective, gentle touch, his heart shielding her from all the pain she'd suffered in too many lifetimes. As much as he wanted her, he also wanted her safe.

"I love you," he whispered.

"I love you," she said, wrapping her hand over his. Then, "Let's close our eyes." She'd have to be quick; she'd have to run away and not listen to him calling out her name.

They were so lost in each other, so lost in their concentration on making this work, that they didn't hear Ali's frantic whispers until he was standing right beside them.

"Master, madame, wait!"

Chase looked up first, dazed and distracted. "Ali?"

Jody lifted her head, her heart pumping. "What is it?"

Ali huffed to steady his breath. "The Yankee soldiers, Captain Markham—he has taken Miss Sarah."

Chase stepped away from Jody, shocked. "What?"

"They're holding her at the old Calhoun cabin. She is very frightened, master."

"Why?" Jody wondered out loud. "Why would he take Sarah?"

"To get to me," Chase said solemnly. "He must have returned to the house for you, and when he couldn't find you, he took Sarah instead."

Jody slumped into Chase's arms. "I didn't make it in time."

Ali shook his head. "No, no. He encountered Miss Sarah on the road. He was on his way to Camille, but she stopped him. They argued, and he forced her to go with him." On a winded breath, he said, "I followed them."

Chase looked over at Jody. "I have to help her."

"No," Jody said, the one word ripping through the still night. "Chase, you can't do that!"

Chase looked from the woman he loved to the man who'd served his family to the death. He knew this was his moment of truth. And he knew this was somehow part of the plan.

Turning to Jody, he held her by the shoulders. "I have to go, Jody. I can't let them hurt Sarah; you know I can't."

"Oh, God," Jody said, lowering her head, a sick feeling curling in the pit of her stomach. She knew only too well what Captain Markham would do to Sarah. Yet she couldn't bear the thought of what might happen to Chase. This was all her fault! She was the one who should be going to face Markham.

She looked up at him, her body still warm from their joining. "Please, Chase, don't do this. Let me go. He came for me. Let me go and talk to him."

"No, Jody." He pulled her back into his arms, his hands moving helplessly through her long curls. "I have to do this one last thing. Then it will all be over, I promise."

She realized there was no point in arguing with him. At that moment, she hated Spence House and its determined ghost, hated her own meddlings and stubborn yearnings. But it was too late to lay blame; too late to rub a magical piece of jewelry or snap her heels and make a wish.

A long, shuddering sob racked her body as she pulled away from him. "I . . . it should have been me. You were supposed to go home."

Chase glanced at Ali, worry showing on his face. "Let's take her back to Camille."

"There's no time," Ali explained. "It would be best if she waits here. She's safer hidden in the woods. The captain most certainly will have watchers around the mansion."

"I'll be fine," Jody said, thinking if they really believed she was going to stay put, they were both living in a dream world. "I do feel safer here by the tree. I'll wait right here."

Chase nodded, then pivoted back to her. "Jody, if I don't come back by dawn, promise me you'll try to make it back to Hampleton without me."

"No," she said stubbornly. "Either we go back together, or not at all." She didn't need to remind herself she'd planned to send him back alone.

"Jody."

"Don't argue with me," she snapped to hide the fear clawing its way up her spine. "I won't leave without you."

"Damn it, Jody, I don't have time for this!"

"Well, neither do I! We don't get a say in the matter, Chase. Just go off and be heroic, but . . . her voice cracked, "come back to me."

He didn't answer that. He only looked at her, his eyes drenching her in so many emotions, she couldn't move or breath.

Ali offered her one of his robes to ward off the chill of the wee hours. Then, from a pocket hidden deep within his many layers of muslin dress, he produced a small pearl-handled dagger. "For your protection, madame."

Jody wasn't sure she'd be able to use the razor-sharp knife, but having it would give her some measure of safety. As she took it, she clutched Ali's massive arm. "Take care of him," she pleaded.

"With my life, madame." Then he gave her a direct look. "Do not try to follow us. You would only complicate things."

She watched as they mounted their horses and rode off into the night. Ali was right, of course. Until dawn. She'd wait until dawn, then she'd wait no more.

Alone, she fell down underneath the shelter of the magnolia and wept.

Chapter Sixteen

"Choose your weapon, master."

Ali stood in the shelter of a mass of small cedar trees, about a hundred yards away from the cabin where Markham was holding Sarah. On the red clay ground before him lay a heavy machete with a gold jewel-encrusted hilt. Next to it lay a smaller light cavalry saber with a curved blade and leather pommel. This one caught Chase's eye. Gold filigree etched its guard cup. It was an exquisite weapon, but Chase wasn't sure he'd be able to do it justice.

"What about guns?" he asked, eyeing the cabin. "Don't you have a musket or a flintlock or something we can shoot? I saw a fine Springfield rifle in the gun cabinet back in the library. How about we go get it real quick. And I did pack the revolvers in my saddlebag, remember?"

Ali shook his head. "We have the element of surprise in our favor. Two guns against so many—it would be foolish. We must kill them slowly, one by one. We'll inch our way on the ground, and distract them." Pulling a small pearl-handled dagger out of the top of one of his high boots, he added, "If I can't overpower them and snap their necks, I'll

262

use this.'' Then, with a shrug, ''But you are welcome to bring along your revolvers.''

Chase understood the tactic, whether he liked it or not. ''Okay, Rambo, but don't you think Markham's expecting us?''

Ali gave him a puzzled look but answered his question anyway. ''I do not know if he has thought this through. I believe young Sarah has interfered with his plans. If he is waiting for us, I do not think he will shoot you.''

Chase nodded. ''No, he wants me alive too badly.''

''And it's very possible that the captain isn't even in there. He could be looking for Agnes Jodelyn.''

That concept chilled Chase to the bone. ''God, I hope not.'' He also hoped Jody had the good sense to stay hidden. ''How many do you think are in there?''

''Four, when I last saw them.'' Ali shifted positions, lifting his head as if sniffing the wind. ''With luck, they will have drunk heavily of the bourbon they stole from Miss Martha, and we will be able to tie them up and leave them alive. Me, I will not hesitate to kill them, but I can see it's unsettling to you. Master John never liked killing either, even though he did it with uncommon valor.'' He nodded. ''Master John has seen the elephant many times.''

Chase picked up the cavalry saber. ''I don't have uncommon valor, and I've never been in the thick of war, but I won't let them harm an innocent girl.''

''Not so innocent,'' Ali corrected, ''but she is just a child. We must do what we can to help her, and hope she's learned this lesson well. Do you know how to wield a sword, Chase Spence?''

Chase shrugged. ''I've had a few fencing lessons—I guess I can parry and thrust and sidestep enough to save my skin.''

Where he lacked skill, he'd use logic. He couldn't let his rage get the best of him. Unlike John Hample, he would not allow his love for Jody to become his weakness. Instead, it would be his strength.

''Use the sidestep as much as possible; remember to circle your opponent, keep him guessing,'' Ali suggested. ''Of course, these men are volunteers, not exactly the best of the Union army. Except for Captain Markham. He is a West Point graduate.''

"Now, isn't that special," Chase said under his breath. Giving Ali a determined look, he said, "I'll take the saber." He couldn't help but enjoy the feel of the slick sword in his hand. And, sickening as the thought was, he'd take great pleasure in slicing it through Markham's gut.

Ali inclined his head. "A good choice, sir. It was my master's. He ordered it from Damascus and he carried it into battle many times. He retired it when Jeb Stuart presented him with a new one. He did not want to insult his commander, you understand?''

"I understand," Chase said, hoping some of his ancestor's honor had rubbed off on him. "I'll try not to mess it up." In the moonlight, he saw a brief inscription scrolled across the glinting steel. "The Sword of *Dahr*. What does it mean?''

Ali bowed low to sweep up his own heavy, jeweled weapon. "Eternity," he said simply before turning toward the cabin.

Eternity. Chase knew the word well, had lived several eternities since he'd left Jody sitting forlorn and heartbroken, underneath that splendid magnolia tree. Now, as he followed Ali belly-crawl style through the damp, dank forest bed, inching along slowly, he wondered if he hadn't lived one too many eternities. He was tired, worried, and so angry that he was ready to kill anything or anyone—just so he could get back to Jody and take her home again.

Slowly, like a giant anaconda, Ali advanced toward the silent cabin, motioning for Chase to do the same. The night had advanced along with them. The coming dawn teased at them through the canopy of trees surrounding the cabin.

"A man sleeps heaviest just before the light," Ali said philosophically, his eyes keen on the cabin.

"Except us," Chase replied, his nonchalant tone belying the apprehension curling in his belly.

"Little sleep, little talk, little food," Ali shot back. "It is the discipline of the Absolute One.''

Chase gave an appreciative nod, wishing the Absolute One would send down an Egg McMuffin right about now. Nah, he'd probably be too damned nervous to eat it anyway. Anxious, he asked "What in hell are we waiting for?"

Ali lifted a hand. "I am making sure no watchers are surrounding the cabin. It is too quiet, but we cannot wait much longer. You are prepared to do this?"

"Hell, yes."

"Then we shall advance. Do not draw your weapon unless you need to. You take care of the child. I'll do the rest."

With that, the two men split up, Ali taking the front of the cabin to distract any guards, while Chase's assignment was to go in through the back to find Sarah.

Chase waited, tapping an impatient foot, his whole body primed for battle. This little adventure could almost be fun, if so many lives didn't hang in the balance. He counted slowly, knowing Ali's plan was to take the men one by one. Ali had assured him he could do this, ten seconds per man.

Chase heard a door creaking open, then started counting. There was a slight scuffle followed by a soft moan. Swallowing, he reckoned Ali had opted to go ahead and kill the first man. Again, Chase counted slowly to ten. Again, he heard a scuffle, this one more spirited, but just as deadly, apparently, from the surreal silence that descended over the woods after the last of the scuffling sounds had echoed out over the thicket. His heart pounding off the seconds in a fast-pitched march, Chase counted again, this time closing his eyes to wait for the sickening sound of a man being murdered. It came, right on cue.

"Okay." He knew Ali would finish off the last man. Unless it was Markham. He hoped it was. He'd asked Ali to hold back on killing the captain. Chase felt he had to be the one to do that job. After waiting, he hopped up and took a giant lunge at the half-rotten door, splintering it away from its bolt, along with all the muscles and tendons in his shoulder—or so it felt—as he fell into the dank cabin.

A muffled scream followed his entrance. Sarah. Well, at least she was still alive. In the semidarkness, Chase saw her sitting on the bed in the far corner. Her eyes were bright with fright; her mouth, thankfully, was tied shut, and her hands and legs were tied enough to make it impossible for her to move from the bed.

He rushed across the dirt-packed floor, his tone soothing as he untied her. "Sarah, honey, it's me. Ch—John. I'm going to get you out of here."

Sarah squirmed her relief. When Chase finally took the filthy rag away from her mouth, she cried out, "I knew you'd come, John, but I wish you hadn't."

"Don't be silly," Chase admonished, anxious to get back to Jody. "C'mon, let's get you home before dawn."

"I'm sorry," she said, her eyes flying to the front door of the cabin. Chase looked at her. Then, a sinking feeling dragging through his stomach, he turned toward the door.

"Major Spence, we meet again," Captain Markham said, his eyes trained on Chase while his revolver remained trained on Ali's temple. Chase went for his own gun, but the captain pressed the revolver further into Ali's skin. "Don't try it. I assure you, I have no qualms about blowing this heathen's head off."

Chase looked from the captain to Ali. "I miscounted, master," Ali said with an apologetic shrug. "He let me kill all of his men, then he ambushed me." The message in Ali's dark eyes was one of defeat. He wanted Chase to take a chance and go for his gun anyway.

Chase knew Ali would die for him, but Chase couldn't bring himself to let it happen. Dropping his hand, he said to Markham, "What do you want from me?"

Shoving Ali into the room, Markham sneered as he held the revolver on all three of them. "Oh, just what should rightfully be mine in the first place. Your wife. After all, I've had her already, before you married her, of course. She gave herself to me, thinking to save you. Imagine my surprise to find you still alive. It won't happen again."

Chase made a move forward, but the gun stopped him. His fists in tight balls, he said, "Leave her alone. She's done nothing to deserve this."

"Oh, but she has," Markham replied, a feral smile showing on his handsome face. "She's betrayed her country, her heritage, and me. I do not take too kindly to being made a laughingstock.''

''You're wrong,'' Chase said, watching the madman in front of him for some sign of weakness. Chase might not know the best military tactics, but he knew in his heart he was going to kill this man, somehow. ''Leave the women out of this; take me, do whatever you want, but don't harm them any further. They're both innocent.''

Sarah sobbed softly. ''It's too late, John. He's already sent his men out to find Agnes.''

The captain looked at her as if he'd only just realized she was still in the room. ''And I have you to thank for all the wonderful information, my sweet child.'' Glancing back at Chase, he said, ''Your naive little sister actually believed I wanted to marry her; she also believed I was only after Agnes for spying. Silly child—Agnes has done little to damage the Union's hold over you rebels. I simply want her to suffer, the way she's made me suffer. And I want to see her rebel lover dead, once and for all!''

''Why?'' Chase asked, unable to fathom such hatred.

Captain Markham bowed slightly. ''Well, because I love Agnes, of course. And once you're good and dead, she'll come around to seeing things my way.''

He moved toward Sarah, reaching out to touch one of her blond curls. ''Little Sarah here agrees that Agnes needs to be disciplined. She supplied me with all the details, whenever I needed them. Let me be the first to congratulate you on your nuptials, by the way.''

''I'm sorry,'' Sarah said again, shrinking away from Markham's touch. ''He . . . he tricked me.''

Chase gave her a reassuring look. ''It's not your fault.''

Captain Markham laughed harshly. ''No, indeed, the fault lies with your brother and his lover—excuse me—his new wife.'' Poking Chase with the gun, he said, ''Ol' Jeb must miss your expertise terribly. My sources tell me Rebel troops have advanced near the Rappahannock River. Union casualties have been heavy, but no matter. I'll make up the loss by handing General Hooker your head on a platter. And this time, I'll hang you myself just to make sure you're

...ad.'' With a sneer, he added, ''I was too busy
... ...our lover last time. Ah, but what a pleasure it was—
...ouldn't contain my excitement. I won't be so enamored
this time.''

Chase blocked out the image of that particularly ugly
scene, wondering just how much Agnes had to suffer at the
hands of this lunatic. Jody would not follow the same path,
he silently vowed.

Wanting to goad the egotistical captain, he said, ''I guess
an outcast such as yourself has to take a woman by force.
How does it feel knowing she loathed your touch? How does
it feel now, to know that she loves me enough to die for
me, and that I will do the same for her?''

The jibe hit its mark. The captain stepped forward, his
nostrils flaring, his words filled with venom. ''I'll show you
how it feels. I'll have my way with her, while you watch,
and then I'll hang both of you.''

Chase took a calming breath, telling himself not to lose
his cool. Markham was a walking time bomb, and Chase
knew if he just kept taunting the man, Markham would explode one way or another. He only hoped Ali would be
ready when it happened.

''She is my wife,'' he reminded the captain, the thought
of this scum bag's hands on Jody enough to make him see
red. ''And you will never again touch her. I'll see you in
hell first. Of course, even the devil himself might turn you
away. You're just not wanted in any society, good or bad.
How does it feel, Captain, to be so vile, so ineffective, that
your own men hate you and criticize you behind your
back?''

The explosion came, hard and swift. The captain raised
his revolver, but he didn't shoot. Chase saw the hit coming,
then felt a white-hot spasm of pain that centered on his left
temple and left fiery stars before his eyes while Sarah's
scream of horror shrilled through his aching skull.

He fell to his knees, a spurt of warm blood curling down
his cheekbone. Knowing he was going to pass out, he gritted
his teeth and shouted, the sound of his own words hollow
in his pain-etched brain. ''Run, Ali! Sarah!''

Ali sprang into action, grabbing Sarah by the arm. "Go, child!" She did as he told her, her skirts ballooning out behind her slight form. "Go home, to Camille," he called, watching her as she spilled out into the now full daylight.

Turning back to Chase, he found Captain Markham's revolver in his face instead.

"Sit down," Markham said, "or I will kill you, and this time I'll make very sure you don't survive."

Ali plopped on the floor beside Chase. Dizzily, Chase raised his head and mumbled, "You were supposed to run, Ali."

"I will not leave you," the giant said solemnly.

"But you have to . . . get back to Jody. You have to protect her . . . that's a command, Ali. Whatever happens, you stick with her—don't leave her side and don't bring her anywhere near here."

Ali watched as he slumped over against the frame of the bed. Silently, he waited as Markham gathered their weapons and placed them on a nearby table, all the while training his own revolver on Chase.

"I want to kill him," Markham admitted. "But I have to wait. I want her here to watch." Pivoting, he held the gun on Ali again. "You will go and get her. You will bring her here to me. Or he will die a slow and torturous death, and I'll burn Camille Plantation to the ground; then I'll take little Sarah as my personal hostage and camp follower. It won't be pretty for a girl with her delicate sensibilities." He grinned conspiringly. "I would love to take dear Agnes, too. But I have other plans for her. I might be forced to kill every one of them—his family that is—for harboring a criminal of war."

Ali knew when to throw all his cards on the table. "That will not be necessary. I will do your bidding."

"Somehow, I thought you might. You have until sunset." Markham summoned him to his feet, then pointed him toward the door by way of his revolver. "And please do not try anything rash. I have your sword; I have his saber. I will not mind using either to chop him apart. Or I could just shoot him and be done with it."

Ali nodded his understanding; then stooping to go out the cabin door, turned to face the captain. "I shall return with Mistress Agnes. I have no fear of you, so when I return, I intend to kill you before you can carry out your threats."

Before Markham could respond, Ali was gone, but the three men he'd killed with his bare hands—not his weighty sword or the dagger Markham had found on him—were proof that he could be a dangerous adversary. Captain Markham wiped the sweat from his brow; then he reached for a bottle of whiskey.

Jody watched the sun lift its yellow head over the horizon, her heart hammering a constant nervous beat against her chest. She'd paced a path underneath the magnolia. If someone didn't come soon, she'd run all the way to that damned cabin!

All sorts of horrible images replayed in her head. Was Chase lying somewhere, bleeding, or worse, dead? Had Markham taken him away as a prisoner of war? Was Sarah being tortured or abused? Where was Ali?

Glancing at the road, she'd already decided she'd wait until full light before setting out for the cabin. Earlier, several Union soldiers had passed by at a fast trot, barely missing her as she'd hidden behind a clump of pine saplings. If she didn't want to be discovered, she'd have to stay back inside the woods by the road. With the road markers as her guide, she thought she could find the secluded spot where the cabin was located. But it would take her an hour or so to get there, at best.

Taking a deep breath, she patted the small dagger Ali had given her, then stepped gingerly through the thick bramble. "Hang on, Chase. I'm coming."

About a half-hour later, a figure appeared up on the road, startling Jody back behind a blackberry bush. With Ali's cloak drawn around her, Jody leaned forward enough to see who was approaching. Sarah!

Rushing out, Jody called to the bedraggled girl. "Sarah, Sarah, are you all right?"

Seeing Jody, the girl immediately starting sobbing hysterically. "He . . . he has John and Ali. He's a madman! I didn't want to tell him, but he said . . . he threatened to do horrible things!''

Jody took the trembling, filthy girl into her arms, her own tears falling silently while Sarah's wailing turned into a kind of soft keening. "It's all right," Jody said soothingly, pulling Sarah back into the shelter of the trees. "Just tell me, are they still alive?"

Jody bit back another sob, lifting her tear-streaked face to Jody's. "Yes, but he . . . he hit John with his gun. The blood—it was awful."

Jody bit back the lump of fear threatening to choke off her very breath. "As long as he's alive, we have a chance of saving him, Sarah." Steadying herself as well as the girl, she said, "Will you help me to save him?"

Sarah began sobbing all over. "Yes," she managed to say. "I never knew Richard could be so cruel. I only wanted him to . . . to—"

"Take *me* away," Jody finished, her heart going out to the girl in spite of what she'd tried to do. "You wanted your life back, Sarah. You wanted to feel safe and secure and happy again. War is a horrible thing, not the romantic noble venture men make it out to be. And if the truth be told, they, too, are as afraid of war and what it brings as we are."

Sarah looked up, her eyes studying Jody's face. "You do understand."

"More than you'll ever know," Jody whispered, the tears falling down her cheeks not only for John Hample and Chase, and this frightened girl, but for her own noble father and her sad, disillusioned mother, too. And—for herself. She'd been too young to understand her father's death. She'd never mourned, she'd just let the bitterness build up inside her until it had turned into a mortal fear of love. Swallowing back her own pain, she said, "When you love someone, you learn to be brave. You'll survive this, Sarah, I promise. And I won't be a threat to you anymore. I'll be gone soon. Then you will have Camille, and your family, and you will find true love. You life will change, but you have to be strong and stand firm."

271

The girl hiccupped. "But I'm such a coward. I told Captain Markham everything—everything—because I couldn't bear all the vile things he threatened to do to me."

"You're not a coward," Jody said, stroking the girl's tangled locks away from her dirt-smeared face. "You did what you had to do to survive. And if we want John to make it, we have to stay calm and think."

Sarah took a long breath. "But how?"

Impatient to get to Chase, Jody tried not to snap at the frightened girl. "You go on home to Camille and get cleaned up. If anyone asks what happened, tell them you got lost picking blackberries." The many bramble scratches on the girl's arms and face would attest to that.

"What about you? What were you doing in the woods?"

"I was on my way to find Ali and John. Ali warned us that the captain took you." Worried, she asked, "Sarah, did he do anything . . . to harm you?"

Silent tears fell down Sarah's pale face. "No, but he talked about all sorts of things."

"Put it out of your mind," Jody advised. "When you find the man you'll marry, it won't be the way the captain described."

Sarah sniffed, then wiped her tears, a new determination evident in her demeanor and tone. "I don't think I'll care to marry for a long time. I intend to take care of my family from now on. I just want to go home. I want to see Mother."

"I know how you feel," Jody said, lifting the girl up. "Now, go. I'm going to the cabin to see what I can do. And I'm depending on you to be strong and responsible."

Sarah nodded. "I will, I promise."

A look of understanding passed between them. "And Tucker," Jody said, her words full of hope and longing. "Please take care of little Tucker."

"He'll always be a part of our family," Sarah said, the look in her eyes devoid of any resentment.

A sense of peace settled over Jody. Knowing Tucker would be taken care of gave her the strength to leave him. She had to remind herself that he'd go on to have a long and full life. "Thank you," she said. "I'm going to my husband now."

"Be careful," Sarah said, a worried look on her face. Then, "Miss Agnes, I'm so sorry for all the suffering I've caused you."

Jody hugged the girl. "You're already forgiven, Sarah." Giving the girl a gentle shove, Jody pushed her toward Camille. "I hope to be home soon, myself."

Never had words been more truly spoken. Sprinting down the dusty clay road, Jody headed to the Calhoun cabin. This showdown was about to end, one way or the other.

Ali stayed to the woods, watching the road with a keen eye. The way he figured it, the captain's remaining troops had deserted him. Obviously, his own men were afraid to have any part of his obsession with Agnes Calhoun. That, or he'd ordered them to remain hidden away. Whatever, Ali would take no chances. He was in a fine quandary, torn between his loyalty to his master—or the man playing his master—and the woman he'd been commanded to protect. He'd stay with the woman, no doubt, but he'd also have to figure out a way to save his master.

But, Ali Rasheem, giant, brave warrior, mystic, and all around good guy, had never come across a woman more determined than Agnes Jodelyn Calhoun, the Second. Now, he watched, amazed, as she flew down the road, her long skirts and his black cape lifting out behind her like a ship's flag, her eyes misty and wild, and in her white-knuckled hand, the dagger he'd given her for protection. The Yanks would be wise to go back North.

Stepping carefully onto the road, he waved to her. "Mistress, it is I, Ali."

Jody, of single mind and intent purpose, stopped so suddenly she almost fell back on her bottom. Gasping for breath, her hair plastered around her face and neck, her arms scratched and bleeding, she let out a soft, keening moan at seeing him alone. "Oh, no, no. Ali, where is he? Please, please, tell me he's not dead."

Ali reached her before she slumped onto the clay dirt.

"No, mistress, he is still alive. I am to bring you to him. But my master has forbidden me to carry out Captain Markham's demands. I am to guard you with my life, and that means I cannot let you go to the cabin."

He wasn't prepared for the burst of unbridled rage that shot through Jody. With a strength that even Ali couldn't control, she pushed him away, then raised up on her feet, the dagger held up in the air in front of her. "Are you telling me after all we've been through, Chase is just going to die and leave me all alone? Are you telling me that I'm supposed to stand back and let that happen? Are you telling me to simply give up?"

At a loss for words, Ali could only nod. Then, before he could form a rational thought, Jody continued her tirade. "I am not Agnes. I will not stand by and let Chase die. Isn't that the whole reason I was brought back, anyway? Aren't I supposed to save him? Didn't you tell me yourself, you watched John die because of Agnes—so Agnes could be saved?" Not giving him time to so much as grunt, she went on. "Well, by God, I won't just stand here in the middle of the road like some helpless ninny. And I don't give a fig what Mr. High-and-Mighty Chase Spence commanded you to do."

Pointing a finger in his face, she glared up at him. "Now, Ali, you will take me to that cabin and together, we will save Chase." Holding up the dagger in one hand and her brooch in the other, she vowed, "And then, I'm going to rub this thing until I turn blue, and . . ." her voice cracked, but she didn't let it stop her, "then Chase and I are going home." Stepping close, she lifted her chin, her eyes glued to the big man. "Do you understand me?"

Ali understood. He understood, that even though he'd been in this predicament once before, with another woman who looked very much like this one, things weren't going to turn out the same this time, because this woman was different. He'd been given a second chance right along with these reincarnates of his master and Agnes. And, destiny be damned, he wouldn't stand by idly this time. He'd go to his master, and his own inevitable death, but this time, he'd die knowing he'd done everything possible to save Chase Spence and the woman he loved.

Placing a hand on Jody's heaving shoulder, he said, "I am with you, Mistress Spence. I will take you to Chase Spence. And I will do my best to help you save him. After that, it is in the hands of Allah."

Jody snorted, then wiped her nose. "Allah, my foot. From now on, I'm calling the shots. Now, lead me to that cabin, Ali."

Ali Rasheem looked toward the East and said a quick prayer. No time for a formal meditation. The wrath of this woman would be much worse than anything the One God could heap upon him. Turning, he raced to catch up with Jodelyn Calhoun Spence.

And he pitied Captain Richard Markham.

275

Chapter Seventeen

Chase looked up at the man standing over him, wondering when his time in this living hell would end. He was so tired, so worried about Jody, so ready to end this, that he didn't care if he lived or died. His temple throbbed, dried blood caked one side of his face and his vision was so blurry, at times he thought he was seeing two Captain Markhams. Not a good thing. One was quite enough to turn anyone's stomach.

They'd spent the better part of the last several hours playing an interesting little game. Chase sat on the hardened dirt floor, his hands tied to the bedpost behind him, his feet bound at the ankles, while the Captain pranced around like the hero of war his overblown ego believed him to be. He'd taunted Chase with so many threats and so many stories about Agnes, that Chase thought if rage could kill, the Captain would be a dead duck.

"Shall I continue, Major Spence?" Captain Markham asked, taking another swig from the bottle of whiskey he held just away from Chase's nose. He'd offered none to Chase, of course. No whiskey, no water, no food. Just the

276

pleasure of his demented company.

Chase didn't answer. What good would that do? The man had told him exactly what had happened between Agnes and all the men in her life. And he'd done it with props—the rest of the letters Agnes had written to John. Somehow, Captain Markham had intercepted a good part of their correspondence and kept it hidden here in the cabin for his own reading pleasure.

Now, like a fox returning to his lair, he paced and snorted, reading more to himself than to Chase.

"Let's see," Markham said, putting his whiskey bottle back to his lips. "Where did I leave off?" Ignoring Chase, he continued reading:

Dear John,

How could we have known all that would happen in the last few months? This war, my marriage to Will, my father's involvement in politics, all of these things have torn us apart, just when we had found each other. I love you, John. Always. I will not be disloyal to my husband, or my father's wishes, but in my soul, you will always be my only true love.

The Captain stopped, his red-rimmed eyes centering on Chase. "No, she was never disloyal, physically. But she sure pined away for you, didn't she, Major? And it didn't take her long after Will was killed, to come running to you for protection. Took her even less time to change her loyalties from Union to Confederate. Traitor. Whore."

He stopped pacing, his head going up like a feral animal's, his nostrils flaring. "Did you hear something, Major?"

Chase rolled his head, wishing the floor would just swallow him up. He'd worked with the tightly wrapped ropes around his arms and hands until he was sure his fingers were bleeding from rawness. He wasn't in the mood to pacify this sick puppy.

"I didn't hear a thing, Captain. Must have been the wind."

Or Ali. Sooner or later, Chase knew, Ali would be back. He sincerely hoped it was sooner, and that Jody was safe back at Camille by now.

Markham continued. "I sent the last letter to you. The one where she begged you to come home. She feared for your family. How sweet, how very noble. She took my threats seriously, as well she should have." His laugh was harsh. "I sent it, and I waited. I knew you would come. I knew I'd soon have both of you exactly where I wanted you."

Chase could see it all so clearly, as if he'd actually read the letter himself. "She needed me."

"I could have made her happy," Markham said, his voice full of hatred. "I intended to marry her, take her away from this God-forsaken place. But she refused my advances; she'd only allow our relationship to be one for the cause—helping those poor, wretched slaves." He asked, "Did you know this place was a station of the Underground Railroad?" Moving close to Chase, he lowered his head, his stale breath smelling of whiskey. "But that's all over now, isn't it, Major Spence? Our sweet Agnes shifted her skirts faster than a foot soldier reloading his rifle. How can you be sure she won't betray you exactly the way she's betrayed me?"

In spite of Markham's bad breath, Chase didn't flinch or look away. He felt a certain amount of pity for the poor, disillusioned captain. But not enough to be kind. He looked up, his eyes clearing enough that he could stare the captain down. "That's so simple, even you ought to be able to figure it out, Markham. She loves me."

The truth was more than the demented captain could bear. Crashing his whiskey bottle to the floor, he dropped his trusty revolver for the first time, then lurched for Chase. "I will not wait for your lover to come to you. I'll hang you right now, with pleasure. And then, I believe I will have her thrown into prison, so she can suffer until I come for her."

Just then, the door burst open and Markham, taken by surprise, spun around only to find Jody's dagger thrust toward his face. But even drunk, he was too quick for Jody. Screaming her wrath, she managed to nick him on the cheek before he pinned her arm with both hands, twisting it behind her back in a painful grip, so that she was forced to drop the knife.

Chase struggled with his ropes, his eyes never leaving Jody. Had he really expected her to stay put?

Breathing heavily, Markham hissed at her. "You're just in time, dear, sweet Agnes. You can have a front row seat at your rebel lover's hanging." Throwing her down beside Chase, he grabbed his gun again, waving it at both of them.

Jody didn't care. She threw herself against Chase, tears of joy robbing her of any rational thoughts. "Oh . . . you're alive. Thank God, you're still alive."

Chase managed a weak grin. "You shouldn't have come here, but damn, it's good to see you."

Markham yanked her away, the gun held so close to her head, her pulse beat echoed through its sleek chamber. "Get up," he said through gritted teeth, "and get that coil of rope over on the table." Pushing her forward, he watched as she did as he told her. "Now, you're going to string that rope across that high beam over there. Get up on a chair and throw it over, my dear. I want you to be part of this. I want you to watch him suffer."

Jody stopped in her tracks. "No," she said defiantly, her eyes going from the gun to Markham's face. "I won't do it."

Chase saw all the warning signs, but poor Markham didn't know the woman he was dealing with had a lot more gumption than her confused namesake. To get her attention, Chase groaned.

Concerned, Jody looked at him. "Are you in pain? What has this monster done to you?"

Chase gave her a meaningful look. "Oh, nothing much, other than trying to get me to admit you're a Confederate spy, threatening to hang me and send you to prison, and reading the missing letters to me. Do as he says. Go ahead. He's going to kill both of us anyway."

Jody lifted her chin back to Markham. "Like hell," she said, her face inches from his. "You see, my love, the brilliant captain here forgot one thing."

Markham gave her a puzzled look, a menacing grin forming his sweaty face. "And what might that be, my dear?"

"Ali-Rasheem," she said, just as the giant rushed into the room with a blood-curdling scream.

Chase watched the action before him as if he were caught in the middle of a slow-motion movie. He saw Ali lunge for the captain, watched as the smaller man fell down, heard the gun discharge, saw the flash of fire that followed, heard the loud pop of a bullet hitting the ceiling, smelled the acrid stench of gunpowder. Hearing Jody's scream, he prayed that she wasn't hit, then struggled as Ali came rushing over to cut his ropes free with Jody's discarded dagger.

"Up, master," Ali shouted, his eyes watching the twitching body of Richard Markham. "He is not dead yet."

Chase shook his ropes free, then rubbed the circulation back into his numb limbs. "Jody?"

"I'm here," she said, rushing into his arms as he tried to stand. "We've got to get you away from him."

Ali threw Chase his saber, and grinning, clenched his own sword in his hand. "Go, master. I'll take care of the clean up."

Jody urged Chase toward the door, but he stopped. "No. I can't leave yet."

"What?" Shocked, Jody halted, her eyes searching his face. "No, Chase let it go. Let Ali finish it."

But Chase knew what he had to do. "Don't you see?" he said on a low whisper. "This is it for me. This is where John Hample lost his soul. He wouldn't admit Agnes had done anything dishonorable, so Markham tortured him by making him watch as his men took her away. John Hample was helpless, Jody. He didn't die right here, but he might as well have. They destroyed him. He tried to get back to her, but he was too late. I have to avenge that."

A sob racked Jody's body. Clinging to him, she said, "No, you don't have to finish it. We've already won. Ali killed the others, and we're . . . we're safe now. We survived; we can go home. Please, Chase."

Gently extracting himself from her arms, he said, "Jody, wait outside."

She stepped in his path. "Don't do this! You don't have to prove anything to anyone. Let's just go home, now!"

"Ali?" Chase called, his eyes on Markham, who was now alert and sweating profusely, "take her outside."

Ali stepped forward, lifting Markham up by his collar. "Master, I will be honored to take care of this swine for you."

The captain looked from one to the other, the paleness of his skin indicating that he wasn't sure which of the two he'd rather have kill him. In a last-ditch effort to save himself, he said, "You'll both die for this. They'll come for you and you'll regret you ever saw me."

Chase looked at Ali. "Oh, we already regret that, don't we, Ali?"

Ali dropped Markham at Chase's feet. "Indeed we do, master. You more so than I." Giving Chase a pat on the back, he bowed. "Have at him, Chase Spence. And do not leave anything for the buzzards. This one is too vile even for those scavengers to pick apart."

Markham's skin turned sickly white at that image. Choking slightly, he said, "You wouldn't kill an unarmed man— you Southerners are too damned noble."

Chase nodded. "Yes, unlike you, we have some principles. Ali, would you fetch the good captain's cavalry sword?"

Ali hastened to Markham's haversack and saddlebag. Spotting a scabbard, he pulled out the regulation sword, then tossed it to Chase. "It is not much of a weapon, sir, but he will not be unarmed."

Jody stood in the doorway, wondering why it was that men always had to make a game out of everything. Ali and Chase were enjoying this, circling the captain as if he were a cornered rat.

"What do you think, Markham?" Chase asked, swaying on his feet slightly, his grin half-cocked. "Do you think this will be a fair fight?" He lifted his own exquisite sword, then bowed low before handing the captain's sword to him. With a cavalier attitude that would have done Errol Flynn proud, he asked, "Are you ready for a duel to the death?"

Jody rushed forward before Markham could answer. "This is ridiculous. Let's leave him and get out of here. He's not worth the effort."

Chase nudged her back, his eyes warning her to hush. "Remember when the captain paid us a little visit the other day, love? He didn't know I was stowed away in the kitchen fireplace of all things, did he?"

Markham hissed like a dying snake.

Chase continued, gaining much-needed strength as he slowly began circling his opponent. "You wouldn't let me confront him then; you had to be brave and talk with him yourself."

Lifting a brow, he added, "Then I found out, thanks to the captain's drunken ramblings, that you intended to meet him here last night, around midnight I believe." At her gasp, his expression hardened. "He actually tried to convince me that you wanted to be with him. Of course, I know you were only trying to do what you thought you had to do, right?" He shrugged. "Well, that's exactly what I'm doing now."

Jody groaned. "Really, is that what this is all about? You have to prove something, to me, to yourself, simply because I tried to save your skin—that's so utterly ridiculous." Stepping between the two men, she repeated, "Let's get out of here. We can argue about who's the bravest amongst us once we're away from this lunatic."

Chase held her at arms length, a determined gleam in his eyes. Lord, he was a handsome devil, and at the moment, an irrational idiot, but she loved him anyway.

"Please," she whispered, "don't do this."

Giving her one final warning glare, he said in a voice sweetened with daring, "Now, sweetheart, you've had your bit of fun, tricking the captain and almost fooling me. Well, now it's my turn!"

With that, he lunged for the captain, taking him completely off guard. Markham quickly composed himself, however, and the fight began in earnest as the two men circled each other. Thanks to Ali's debilitating blow to Markham's gut, Chase's odds were now slightly better.

Jody backed against the wall, shaking her head at the

stupidity of the male species. What did she care if Chase got his insides split apart? Burying her head in her hands, she knew she cared a lot. She'd marched through time and hell, to get to this point, so she could save him and take him home. Now, she had to watch as he tried to prove his manhood. Oh, if she ever did get him back to Hampleton, she'd give him a good piece of her mind!

Markham thrust his sword toward Chase, but Chase gracefully sidestepped the blow.

"Excellent, master," Ali said encouragingly, like a trainer on the sidelines of a boxing match. "He is weak; it will not take you very long to bring him to his knees."

Chase grinned, then parried with his left hand, avoiding yet another of Markham's ineffective strikes. "I do believe you're right, my friend. He seems a bit disconcerted, don't you think?"

Ali grinned an ugly grin; then he folded his hands across his huge chest. "Yes, master. Captain Markham seems a bit out of his element without his loyal band of followers to do his dirty work."

Markham's rage grew as bloodred as his sweating skin. Chase thought if the captain had had all his senses about him, and about a fifth less whiskey in him, he would have seen that Chase and Ali were orchestrating him right into a corner. It didn't take a smart man to figure out where Markham's brilliant career had gone wrong. The man couldn't control his temper. This would prove to be his ultimate downfall.

Angry now, he lunged toward Chase and came perilously close to slicing through the sleeve of Chase's sweat-smeared white shirt. "I'll kill you, Spence, I swear it."

Chase looked completely at ease. He sidestepped just in time, then looked for his advantage, his every word as taunting as the silver flash of his sword in the waning afternoon light. "How many times have I heard that?" He winked over at Jody, then made a wry face at her boiling look.

Markham used the distraction to pierce Chase's forearm with the blade of his sword. That brought Chase's attention back to the man dancing before him.

"For heaven's sake, keep your eyes on him!" Jody shouted, the sight of blood on Chase's shirt making her queasy.

"Whatever you say, love," Chase replied, his sword slicing through the air near Markham's chest, his whole expression and demeanor now full of serious intent.

Jody watched, amazed that Chase had such a killer instinct buried inside him. Apparently, he'd inherited more of John Hample's bravery than he'd let on. Apparently, he himself had just discovered this darker side, and from the intensity of his actions, he planned to use it to its full advantage. Like a seasoned swordsman, he executed the proper stances, dancing with a graceful glee back and forth around the confines of the cabin. Each time Markham lashed out, Chase parried, then danced closer, his sword swishing through the still, hot air in a deadly rhythm.

The captain managed to keep backing up, but soon the only thing between him and the wall was about an inch of air. Realizing his mistake, he looked across at Chase just as Chase lifted his sword to come slicing down through the stale, musty air.

The hit met flesh across the captain's right sword arm, causing him to drop his weapon and grasp his bleeding shoulder, an expression of intense pain deforming his face into a twisted grimace.

Chase backed away, his breath coming in little spurts. "I do believe I have the advantage," he said to Ali.

"Yes, you do." Ali leaned forward, his big hands resting on his waist. "Time to finish the job, master."

Captain Markham looked up at Chase, then stumbled forward, trying in vain to grasp out at something, anything, while blood poured down his arm and over the hand holding his wound.

Spotting Jody cringing against the wall, he lunged for her in one last effort to claim her for his own. "Agnes—"

Jody screamed as he grabbed at her skirts, his bloody hands reaching up for the column of her neck. Before he'd ever touched her skin, the steely point of Chase's sword rammed into his mid-section, leaving him gasping for air as he twisted and fell heavily to the floor at her feet.

It was over. Chase dropped his sword and pulled Jody away from the gruesome sight of the open-eyed death scowl on Captain Richard Markham's twisted face. Taking her in his arms, he urged her outside into the sweet dusk, gulping in fresh air as he kissed her and soothed her tears.

"It's all right," he said, holding her tight. "It's all right now."

Jody knuckled him in the back with her balled up fists. "You could have been killed."

He lifted her chin with a finger. "Well, how about you? Planning to sneak away to meet that madman, then coming here today after I told Ali to keep you away—"

"I couldn't stay away!" she said, her eyes brimming with hot tears. "I couldn't let you die."

"It wasn't meant to be," he said, his harsh look turning tender. "This, Jody, this was meant to be." He kissed her, long and hard and lovingly. "Now, my darling, now we can go home."

"I'm ready," Jody said, taking his hand in hers. "I have the brooch right here. If we hurry, we can make it back to the magnolia before full dark."

Chase nodded, then turned to see Ali standing at the door of the cabin. "Wait," he told Jody.

Ali smiled broadly. "Master, I have something for you to take with you, as a token of this great adventure and your destiny." Ali held out the sword Chase had used to kill Markham. It was clean now; no trace of Markham's blood on it.

Chase took it. "Thank you." Then he looked inside the dank cabin. "There's something else I'd like to take back, too."

Ali inclined his head slightly. "Your love letters to your lady, and hers to you? I saw them lying about on the table. That son of a goat in there has defiled them with his touch."

Chase laughed, then headed inside to collect the letters. Stepping gingerly around Markham's body, he hurried back out to Ali. "Well, friend, we'll just have to un-defile them, won't we?"

Ali grinned. "You will have all the time in the world to do so, I imagine."

Jody walked over to the two men. "Ali," she said, taking the big man's hand in hers, "I want to thank you for helping me save Chase."

Ali bowed his head. "It was my duty, madame."

Chase slapped him on the back. "Well, apparently, you did such a fine job, you didn't go and get yourself killed, after all."

Ali looked up, his eyes filling with awe. "It is true. I am indeed still alive, am I not?"

"You are indeed," Chase said, shaking Ali's hand.

Jody poked Ali on his rock hard chest. "Go back to Camille, and get to know Dancy. She's a really sweet woman, you know?"

Ali rubbed the stubble on his chin, then grinned. "I do know—and perhaps it is time I pay more attention to my own amorous yearnings."

Chase took Jody by the arm to gather her close. "Can we depend on you, Ali, to take care of things in our absence?"

Ali clasped him on one shoulder. "Most certainly, Chase Spence, most certainly."

With a final wave of farewell, the giant man slipped on his Arabian stallion and rode away into the misty, mystical dusk.

Part Three
Home Again

Chapter Eighteen

An hour later, Chase and Jody stood underneath the magnolia tree holding each other tightly, the letters, the sword, and the brooch clutched between them.

"Okay, Dorothy," Chase said, his breath tickling her earlobe, "tap your heels together and think about home."

"Whatever it takes," Jody said, her hands wrapped around the brooch. "John Hample, we've accomplished our mission. We got married, and now know each other in the Biblical sense, we killed Markham, and we saved Ali and your family. Can we please go home?"

The wind shifted, blowing over them with a soft, warm intensity. The trees swayed and danced, their soft waltz a perfect symmetry to the two anxious hearts beating together beneath the magnolia tree where John Hample Spence had first fallen in love with Agnes Jodelyn Calhoun.

Jody lowered her head against Chase's chest. "I'm so scared."

He covered her hair with his free hand. "You—scared?" He chuckled. "We're safe now, Jody. Hold on to me."

Then, a great flash came, like a charge of lightning, filling

289

them with a kinetic energy that took their breaths away and left them disoriented and dizzy. Chase held her in the shelter of his arms, refusing to let her go even when his head seemed about to burst right off his body. Jody kept her eyes closed and her face buried against Chase's chest, listening for his heartbeat, using it as her guide, her lifeline.

The flash died away, and everything went completely still.

Swaying against Chase, Jody opened her eyes to look around. They were standing in the same spot, but . . .

"Chase, look! Look at the tree!"

Chase relaxed his protective grip on her to swivel around. "Same tree, just about forty feet taller," he said, letting out a whoop of joy. "We did it, Jody! We're home."

Jody danced around in the dusky pink light, her eyes on the welcome sight of Spence House looming in the distance. "We're here. We made it. We're home again."

He pulled her into his arms, kissing the tears away from her face. "Yes, and now, we can start our new life together. We can really be married and live here, in our house."

Jody stopped dancing, her heart dropping to her feet as reality hit with all the force of a tornado. "Chase, what are we going to tell everybody?"

"About what?"

"About us? Where we've been, what we've done. That we got married?"

He touched her cheek affectionately. "We'll tell them the truth."

She scoffed. "Yeah, sure. Well, we traveled back in time, pretended to be someone else, got married, then killed a Union officer. That'll go over real well just before they call the people from the loony bin to come and cart us away."

He smiled, loving every inch of her. Ironically, she was acting like the logical one right now. "No, silly. We'll tell them that we were so madly in love, we ran off and got married. We've been on our honeymoon."

"Without a word to anyone?"

"We're in love, we weren't thinking straight."

She eyed him, her mind clicking. "Well, that wouldn't exactly be a lie, would it?"

He yanked her into his arms. "No, that's not a lie. We are madly in love." A little catch of doubt in his voice, he added, "Aren't we?"

Jody leaned her head on his shoulder, pushing her own doubts away. "Yes, we are. That much is very true."

She didn't tell him that she was still deathly afraid of loving anyone, that all her doubts and fears remained as firmly planted in her mind as this old magnolia had remained firmly planted in the ground. She'd tell him all about that later, maybe. Right now, she just wanted to curl up and sleep for a year or so. With him by her side, of course.

Chase noticed her withdrawal, but chalked it up to exhaustion. "C'mon," he said, pulling her across the garden. "We'll take the company truck parked out back and go to the lake. We'll get cleaned up, and first thing in the morning, we'll set the plans in motion to rebuild this place."

Jody didn't argue with him. She'd won, after all. She'd saved this big, old house. She'd experienced two lifetimes. And she'd fallen in love with the most wonderful, aggravating man alive. What more could she ask for?

As they walked down the overgrown drive, she glanced up at the empty, dark house. For the first time, a fear crept into her overly confident psyche. That old saying, "Be careful what you ask for, you just might get it," came to mind.

"I wonder if John Hample's at peace now."

Chase stopped, looking up at the desolate house. "Jackson knew, Jody. He found John Hample there in the yard where I landed. John told him everything before he died. Jackson probably told the Chancellorsville story to protect Sarah. Papa Spence had just died, Miss Martha was ill— Jackson did what he had to do to save his family. Then he took John's body to the magnolia, that would have been John's last request, and found Agnes dead there." He turned to look up at the magnolia. "I think they're both buried in that grave, and I think Jackson buried them together because he knew how much they loved each other. In fact, I'm sure of it."

Jody shuddered and pulled Chase close. "Then he saved as many of the letters as he could find. I wonder if John ever got to read any of her letters.''

"I think he did," Chase said. "He answered her a few times. He talked about how he'd marry her and how they'd build their dream house in the new town." Tapping the tin box, he told her, "They're in here now, with Agnes's. We brought them back." He kissed her, then tugged her forward. "There's a lot we'll never understand, but we did what we set out to do. We avenged John's death, and this time, we saved part of Agnes, too."

Jody took the hand he offered her, so many questions running through her mind. She'd survived; she'd helped John Hample right his great wrong. She'd lived up to the task.

But what if she couldn't live up to her own expectations?

"It's just so romantic," Katie said again, wiping her red-rimmed eyes as they sat in Siwell's sipping sodas. "The whole town's talking about it, you know. How you stopped him from taking that house down. How on the very same day, he asked you to run away with him. I still can't believe it. Jody Calhoun, the only woman in this town who'd declared she didn't need a man to be happy, the only woman left who'd sworn she'd never get married because it only caused heartache, eloping with the most eligible, the best-looking man to ever set foot in Mitchell County! And not telling a soul where you were. Do you know how worried we all were?"

Jody sighed heavily, wondering why she felt so tired and forlorn, when she should be on top of the world. "I know. Grandpa's only told me about a thousand times. I swear, from the looks I'm getting right now, you'd think I'd run off with the city coffers or something."

Her tone rising with each heated word, she said, "This is my life, you know. This is my business, after all. I am a grown woman with a mind of my own. I didn't think I needed to clear it with everybody in Hampleton, Georgia, before I decided to go out and find myself a life."

Several nearby lunch customers stopped chewing long enough to listen to her tirade. Katie, long used to this kind of defensive reaction from her dear friend, smiled knowingly and patted Jody's hand. "Are you okay, really?"

"Really, I am," Jody said. She was about to tell her best friend that, no, she really wasn't all right, that she was scared to death of a lifetime commitment to Chase, even though she loved him to distraction, when footsteps echoed on the tiled floor and the man himself walked up to their booth.

Chase looked every bit as delicious as an ice cream sundae with a cherry on top, Jody decided, her gaze landing on her new husband's smiling face. And he was definitely just as yummy, and virtually calorie-free. He was doing everything he'd promised, too, and more.

To appease the city council, after he informed them he wouldn't be tearing down Spence House after all, he offered to buy up the entire block surrounding Spence House, and based on Jody's original idea of a Victorian village full of shops and eateries, (which she'd finally been able to discuss with him), he came up with a plan. The town would still have its shopping center and office complex, except now, everything would have a theme based on the history of Hampleton.

This would include antique stores, craft and gift shops, coffee shops and tea rooms, all those things tourists loved, including scheduled daily tours of Spence House. He was quick to tell the town leaders that it had all been Jody's idea, and he was ready and willing to see it through after careful analysis and several studies of other such small towns that had done the same thing. It was whimsical and risky, but Chase knew it would work. He had his ancestor's vision.

While the politicians and concerned citizens mulled that over, he began rebuilding Spence House, working his crew day and night to make the house secure, while Jody was in charge of the furnishings. Buying antiques was a lot more fun when you got to keep them for yourself. Having Chase and Spence House was more than a dream come true. It was almost too perfect. And therein lay her worst fear.

Chase's gray eyes swept over her, making her melt into

the cool vinyl of her seat, making her think of their nights alone in his little cabin, and all the nights they'd have together from now on, if she'd just get over this silly fear.

"Hi," he said, his eyes only for her.

"Hi," she said back, aware that every woman in the place was drooling into her blue plate special. "You looking for me?"

He smiled, and Jody could have sworn she heard a collective sigh emitting from their overly interested audience. "Yes, I was. But then I heard you the minute I entered the front door."

Katie piped up. "She's a little testy about the small town rumor mill." Patting the seat next to her, she inclined him to join them. "You know, Chase, you really haven't been fair to poor Jody."

Concerned, Chase glanced over at Jody. She did look a little pale. "How's that?"

Katie ignored Jody's warning glare and continued. "Well, darn it, we've all waited so long for the day she'd finally walk down the aisle, and what did you do? Took her away, where none of us even got a chance to see her as a bride or celebrate with her." Stabbing her crushed ice with her bent straw, she added, "It's just not fair. You ought to marry her all over again, to stop all these rumors flying about."

"I will," he said, his eyes never leaving Jody's drawn face. "How about it Jody? Want to marry me again—at Spence House?"

Jody's shocked expression was priceless, but Katie's comment went even further. "Oh, that'd be perfect. I mean, you've been working so hard on that house since you two got back. You must be spending a bundle, trying to get it back in shape and all. What better spot to get married, huh, Jody?"

Jody had to sit on her hands to keep from clawing away at both of them. How could they conspire against her like this? How could he put her on the spot like this, when he knew she'd been having doubts about the whole thing? She'd tried to talk to him, tried to tell him, but every time they were alone together, well, one thing always lead to another and . . . talking hadn't been a main priority. But, that was just like him, sweet-talking, instead of really talking.

Chase sat watching her, reading her thoughts like a front page. Ali had been right—they could almost read each other's minds. And he'd known, had *felt*, from the moment they'd returned, a kind of distance in her. She wouldn't admit it, but Jody Calhoun, time traveler, ghost chaser, fearless dagger-toting enchantress, was scared to death of facing reality.

And the reality was, that he loved her and she loved him, and they belonged together. You'd think going back in time to help some tarnished souls would have convinced her of that. Ah, but Jody, she was different. She was one tough case.

Leaning forward, he cupped his hands around his mouth. "What do you say, Jody? Want to get married all over again, for real, at Spence House, with the whole town as our witness?"

An evasive little light came on in Jody's eyes. "Uh, the house . . . it's not nearly finished, Chase. We couldn't possibly—"

"Yes, we could," he said, aware that half the town was listening. "And we will." Raising up, he pulled her to her feet. Then winking down at Katie, he said, "Thanks. What a wonderful idea." Before Jody could protest, he shouted out, "Hey, everyone, you're all invited to a wedding, at Spence House, as soon as we get it back in shape. I love Jody so much, I want to marry her all over again." Just to prove his point, he pulled her squirming body close and gave her a big, wet kiss that left her panting and angry, while everyone else applauded with delight.

Katie hopped up. "We'll be there, won't we?"

Everyone agreed, laughing and buzzing about. The news traveled the streets of Hampleton faster than a FedEx man on a last-minute delivery. The questioning rumors turned into self-righteous accolades: that Chase, he was a true Spence, a good man, good for this town, by golly, and especially good for that wild, independent-thinking Jodelyn Calhoun. Why, he'd put this town on the map and settle

Jody down to boot! The whole town was excited about the romantic wedding Chase had planned for Jody at Spence House.

Everyone, that was, but the bride.

"How could you do that?" she asked later, as they sped down US 98, along the Florida coast, to take care of some of Chase's other business. "Just because I married you a hundred and thirty or so years ago, doesn't necessarily mean I'm ready and willing to marry you in this century! In fact, I'm so mad at you right now, I don't think I'd marry you if you got down on your knees and begged me."

Chase held one hand on the car's leather-encased steering wheel and the other one on Jody's arm. "That's exactly why I want to marry you again. Heck, Jody, you're so damned afraid of making a commitment—I'm fearful you'll turn tail and run away if I don't make an honest woman out of you." Leaning close, he said, "That is what this little stand-off is all about, isn't it? You're a small town girl; you wanted a big wedding with all the trimmings; you can't take the looks and the whispers. I understand, and I . . . I want to make things right."

Lord, that was so sweet, she almost forgot she was mad at him. But not for long. "Chase, we weren't really married, anyway," she reminded him. "It was just part of the plan. It was just a fantasy."

Spotting a pull-off that gave them a fabulous view of the Gulf Coast, Chase stopped the car, then turned to her. "Jody, it might have started out as a fantasy, but now, it's very real. I love you. I want to marry you—again. Do you still love me?"

The vulnerable quality of his question tore through her. "Yes," she whispered, her eyes on the waves crashing against the pier in front of them. "Yes, I'll always love you. But there's so much to consider. My mother, Grandpa—"

"They're doing great," Chase pointed out. "Maria accepted our story more calmly than anybody else, and Mitt told us how she stepped in and helped him with The Treasure Chest the whole time you were gone. Plus, he's got

Miss Edith to take care of him now. Your mother's going to be all right, Jody. She's seeing her therapist. I'll see to it that she never wants for anything.''

He had been terribly sweet about that, she had to admit. ''She does love that old piano we found for Spence House,'' she said. ''Getting back into her music has been the best therapy for her.''

He nodded. ''Well, you did say she loves to sing. That's why I bought the piano.'' Shaking his head, he said, ''But let's not get off the subject. Your mother is going to be okay. And your grandfather seems really happy for us.''

''Oh, he is. He's always liked you.'' She lowered her head, then looked out at the water again. ''Of course, he was pretty miffed with us for running off, but he's over that.''

''So you've run out of excuses.'' Lifting her chin so she'd look at him, he said, ''You can't give up your own happiness just to babysit your relatives. They don't expect that of you.''

''No, they want me to be happy,'' she admitted, her heart bursting with fear as well as joy.

''So do I.'' He leaned over to kiss her. ''But I agree we've got a lot to sort through. Hey, I came to Hampleton to tear down a house and build a business complex. Now, I'm hopelessly in love, and knee-deep in restoring an ancient house—not to mention our little escapade back in time. I'm having my doubts, too, sweetheart, but not about us.''

She glanced over at him. ''I'm sorry. I hadn't stopped to think about how all of this has changed your life, too. But that's my point, exactly. Are you ready for this? Are you ready for me?''

He leaned his head back on the head rest. ''Well, you did hit me with the force of a hurricane, but I think I can learn to live with you.'' He winked at her, then touched his mouth to her earlobe, his words husky in her ear. ''Yeah, I'm ready for you. Always.''

Jody closed her eyes and moaned. ''Yes, there is that.''

''And there'll be lots more of that when we get to the beach house. I'm going to pamper you and make you relax.

297

You seem so tired and withdrawn. Is this about us, or is there something else?"

She raised her head, her eyes searching his. "I . . . I haven't been feeling like myself. I've been having dreams about Agnes. I guess I still need some answers." Giving him a smile, she said, "I'm going to go through the letters and read them again. Maybe that'll help."

Chase leaned back on his seat. "It does all seem like a dream, doesn't it? Sometimes I wonder if it really did happen."

"Me, too," Jody admitted.

He glanced over at her. "How about I take you to meet Aunt 'Nette while we're down here. She might be able to answer some of our questions."

That perked Jody up. "I'd like that."

He took her hand in his, kissing it before he started the engine. "Maybe you'll feel better after you rest some. You've been working too hard with the house and the plans for the village. The ocean has a way of healing; it'll be good therapy for both of us."

"I'm sure I'll be fine," she said, her tone not as reassuring as it should have been. The queasy feeling in the pit of her stomach only added to her doubts.

They reached the beach house just as the sun was setting over the blue-green ocean, and Jody's anxieties were setting firmly in the center of her stomach. Her elation at being with the man she loved warred with her doubts and despair. Why did she feel as if something had been left unfinished?

As Chase pulled the car up a steep circular drive, she saw the cedar house looming before them, its shape all angles and planes against the backdrop of the sea.

"It's beautiful, Chase," she said, her eyes taking in the cedar deck leading to a set of double glass doors.

Chase down-shifted the car, then came around to open her door. "Are you going to spend the night in the car?"

"Of course not," she said, slipping out of the seat too quickly. Dizzily, she grabbed at Chase's arm.

"Hey, are you all right?" he asked, his hands supporting

her elbows. "You're as white as that ocean foam out there."

Trembling, Jody leaned back against the car. "I . . . I don't feel too hot. I guess I got out too fast. My head's spinning."

Chase came to her, pressing her body back against the heated metal. "I didn't mean to upset you, Jody. About the wedding, I mean." Lifting his hands through her windblown hair, he looked down at her. "I love you, but I don't want to pressure you. If you're having doubts—"

"Oh, Chase," she said, tears springing to her eyes, "please don't think I don't love you. I do, so much. Maybe too much. I don't know what's wrong." Wiping her eyes, she tried to laugh. "Look at me, I'm a basket case."

He pressed her close. "What can I do to help you?"

She took in the scent of him, male and musky, fresh and alive. "Just hold me."

He lifted her up into his arms, cradling her close as he carried her up onto the deck. "I will, all night. I'll hold you until you're not afraid anymore."

Jody rested her head on his chest. "You're carrying me over the threshold? That's so sweet."

He managed to get the door unlocked with her still in his arms. "You're my wife, and this is our honeymoon. I want to carry you all the way up to my bedroom." Stopping just inside the door, he asked, "That is, if that's where you want to sleep?"

"I want to be near you," she said, nuzzling her head against his chest. "But I still don't feel too great."

"I'll take care of you," he promised.

Hours later, Jody lay in Chase's big bed watching the fire he'd built in the massive stone fireplace in his bedroom. A storm was coming in off the coast, making the night chilly. Or at least Jody felt cold, as another round of shivers danced up her spine. She should be relaxed; Chase *had* pampered her, bringing her hot chocolate in bed, massaging the tense muscles in her neck. Heck, she should be floating like a piece of driftwood by now, but she was afraid to go to sleep.

"Still awake?" Chase said, coming into the room from

downstairs. "Sorry about the phone call. I'm afraid I've neglected my office down here; I've got a lot of catching up to do tomorrow. But no more tonight. I promised my wife I'd hold her, and that's what I intend to do."

Warmed by the fire and soothed by the ocean's timeless lull and Chase's attentiveness, Jody managed to relax at last. The time floated by, and still Chase held her, never asking anything of her, never forcing her to admit her worst fears or her best hopes. He simply did what he'd promised her he'd do; he took care of her.

And for that she loved him even more.

The nightmares came around dawn, bringing her up off the pillow to reach out in the misty air.

Chase was there, soothing her, coaxing her into his arms. "What did you see, love?"

Jody gulped air, then rose off the bed to push open the glass doors leading to a deck off the bedroom. The chilly salt air hit her feverish skin like a balm. The storm had passed, leaving a silent, misty rain in its wake.

Chase came out to wrap her with a cotton throw, his arms circling her waist as he stood behind her and kissed the top of her head. "Want to tell me?"

"I dreamed that Captain Markham killed you. I didn't make it in time to save you. He tortured you, trying to get you to tell him where I was. But you never did, you wouldn't. Then he came for me, and Ali tried to save me, but they shot him. They carried me away."

Chase swallowed the rage permeating his entire system. "Baby, this isn't a dream. I think this is what really happened to Agnes and John."

Jody twisted around to face him, her expression full of terror. "Then they suffered more than either of us can begin to imagine. They carried me away, Chase, to a place . . . a dark, stinking place, a prison of some sort, with chains and rats and filth. I could smell the filth, the death, all around me." She collapsed into his arms. "Oh, God, I'm so glad we're safe. I'm so glad you're here with me, and we're alive."

Worried about her state of mind, Chase urged her back inside. "I'm taking you to a doctor today. You've been through too much. You need a complete checkup."

Lifting her arms away, she glared at him. "You think I'm crazy, don't you?"

"No, Jody. I was there, too, remember? I heard Markham threaten to take you to prison. I believe you, but I'm still worried about you."

"I'll be all right," she insisted, even as a spasm of weakness came over her. "I'm fine." She was strong; she'd never crumbled the way her mother had. She couldn't give in to these fears and paranoid doubts. "I'm perfectly capable of taking care of myself."

Then she turned around and fainted in his arms.

They sat in the doctor's office as if they were waiting for an executioner to come and take them away. Chase tapped his fingers on the arm of a replica Queen Anne chair while Jody stared at the imprint on the paisley Persian rug.

Dr. Dennison had gone over Jody with a fine-toothed comb, doing every conceivable test possible, just to soothe Chase's concerns—he was a major contributor to the hospital's funding, after all—as well as to assure Jody that she wasn't going insane. Chase knew he'd badgered the old family friend into going overboard, but damn it, he couldn't bear the thought of something being wrong with Jody. She'd always seemed so healthy, so vibrant. He'd do whatever it took, spend whatever money he had, to put the sparkle back in her eyes.

The doctor entered the room, and both of them jumped to attention. Chase automatically took Jody's hand. "What's the verdict, Doc? Is she really sick, or just full of meanness?"

The doctor, debonair and fit himself, laughed at Chase's lousy attempt at humor. "Relax, son," he said as he tossed Jody's file down on the tidy desk. "What ails your wife is common to most women. She'll pull through just fine, I suspect."

Chase took a deep breath. "Then there is something wrong?"

The doctor leaned back in his swivel chair, his eyes bright with a secret. "Depends on how you look at the situation."

Impatient, Jody snapped, "And just what is the situation?"

"You're pregnant!" Dr. Dennison announced happily. "I can't believe it. I delivered Chase and now, well, I'd be honored to deliver his first child."

Chase looked from the slaphappy physician to his shocked wife, his own wind knocked completely out. "A baby?"

The doctor laughed. "Yep, that's what we call 'em around here."

Jody sat still, one hand clutching her stomach. "I'm going to have a baby? That's why I've been feeling so rotten?"

"Oh, yes." The doctor rose to shake Chase's hand. "That's the way it'll be for about the first three months. It'll get better with time, but you are a bit run-down. I'm giving you some vitamins and I expect you to be back in a couple of weeks for a checkup."

They stood up, still reeling from this incredible news. "I'll make sure she shows up," Chase said, his words full of awe, his eyes on his wife.

"Congratulations," the doctor said as he made to leave. Looking at Jody, he added, "This is good news, I hope."

"The best," Chase said, while his wife only stood staring. "She's just a little shocked, I believe. We haven't been married long."

The doctor smiled. "Well, you've been together for a while, at least. She's four weeks pregnant."

After the doctor left, Jody looked up at Chase, her eyes filling with tears. "Four weeks. My God, Chase, do you know what that means?"

"Yeah," he said, "we've only got eight months to get ready."

"That's not what I'm talking about," she croaked, sniffing back a sob, her gaze lifting to meet his. "We've been back here three weeks, but we've been married . . . we've

302

been intimate for over four weeks."

Chase stopped teasing, his eyes going dark. "Then that means our baby was conceived—"

"Over one hundred and thirty years ago," she whispered. "Is that possible?"

He looked down at her, his hand automatically splaying across her stomach, his eyes wide with wonder. "On our wedding night?" he asked, "or maybe in the attic—no, I bet it happened under the magnolia. Remember, how we couldn't stop ourselves, how much we wanted each other, needed to be together. I still think about that, even now, when we're making love. It must have happened then."

Jody moaned, her own memories sending a sweet heat rushing through her system. "Yes, that must have been it. Funny, but I kept blaming myself; I kept thinking if only I hadn't seduced you, you would have made it home without having to deal with Markham. But then, Sarah might have died and Lord knows what Markham would have done to your family. Is it possible, Chase, that it did happen there?"

Chase placed a gentle hand on her face, his eyes holding hers. "Jody, love, don't you know by now—anything is possible. We're married and we're going to have a baby. Everything is exactly the way it should be."

Jody let him escort her out of the office, watching as he smiled and shook hands with everyone in his path. She prayed he was right. She hoped she didn't let him down.

Chapter Nineteen

"Now remember," Chase warned as they stood waiting for his great-aunt Jeanette to answer the doorbell, "she's old and eccentric. And she's blunt and a bully—don't let her upset you."

Jody shot him a determined look. "After this morning, nothing would upset me." Her hand on his arm, she asked, "Chase, how do you feel about the baby?"

He bent low to whisper in her ear. "Do you even have to ask? I've been grinning since we left the doctor's office."

"I did notice," she reasoned, "and that's what scares me. You look like Jack Nicholson as The Joker. Are you sure you're not faking it a tad for my benefit. I don't expect you to remarry me just because of this."

He stopped grinning. "Oh, I get it. This is just another excuse to not marry me. You don't want me to be noble and marry you simply because you happen to be carrying *my* child."

"Exactly," she said, her heart pounding. "I can raise a child on my own."

Jabbing the doorbell again, he put his hands in the pockets

of his khaki trousers. "Oh, sure you can. You can move mountains, change history, save mansions. In fact, you're so self-reliant, I'm surprised you even needed me to conceive this child!"

Affronted, Jody glared at him. "Well, you don't have to get nasty. I just didn't want you to feel *obligated*."

Steaming, he rocked back and forth on his heels. "I am obligated, to you, to our child, to our future. What do I have to do to prove that to you, Jody?"

She didn't have time to answer. The door opened on a petite woman with short white hair that lay like cotton puffs around her cherubic face. A pair of designer glasses sat perched on Jeanette Spence's pudgy nose, the rhinestone studded chain connecting them to her neck glittering in the late afternoon sun. She wore a pink silk blouse and a white gabardine skirt with matching white soft leather slippers. But her eyes were anything but soft. They glittered as hard as a diamond, their depths changing from blue-gray to icy blue each time she shifted her head.

"Well, don't just stand there," she said, backing into the room, her weight supported by a sturdy mahogany walking stick with an ornate magnolia blossom carved on its handle. "Sorry I took so long. The nurse has left for the evening, and I'm alone. It takes me a while to get around."

Chase tipped his head to kiss his aunt. "That's okay. We were in the middle of a heavy discussion anyway." The look he sent Jody told her they weren't finished, either. Then to his aunt, "You're looking good, Aunt 'Nette."

"I'm adequate for eighty-nine," she said. "And you look pretty fit yourself."

"I'm doing all right," Chase said, pulling Jody forward. "Aunt 'Nette, this is my wife, Jody Calhoun Spence."

Jeanette Spence tipped back her head to reveal a wrinkled pink throat close to the same shade of her blouse. Her cold eyes moved over Jody with precise intent, never wavering until she seemed satisfied she'd seen every inch.

Jody tried not to squirm under that scrutiny, but a telltale flush rose up her chest and arms, making her feel all hot and bothered. "Hello, Miss Spence," she managed to say.

Jeanette grunted, then said, "Mitt Calhoun—he's your grandpa?"

"Yes, ma'am," Jody replied, her Southern upbringing making her mind her manners. "He was married to Rose— my grandmother. But she died a few years ago."

"I remember them," Jeanette said, waving them into a cluttered sitting room. "The Calhouns always farmed the land, sharecropped for my papa for many years."

"From way back," Jody agreed. "Many years after the Civil War."

Eyeing Jody with that glinting stare again, Jeanette replied, "Uh-huh."

Wondering what that knowing grunt indicated, Jody sat down on the edge of a Louis XV style chair, feeling every bit like a five-year-old in Sunday school. But when she finally found the courage to face Miss Jeanette Spence, she caught a glimpse of the softness behind the steely glance.

Miss Jeanette was smiling at her.

As the evening progressed, Jody grew more comfortable with Chase's formidable aunt. They had a delicious dinner which the nurse had left—roasted chicken, steamed rice, crispy vegetables—things Jody would have to eat now that she was expecting, then decaffeinated coffee and tea cakes. For the first time in a long time, Jody had somewhat of an appetite.

Aunt 'Nette and Chase both seemed to approve. As they settled down with their coffee, the old woman looked over at her nephew and his new wife. "Now, tell me how you got hitched, and, oh, tell me all about your plans for Spence House."

For once, Jody left the talking to Chase. He explained how Jody had rushed to save the house and how they'd fallen in love, leaving out the little episode about John Hample's ghost sending them on a quest. With painstaking patience, he told Aunt 'Nette what steps they were taking to save the house, including everything from the regulations regarding asbestos—the house had to be safe for the baby (which he didn't mention to his aunt)—to his plans for energy-saving features and new copper plumbing to replace the original brass pipes.

Jody listened, fascinated, as his face lit up and his eyes touched hers. He was really getting into this, more than she'd ever hoped. The fact that he was doing it for her, for their future, only confused and scared her even more. She couldn't let him down, she couldn't cause him any further heartache.

Jeanette's keen gaze shifted from Jody to Chase. "Well, well. Sounds like you've got a bright future together. I want to give you something, for the house, as a wedding gift."

Jody smiled her appreciation. "That's very sweet of you, Miss Jeanette."

"Call me Aunt 'Nette," the older woman responded. "And I'm not being sweet, my dear. I left Spence House in a hurry, and didn't look back. It's time I remember my responsibilities."

Taking that as her cue to get some much needed answers, Jody leaned forward. "Why did you leave, Aunt 'Nette?"

Jeanette Spence sat up straight in her green brocade wing chair, her eyes moving slowly over the two young people sitting across from her. Lifting her chin, she leaned her head back so that her white hair mushed against the lacy crocheted doily resting on the chair's worn back. "That, my dear, is a long story."

Summoning her courage, Jody pressed on. "We really need to hear it."

Aunt 'Nette let out such a long sigh, it fluttered the pink lace at her collar. Carefully, she propped her feet on a footstool cross-stitched with the words, "Take A Load Off." "I lived there alone, you understand. I could have been imagining things. It was such a big, lonely, old house." Staring across at Chase, she said, "You do remember when I had your father move me down here?"

"Sure," Chase replied. "I hope he didn't bully you into anything."

"Heavens, no! I've never let any living man bully me. But . . . a dead one sure scared me. As I said, I could have been imagining things—things that go bump in the night."

Jody sat up. "Like a ghost, perhaps?"

"Perhaps," Jeanette said, her eyes widening. "Have you seen him, dear?"

"Yes, I have," Jody admitted. "He's talked to me."

Aunt 'Nette seemed relieved. "Thank God I'm not as crazy as I thought I was. I saw him, too, walking through the house, wearing a Confederate uniform. He acted quite daft, as if he were searching for something or someone. He turned up out of the blue, and he seemed determined to stay. I wasn't exactly scared of him; I just got tired of him making all sorts of noise during the night. I couldn't sleep. It was quite disturbing, so I left. I was afraid everyone would think me a senile old maid if I told about him."

"You're not senile," Chase assured her. "John Hample's ghost is very real."

Jeanette gasped. "Uncle John? So it was him! I thought as much. Well, what in the devil does he want?"

"His lost love," Jody said. Quickly, she explained all that had happened, placing her faith in Aunt Jeanette's ability to keep an open mind. When she was finished, the old woman sat nodding.

"That makes sense to me," Jeanette said, raising up to search the desk behind her chair. "All the more reason to give you something I found—your wedding gift."

Chase and Jody watched as she sat down between them, a heavy photo album planted across her lap. "This is my family album. I want you to have it—to carry the memories into the next generation. There are pictures of our ancestors in here, some reproduced from daguerreotypes." Leafing through the pages, she said, "I especially want you to see this one."

Chase and Jody both looked at the picture she pointed to, then at each other. Jody's hand went to her throat.

There in yellowed black-and-white, was a picture of John Hample and a woman. He wore his Confederate uniform, while the woman wore an ivory lace-covered dress with a high Victorian collar. On the collar was the brooch Jody had carried through time, and now had in a special box at Chase's cabin.

"It really happened," Jody whispered, her voice husky with emotion. "Oh, Chase, it really happened."

Chase finally spoke. "But . . . we didn't have a picture made. How did they?"

Aunt 'Nette explained. "It was taken when John first moved her into Camille; a traveling photographer, I believe. There are others here, some taken during the war, some after." She indicated the carefully preserved pictures in the album. Miss Martha and Papa Spence, with all the children. Jackson and John Hample standing in front of the house. And . . . Sarah, holding little Tucker.

Jeanette patted Jody's hand. "When Chase called and told me about meeting you, who you were, and that he'd married you, a peaceful feeling came over me. I always thought John and Agnes's story was such a tragedy."

Jody wiped her eyes. "I've read all their letters to each other. They were so in love. Now I know how much they suffered, and how they died, but we're going to make up for all that."

Jeanette practically beamed. "She was forced to marry her cousin, Will—a common practice back then, marrying distant cousins. You two will have a different story to tell, that's for sure."

Jody looked over at Chase. "Very different."

"They never made their vows official," Jeanette said, her voice low and dreamy. "But they died because of their love—knowing the noble character of Uncle John, I imagine that has been a burr in his bonnet . . . er . . . cap ever since, I suppose." She pointed to the tintype. "This picture of them together, and the brooch you now have, was his only link to her."

"We have one other link," Chase said, his eyes touching on Jody.

Missing his point, Jeanette gestured to the figures in the picture. "Look, you're both the splitting image of them. Why, it's uncanny."

They all laughed at that understatement.

* * *

Hours later, Chase and Jody stood on the beach, watching the ocean roll into shore.

"Okay," Jody said, wanting to find some closure in all of this so she could make some decisions about the future. "We know we're the reincarnate souls of Agnes and John, we know we did go back and change the outcome of things, and we know that my showing up in Hampleton all those years ago probably got John Hample all stirred up."

"Yes, yes, and yes," Chase said on a teasing note. "We not only verified everything, heck, we lived it."

Jody turned in his embrace, her golden hair whipping around them in the salty ocean breeze. "Maybe it's time to let go and think about the future for a change."

"Can you?" he asked, his tone carefully controlled.

"I'm willing to try," she answered, then kissed him to prove just how willing she was.

"Will you marry me again?"

"I'm willing to try," she repeated, pulling away from him to head back to the beach house.

"Jody?" he called after her. "Don't run away. Do you want to be my wife or not? Do you want to have my baby? Do you know how much I love you?"

She turned, facing the wind, facing the sea, facing her doubts. "Yes, yes, and yes," she said, smiling. "Come to bed, Chase."

The nightmares came back, sharp and clear, and detailed. She was struggling for each breath; she'd been walking, riding, begging for food; she was sick, very sick. Chills racked her body, and memories, black and horrible, moved before her eyes like shadows in the trees. She had to make it back, back to the spot where she was supposed to meet John.

They'd been separated, by this war, by Richard Markham's evil schemes, by forces beyond their control. A prison—he'd held her at a prison, telling her she'd be hanged as a spy. Richard Markham had held her prisoner, taunting her, using her, abusing her till she'd almost died. But she'd fought back, she'd survived, she'd convinced him to let her come home to Tucker, to her son. But first, she had to find John. He'd be waiting for her. He'd promised.

She had only a few miles to go, then she'd be home again, safe in John's arms. Safe at Camille. John would protect her, and soon, they'd be married and they'd build their home on the land near the magnolia tree. They'd plant wisteria, trails and trails of wisteria. And together, they'd raise the child she was carrying. John's child.

The dream shifted and she walked one last step, falling down on her knees underneath the young magnolia tree. She'd made it back. She'd wait here for John. He'd come soon.

Then the blood came, pooling on the skirts of her torn, dirty dress. She was dying, bleeding from her womb. The pain was so intense, she screamed, calling for John to help her. "Please, please . . . John, please don't leave me here alone. Don't leave our child."

She sank to her knees, the blood warm and sticky against her legs. She rested, her head falling across the rough trunk of the tree. All was lost. John wasn't coming, and her baby, his child, was dying inside her womb. She had nothing to live for.

"No!" The screams tore through Jody, bringing her up as she thrashed about the bed. "No!"

"Jody, baby, wake up." Chase stilled her, holding her tightly against his chest. "You're all right. We're safe. It's all over now, love."

She cried until the tears couldn't come any longer, until she could only sob the dry heaving sob of someone who'd seen the worst and survived. Then she looked up at her husband. "I know what happened, Chase. I know what happened to Agnes. She had been held by Captain Markham. He held her as a prisoner for days, weeks, maybe, then when he'd broken her completely, he allowed her to return home, for Tucker's sake. But she never made it. She died underneath the magnolia."

Chase reached out to her, trying to console her. "But you didn't, darling. You made it home. You're safe now."

311

She raised up, her eyes wide with pain and horror. "It's the baby, Chase. Our baby. That's why John sent us back. Agnes was carrying his child, but . . . she lost the baby. They both died. John promised to save her, but he couldn't."

Chase urged her back into his arms. "It's all right now, Jody. We did save them. We're safe, and we're together. And I swear to you, I will take care of you and our baby."

She looked up at him, her heart aching sweetly from sheer love.

"I do love you, Chase. This was what was holding me back. I had to know, to understand how someone could sacrifice so much for another human being. I couldn't understand Agnes's devotion, or John's noble, heroic actions. I only knew I'd do anything—even die—for you. And that scared me."

Grasping his bare arm, she poured out her soul to him. "You see, my mother loved my father like that. She worshiped him, long after he'd died. It made her miserable. I wasn't sure I could let myself really love you. I kept thinking if I pretended it had all been some sort of fantasy, I could keep the memories, even if I lost you."

He sat up, touching her face with his hand, his own heart breaking for her pain. She'd been abandoned, by her heroic father, by her fragile mother, and now she actually thought he might abandon her, too.

"You're not going to lose me. You're not going to fight me off anymore, either. We belong together and we can be happy. You have a right to be happy. I'll see to it, Jody."

The emotion in his voice shattered the last of her fears. She was open now, bare, reborn in his love. She needed to reaffirm everything they'd shared. She reached for him, pulling him to her, taking him down, down on the big, soft bed. Outside, the ocean cried its rage, pounding the sandy shore, rearranging it, changing it, clinging to it as Jody clung to Chase.

"We will be happy," she said, the vow steeped in love and hope. "We're going to have a baby."

He saw the fresh wonder in her eyes, realized she'd only

just now accepted all that had happened, all that would happen.

"I love you," he said, as he moved over her, fitting himself close to her.

"I love you," she responded, opening to his love, his touch, his tender endearments. "And I'll marry you again."

A lazy afternoon breeze played through the streets of Hampleton, Georgia, teasing its way through white magnolia blossoms and dainty strands of trailing purple wisteria flowers. The gleaming porches of Spence House were decorated in pink running roses and sweet-smelling white lilies. Wisteria draped the open doors. The whole house gleamed with cleanliness. And from her place in the top floor cupola room, Jody surveyed it all, wonder filling her soul.

In a few minutes, she'd be getting married right out there in the garden, underneath the magnolia tree that had sheltered the hopes and dreams of so many generations. John Hample's grave marker was still here. Now, the Sword of *Dahr* graced its gray stone, protecting a love hard won, a love that couldn't be denied, an eternal love. And, next to John Hample's gravestone stood a new one, a memorial to the woman he'd loved. A memorial to Agnes Jodelyn Calhoun Spence.

Patting her growing stomach, Jody moved down the steps into the bedroom Chase had presented to her as a wedding present. The whole house was restored now, each fireplace shining with ornately carved rosettes. Each scroll of fretwork, each carved cornice, was polished to perfection. Each alcove, each bay window, breathed a fresh new life, welcoming the light in to replace the gloom that had haunted this old house for so long. But this room, this was the heart of the house.

Chase had brought her up here last night. He'd gone to such lengths. He'd placed scented candles all around the big room, their perfume mingling with the fresh-cut wisteria blossoms he'd threaded across the furnishings. The room had been freshly painted a soft white. It had been empty, except for one handsome object, a bed, placed in front of the bay window overlooking the back gardens.

Jody stood looking at the big man bed standing like a throne in the middle of the room. Her grandfather and Maria had given her a crocheted lacy white spread and crisp white linen pillow cases and sheets to cover the bed. It was beautiful.

She'd filled the room with other pieces: the wicker she'd saved at The Treasure Chest, sunflowers and ferns, paintings and knickknacks. Love.

Last night, Chase had pulled her down on that bed to kiss her breathless, telling her, "You taste like peaches and cream."

"And you," she teased, "are still a good kisser. And a sweet talker. We aren't messing up this bed until our wedding night, city boy."

"Uh, shucks."

He behaved though, taking her up to dance her around the room. "Isn't it amazing that my headaches have gone away?"

Jody grinned. "Oh, I think you'll always have one major headache the rest of your life."

"You?" He pulled her close. "That's one headache I can live with. Of course, we'll probably never be alone again, thanks to the stories circulating about John Hample's ghost, and the legend of his love for Agnes Jodelyn."

She grinned. "Best marketing ploy in the world." At his disapproving look, she added, "Well, we had to explain the sword and the new grave marker somehow."

There was a knock on the door. Maria entered the room, a bright smile on her serene face. "It's almost time."

"I'm ready," Jody said, patting her hair. "How do I look?"

"Like a dream," Maria said. "That Victorian dress is so lovely, and your brooch is exquisite."

Jody smiled, her nerves settling down in spite of the excitement. "I had the dress copied from the one in the picture."

Maria looked at the portrait sitting on the wicker vanity table Jody had brought in today. "They do look very much like you two. Your story is really amazing. I can't believe Chase's aunt remembered all of that, though.''

Jody shot her a wry smile. "She could have dreamed it, but I believe it's a true story." She didn't have the heart to tell her mother she'd *lived* it. Maybe later . . .

Jody took her mother by the arm. "No, we're different, Chase and me. We're going to have a long and happy life together."

Maria guided her daughter down the stairs. Outside, the fiddlers they'd hired for the ceremony began to play a haunting melody. Jody remembered another wedding, and the music of a lone flute. The house lay empty now, but soon, laughter would fill the newly redecorated rooms. Maria and Jody reached the bottom of the stairs, their hands clutched tightly together, when tinkling laughter coming from the parlor caused them to pause.

Holding to her mother's hand, Jody tiptoed across the wide hall to peek in at the open parlor doors. Behind her, Maria's surprised gasp spilled into the waning light.

There, bathed in a soft shaft of sunlight, a man and a woman danced to a timeless song that only they could hear. His dark hair appeared burnished with gold and his Confederate uniform shone as his gentle gray eyes laughed down at the golden-haired woman he held in his arms. The woman wore an ivory lace dress with a high Victorian collar, and pinned to her throat was a brooch made of pearl clusters and intricate gold filigree.

Fingering her own brooch, Jody bit back the tears forming in her throat. Silently, she and Maria watched the phantom couple as they glided across the room, their feet barely touching the polished oak floor, their gazes so locked together, they didn't seem aware anyone human was watching them, or that time had stopped to bring them together. On and on, they danced, swirling around the room, coming so close, Jody could feel the cool rush of air they created as they moved across the floor.

"Aren't they beautiful?" her mother whispered, her voice raw with pain. "Oh, Jody, they did find each other again."

Unable to speak, Jody lowered her head to let the tears

fall down. She vowed to spend the rest of her life, no, the rest of eternity, loving Chase.

"It gives you hope, doesn't it?" Maria said, her hand gripping her daughter's. "Maybe I'll be with Bud again one day, and we can dance like that. Wouldn't it be wonderful?"

"Yes, Mama." Jody hugged her mother close. "I'm so sorry you've been lonely all these years."

"I'm okay now," Maria whispered. "This makes up for all of it."

Jody had to agree. As they stood watching, the couple once again whirled close, but this time, they stopped dancing and glided past Jody and Maria, moving toward the stairs.

Still unable to move, Jody watched them, wishing she could tell them how much they'd helped her to heal. As if sensing her need to communicate with him, John Hample Spence turned and looked down at her, his gray eyes locking with hers in a brief look of total understanding and gratitude. Bowing his head, he took his lady by the arm and guided her up the stairs until they both faded out of sight.

"Was that real?" Jody asked in awe.

"About as real as anything in life," Maria answered sagely.

As they moved toward the back of the house where Mitt waited to take Jody down the stairs to the garden, he smiled and handed her a letter. "It's from Chase," he explained, taking her bouquet so she could open it. "He said you should read it before you go out."

Jody opened it, her hands shaking as she recognized the now familiar scrolled handwriting of John Hample Spence. It was one of his love letters to Agnes.

4 May, 1863
Kelly's Ford, Virginia

My Dearest Agnes Jodelyn,

It is four o'clock in the morning and I miss you, my love. We're going into an important battle today, and I have been given the honor of accompanying General J.E.B. Stuart onto the field. But I wanted to have the equal honor of writing you one last time, if by chance I do not make it across the Rappahannock River with these other brave soldiers.

I wanted you to know, my sweet Agnes Jodelyn, that if I could choose a place to die, it would be in your arms. Since I cannot be with you just yet, I shall keep your letters near my heart, until that day when we can be together again, dancing underneath the magnolia tree the way we did when last we saw each other. I can still smell the wisteria. I can still see the white magnolia blossoms over your head as I held you close.

Nothing can ever change my love for you—not time, not death, not eternity. Know that if I do not make it through this day, I will be waiting for you somewhere in a more beautiful, more gracious place, and somehow, my love, we will be together once more. I won't rest until I can hold you in my arms, as my wife, as my only love—for all eternity.

With all my heart,
John

Jody held the letter to her chest. He'd written it the day he'd been injured. Then he'd come home only to die at the hands of Richard Markham. Chase wanted her to see, they were the same, yet they were very different.

Tucking the letter inside her bouquet, she took Mitt's arm, and with her mother by her side, walked through the garden to find Chase waiting there for her, in their special spot. At the sight of her, he stood still, his eyes filled with so much love, she wanted to rush the last few steps to be in his arms.

As Mitt handed her over to him, Chase leaned close to whisper in her ear. "Are you ready for a lifetime commitment?"

"No," she answered honestly. "I'd rather spend eternity with you."

"I think I can settle for that," he said, tugging her close.

She smiled up at him, a warm peaceful feeling settling over her soul. It was so good to be home again.

An Angel's Touch
Carly's Song
Lenora Nazworth

Carly Richards has come to New Orleans to escape her painful past. She certainly has no intention of getting involved with some reckless musician with an overzealous approach to living and an all-too-real lust for her. Sam Canfield is simply the sexiest man she's ever seen, but Carly is determined to resist being mesmerized by his sensuous spell.

Sam thinks he's seen it all in his day. But one enchanted evening, his world is turned upside down when a redhead with lilac eyes stumbles into his path and an old friend he thought long gone makes a magical appearance on a misty street corner. Soon, the handsome sax player finds himself conversing with an elusive angel, struggling to put his life together, and attempting to convince the reluctant Carly that together they'll make sweet music of their own.

_52073-7 $5.99 US/$7.99 CAN

THE OUTLAW HEART

VIVIAN KNIGHT-JENKINS

Bestselling Author Of *Love's Timeless Dance*

A professional stuntwoman, Caycee Hammond is used to working in a world of illusions. Pistol blanks firing around her and fake bottles breaking over her head are tricks of the trade. But she cannot believe her eyes when a routine stunt sends her back to an honest-to-goodness Old West bank robbery. And bandit Zackary Butler is far too handsome to be anything but a dream. Before Caycee knows it, she is dodging real bullets, outrunning the law, saving Zackary's life, and longing to share the desperado's bedroll. Torn between her need to return home and her desire for Zackary, Caycee has to choose between a loveless future and the outlaw heart.

_52009-5 $4.99 US/$5.99 CAN